A Curio for the Count

Gems of London
Book Two

Elizabeth Ellen Carter

ARE YOU SIGNED UP FOR DRAGONBLADE'S BLOG?

You'll get the latest news and information on exclusive giveaways, exclusive excerpts, coming releases, sales, free books, cover reveals and more.

Check out our complete list of authors, too!

No spam, no junk. That's a promise!

Sign Up Here

www.dragonbladepublishing.com

Dearest Reader;

Thank you for your support of a small press. At Dragonblade Publishing, we strive to bring you the highest quality Historical Romance from some of the best authors in the business. Without your support, there is no 'us', so we sincerely hope you adore these stories and find some new favorite authors along the way.

Happy Reading!

CEO, Dragonblade Publishing

Additional Dragonblade books by Author Elizabeth Ellen Carter

Gems of London Series
Deceiving the Duke (Book 1)
A Curio for the Count (Book 2)
A Sweet Tale of Blessing (Novella)

Heart of the Corsairs Series
Captive of the Corsairs
Revenge of the Corsairs
Shadow of the Corsairs
Tidings of Comfort (Novella)

King's Rogues Series
Live and Let Spy
Spyfall
Spy Another Day
Father's Day (A Novella)

The Lyon's Den Series
The Lyon Sleeps Tonight

Pirates of Britannia Series
The de Wolfe of Wharf Street

Also from Elizabeth Ellen Carter
Dark Heart
Warming Winter's Heart
The Ghost Bride

A Curio for the Count

To find his future, he must own his past…

Raised as an Englishman, Armand Danger, Comte de Ytres, is troubled by a dream from his childhood that leaves him speculating on his French past.

He is convinced that the answers he seeks can be found in an elaborate clock which belonged to his father who was executed during the French Revolution.

Miss Jade Bridges works as a valuer in her family's London antique shop and auction house. One day she receives a mysterious letter from an anonymous client willing to pay any price for a very specific statue clock.

While in pursuit of the clock, Jade and Armand meet, and there's immediate attraction. But how can it amount to anything when they are rivals for the very same object? As the couple grow closer and attraction deepens, they agree to join forces to find the timepiece together.

Then an antique dealer is killed. It appears someone else is willing to extract a fatal price to possess the clock for themselves.

Why is someone willing to commit murder for this curio for the count?

"The clock talked loud. I threw it away,
it scared me what it talked."
—Tillie Olsen

Acknowledgements

To the wonderful team at Dragonblade Publishing, with amazing publisher Kathryn Leveque and superlative editors, Cynthia Blackburn and Scott Moreland. Thank you for everything you do.

Dedication

To my fantastic neighbors, Debbie and Graham. I'll never forget how my husband Duncan and I nutted out the plot of this tale while taking down the thirty meters of old fence between our yards! And to Brooke and Hannah. Thank you for letting me "borrow" the name of Mickey Mattis.

PROLOGUE

Witherick House
London
1818

THE NIGHTMARE WAS not new. He'd had it many times before. But in it Armand Danger saw himself as three-years-old once more.

It was mostly dark, and he was running, running, running. First awakened by his nanny, then dragged along by his *maman*.

Out of bed. Down the darkened corridors. Into the woods. Out to sea.

He was frightened, but then he saw his papa in the study, so everything would be all right.

And yet, what was once a neat and orderly room was a snow-storm of paper glowing white in the lamplight.

Paper became flame.

Three-year-old Armand ran once more.

The thudding of his heart became the sound of the tattoo of drums outside, where the flames chased him faster and faster, away from the safety of his home to the place where he dreaded to go.

The giant lady pointed the way. He went as she directed.

To the building that was the home of the Dead.

The rap, rap, rap of the drums became a tick, tick, tick of a clock keeping time. The giant lady was now tiny, but the tick, tick, ticking she made was insistent, maddening. So much so that papa ripped the swinging ball from her hand and broke it into pieces.

The tiny lady was now silent.

Armand half-emerged from his sleep, aware his heart pounded double time, but unable to force his way back to wakefulness.

The nightmare continued in its disjointed awfulness.

He had a dread fear of this place where the Dead lived.

The Dead *lived*.

How could the Dead live? Unless they were not truly dead?

He'd seen the wizened body of his *grandmere* in rigor, old, desiccated. Would she be like *that* if the dead lived? Mouth open, sunken cheeks, hands clawed?

His mother and father argued. That frightened him more than being among the dead that lived. He cried and cried, but no one paid him heed.

The rap, rap, rap of the drums came closer and closer. The pounding in his ears became the pounding of his heart.

The tiny lady was giant again, and they ran away from her – but only he and his maman. Not Papa.

The flames of Hell chased them, louder, hotter, larger than he'd ever experienced. That must be his punishment for being in the home of the Dead.

Je suis désolé, je suis désolé! I'm sorry, I'm sorry!

The words, a mix of English and French, were on Armand's lips as he woke. Decades had passed since that terrifying night, but his heart still hammered in his chest as though he were that young boy once again.

He sat up, knowing sleep would now elude him for some hours. He scrubbed his stubbled face and went in search of a brandy. A large one.

Why did he have this dream *now*? It had been years since it last tormented him, and yet the power of it still managed to catch him unawares, creeping up on him as he slept.

He retreated to the library, the banked fire still radiating enough heat to be comfortable. He poured a measure of the amber liquid into the glass closest at hand, a whisky tumbler. Worse than being disturbed from sleep was the restlessness that came after and impossible to shake. It would be foolhardy—not to mention too damned cold – to go out and walk the dark, deserted, early morning streets to enervate the dream and give some hope of gaining at least a couple of hours' rest before dawn.

And where would he walk? To some undefined *there* and back again? To paint a target on his back for murderers and footpads who used the cover of darkness for their sins?

He pulled a copy of yesterday morning's paper towards him.

Perhaps reading the doings of the *ton* and the machinations of those who sat in parliament would distract him.

He skimmed a few paragraphs, the words slipping through his mind like sand through his fingers. Nothing captured his attention, but it was still better than the dream.

Armand turned the page. His eyes fell across an advertisement.

Curios for the discerning
Highly sought-after desirable objects found
Discreet valuations and disposals Our specialty.
Auction on Saturday.
Bridges & Sons
Southwark

Curios and Jewelry
Bridges & Sons
Bond Street

Armand stared at it a moment and was struck by a sudden resolve. He tore the advertisement from the page and slipped it into his dressing gown pocket.

CHAPTER ONE

Bridges & Sons Auction Rooms
Southwark, London

AS SHE PUT the final polish on the glass of an eighteenth-century gilt rococo mirror, Jade Bridges decided that running her family's business, an auction house, was not very much different to running a playhouse.

There were seats for an audience and a stage for the auctioneer who led the bidding as a conductor might direct an orchestra. Sometimes there was high drama and other times low comedy. Occasionally, there was pathos as people said farewell to objects held as dearly as the late loved ones who'd owned them.

Then there was the backstage, the part the audience didn't see, a place of chaos finely balanced on the better side of anarchy.

Jade performed one of two roles in the play and knew her part well.

She wryly examined her reflection in the mirror and tucked a loose strand of light brown hair over her ear. She wore an unremarkable day dress beneath a dun-colored apron of a type that all the staff wore over their clothes.

Well, there was no mistaking her for one of the fashionable set *today*, was there?

The gown of jonquil yellow silk she'd worn to a dance the

night before last had been put away, along with the suite of citrine jewels she'd worn with it.

Those had caught the eye of the Duchess of Chisworth, who'd regarded them covetously all evening.

Jade had a five-pound wager with her brother as to who would be enquiring after them at their shop in Bond Street.

The husband? Or the lover?

Edward had his money on the Duke. Hers was on the lover. Her brother called her a cynic over her choice, but that wasn't true—not really. She was simply practical, having seen enough of the *bon ton* to recognize that love and marriage didn't always go hand-in-hand. Neither did constancy and faithfulness.

Jade stepped away from the mirror and examined the scene before her.

Her brother strolled in.

Ah, here was the star of their performance.

"You're late," she called out.

"You're five pounds richer, so I shouldn't complain if I were you," he replied.

Jade grinned.

So, it was *the lover.*

The porters, overhearing their banter – and knowing of the bet – clapped and cheered.

Jade left the mirror and hurried toward the counter where the list of auction items waited for Edward.

"So, who *is* the buyer?" she asked, handing Edward his notes.

"Colonel McAufille."

Jade cocked her head. "Interesting. I had no idea. He's kept *that* very circumspect."

"And that's why the *ton* comes to us," said Edward. He glanced over the sheaf of paper, familiarizing himself with the items up for sale before glancing about the room and eyeing the location of the major pieces. "We keep our eyes open, and our mouths shut."

It was a principle their father had taught them, a lesson from his father before him. It was the philosophy that had kept Bridges & Sons in business for the better part of one-hundred-and-twenty years.

"We have only eight registered bidders on the books, but we'll see soon enough who comes in for the viewing," she told him.

Edward skimmed through the sheaf of paper like an actor running his lines one final time before opening the curtain.

As he did, Jade looked at the bright, blue autumn sky through one of the high-set transoms. A fine day was both a blessing and a curse. If the day was raining and miserable, people stayed in. If it was sunny and pleasant, people stayed out. Today, she was hopeful of a large crowd at today's auction. It would be a long one with more than two hundred lots under the hammer.

"If we can shift just half the lots today, we'll have made a pretty penny," said Edward, reading her mind.

"I'll be happy if we can sell some of the larger pieces of furniture," she countered. "We need the room to deal with the cartload of furniture you brought back from Tunbridge Wells last month."

A dozen long case and mantel clocks chimed the ninth hour at more or less the same time. Pete, the Bridges' family's longest-serving auction porter, took the cacophony as his cue to open the doors.

Throughout the morning, a regular stream of viewers came through the doors. Some registered their names to leave absentee bids on various lots. Others elected to stay and bid on the items directly.

Many of the objects in today's sale were from stately homes. Some came from wealthy owners divesting the old for more fashionable furniture and knick-knacks. Other lots came from deceased estates. And more than a few items were from impoverished nobility slowly and discreetly selling off the family silver.

Jade reflected on how the auction house and associated shop had grown increasingly prosperous over the past twenty years, thanks to the rising middle-class of merchants who desired the trappings of the aristocracy and had the money to pay for it.

She was proud to know that her family had been a feature in London society for four generations – although an unacknowledged part of it.

Jade had grown up with the trade and absolutely loved it. Her father was equally delighted to have his second child take an interest in the business, although her mother did her best to ensure that she was educated as a lady.

Both forms of schooling had proved their worth. Edward quite happily acknowledged that she could pass in high society much more readily than he and her skill as a valuer was equal to his.

That made her an especial asset when clients wanted to employ their services surreptitiously while maintaining appearances.

Jade received invitations from the Beau Monde, usually with the excuse of making up the numbers. In truth, the invitations accompanied a commission to discreetly value an item for an owner without it being widely known that it was for sale or suspected of being a fake.

Today, however, she was just one of the workers. She would assist with drawing attention to each lot, collecting the money at the counter, and accounting for afterward. Then their clients would be paid. Less Bridges & Sons' eleven percent commission, of course.

Jade spied a number of regulars. She greeted them with the familiarity of friends, rather than customers.

Among them were the second-hand dealers who pretended nonchalance, but keenly examined each piece that caught their eye. And there, sitting in their usual position, three rows from the front to the left-hand side, were the two widows.

The auctions were a day's entertainment for the old dears. They would each pay their ha'penny for two copies of the catalog, but they never bid on, let alone buy, a thing. They did, however, have a discreet bet between friends. Jade had learned a long time ago that they chose ten of the best items in the catalog. Each wrote down their estimate of how much it would fetch under the hammer.

She could never find out which of the old ladies was the most successful at the game. Nevertheless, they came back month after month carrying a little wicker basket which they stowed under their seat.

The porters were particularly attentive to them because the first thing out of that basket each month was a cake just for them. It had become a much-anticipated afternoon teatime treat for the workers in the back room.

The clocks struck one in chorus.

Jade looked about the room. Of the sixty in attendance, there was one man who stood out. He was tall. Hair as black as polished ebony, swept back from a hawkish but youthful face. Not quite thirty years of age was her estimation. He spent such a great deal of time examining the furniture that at first she thought he might have been a new dealer, but he was too finely dressed for that.

Jade never worried about being recognized by the upper classes. Their steward or man of business would attend these auctions on their behalf. So, what was it that made her wonder if she *had* seen him before? Then she twigged. It was not the man's face, rather it was the cut of his suit she identified. It was from a tailor in Bond Street.

Had he registered to bid?

Jade casually made her way to the counter and examined the register. Her action caught the eye of a middle-aged woman who wore a dun apron like hers.

"'E's a bit of a looker that one," observed Dottie. She was Pete's wife who helped out on auction day.

"Who?" asked Jade without betraying interest.

"The man whose details you're looking up."

"I'm doing no such thing!"

Dottie patted her arm, nodding with a knowing look, before

moving away to attend to some other matter.

Jade found the entry.

Armand Danger, St James' Wood.

She watched him while attending to the registration of the late comers.

Finally, Edward stepped up to the podium. He struck the gavel on the lectern three times to bring the auction to order.

Jade watched this Armand Danger take a seat beside the widows. The man seemed to have charm in abundance. The old ladies were talking to him like they'd known him forever. They even offered him a piece of cinnamon bun which he politely refused.

Then the auction was underway, and the hard work began as porters bustled about the room adding paper tags to sold objects on which was written the registration number of the successful bidder to account for each sale.

The day progressed. Unsuccessful bidders drifted away, successful ones approached the counter to pay for and claim their lots.

Only a few were guaranteed to stay for the entire event – the two widows, as well as one or two of the second-hand dealers.

"Your friend seems keen," observed Dottie. "He's still here."

Danger.

Such an unusual name for such an uncommonly striking gentleman. There was something about him that niggled the back of her mind – other than simply the name of his tailor.

No, they hadn't met before. She would certainly remember if they had. It was his name…

By the time the hammer came down on lot number seventy-five, she remembered.

Count Armand Danger. He was a French *émigré*, adopted as a child by the late Earl of Rosemont after he married Armand's mother, the widowed Countess of Ytres.

Jade matched his number, thirty-five, to items he had bought so far. No objects d'art, so far, just solid, well-made pieces of furniture.

Dottie read over her shoulder and *tsked*.

"Looks like he's planning to set up a home of his own," she said. "I think you missed out there, ducky. The only reason I know of for a man to start building a nest is if he plans to wed."

"Or he's setting up home for a mistress," Jade added.

"You!" Dottie's shock was not all feigned. "You've been mixing with those rich folks for too long. Besides, it's the mistress what does her own dressin', if you know what I mean."

She shook her head sagely. "Whatever happened to the good ole days when a young woman would settle down with a nice young man and have plenty of babies, I ask you?"

"It's far too late for me to find a nice young man, Dottie," said Jade, making sure she added a mock tragic air to her tone. "I'm left on the shelf, just like that rococo mirror over there."

Her theatrics attracted scorn.

"Bah! You're nothing of the sort. You're just too fussy, that's your problem. I've always held it was a big mistake your father encouraging your interest in this business. You've become too used to mixing with them aristocrats to settle for a humble clerk, and yet they won't accept you in their circle."

Jade held her tongue.

She'd known Dottie all her life, which gave the older woman certain license to speak her mind, but it didn't mean Jade had to like it – especially when it was so close to the truth.

The fact of the matter was, she enjoyed the work and was good at it, but it had come at a cost. At twenty-five, the only ones offering marriage were older men, believing they were doing her, an old maid, a favor – or whose real interest centered on inveigling their way into the Bridges' family business.

Neither reason commended the wedded state.

The afternoon wore on, leaving Jade no time to further rue her spinsterhood. The counter became increasingly busy as more of the attendees came to settle their accounts and take their purchases or make arrangements for delivery.

She spotted Count Danger in the queue waiting in line with everyone else. A man of his status might be expected to use his rank to be served quicker, but instead, he seemed content to bide his time until it was his turn.

Jade scanned down the list of items he'd bought. The most expensive was a dining suite in the Louis XVI style in mahogany and brass trim – a table and leaves to seat eight, with chairs and a matching enfilade buffet with marble top. Next there was a small parlor set with carved giltwood gold leaf and cane settee, two matching chairs in a rose-pink striped fabric, and two marble-topped pedestal tables.

She knew the pieces. Excellent quality; originally French.

There were some smaller lots as well – mostly unexciting household accoutrements.

Before long, he stood before her. His dark eyes watched her total his account.

"One hundred and five guineas, sir," she said.

"I hadn't intended to buy so much today," he said, with no trace of his original home's accent.

"Your first auction?"

He nodded, withdrawing a banker's draft from his inside coat pocket. Jade caught his scent – a hint of grapefruit and jasmine with an underlying woody note.

"You show excellent taste, if I may say so," she said.

Danger looked up from writing his particulars on the cheque and gave her a smile. His dark eyes sparkled.

"Why, thank you."

Jade had no idea why those three words made her blush, but they did.

"Might I suggest that a Sevres dinner service would be an excellent accompaniment to such an exquisite setting."

"Do you have such a service? I didn't see it here."

Jade handed him a card.

"Our shop on Bond Street, sir."

Danger took the card and made a deal of studying it.

"Your card has an error."

Jade frowned.

"I see it says 'Bridges & Sons'. It ought to read 'Daughter', if I am not very much mistaken."

Jade hid a smile.

How very perceptive.

She couldn't help but feel a little flattered by his notice That was a point in his favor, as far as she was concerned but she wouldn't give him the satisfaction of letting him know that.

Jade inclined her head. "I shall be sure to let management know about the oversight."

"Wednesday morning?"

"Our shop is open five days a week, sir, or by special appointment."

He offered her a relaxed smile. "Will *you* be there on Wednesday morning?" he asked before leaning in a little closer over the counter as though he intended to share a confidence. "My sister-in-law tells me that men cannot be relied upon with respect to matters of taste."

Was he flirting with her?

"I'm sure she cannot have been referring to you," she replied.

"*Two* compliments, Miss Bridges! I think you mean to fair turn my head."

Jade laughed.

Oh yes, the man was flirting with her, and she really ought to put an end to this. It was more enjoyable than it ought to be.

He handed over the cheque. Jade made a note of it in the ledger.

"When do you intend to take delivery?"

His open expression faltered a moment.

"Ah, I hadn't quite thought that far."

Really? How curious.

Jade schooled her expression and picked up a pencil.

"Never mind, sir. We will arrange a carter. What address?"

Danger's frown deepened.

"I don't exactly know yet." His tone was serious, quite at odds with the light-hearted teasing of moments before.

Jade regarded him more fully. *What kind of man buys a large amount of furniture and has no home to put them in?*

"Can I store it here?" he asked. "My, ah, domestic arrangements are not quite settled."

Ordinarily, the answer would be *no*. The policy of the auction house was clear. And yet for some reason Jade felt sorry for the man. It had been his first auction, after all.

Over his shoulder, Jade saw Edward speaking with one of the porters. Her brother wanted the floor space cleared too. But he was going to Berkshire in the next couple of days to attend a house sale. He'd be away for nearly three weeks, so what he didn't know…

Jade leaned forward confidentially.

"We don't normally do this, sir, but I can allow you two weeks. My brother is to attend a house sale shortly and will return with at least three cartloads, so you *will* need to make your arrangements before that."

The look of relief on his face touched her heart.

"I'm in your debt, Miss Bridges. I will see you on Wednesday."

Seemingly mindful of those still waiting to be served, Danger gave a short bow and went on his way.

Jade turned to her next customer.

Bah! No doubt Dottie would think that she'd turned soft in the head for giving into the charming count but still, she could not dismiss that for a moment there, Danger had looked like a lost boy.

What was his story?

It surprised Jade to realize how much she really wanted to know.

CHAPTER TWO

TWILIGHT FELL OVER London, the sky painted purple and turned familiar buildings into silhouettes in black.

Armand rapped on the roof of the hackney he'd hired and gave the driver a change of instruction. Not Witherick House at St James, but on to White's. There might be an expectation he'd be home for dinner, but he'd been vague about his plans when his sister-in-law, Arabella, asked about them this morning.

Neither she, nor Barnet, his estimable valet, had reminded him of such obligation when he left, so he doubted his presence would be missed.

Now, to his more immediate problem. He'd never set up a household of his own and had no real idea how to go about it. In truth, the idea of it had only been half-formed in his mind when he went to the auction house.

A house full of furniture required a house. He'd quite over-looked that fact until the rather attractive Miss Bridges had reminded him of it.

Witherick House had been his home for more than twenty years – ever since his widowed mother Nicole, the Countess of Ytres, married William Spencer-Lane, the Earl of Rosemont, himself a widower.

Armand had only vague memories of the time before that, when he and his mother shared one room in a boarding house, having arrived in England with other French *émigrés*.

Prior to that, his recollections were indistinct, but he clearly remembered how he felt. Confusion. Terror. Of being pulled out of bed one night and spirited away from everything he had ever known.

Never seeing his own father again.

But how fortune could smile too. How grateful Armand had been to discover that not only was his new stepfather a kind man, but he was also father of a boy his own age, Charles, with whom he had become fast friends.

Two years ago, Charles became the Earl of Rosemont, and a year after that he married a young beauty by the name of Lady Arabella Forsythe. It was a well-suited marriage that proved to be a love match as well.

Was that one of the reasons for this sudden restlessness he felt?

Possibly.

A marital home was no place for a bachelor brother, despite Arabella's best efforts to change his single state.

Having arrived at White's, Armand acknowledged a couple of people of his acquaintance – the Earl of Runcorn, and the new Duke of Auchen – before attracting the attention of Viscount James Howlett. Howlett had mentioned a desire to divest himself of a townhouse in Mayfair in the past month.

Negotiations for the property were conducted over a meal and drinks that very night.

Armand returned home to Witherick House basking in the glow of the day's achievements – not to mention a glass or three of very fine claret. In his mind, things were going swimmingly until Barnet met him at the door.

"A word to the wise, sir," he said in hushed tones. "The Countess is somewhat displeased by your tardiness."

"Tardiness?"

"Yes, my Lord. Apparently you were expected for this evening's card party."

"Was I? I don't recall that."

Barnet said nothing but gave him a look which told Armand that *he* knew no such appointment was in his diary.

Armand tamped down a frisson of annoyance.

He liked Arabella a great deal. She was a lovely young woman, ideally suited to Charles, but just because *she was* happily wed, it did not give her license to try to entice him to a similar state.

No doubt she thought herself clever this morning in not rousing his suspicions, but he knew that if he were to go into the drawing room right now, he would see an odd number around the card table, and some unfortunate young woman wondering why she was the gooseberry.

"I've taken the liberty of laying out your evening dress. You will have time for a quick wash, but not a fresh shave," Barnet continued.

"There's no chance of quietly going up to my rooms unobserved and staying there?" Armand asked hopefully.

Just then, the door to the drawing room opened, and Arabella emerged. Her blond hair was styled just so, and she wore an evening dress in cornflower blue.

"Armand, dear!" she said in a voice designed to carry to the guests inside the room. "I'm so glad business didn't keep you as long as you'd expected."

Barnet offered him a commiserating look.

Arabella closed the door and marched right up to him.

"Why didn't you tell me you were going to be out all day and half the night?" she said. "What must Lady Beverley think? She was counting on you to be her partner at whist this evening."

Armand struggled to keep a rein on his temper.

Firstly, it was not later than nine o'clock, so he'd hardly been out all night. Secondly, he'd encountered Lady Beverley a half-a-dozen times over the past six months, and never once had she expressed an especial interest in card games. Thirdly, his sister-in-law had no right to order him about as though she was his wife.

Those three observations were on his lips to say when Arabella gave him her lost puppy eyes.

"Oh, please don't be cross with me, Armand."

Damn it, the woman knew his weakness.

He shook his head slowly, rolling his eyes as he did so. "This is the last time I let you have your way, Arabella," he said.

Charles's wife giggled and clapped her hands together.

"She's a *lovely* girl, Armand," she enthused. "I know you'll like her once you get to know her better. Just be pleasant to her this evening. She's very accomplished, you know."

Armand nodded wearily and headed up the stairs. His resolve was fixed. He'd negotiated with Howlett to purchase his townhouse. He'd bought furniture to go in it. He would have a home of his own, and he would tell Charles of his decision tonight.

LESS THAN FIFTEEN minutes later, Armand entered the drawing room freshly washed and dressed to his valet's satisfaction. He greeted Lord and Lady Hartnell, then halted a moment at seeing a young woman with light brown hair with her back to him.

Miss Bridges?

The young woman turned, and he was disappointed to find that she was not who he thought at first glance. Nevertheless, he pulled out a smile to wear and bowed to Lady Beverley Sinclair.

Finally, Armand acknowledged Arabella and his stepbrother. Charles wore an expression of watchful amusement. Yes, he too was aware of the reason for Lady Beverley's presence, but Armand knew his stepbrother well enough to know he only lightly tolerated his wife's matchmaking efforts.

"So, what business kept you so late?" Charles asked conversationally as he shuffled the deck for a new hand.

"I was at an auction house."

"What on earth for?"

It was a matter he would have preferred to discuss privately, but, at present, Armand couldn't think of an excuse that wouldn't look patently false.

"I was buying furniture for a townhouse."

"Whose?" asked Arabella.

"My own."

Armand saw his sister-in-law's eyes widen in surprise.

"Perhaps our bachelor is ready to settle down after all," she said, giving Beverley a meaningful look. "Furniture, you say? You need a woman of good taste to advise you, Armand." She turned to her guest. "Do you not agree, Beverley?"

"Indeed, you are right Arabella," she replied with a winning smile. "Perhaps it is a small service I can offer, my Lord."

Armand didn't want the poor woman laboring under false hopes.

"I'm afraid the position has already been filled, my Lady."

Arabella set down her wine glass heavily, ruby liquid sloshing over the rim of the glass and onto the green baize of the card table. Lord Hartnell, seated at Arabella's left, gallantly furnished his hostess with his handkerchief while a footman stepped forward to stop the wine from dripping onto the silk of the chair and into the wool of the rug.

"Yes, the young woman at the auction house suggested a fine Sevres dinner setting for my sideboard," Armand continued.

Arabella quickly composed herself and laughed.

"Oh, a *shop* girl! I shall grant that you gave me a start. For a moment I thought you were going to announce your engagement!"

Inwardly Armand winced. To dismiss Miss Bridges as simply a shop girl was to do her a disservice, he was sure.

Nevertheless, his news dominated the conversation for the rest of the night, and, as a result, Armand did not have to go out of his way to entertain Lady Beverley. But as the guests departed for the evening, he knew there would be a call for a full accounting.

Charles invited him to the library for a brandy.

"I had no idea you were unhappy here with Arabella and me," he said, handing him a glass.

"I'm not. But now you're a married man, and one day will be a family man. I thought it time for this old bachelor to find digs of his own."

"Are you sure? You're always welcome to stay. This is your home as well as mine."

Armand saluted him with the glass before taking the green leather Chesterfield chair by the fire.

"Are you sure there isn't another reason?" said Charles, slouching comfortably in the matching chair opposite.

"You mean Arabella." It was a statement, not a question. "Your wife means well, and I love her as a sister, but this is the fourth young lady she's virtually thrown at my feet since you returned from your honeymoon."

"I've warned her against meddling in other people's affairs."

"I know you have, and I appreciate it. But it seems that, once she believes she is in the right, she won't stop, and that means marrying *everybody* off. But it's not just that…" Armand paused and collected his thoughts. "It's just time I forged a life of my own, you know?"

"I still consider us brothers, Armand. I don't want that to ever change between us."

Armand set down his glass and fixed his brother's eye.

"You have my word on it, Charles. But I have been conscious for quite some time that as Earl of Rosemont, you have responsibilities of your own. When I was young, my own past and title meant nothing. But I envy you your history now. You have something to look back on, something tangible to hold *now* that connects you to this place."

"Maman never spoke of France much, did she?"

Armand gave Charles a fond smile. The man had been a babe-in-arms when his own mother died and a lad of only six when the Earl had remarried. Armand's *maman* was the only mother Charles had known, just as William was the only father Armand really knew.

Now he wanted to know. There was so much he didn't know

about his father and his past and Armand was beginning to fear that he'd left it too late.

After a period of silent contemplation in Charles's easy company, Armand ventured to put into words something which he'd struggled to understand himself, let alone articulate.

"I don't know who I *am*, Charles," he said softly, sounding out the thought. "I feel undeniably English, but I am also French. For the longest time I thought my family history didn't matter. But as time goes on, I realize I'm adrift. I need a compass."

"Arabella would say you need a rudder – a wife to chart your course," said Charles.

Armand snorted. "Yes, indeed. That *is* what she would say."

Charles straightened out of his slouch.

"For what it's worth, I think you're doing the right thing."

Armand drained the brandy.

"That keen to be rid of me?" he laughed. "You and Arabella will no longer need to be on your best behavior upstairs."

"Ha! It will be *you* with freedom to misbehave!" Charles answered. Then he sobered. "You will be the master of your own ship, my dear brother. That is a good thing."

There was silence between the two men for a period of time before Charles asked something that had clearly been on his mind for some time.

"Do you think you'll go back to France and find out what happened to your father?"

Armand stared into his empty brandy glass, where reflections of flame from the fireplace danced golden. He shrugged his shoulders, letting out a huff.

"*Maman* refused to talk about him," he said quietly. "It was as though she had locked the door on those memories, and they were never to be revisited. I remember when I was about thirteen, I even asked your father about him."

"I never knew that," Charles said quietly.

"He was reluctant to say anything at first, you know, given how *Maman* felt. Then one afternoon he asked me to come to see him when you and she were out. He bade me to sit in this very room, closed the door and unlocked that cabinet over there. He set before me a box of letters *Maman* brought with her from France, and several clippings from news sheets. My father – his name was Robert – was executed by guillotine a month after *Maman* and I arrived in England."

Armand looked up to find Charles's head down, seemingly contemplative. But then he lifted his head and met Armand's gaze. "I thought that was the case," he said. "But there never seemed to be an appropriate way to bring it up – especially considering how delicate *Maman*'s disposition became over the years."

That was true. She'd changed markedly after the death of her second husband – so frequently lost in a world of her own. And then, a few years later, she took up correspondence with a French cousin. Soon after Charles and Arabella's wedding, she'd accepted an invitation to visit Giselle Perrin and her son Gerald. Three months later, Nicole wrote from Arras to say she would not return to England. She wanted to stay in her homeland now that a king was back on the French throne.

"Have you thought of going back and reclaiming your family's lands?" asked Charles – apparently his train of thoughts had followed Armand's own.

"I don't even know if they are there to be had."

At Charles's frown, Armand waved his hand and continued. "I have some vague idea *where* they are of course, based on the title, but..." he drained the last of his drink. "I imagine there's nothing left of the estate and what there is, would be home to squatters. I don't intend to throw people out of their homes even if they did throw me out of mine."

He set the glass down on the side table and got to his feet; Charles remained where he was.

"You haven't even told me where you intend to live," he said.

"Mayfair. Howlett has taken up an appointment in New South Wales. I'm buying his digs."

"Living a couple of blocks away is better than a couple of continents away."

Armand nodded. There was nothing else to say but he was glad to have had this conversation.

"'Night, Charlie."

Charles got tiredly to his feet and suppressed a yawn.

"At least I can go to sleep reassuring Arabella that this turn of events is nothing to do with her." He gave Armand a smile. "Well, not entirely, anyway."

CHAPTER THREE

Bridges & Sons Curios and Jewelry
Bond Street
Six months later
February 1819

TUESDAY WAS USUALLY a quiet day in the shop. Jade used it to her advantage to work on the order of lot items for the upcoming auction's catalogue. Normally this was Edward's job, but he, along with three men from the auction house, was in Norfolk at a house sale. They hoped to buy a good proportion of high-quality paintings and furniture from the deceased estate.

As a result, Jade and the other staff who remained in London worked especially hard to ensure things were ready for next Saturday's auction.

"There's a letter for you, Miss Bridges," said Seton.

The man had been with the family for years. Although at the older end of middle-aged, he was wiry and strong, turning his hand to anything from coach driving to cataloguing, and being a general dog's body. That made him invaluable as far as Jade was concerned.

She accepted the letter and slipped it into the pocket of her dress while she carefully wrote out the list of lots for the auctioneer. At her elbow was a newly sealed envelope of her own. She glanced at it with a smile.

Armand Danger had become quite a regular in the auction house over the past six months.

Her smile became a grin.

She knew what his townhouse looked like without ever having set foot in it. And, in her upcoming auction, there was a high-quality Turkish rug and a pair of tall vases that were perfect for the oak pedestals he'd bought the previous month. In her letter to him, she also took care to make mention that a rare set of 18th century Jacobite wine glasses might also find a home on the side table in the study, along with a cellarette for the dining room.

Edward would be pleased for the quick turnover of the glasses. He told her he'd paid over the odds for them because he felt rather sorry for the young buck who sold them. The young man had overextended himself and needed to quickly replenish his funds to satisfy a gambling debt.

Jade already knew of the man's misfortune. His debts had been the subject of gossip in some drawing rooms for quite some time. But in coming to Bridges & Sons, the young man's embarrassment was solved and not breathed to another living soul.

After a little while, the unopened letter nagged at her. It was unlikely to be a bill because the package was too thick to simply contain an invoice. Nor did she recognize the spidery handwriting.

Curiosity got the better of her.

Jade set her pen down, pulled out the envelope, and broke the seal. The first thing she saw was a detailed sketch which seemed familiar. It was a statue clock. A robe-draped Grecian woman held the timepiece aloft in her right hand. A gridiron metal pendulum dropped beneath the face of the clock and terminated in a brass ball bob with an adjusting nut at its base.

The author had even gone to the trouble of noting the clock's height as twenty inches. Jade smiled to herself. She knew the type of clock well. It was quite a popular piece. In fact, she was pretty certain there was one in their auction room right now.

She set the sketch down and picked up one of two enclosed notes. The first was a Bank of England draft for fifty pounds.

Jade frowned. She picked up the second note, a handwritten letter.

Dear Miss Bridges,

I wish to offer you a commission. To that end I have enclosed the sum of fifty pounds.

I am looking for a particular object – a clock, but not the common type every household of a middling income apparently seems to acquire.

I have no interest in the cheap copies. I wish to possess the original from which the copies were cast. Its dimensions are similar to the common type, but not exactly. The statue is cast in bronze, not spelter, and it will be signed by the sculptor.

There is little more I can tell you, but I am in earnest. I want to have this clock and your reputation for sourcing such curios for the discerning is what brings me to write to you.

I wish to keep my identity confidential. Inform me of your acceptance of this commission by placing the following advertisement in The Times. Use these words and no others:

TKA to VMA

Grandmother is now quite well.

*If you do not wish to accept my commission, then the fifty pounds is my loss, but I venture the chase is as much value to you as the monetary reward. And you **will** be rewarded handsomely and be satisfied to know I am prepared to pay any price to possess the clock.*

The letter was unsigned.

Jade examined the envelope again to see if there was any clue as to the sender. There was none. She examined the bank note, holding it up to the light to see whether the paper had the tell-tale watermark assuring of its authenticity.

It did.

She returned her attention back to the letter. The heavier, more angular letters were indicative of a male hand. The letter was on high-quality paper which suggested the gentleman had wealth. His word choice indicated an upper-class upbringing.

Curious.

Lastly, Jade considered the sketch of the clock. She would need to examine this picture against the one at the auction house to see the specific differences, but in all, she was hard pressed to identify any real distinction.

She gathered her letter and pondered the last thing that bothered her. The man had written to *her*. Not to Bridges & Sons as a whole. And not to her brother.

Why was that?

It wouldn't be one of the regulars at the auction house or the shop – they would simply approach her directly. Members of the aristocracy would send a man of business, a solicitor, or some other agent acting on their behalf if they did not wish their identity known. Never before had she received a completely anonymous letter.

"Excuse me, miss."

Jade raised her head and acknowledged the boy who stood at the threshold of her study.

"Do you have any errands for me?"

Jade glanced down at her paper-strewn desk, then back at the boy.

"No, thank you, Jack. Ask Mr. Seton to have the carriage readied for me, will you? Then go see if you can help Billy with shop inventory."

The boy nodded and left.

She had been at her desk for far too long and the fine, late winter day beckoned. Normally she would have given Jack the task of taking the handwritten catalogue to the printers for setting but doing the task herself gave her an excuse to stop by the dressmakers to check progress on the new evening gown she'd ordered. Then she could drop her letter at Count Danger's door before heading to the sale room to see how Dottie and the porters fared in Edward's absence.

She pulled out the mysterious letter once more and read it again. She wished Edward was there. She would have sought his counsel, although she had an idea what he might say: "Business is business, and fifty pounds is fifty pounds".

The author had not asked for anything illegal – let alone immoral – so why did the request weigh on her so much?

In the end she decided it was simply some eccentric and when she took the note to the bank, the bank teller didn't blink an eye when she handed the paper across the desk. At that moment Jade knew she was committed to finding this clock. She ordered Seton to stop at the newspaper office to place the advertisement letting TKA know his "grandmother" was well.

When she arrived back at the auction rooms, she found the clock in stock, sitting on a small, marble-topped wine table. Jade pulled out the sketch purporting to be of the original and studied it closely. The sketch was annotated, drawing attention to details an original would have. 'Features distinct, not soft' read one note. Indeed, the details as sketched were very crisply drawn, whereas the woman cast in spelter was less well-made. The intricacy of the spray of flowers on which she stood on paper was only hinted at in the reproduction.

On the base of the clock was the figure's name, *Thalatte*, clearly shown in relief. But on the spelter clock, the name only became visible under the brightest of lights angled just so.

Held aloft in Thalatte's right hand was the clock itself. The bezel was decorated with cast ribbons. The face was white enamel with black Roman numerals. So far that seemed to match the sketch, as did the brass pendulum.

"You've been staring at that clock for a while," said Pete. "Is there something wrong with it?"

"No, nothing like that," said Jade. "It's just that a customer has written to ask me to find one just like this."

"So why not sell him that one?"

"Apparently he wants the original."

"Oh-ho! Good luck with that, I say!" Pete laughed. "If it still exists at all, it'll be in France – that's where all these types of clocks have come from."

Jade shook her head. "He must think it's in London – or England at least, otherwise why not pursue enquiries in France?"

"Ask him."

"I wish I could. This mysterious client wishes to remain anonymous," she said, then added *sotto voce*, "I must contact him through placing an advertisement in *The Times*."

Pete's face lost its humor. "That don't sound right at all, Miss Bridges. Do you think you ought to wait for Master Edward to come home before pursuin' this?"

Jade shook her head.

"I can't see the harm in it. It's just a clock after all, not a fortune in doubloons from the Spanish Main."

Pete gave the clock another glance. "If there's anyone who can tell you more about it, it's that jeweler fellow at Hatton Garden."

Jade nodded. "Good idea. I'll make an appointment with Eli on Monday. Hopefully he will know more."

ARMAND EXCHANGED A knowing glance with his brother as Arabella poured them tea and regaled him with Lady Templeton's virtues.

"I've known her for years," she continued, "and don't worry, Armand – I have made her no promises. But it would be *so* wonderful to have your company."

His sister-in-law had been extremely solicitous to him whenever he dined with them. At each visit, she went out of her way to make him feel welcome. He ought to feel guilty that Arabella thought she still had to make amends for his decision to start a household of his own.

Yet he could not feel too badly about it. So far, she seemed to have learned her lesson about meddling in his love life. There had been no more contrived "accidental" meetings with eligible young ladies. Indeed, in the months since the unfortunate incident with Lady Beverley, Arabella took pains to tell him the guest list in advance.

He decided to put her out of her misery. "I accept the invitation. I look forward to meeting Lady Templeton."

"Oh, Armand! Do you mean it?"

He half rose from his seat and kissed Arabella on the cheek.

"Of course, I do. We will make a pleasant evening of it."

Charles shot him a look of thanks. Armand could only imagine what life had been like for his brother in his absence.

No. He was not ready to enter the marriage mart, but there was no harm in considering his options in that regard. Now he had a home of his own, it was quite probably about time he *did* consider settling down.

He smiled to himself. He'd taken a great deal of satisfaction in attending to the details of furnishing a home himself. It had given him a purpose for the past six months.

He'd begun to understand who he was as a *man* – not as the stepbrother of the Earl of Rosemont and the son of an *émigré*. And, on that journey, he'd discovered something interesting about himself – as English as he considered himself to be, his aesthetic tastes were decidedly Continental.

Arabella had found some of his decorating choices quite surprising. In truth, the only person who seemed to fully understand him in that regard was that delightful Miss Bridges from the auction house.

He found himself looking forward to attending auction day and not just for the satisfaction of bidding successfully on objects he wanted. There was Miss Bridges herself. He had come to rely on her discretion and good judgement. If there was anything she thought he might like, she would send him a letter outlining said pieces. And he bought them. Every single one.

So far, she had not steered him wrong.

"Will you not join us at Countess Beatrice's for the card party?" added Arabella. "You'd be more than welcome."

"Not today, thank you. I have an appointment in Southwark."

"Ah, your romance with the shop girl," said Charles with amusement.

"Stop that!" Arabella admonished. "That's a dreadful thing to say. I ought to confess to you that I recently met your Miss Bridges. She was pointed out to me at Lady Meadowbank's party the other night. She happened to be wearing an exquisite pair of turquoise earrings."

Arabella gave her husband a hopeful glance.

"Duly noted, my dear," said Charles, his eyes twinkling, fully aware Arabella's birthday was coming up next month.

So, it was with good spirits he left Charles and Arabella to attend the viewing ahead of the auction so he could examine the pieces Miss Bridges – Miss Jade-like-the-gemstone Bridges – so thoughtfully identified for him.

Jade.

It was an unusual name. One day he intended to ask her about it.

He arrived at the auction rooms and spotted her immediately. Her back was to him as she concentrated on polishing a set of glassware. Over her dress, she wore a dun-colored apron tied at the back which accentuated her trim waist. Dottie, the chief porter's wife, spotted him. He caught the beginning of a grin from her as she turned away and tapped Jade on the shoulder.

Miss Bridges turned in his direction. Armand acknowledged her with a nod but did not approach. Instead, he made his way to the first item on his list, the cellarette, aware she watched him for a moment before she returned to her work.

This was the game they played.

Every month he would arrive for the viewing, and she would

pretend he was nothing more than any other customer. Then, when it came time for him to collect his goods at the end of the auction, he would flirt outrageously with her, and she would give as well as she received.

At first, he'd thought it nothing more than a professional act to flatter a customer, but as the months had gone by, he'd sensed something more sincere about her.

How refreshing it was to converse with a young woman as an equal!

The ladies who Arabella cast before him were pleasant enough, but one had to walk on eggshells around them, lest their sensibilities be offended by a little frank speaking. And the only other type of women with whom he was acquainted were quite another thing entirely – more at home in a bedroom than a drawing room.

Miss Bridges was neither, and yet, somehow, more than both.

He liked her. If circumstances permitted, he might even consider her a friend. She always seemed to be in good spirits and was outgoing without overstepping the mark.

Armand freely acknowledged that he could easily send someone else to bid in his stead, or have an artisan make something especially for him. But he didn't.

The reason why he came back here month after month had become less the need to furnish his townhouse, and more a need to enjoy the camaraderie of the regular bidders and the staff at Bridges & Sons Auction House.

He was especially fond of the two elderly ladies, Aunt Eunice and Aunt Margaret, who always brought a tin of cake and played their guessing game on each lot.

He'd got to know the porters by name too – Peter and his wife Dottie, Seton, Billy – as well as Edward Bridges, the 'son' in Bridges & Sons. And he'd also learned to spot the dealers among the regulars. They were friendly enough but kept to themselves.

Armand closely examined the cellarette and mentally assigned a figure he was prepared to bid up to. Next, he approached the cabinet that held the set of Jacobite glasses. An unexpected nostalgia washed over him. He remembered these – or ones very much like them – back home in France.

"I thought you'd appreciate them."

He turned swiftly at the voice. Miss Bridges stood just behind his shoulder where she could see the cabinet of glassware.

Armand took in her figure and face.

"There's much I appreciate."

A blush lit her cheeks, but she didn't move away from him. She simply raised an eyebrow, gave him a knowing look. And absolutely no encouragement.

He dropped his teasing tone. "No, I do like them." He turned back to the cabinet. "I like them very much. I'm surprised how simple inanimate objects can be the key that unlocks a memory."

"You remember a set like these?" she asked softly.

Armand regarded her again and nodded. "I don't know how. I was young when I came to England—not more than three-years-old."

He thought he saw understanding in her eyes and wished she might have said something more, but Miss Bridges was called away.

Suddenly, the auction room was busier than it had been just a few minutes before. Or perhaps it had been that, when he spoke to her, no one else existed except them.

Armand nodded hello to his "Aunts" before examining the edges of the Turkish rug, running his hand over its smooth nape. Finally, he registered his attendance as a bidder and received his catalogue from Dottie. He flicked through the pages. Fortunately, the lots he wanted were listed early.

That might afford him time to get to know Miss Bridges a little better.

He rather liked that idea.

CHAPTER FOUR

J ADE RETURNED TO the desk, thoughtful.

That was a most unexpected exchange with Count Danger.

She was used to his harmless flirtation and the compliments that meant nothing. He was not the first man to have flirted with her, and it had nothing to do with conceit to acknowledge it. With most, it was a pleasant way to pass the time. Those few men with overt lascivious intent were recognized and watched carefully by the porters – and quietly dealt with before they became a problem to her or any other female in the auction rooms.

As such, Jade had never given such banter any weight. At least, with other male customers. With them, it was part and parcel of business, a means to an end – that end being a happy customer paying a fair price, willing to purchase again, and amenable to telling their friends.

But with the count, it had steadily become something else, and today he had shared a vulnerability with her, a private part of his mind.

Somehow that seemed more intimate than any innuendo.

Jade watched him make his way to his now customary seat next to the aunts, stopping on the way to share a word or two with the porters.

She shook her head.

It was tempting to believe she only imagined this alteration in the relationship, except she knew better. Did he feel it too?

Just before he sat, Danger glanced back. Their eyes met once more. Their gaze held a moment.

Oh my, yes. There was no mistaking that.

Jade pulled her eyes away and feigned interest in the ledger before her.

The count was a very attractive man. That much was beyond doubt. In the six months she had known him, he carried himself with nothing less than the self-assurance of a person who was comfortable with himself and his place in the world. It was an attitude shared by all members of the ton.

Indeed now, as he accepted a piece of fruit cake from the aunts and engaged them in animated conversation, he was still the urbane and sophisticated man who had first entered her sale room all those months ago.

But now she saw him… *differently…*

She'd had Count Armand Danger nicely catalogued, and now he was doing something unexpected.

Surprise gave way to annoyance.

How dare he do that!

The smart rap of the gavel falling onto the lectern threw her out of her musing. No more thinking about handsome wayward men. There was work to do.

Dottie joined Jade at the desk and watched the fall of the lots.

"Your beau has done well for himself," she said. "That cellarette should have gone for another five pounds."

"It would have done if old Frank was here," Jade replied. "And the count is *not* my beau."

"Uh-huh."

Jade gave her a mock glower.

"What's he like?" Dottie continued. "Have you seen him outside this place? After all, you're the one who goes to all the big houses."

Before answering, Jade attended to a bidder who wanted to

collect his lot and leave early. When she had finished, she was relieved to find Dottie now similarly occupied with another customer.

What was *he like?*

She had seen him from afar just the once, at the Earl of Huntington's ball about three months earlier. She and Edward had received an invitation from Lady Villeneuve as thanks for sourcing a painting by the artist JMW Turner for her collection.

Jade had attended enough of these functions to feel quite at ease amongst the world of the aristocracy but Edward fidgeting with his cravat reinforced that her brother did not feel the same way.

"Is it time to go home yet?" he had muttered under his breath.

"Don't be such an infant," Jade had whispered back. "We've only just arrived."

"I feel conspicuous standing here."

"Well, I want to see who has been invited this evening. And besides, there is no better way to show off the emeralds than near the receiving line."

Indeed, they stood close enough to hear the majordomo announce the name of each guest as they arrived.

"The Earl and Countess of Rosemont. The Count Danger of *Ytres* and Lady Sarah Moore," the man announced.

Jade had to own that her heart had raced a little on hearing Armand's name. She spotted him in the throng immediately. His evening dress was cut to perfection, a sapphire blue cravat secured with a pearl pin making him even more handsome than ever.

Tonight, she wore the finest gown she possessed, a watered silk in silvery gray, and with an impressive collection of emeralds from the shop. Would he recognize her? Danger had only ever seen her in her working attire. Inexplicably, Jade wanted him to see her as she was now.

"Perhaps we should make ourselves known to our client over

there," Edward had said with a playful glance her way.

It was on her lips to agree when she noticed the woman on Danger's arm. With blond hair set in charming ringlets against a blue pearlescent gown, she was the most beautiful woman Jade had ever seen.

Edward took half a step in that party's direction, but Jade gripped his arm.

"No. I'd rather not."

Her brother shot her a questioning glance but didn't receive an answer. What could she say? There was no good reason *why* they shouldn't be acquainted in this setting. So, what could explain the slight disappointment she felt on seeing the Count in his natural habitat?

It was a reminder that she did not truly belong in that rarefied world. She ought to be content with who she was – the daughter of a successful trader and merchant.

She watched him greet their host and begin to turn away, no doubt to survey tonight's assembly. Jade waited, wondering whether he would spot her in the crowd.

You're being perfectly foolish. He won't see you. He doesn't expect to see you here, so he won't.

Jade decided she didn't want to risk that disappointment.

Before he looked in her direction, she turned on her heel and retreated further into the throng.

For the rest of that night, Jade went out of her way to avoid him and, indeed, was grateful to leave just as soon as Edward determined they could quit without causing offence.

THE GAVEL WENT down once more, and the sound was a judgement, a sentence pronounced. A reminder that she had work to do.

The next lot was the spelter statue clock. These were always popular in the sales room. Jade set her work aside and watched the bidding with interest.

The auctioneer, a stand-in since Edward was still away, raised his gavel then paused, waiting for the room to settle before beginning his performance. He started with an outrageously high amount. No one bid. He named a lower amount. Silence. Then an amount lower still.

A hand went up.

The auctioneer named a price five shillings above the opening bid. He swept his hand across the room, using the handle of his gavel as a pointer.

There was a second bidder. And a third.

The bidding went up past the reserve. Jade breathed a small sigh of relief. The higher the amount the item went for, the greater their commission. The reserve meant they would break even. Amounts above that were profit.

The bidding increased – far more than these clocks usually fetched. Jade scanned the crowd and stopped at the count who at that very moment raised his hand.

"It's not worth that amount," whispered Pete, who'd come alongside them.

"True enough," said Dottie, "but Mr. Purdeau's son will be very happy with his windfall."

Jade added nothing to the whispered conversation.

Instead, she thought about her mysterious commission. She'd examined that clock closely. It wasn't the original, but was there something about it that she'd missed?

She frowned.

Was someone else looking for the clock?

And why had Danger entered the bidding when he surely appreciated the price it had now reached was far more than it was worth?

"The count is one of the bidders," she said. "Do we know who the others are?"

"Number five," said Pete.

Dottie ran a finger down the registration list. "Mick Mattis."

Jade nodded absently. She knew him. He was a dealer of dubious honesty and worse manners who came to London twice a year and took home goods to sell at three times the price at his shop in Dublin. She spied him toward the back of the room, standing to one side.

Mattis was the first to drop out. He waved his hand under his chin to silently declare he'd had enough.

The count continued bidding against someone Jade didn't recognize.

"Who's the other one?" she asked.

"Number sixty-four," Pete answered.

"Not a regular. Given his name as Smith," announced Dottie.

The auctioneer pointed to the mystery bidder.

The man chose to state his price. "Seventy-five guineas."

Jade gasped, as did the room. The bid had leapt twenty guineas past the count's previous offer.

She watched Danger straighten in his seat.

"Against you, sir."

There was a moment's pause before the man's answer – an emphatic shake of his head.

No.

"Then going once, going twice, going three times…" said the auctioneer.

The hammer dropped. The room burst into applause in appreciation of the vigorous and costly contest.

⟫⟫⟩✦⟨⟪⟪

ARMAND HAD BOUGHT the cellarette and the Turkish rug in short order. The only other lot he'd intended to bid on was the glasses, but they were still a little while away.

He exchanged a smile with Aunt Eunice who was so far winning the guessing game against Aunt Margaret. He'd not been paying much attention to the lots as they fell.

Until he saw the clock…

I recognize that, but from where?

He told himself he must have seen it in a drawing room

somewhere. A porter indicated it stood atop a tall chest of drawers. The pendulum swung back and forth.

Tick-tick-tick.

Rap-rap-rap.

Armand felt as if he had plunged from a great height.

The Lady!

The clock from his nightmare!

As the auctioneer started the bidding, Armand stared at the timepiece, trying to work out from where – beyond his night-mares – he knew it.

The pendulum swung hypnotically.

He saw it on a mantel over a fireplace. A mantle in a study.

Without thinking, he put his hand up and joined the bidding.

His father was in the room, at his desk. His father smiled down at him.

Armand put his hand up once more.

In his mind's eye he saw his father's face clearly for the first time in years.

He held on to the vision and nodded once again to increase his bid.

It didn't matter if it was *the* clock. There was enough of a resemblance that it brought his father back.

He bid higher.

One of his two rivals dropped out, waving a hand under his chin to announce his defeat.

The remaining bidder sat somewhere behind him, out of his field of vision. But he was aware Aunts Eunice and Margaret regarded him with a great deal of interest.

Armand affirmed a counter bid with a nod of his head. The other bidder did the same.

He suspected he was bidding far more than the clock was actually worth, but curiosity and ego got the better of him, driving the price higher.

"Seventy-five guineas."

The mystery bidder's voice carried across the room. Armand

took note at the gasp from the audience. That was more than twenty guineas more than his current bid.

A curt shake of the head from him, and the bidding was over. The room burst into applause. Armand acknowledged the audience as he turned around to find the successful bidder.

Why did he want the clock so much?

He excused himself to the aunts and slipped to the back of the room from where he could observe the man who had made his way straight to Dottie to pay for the clock. Apparently he intended to leave with it immediately. The bidder's back was to Armand, who could see nothing extraordinary about him from that angle. His clothes fit him well, but they didn't seem that expensive.

Armand moved a few feet to one side, trying to see the man's face, but couldn't. All he could see from his new position was Miss Bridges in the background, observing them both.

Pete helped Dottie partially dismantle the clock, detaching the pendulum and wrapping it in an old newspaper before wrapping the statue. Having paid for his purchase, the successful bidder left quickly without turning round.

Armand might have gone after him, except the auctioneer announced a new lot, the Jacobite glasses. He did not intend to lose *those*. He returned to his seat.

A few moments later the glasses were his and for a good price. It took the sting out of losing the clock.

He fronted at the counter to pay for his goods, just behind the other man who had been outbid for the clock. He was chatting to Miss Bridges then, noticing him, stepped to one side to include Armand in their conversation.

"To be sure, he was a keen one, wasn't he?" said the man in an Irish accent.

"Do we know who he was?" Armand asked, making sure to keep his tone only mildly curious.

Miss Bridges shook her head. "No, I've never seen him before."

Armand introduced himself – without the title – and learned the Irishman was a second-hand dealer by the name of Mattis.

"I'll tell you what I *do* know," the Irishman said, "he's well and truly paid over the odds for that clock. Anyone would have thought it was the original."

At that, the delectable Miss Bridges straightened, schooling her features.

I wonder why?

Armand returned his attention to Mattis. "Original?"

Mattis shrugged. "Well, there *had* to be an original casting of it. I was told it was a Frenchie piece, belonged to one of them aristos before, you know..." The man whistled and drew one hand down in a chopping motion until it hit the palm of his other hand.

Armand gritted his teeth but said nothing.

"No one knows if it still exists," Mattis continued, "but after the Revolution, some enterprising chappie was turning out these cheaper spelter pieces."

Armand responded with an insouciant shrug. "A very pretty penny our rival paid indeed."

The Irishman doffed his cap to Miss Bridges. "Right-o! I'll be off then," he said. "I'll be seein' ye tomorrow, lassie, to see about cartin' the rest o'my goods and chattels."

Miss Bridges' attention remained on the Irishman while he exited the auction house with a bagful of smaller items. When she turned to him, Armand was pleased to see her gaze drop to his lips before meeting his eyes.

"Well, Miss Bridges," he said. "What are we to do?"

Her eyebrows raised at his teasing tone.

"My lord, had I known how fond you were of the clock, I'd have drawn it to your attention," she said, her voice serious.

He shook his head and laughed. "Don't trouble yourself about it. It just happened to be an idle fancy."

"That was a lot of money to offer on an 'idle fancy'," she said.

Armand sobered.

"It reminded me of something I lost."

The look of sympathy on her face warmed his heart.

"I can understand that. Would you like me to look for another one for you?"

"It isn't necessary," he said. "It's only a clock. But I am interested in knowing more about the original."

Jade stiffened and took half a step back, as though she were about to bolt. "I shall be delighted to tell you anything I find out about it."

Now it was *his* turn to raise his eyebrow. *What was she trying to hide from him?*

He put his hand on hers before she withdrew further.

"You looked beautiful at Lady Huntington's Ball," he said.

Her eyes widened. She licked her lips nervously a moment before she gently removed her hand from beneath his.

So, he *hadn't* been mistaken. It *was* her at the ball.

Why?

The play of small expressions on her face fascinated him—surprise, embarrassment – and perhaps a little curiosity of her own.

Then she recovered her composure, and it was delightful to watch, an emerging fullness to her lips, a slight flush to the cheek, then the brightness in her green eyes.

"Given the attractive lady on your arm, I *am* surprised you'd deign to notice a mere shop girl."

Ouch.

Dare he imagine that the putdown suggested a mote of jealousy? A hint that she regarded him more than just a mere customer?

He was intrigued by the idea.

"I didn't notice a shop girl," he said. "I saw a beautiful woman in emeralds who had more envious glances toward her than half the titled ladies there."

Her gaze did not leave his.

"Then why did you not make yourself known to me?" she

asked.

"Difficult to do when *you* went out of your way to avoid *me*."

Miss Bridges flushed red, telling him he'd guessed true. It *had* been deliberate.

She drew him a few paces along the counter, so that Dottie could serve another customer. "I imagine you're wondering why someone like me gets invited to an event as notable as the Huntington Ball," she began, her voice lowered.

"No, I was wondering whether or not you'd accept if I asked you to take a ride through Hyde Park with me."

She regarded him cautiously a moment before glancing away. When she turned to face him, her expression was one of indulgent amusement.

"What about your reputation, good sir?" she said, a delicate eyebrow arched. "No, you shan't get around me like that. I promised I'd tell you what I find out about the original, and I will."

"And then you will let me buy it."

Her expression upended a moment before righting itself. The smile was gone.

"I cannot. It is promised to another client."

"I'll better his price. Who is it?"

"I can't tell you that! Bridges & Sons has never breached a confidence in the one hundred and twenty years we've been in business, and I don't intend to do so now."

Armand faced defeat for the second time today. He acknowledged as much with a slow nod of his head but in truth was not particularly deterred. If he was a man possessed of a more sensitive ego, mind you, the rejections might have cut to the quick. If he acted now, there might be something to salvage from the bruising...

He turned over a check to pay for today's purchases.

If he hurried, he might just catch up with someone likely to be far more forthcoming about the clock.

CHAPTER FIVE

N O, *I WAS wondering whether or not you'd accept if I asked you to take a ride through Hyde Park with me.*

Jade blinked after him as he left.

Who on earth did the man think he was, making such a presumption? Was he having a laugh at her expense?

Dottie nudged her shoulder with her own. "Well then, I think you've made a conquest."

She gave her friend a sour look. "That's perfectly ridiculous." Jade knew she was being peevish but couldn't help herself. Dottie clucked her disapproval.

Then there was no time to think any more about the count. The auction reached the final act, and more and more people came to the counter to settle their accounts.

"We're fifteen lots from the end," said Dottie. "And only a few bidders left. Why don't you go and make a start on the books now? It'd be nice to get home a little earlier tonight."

It was a sensible suggestion to which she readily agreed. Jade gathered up the ledgers and headed to the back office to reconcile the accounts. Edward would be pleased to see that task already attended to when he returned.

Peter followed with the cashbox, and Jade set to work.

Why did the count's words trouble her so much?

Because she liked him.

She liked him a lot.

Yes, he was handsome and affable, but he also seemed to be good company. She'd noted the easy, friendly manner he had with the porters. That he was kind and considerate to the aunts was yet another point in his favor.

But *why* hadn't he left well enough alone?

An aristocrat didn't offer a girl like her a carriage ride through Hyde Park where, during the fashionable hour, people were there to see and be seen. What could squiring around someone of her class possibly offer him? Perhaps it was to turn her head and make her amenable to double-crossing her secretive client.

Jade discounted the notion as soon as it entered her head. He didn't seem the type to behave underhandedly. In all her dealings with him so far, she had found him direct, and decisive, and honest.

The truth of the matter she knew in her heart. She'd *allowed* her head to be turned. Allowed herself to entertain, even for the moment, the possibility that a passing flirtation might become something more serious.

It is the fastest way of getting your heart broken.

Jade always knew that she was caught between two worlds. It was just the way it was, and she'd been content with that.

Thanks to her mother's insistence on her having a lady's education, it was not so outlandish a fantasy that she might make a gentleman a good wife – elegant, cultured, sophisticated, and able to run a household. But by the same token, she could be equally happy working alongside a husband on a business of their own.

Yet so far, in her experience, it seemed as though the men of both of those worlds were looking for another type of woman altogether.

It was her own fault.

She had been eager to take on her father's role as valuer. She saw it as a point of pride that a woman could be as knowledgeable and authoritative as a man in such affairs. It was also true that her word was accepted only because of her family's reputation.

How fortunate was she that Edward had quite willingly relinquished the role of dealing with the well-to-do to her? He had little patience for the world of airs and graces. Moreover, he feared he would make a fool of himself or speak an ill-judged word to someone of influence.

Jade, however, relished the challenge.

In a few nights' time, she would be attending Lord Leverstone's card party. He had asked for her specifically to discreetly value some of his wife's jewelry. Edward did not have the patience, let alone the conversational skills, to sustain an evening in polite company.

In encouraging, nay, *participating* in this flirtation with Count Danger, she was putting everything she'd worked for at risk.

Danger by name, danger by nature…

She wrinkled her nose and continued to work on the ledger.

ARMAND QUICKENED HIS step to catch up with the Irishman.

"Excuse me!"

The man didn't hear him and headed toward one of the cross streets where hackneys waited.

Now he was close enough to clasp a hand on the man's arm.

"Hey, Mattis!"

The shorter man rapidly turned, his cloak billowing out to reveal a short knife in his left hand. Mattis wore a murderous snarl which slowly disappeared as he recognized Armand.

"You're the gent from the auction house," he said. "What ye be wantin' then?"

"I want to know more about the clock."

"What? That clock at the auction house?"

Armand nodded.

Mattis' knife disappeared as fast as it had appeared.

"You're a keen one, ain't ye? Well, as it happens, I have already acquired two, an' the third would have been a little icing on the cake."

"I'd like to see them."

"What for? You said you wanted the original."

"I do."

"Then which is it?"

Armand's annoyance grew.

"Just show me. I'll make it worth your while."

Mattis stared at him long moments as though hoping to divine his thoughts.

"All right," he said after a moment. "You pay the fare, make it worth my while, buy me a pint afterward, *then* we'll get along like old friends, won't we?"

Alarm bells were sounding in Armand's head, but he ignored them.

If he could get a closer look at the clock, he might understand what it was that reminded him so much of his papa. Dear God, even now he saw his father as clearly as if he were before him. So, it *had* to be connected to a memory deep within him.

"You have an agreement," said Armand. "Give me the address."

It turned out the fare was an expensive one. The cab took them to the far side of London, to the Isle of Dogs. And, for ten minutes after that, Armand trailed behind Mick Mattis as they walked past rows and rows of warehouses.

The afternoon sun was sinking low, casting long black shadows.

Men could disappear here...

Mattis carried a knife. Armand regretted not having the same. Next time. If there *was* a next time...

The Irishman stopped, unlocked a side door to one of the warehouses, and entered. Inside, the cavernous space had been partitioned off. The dealer only appeared to have a quarter of it, but it was already filled with crates, partly filled with straw to protect his purchases for their voyage across the Irish Sea.

Armand waited in the doorway as Mattis lit a couple of lamps before rummaging in one of the crates.

"It'll be five guineas."

"For what?"

"To look at," Mattis replied, giving him a speculative look.

Armand skewered him with an expression of his own. "To *look* at?"

"Ye promised to make it worth my while…"

Armand crossed his arms.

Mattis shrugged. "Take it or leave it, me old chum."

Armand sighed.

"Five guineas it is."

With all the aplomb and flourish of a magician performing a trick, Mattis lifted the clock from the crate.

"Here she is. The Lady herself. Or one of her, anyhow."

Armand approached, bringing with him one of the lamps.

"Thalatte."

"'ere, you said that strange."

"Your 'lady', as you call her, is a very specific one, part of the Greek Horai, Thalatte is the personification of spring, youth, and beauty."

"And she is a beauty – and heavy." Mattis nodded over to his right. "Clear off the top of that crate for me."

No sooner had Mattis set the sculpture down than Armand immediately picked it up to feel the weight of it for himself.

"For the original, you'd be looking for bronze," Mattis added. "Much heavier. This is only spelter." He delved into the other crate and produced the pendulum.

The ghosts of memories that lurked in the shadows of Armand's mind didn't reveal themselves as he ran his hands over the statue. And for that he was glad. He needed to keep his wits about him, especially around a man who no doubt thought him to be a dupe.

"You said these copies started to emerge after the Revolution," said Armand. "What of the original?"

"I don't rightly know. The story goes that it was made especially for some aristo family in the last century, and after they got the chop, it fell into the hands of a sculptor who made the copies."

Some aristo family. *His* family…

Armand turned his attention to the decorative pendulum.

"Do you know who the sculptor was?"

Mattis shook his head. "If you speak French—" he began.

Armand smiled wryly.

"—you could check if the design was patented."

Armand frowned. Something wasn't right – not with Mattis, but with the pendulum.

He looked closer. With his father's clock, each piece of the pendulum was separate. He traced a finger at the base of it, just ahead of where it connected to the bob. There should have been linking joints, but the assembly was smooth. This pendulum, apart from the bob, was cast in one piece.

"Something troublin' yer lordship?"

Mattis was too keen-eyed by half.

Armand made sure to look at him directly.

"No."

"Then I'll take me money, thanks."

Armand squared his shoulders. He most certainly did not come down in the last shower. If he pulled out his purse now, the second-hand dealer would probably pull out a knife.

"No," he said again.

Mattis' eyebrows disappeared into his ill-kempt gray hair. His lips thinned in unmistakable anger.

"You get your money. But I also owe you a pint."

At the reminder of the second part of their bargain, the Irishman's posture eased, and Armand felt in control once more.

Daylight had almost disappeared by the time he'd hailed a hackney. Mattis stayed close, especially as they'd walked past three pubs before they arrived at a major thoroughfare and there was still no sign of his payment or his beer.

Armand had allowed himself to be led around for hours. Now it was his turn to lead.

He didn't know the docks. He didn't know the type of curs and cutpurses Mattis associated with. That's why he wanted to be on more familiar ground, so Armand picked a more respectable establishment, *The Swan with Two Necks*, to transact and conclude their business.

He ordered a pint for Mattis, found a table, and passed the five guineas to him. Armand remained standing.

"I thank you for your time, Mr. Mattis," he said, sliding his card across the table also.

"What's this for?" the Irishman asked.

"An address for you to send the clock you just showed me."

Mattis emitted a raucous laugh.

"No, no, no, yer lordship. Five guineas was to *look* at it. You want to buy it; it'll be another ten."

Armand regarded him with scorn. "You jest."

"No – you do. This afternoon you were willing to pay fifty-five guineas. I'd be asking that, but I don't imagine you're carrying that much, and I don't hold with taking cheques."

Armand sighed. It mightn't be the original, but he did *want* it. "Very well." He counted out another ten guineas. "Make sure you send it."

Mattis looked offended. "You can trust *me*, yer lordship."

Armand grimaced. "I'll await the delivery." He turned to leave.

"Are ye not going to stay a drink? For the satisfactory conclusion of our business?"

Armand turned back. "No, I must decline."

"I suppose you have lordly stuff to do."

"Something like that."

"Can I ask ye one thing?"

Armand paused.

"What's so fascinatin' about The Lady clock? The original one, I mean." Mattis tapped a finger on the side of his nose.

"Don't think I didn't notice that pretty young thing at the sales room giving the clock a good going over before the auction. Not to mention the expression on her face when I made a joke about the original."

Mattis looked thoughtful a moment.

"Is *that* what this is about? You, the lassie, the mystery bidder… you're *all* after the original!"

Armand remained tight-lipped. Happily for him, Mattis' pint arrived. The Irishman took a big, thirsty swallow. Then he banged his mug down on the table and swiped his forearm over his mouth before he said, "Bah, keep your secrets, but I'll tell ye for nothin' that you're all on a fool's errand."

For a moment Armand thought to ask him why, but he suspected the man didn't know. He was a braggard with a few other vices combined.

He turned to walk out.

"Keep your eye on the Bridges girl," Mattis called out after him. "She's a clever one that, a bit too clever for my likin', but if you want to lay on hands on the real clock, you'd better lay your hands on her. May as well combine a bit of pleasure with business, eh?"

Armand fought a surge of anger. He squeezed his fists tight to prevent himself from launching at the smug bastard. He turned on his heels without a second look back and searched for a hackney.

HE'D PUT A couple of miles distance between himself and Mattis by the time he passed the Houses of Parliament, yet the disgusting man's words still played in his head.

There was no question about it now – Armand wanted the Thalatte statue clock. The desire grew hotter by the minute.

A quest.

That clock had been in his family. If he could prove that it would be something to point at to say that his father lived on. What if there was more? Did he want to go back to France to see whether anything remained of the family estate?

If he'd asked himself a year ago, he'd have said no.

Now… now he wasn't at all certain of his answer.

Armand closed his eyes leaned back into the seat of the hackney carriage and remembered the feel of the brass pendulum in his hands. The one he had seen today had been cast in one piece. But he had the distinct memory of the two outer rods detaching from the center shaft. His father had actually shown him how it all came apart, or at least that's how it appeared in his dreams.

The clock going tick-tick-tick, then falling silent. His father unhooking the pendulum from the clock and dismantling the parts …

For the life of him Armand couldn't imagine why. Certainly not to clean it. They had no shortage of servants. Cleaning was *their* job.

His stomach plummeted like he was falling. Armand opened his eyes and steadied his breath. It wasn't a dream. It was a *memory*. He was as sure of that as he was of his own name and one just as vivid as the one he had recalled at the auction room.

Mon pere…

He wished he'd had the opportunity to say goodbye. But he had been a child, little more than an infant. He'd no idea of what was to come.

But these dreams, these memories of his. There had to be something more, but what was it?

Armand wracked his brain for an answer but was still no closer to finding one by the time he arrived back at his townhouse in Mayfair. The only time answers seemed to come to him was in his dreams. Perhaps he should start *there*.

And, although crudely put, Mattis *did* have a point about Miss Jade Bridges. She was clever – not to mention excellent at what she did. If she had been commissioned to find the original Thalatte clock, then he had no doubt she would find it.

What could he do? Seduce her into giving up her secrets? Hardly…

He continued to ponder the question as he walked through

the front door and made his way up to his bedroom to begin readying himself to join some of his companions at White's.

While Barnet laid out his clothes, he undressed and washed, laughing inwardly at his own pondering.

Seduce Miss Jade Bridges?

He must have been tired, because, at that moment, a vision of having her in his arms flashed before his eyes, and in the very next instant she was in his bed.

There were just a few problems with all of *that*.

First of all, he was not in the habit of seducing women to simply get what he wanted. Secondly, he actually liked Miss Bridges – *genuinely* liked her. The idea of toying with her to achieve his ends left a sour taste in his mouth.

But she *did* like *him*.

Perhaps he could play on that and use charm to cajole her. Maybe if he told her the whole story, she might feel sorry for him as a friend.

Even that seemed cynical.

Which left him exactly where he started, with no clue as to how to proceed. At least he could vow to himself one thing. He would never, not ever, seduce Miss Jade Bridges.

One part of his body expressed distinct disappointment at that decision.

CHAPTER SIX

TICK-TICK-TICK.

The clock on the mantlepiece ticked for over a minute.

Jade waited in silence for her brother to read the letter from her mysterious client. She didn't need his approval to do her job, but she did want his counsel. Two minds were better than one, and she trusted her brother's judgement.

Finally, he lifted his eyes from the letter and said, "Where do you intend to start?"

"Back at the very beginning. I plan to see Eli Rosenbaum at Hatton Garden. I hope he can tell me the history of the original, or at the very least the name of the foundry where the statues were cast. Then I'll write to them to see if *they* can provide any further information."

Edward nodded thoughtfully.

"I'll make some enquiries – a statue clock, twenty-inches in height, bronze base," he recited. "I'll tell you what I hear."

Jade acknowledged her brother's help with a smile. "And, yes, I know the usual conditions apply."

Those conditions were something they had agreed between themselves when they took over running Bridges & Sons on their father's death. At all times on matters of business, they were to know the whereabouts of each other, the nature of the business they were attending to, and when they were expected home.

"And speaking of which,' she continued, "Lord Leverstone is sending a carriage for me at six o'clock tonight."

Edward returned the letter and the sketch of the clock. "Remind me again what that job is?"

"Jewelry valuation," she said. "I think he suspects his wife of selling off stones to support her current lover. She denies everything of course, but his suspicions just won't be assuaged."

"So, who are you *playing* tonight?"

Jade laughed. "The younger daughter of one of Lord Leverstone's business associates. I thought of pretending to be a Bavarian princess again, but twice in one month might get people asking questions."

"Oh, how I remember how you hated being made to sit down at your language lessons," Edward teased.

Jade remembered it well. French and Italian before lunch. German all afternoon. "That's because I was envying you working alongside father, while Mrs. Kuiper had me conjugating verbs!"

"Well, chances are that I won't see you until tomorrow morning. I'll be at the warehouse all day cataloguing the final goods from the Berkshire house sale. Oh, by the way, what dress are you wearing tonight?"

Jade frowned. Edward rarely took notice of what she was wearing.

"An older one. Claret in color, if you care to know such things."

"Would garnets go with it?"

"They might. Do you have some?"

"I brought them back with me from Norfolk. They're not very expensive, so they might pass muster adorning 'the younger daughter of a business associate'."

OVER THE PAST few years, many gem dealers, goldsmiths, and jewelers had set up shop in Hatton Gardens to escape the less than savory reputation of nearby Clerkenwell.

One of them was Eli Rosenbaum, who had become a close friend of the Bridges family. After her father taught her the basics of gemstone valuation, it was Eli who refined her skill in the art. However, it had been some little time since she'd visited.

Jade found the older gentleman as spry as usual despite his gray hair and hunched shoulders. He greeted her with a kiss on both cheeks and an insistence that she have a cup of tea with him.

"How are you, my dear friend?" she asked.

He shrugged his shoulders. "I can't complain. No one ever listens to you anyway when you do, isn't that right? Now tell me about your brother; it's been too long since he has sent me some of his finest pieces. You must tell him to do his job properly!"

"I'm afraid Edward is going to disappoint you again."

Jade opened her reticule and pulled out a smaller bag filled with broken bits of gold jewelry which were only good for scrap.

"Tsk, tsk, tsk." Eli shook his head slowly in mock exasperation as he peered into the bag. He poured the gold onto a tray and set it on a pair of scales.

"Still, one cannot overlook the discarded and broken, because there is treasure there as well." He placed several small weights on the scale's other tray and waited for the scales to balance, then announced. "Three ounces. Nothing to be sneezed at."

The old jeweler wrote up the amount before pouring the scraps of gold into a larger bucket where other bits waited to be melted down and refashioned into newly desirable objects.

"I'll send my boy around on Monday with the payment," he said before settling himself opposite her once more. "Now, my dear. You didn't come down all this way on such a simple errand. Tell me what really brings you to see your old friend."

Jade gave him a bare recitation of the facts – avoiding mention of the mysterious nature of her client. Only that the man wanted the original of this particular clock.

"I learned by chance that the statue was originally French and was copied in the years after the Revolution, but I wonder if you can tell me more."

Eli perched a pair of half-rimmed spectacles on his nose and examined the sketch.

"I can tell you three things about it," he said. "The first is that her name is Thalatte. She is one of the Greek personifications of spring. She has two sisters, Auxesia and Carpo, who also represent the seasons.

"Secondly, I believe the artist was an 18th century sculptor who was commissioned to make several life-sized statues for a wealthy man in France. The client's favorite of those was Thalatte, and he asked the sculptor to make a miniature bronze of her for a clock."

"Do you know who the client was?"

"Alas, I do not. Not my field of expertise. But I can tell you something about the clock – and that is the third thing."

Jade leaned forward on her chair.

"Here is a surprise for you. The clock itself is not French – it's English. This is very much the work of George Graham. He invented the deadbeat escapement to help keep time in clocks like this. It was certainly an expensive timepiece in its day."

"I'd love to see the workmanship in detail."

"Wouldn't we all! But as much as I can tell you *who* and *what*, alas, I cannot tell you *where*. After the Revolution, so many families were executed or fled. The *sans-culottes* sold off the goods looted from aristocratic homes. I imagine that some clockmaker was so taken with her that he decided to make inexpensive copies."

Jade was thoughtful. "My client must think it's here in London, otherwise he wouldn't have commissioned *me* to find it."

"Perhaps London's where you start – with the clockmaker. Graham is long dead, but the Worshipful Company of Clockmakers might have a record of it."

Jade rose to her feet and gathered up her wrap. She folded the sketch and placed it in her reticule before taking Eli's hand and squeezing it.

"Thank you," she said. "You've given me a place to start."

Eli beamed.

"My dear Jade! If I didn't already have a son to take over the business, I would have asked you. You have a jeweler's eye. *Bah!* I would have taken you on as an apprentice if you had been a boy!"

Jade laughed and gave the man a hug. "If I had been a boy, I would have accepted."

She left Monsieur Rosenbaum and continued down the street considering her options. It was still early in the day, and there were errands to be run. Her next appointment was only a few blocks away. To walk there would be much faster than trying to hail a hackney and negotiate the traffic.

As she approached a cross street, Jade was shoved sideways into an alleyway. She cried in alarm, as her arm was wrenched.

My reticule!

Jade found air enough to scream. She determinedly hung on to the strap.

Someone else yelled. but Jade's attention was on the thief, his features obscured by a brown felt hat tugged low across his brow. A scarf of the same color was pulled up over his chin and mouth. She would not forget his eyes – gray rimmed with blue.

Jade's assailant was larger and stronger. He tugged the reticule harder. Jade stumbled back into the street after him. The bag slipped from her grasp.

She fell to her knees, blinking back tears as she noticed a flash of someone sprinting past to give chase. She felt the weight of curious glances of passers-by, but no one expressed enough concern to stop and ask after her welfare.

Jade squeezed her eyes tight – she would not fall to tears in public – and got to her feet. Apart from the bump to her knees and damage to the lace on the sleeve of her dress, she was uninjured – physically, at least.

But without her reticule, she had no fare to get home. And now, thinking of its contents, the loss of the drawing of the clock stung most of all. Still, it might have been worse. If it had happened on her way into Hatton Garden, there would have been three ounces of gold still inside. She let out an unsteady breath.

"Miss Bridges!"

The man who'd taken off in pursuit of her assailant now jogged back towards her.

Count Armand Danger.

Jade didn't know if she wanted to laugh or cry.

She swallowed against a lump in her throat and faced him with what she hoped was a controlled expression. His was full of concern.

"Are you all right? Are you hurt?"

She attempted a smile.

"Quite unhurt, thank you," she said before her body made a liar of her. Her stomach roiled, and heat rushed through her, leaving her dizzy.

Shock.

The count wore a grimace and held her elbow.

"My carriage is just around the corner."

She meekly followed and let him aid her into his carriage. He ordered the driver back toward Mayfair.

Tears neared the surface once more. If he showed any more sympathy, she would be undone.

"I'm sorry I was unable to retrieve your purse, Miss Bridges," he said, watching her closely with his warm dark eyes.

"You were very kind to come to my aid at all, my lord."

The sound of his title spoken by her seemed to jar him.

"I think we've known each other long enough that you should call me Armand. Agreed?"

Jade let out a hiccoughing laugh and nodded. Tears rolled down her cheeks regardless.

Armand offered a sympathetic smile, along with a snowy white kerchief. She used it to wick away tears. She felt warm once more, but it was not the flash of heat born of shock, but rather a steady warmth, comforting and safe.

"Thank you... Armand."

He smiled. His name from her lips seemed to please him.

"I can take you directly home."

"No, please don't. That's not necessary. I just need a little time to recover myself. There is no need to make my brother worry."

"As you wish, Miss Bridges," he said.

"Jade."

Armand cocked his head.

"If I have the liberty of the use of your Christian name, it seems only fair to return the favor," she said.

"*Jade.*"

Never had her name ever sounded so sensual as it did from this man's lips.

She expected Armand to override her wishes and take her home regardless of her protests. Instead, told the driver to stop at a teahouse.

"I do not question the restorative powers of a cup of tea," he said.

The carriage came to a stop outside a tearoom on a market street in a genteel part of the city. The place was charming, with white and blue gingham curtains and matching tablecloths. The service was pleasant and discreet.

After two or three sips of the rich brew, Jade was beginning to feel genuinely better. There seemed to be no hurry on Armand's part to bring his involvement to an end. He waited until she had almost finished the cup before speaking.

"Apart from the purse itself, did you lose much of value?"

She shook her head. "No, not really. A few coins, a handker-chief, a vinaigrette and a sketch of an item a client ask me to find. That's why I was at Hatton Garden; I'd gone to see a jeweler friend."

"What was the sketch of?"

Jade hesitated. "You won't believe it."

"Try me," he smiled.

You know of his interest. You're only courting trouble, a little voice told her. She glanced down at the tablecloth and back to him.

"It was a clock. One very much like the one you bid on a few days ago."

She watched his expression shift. The gaze narrowed, the jaw tightened, and his lips compressed, but only for the barest moment. She might have missed the change if she had not been watching so closely.

She set down her teacup and regarded him expectantly.

"This clock is more than an idle fancy for you, isn't it?" she said.

Armand's eyes flickered away from hers briefly.

She was right!

Armand shook his head briefly before picking up his own cup. He took a sip and set it back down.

There was a play of emotions on his face which Jade found difficult to read. After another moment's silence, she decided the shake of his head was his way of politely refusing the question. She was wrong.

"I believe the clock originally belonged to my family before the Revolution," he said evenly. "And I am desirous of having it back."

Jade started.

The original belonged to Armand's family?

That complicated things indeed. Someone who had a genuine claim against that of a collector. What should she do?

"I'm sorry," she said softly. Armand frowned, so she continued to ensure there was no misunderstanding. "That you lost your family. They were evil times indeed."

He nodded his understanding.

"You know, I have you to thank for my quest."

Now it was her turn to frown. Armand's lips upturned into a small smile.

"You took an interest in the furniture and other pieces for my home. You seemed to know me and my tastes so well, a mixture of French and English… and it has since made me recognize that I need something more to connect me to my past than simply my name."

"The clock?"

"It was in my father's study on the mantle," he said. "I hadn't noticed it in the auction room until the porter pointed it out. At that moment, a memory of my father came back to me so clearly it was as though he stood right in front of me. You might think it foolish that a mere *objet* can hold such a pull—" Jade shook her head, it was not foolish at all "—but given everything my family… that *I* have lost, the original clock is more than just a fancy timepiece to me."

Jade picked up her cup and drank some more tea to cover a wave of sympathy, all the while mindful that he watched her every action like a hawk. A little thought nagged at her. Was Armand Danger her mysterious client?

No. There was something not quite right about that. The writing on the letter was in a different hand.

He reached out a hand and placed it over one of hers. Awareness of him spread throughout her being.

"Help me find it," he whispered intently.

Oh, how she was tempted. Her eyes fell from his eyes down to his sensuous mouth. How easily she might be seduced by four simple words.

But she had made a promise. No, *more* than that. She had a *contract* with her client. Whoever the mysterious man was, it was *he* who had retained her services. She looked back up at his eyes.

"It is promised to another."

She waited for him to laugh and tell her that he'd been the one who'd sent the mysterious commission. But he did not, instead Armand withdrew his hand from hers. She felt a stab of disappointment.

"You will not help me?" he asked.

Jade sighed. "It's not that I *will not*. I *cannot*. Not if you want that clock. If I find it, I'm honor-bound to tell my client and purchase it on his behalf."

Armand let out a small huff of frustration. "You can at least tell me his name. I told you before I'd be willing to buy it from him."

"I don't know his name."

Jade smiled at Armand's confused expression.

"His commission arrived without name or return address. I communicate with him through an advertisement in *The Times*," she said.

The confused look turned to deep concern.

Her spirits lightened. She could bear his concern, but not his disappointment.

"Do your clients always employ such cloak and dagger methods?"

She raised an eyebrow. "You might be surprised – although none so elaborate as this. Everyone has secrets to hide, which means I have secrets to keep."

Armand leaned back in his chair, folded his arms, and let out an audible sigh. "Does that mean we are to be at odds, *Miss Bridges*?"

She held back a wince of disappointment that he had returned to calling her Miss Bridges, and she mustered an even voice.

"I truly hope not. But you must appreciate my position. I do not withhold information out of caprice. This is my *livelihood*, my family's business. Reputation is everything."

"Then you leave me with no other option."

Jade straightened her spine and watched him closely. She wasn't afraid of him, but she was on her guard. It wouldn't pay to underestimate him.

"I wager that I will find the clock before you," he said, a smile in his voice as well as on his lips.

Jade felt her shoulders relax. How dare he be so infuriatingly handsome? His very look did something to her insides – and well he knew it.

Two can play at that game.

"You seem cocksure of yourself, *my lord*."

One part of his mouth rose to present a powerful, self-assured expression. Jade found herself with the uncomfortable realization that she wanted those lips on hers.

"I'm not without wit and resources, my dear Miss Bridges."

"I dare say you are not."

"Then you accept my wager?"

"We have not yet agreed on terms."

Armand roamed her face with his eyes and ventured lower, taking time to peruse her form. It was as though he ran his hands over her, but she could not bring herself to object.

"I have not yet decided, but it should be one that leaves neither of us dissatisfied."

Oh, this was *such* a dangerous game to play, but she was enjoying herself far too much to put an end to this most inappropriate conversation.

"Such an unformed bet might lead to disappointment," she replied. "What if neither of us finds the clock?"

"We should do whatever is in our power to prevent there being a stalemate. Do we have an agreement?"

The teahouse clock chimed three.

Jade rose to her feet and held out her hand. Not as a lady might, palm down, waiting for a gallant to touch briefly, but as a man would – to shake hands.

"I agree," she said.

Armand rose also and shook her hand in the manner she had offered but did not let go afterward. He took a pace forward, forcing her to look up at him. Tension snapped like electricity between them.

He leaned forward, close to her ear, and whispered, "May the best man win."

CHAPTER SEVEN

ARMAND EXITED HIS carriage at Holborn and informed his driver that Miss Bridges had use of it for the rest of the day.

He'd left the tearoom unsettled after his interlude with Jade. That surprised him.

Their relationship had been turned on its head today, and he wasn't sure how he felt about it. An unserious, light-hearted mutual flirtation had deepened into something more tempting, and he had no idea how and when it happened.

He wanted to kiss her. And he was assured enough in his own desirability that Jade would have kissed him back. That wouldn't necessarily have been a problem, except he wasn't sure he'd be able to stop at kissing.

The surprise was at the depth of his musings. It had gone from a pleasant anticipation to a burning desire in the space of moments.

Attraction became fully fledged arousal. So, for her sake as well as his own, putting space between them was the wisest course of action. It also put him within walking distance of the British Museum. The exercise would do him good. It would straighten his head and might even bring him closer to finding the clock if he could discover the name of Thalatte's sculptor.

Reaching the museum, Armand spoke to a curator who directed him to a series of books on French sculptors of the mid-to-late eighteenth century. He began methodically turning over page after page, poring over plate after plate, examining any design that looked familiar.

After three books, he reached for another. This was more promising. It was full of sculptors inspired by classical figures.

He squeezed his aching eyes shut a moment and turned over the page, and then another. Then one more.

The museum clock struck six.

Just one more page, perhaps two…

There! Thalatte.

Armand let out a steadying breath.

The subject's hair was piled high on her head in the fashion of a previous century, her slender figure artfully draped to hide her nudity, but not the curves beneath. Instead, it was molded to her body as if blown by a breeze, giving the sculpture life. The sleeve of her garment had fallen over her right arm as she pointed. She stood on a rock, her feet bare. A spray of roses tumbled from the rock and onto the plinth.

Tick-tick-tick.

Rap-rap-rap.

The giant lady from his nightmares.

He knew the face. He would recognize it anywhere.

Armand forced himself to look at the illustration, searching for details as to the identity of the sculptor and the man who commissioned it.

In the end, he found a signature of the artist.

Boyer.

"Excuse me, sir."

Armand turned around, and a wizened clerk peered at him through thick glasses. "The museum is closing. sir. I shall have to ask you to leave."

"Forgive me. I lost track of the time."

The old man glanced at the book open on the table before Armand and gave him a gap-toothed smile. "It's good that you found something of interest. Shall I reserve the book for you?"

"Yes... no... I'm not sure, but I think I've found what I've been looking for."

⫸⫷

BARNET WAS BESIDE himself by the time Armand returned home.

"Sir, did you forget your evening with the Earl and Countess? You will not have time for a full bath, so I'll have hot water brought up to your room."

Armand frowned. "What time is it now?"

"It's just after a quarter to seven."

"Then there's plenty of time. Charles' dinner parties don't start until nine o'clock."

Barnet no longer hid his exasperation. "Forgive me, sir, you are going to the opera, and your brother is coming by at half-past *seven*."

With a muttered oath, Armand took the stairs two at a time, shucking out of his clothes the moment he entered the bedroom. Barnet followed close behind with shaving accoutrements, and, a few minutes after that, a footman appeared with a jug of steaming water.

As Barnet prepared the lather, Armand wetted down his face.

"I've been highly distracted today," he offered by way of apology.

"I rather thought you were," the manservant replied in a familiar manner that he only used outside earshot of other servants. "When your driver arrived alone, I was concerned that some ill had befallen you."

"Not to me," said Armand, setting his jaw just so as the straight razor Barnet wielded scraped down his cheek. "But to Miss Bridges, the young lady from the auction house. She was accosted by a cutpurse in the street and had her bag stolen."

"Dreadful! I trust she wasn't hurt?"

"A little shaken. She didn't want to return home in a distressed state, so I had a cup of tea with her until she'd composed herself and offered her the use of my carriage. I stopped by the British Museum and spent a couple of hours there, researching sculptors."

It sounded perfectly reasonable when Armand said it out loud. The look Barnet gave him suggested otherwise.

"In the fifteen years I've known you, sir, never once have you expressed an interest in the fine arts," he said, shaving away the last of the whiskers and handing him a warm, wet towel. Armand patted his face clean.

"There's a lot you don't know about me," Armand announced stiffly.

Barnet looked up. Armand saw his face reflected in the mirror. The man was amused. "You don't need to explain yourself to me, sir. As I believe they say, no man is a hero to his valet."

Armand tossed the hand towel at Barnet's retreating back while he launched himself out of his chair to the bowl where he quickly and thoroughly washed.

"The emerald waist coat tonight," Barnet announced. "And I've picked out the gold cufflinks and matching cravat pin. Simple, but impressive."

"Who am I supposed to be impressing?"

"Lady Cornelia. She is an old family friend of Lady Arabella. You agreed to the arrangement two weeks ago."

"Yes, I recall," he sighed. "Well, old man, you'd better get me spruced up then."

Armand finished buttoning his gloves as Charles and Arabella arrived with Lady Cornelia Fairclough. He shot Barnet a grateful look for the little tray of liqueurs he presented to his guests while they waited for him.

Lady Arabella made introductions. With honey-colored hair and cat-like eyes, Lady Cornelia was undoubtedly a beautiful woman.

"You have a fine home, my lord," she offered.

"It is made finer by the presence of two lovely ladies."

Arabella beamed her approval. Lady Cornelia lowered her eyelashes in a show of modesty that Armand wasn't sure she actually possessed.

"Will sir be requiring supper?"

"Oh, please do, Armand," said Arabella. "I haven't seen that Turkish rug you purchased."

Armand took his sister-in-law's hand and kissed it.

"It is settled," he said, then he addressed Barnet. "Tell Cook to prepare something for supper."

"Very good, sir."

Arabella looked pleased. Lady Cornelia even more so.

Armand tried to muster the appropriate amount of enthusiasm and found that he couldn't.

There was a beautiful young woman on his arm who made no concealment of her interest and a fine evening's entertainment promised in the company of the people he loved best – yet his thoughts were of Jade.

How was *she* spending her evening?

"OH MISS! WHAT happened to your dress?"

Jade peered over the edge of the bathtub and glanced at the torn lace in her maid's hands.

"Oh that? Nothing really. A cutpurse stole my purse today and—"

"Oh Miss!" the maid repeated. "Nothing good comes from going out on your own."

Jade picked up her sponge and continued with her bath.

"Calm down, Suzy, I'm unhurt, and the dress can be repaired. Although I am disappointed to lose my vinaigrette." She paused, thinking about what else she might regret. Edward's censure for one... "Say nothing to my brother about this," Jade instructed. "He has other things to worry about."

"And you're going out tonight, too!"

Jade sighed at Suzy's fretting.

"I'll be picked up in a perfectly respectable carriage, going to a perfectly respectable address, and participating in perfectly respectable activities. I've done this a hundred times before, and you've never fussed like this."

"You've never been assaulted before."

"It was on the street, and it was just the once."

Jade stood up in the bath, letting water drip into the tub before climbing out.

Suzy gasped. "Your knee!"

A glance down revealed that one of her knees bore a growing bruise.

"That's nothing, Suzy. I get worse bumping into furniture in the auction room."

"But what if something dreadful had happened?" Suzy asked handing her a drying cloth.

"That was hardly going to happen in the middle of Hatton Garden in the middle of the day. Besides, the gallant Count Armand Danger came to my rescue."

Jade dropped the name deliberately. Suzy's eyes lit up.

"Dottie told me all about him. She calls him your beau and says he fancies you."

"He fancies a certain clock even more."

The maid's countenance crumbled as though she was the one whose feelings had been rejected. It was all Jade could do to stop herself from laughing as Suzy dressed her. Not that she meant to be unkind, but the truth of the matter was the count's interest was purely professional.

It was. Wasn't it?

Oh, that was a dangerous path to tread. Jade mentally shook herself and instructed Suzy to fetch the pear-shaped garnet earrings her brother brought back from Norfolk.

Jade sought out another reticule, this one black and beaded. She added a few coins, a white linen handkerchief, a pair of tweezers, and a jeweler's loupe.

As Suzy styled her hair in a fashionable but simple style in keeping with her guise, she watched her reflection in the mirror. Despite her confident air, Jade felt uncharacteristically nervous. The theft had upset her more than she was willing to admit.

It was another good reason to go to Lord Leverstone's this evening, however. If her brother got wind of the misfortune that happened today, or learned of her skittishness now, he might relegate her to the role of shop girl in a business they ran as equals. Carrying on without hysteria or fear would prove to him that she was capable. Moreover, it would prove a point, to herself most of all.

Jade employed her nervousness to good effect at Lord Leverstone's card party. It played particularly well in her role as the younger daughter of an acquaintance, there to make up the numbers.

Lady Leverstone was an attentive hostess, and a good twenty years younger than her husband. She introduced Jade to a most unprepossessing young man whose lank, pale hair lay flat over a round and doughy face. He seemed to think being paired with her for the evening gave him the right to try to hold her hand during dinner.

Then she found herself partnered with him for whist where he took to biting his full, almost feminine, lips whenever he had a bad hand. Which was often. While the man pored over his cards, Jade observed their hostess. Unless she was an exceptional actress, Lady Leverstone was quite oblivious to her husband's ruse tonight.

Following the fourth rubber of the evening, light refreshments were served. That was the prearranged time for Jade to excuse herself and make her way down the hall to the library. She closed the door after her and approached the well-lit desk where an open leather case box sat.

Inside were the Leverstone diamonds which, she had been told, were gifted to the family by Charles II himself.

She picked up a necklace and felt the weight in her hand.

A few moments later the master of the house, a distinguished man in his late fifties, arrived and locked the door behind him.

"Are you sure you know what you're looking at?" he said. It was a question he'd asked at their initial interview.

She set down the necklace.

"My lord, you are welcome to take the box to any jeweler in London if you have doubts over my credentials."

He dismissed the complaint with a wave of his hand.

"No, no, just get on with it. The choker and those earrings. They're the ones I'm interested in."

Jade sat down behind the desk and opened her reticule. She placed her white handkerchief on the desk and extracted her loupe.

The first piece she examined was the diamond choker with its graduated stones.

She found that talking her way through the process reassured many clients that she truly knew her craft.

"Paste stones, although a beautiful ornamentation, are not as hard as diamonds," she said. "They will scratch and chip."

Jade ran the pad of her thumb over the stones in the choker.

"Leaded glass is, of course, crystal. So, the facets of paste gems will feel sharp."

She picked up the loupe and looked at a stone here and there, before setting it down and picking up one of the earrings and going through the same process.

"Do you know anything about paste, Lord Leverstone?"

Jade did not wait for him to answer.

"The glass achieves its color by the addition of metallic oxides in its molten state. Cobalt gives you blue. Copper gives you green, or red, depending on how it is used, although that is very tricky to do well. But among the best of their type, the results are very, very good."

Out of the corner of her eye, Jade could see Leverstone shift from one foot to another in ill-concealed agitation.

Jade held an earring up to the light and turned it this way and that. Then she did the same with its twin.

"Lead crystal can scintillate like real diamonds. What paste stones lack is the ability to display different colors when viewed from different angles."

She set the earrings down and put her loupe away.

"The choker has genuine diamonds. The earrings do not."

"Bitch!"

Although sure the epithet wasn't directed at her, Jade made sure she remained on the other side of the desk and thanked her lucky stars that she took the advice of her late father to always receive payment in advance.

The man stared at the jewelry case. His closed, pinch-mouthed expression revealed louder than words what he suspected:

His wife was having an affair and had been slyly replacing gems for paste and selling the stones to give cash to her lover.

And Jade had given him evidence of her infidelity.

She thought of offering to inspect some of the other pieces, but angry men often take their resentment out on the bearers of bad news. "Perhaps it is time for me to leave," Jade said softly. "Best tell the other guests that I've come over faint and have had to go home."

She wasn't sure whether the man had heard her. But after a moment he nodded once. Jade took it as her cue to leave.

There was no footman at the front door, so Jade retrieved her own cloak and let herself out.

It was not that late – about ten o'clock by her estimation – but it wouldn't do to be hanging about the street even in a good part of town. She secured the cloak, pleased for the foresight to wear leather shoes instead of satin dancing slippers.

She walked the couple of blocks toward the theater district, where she would be sure to find a hackney to take her home. Light spilled from the opera house. Carriages lined up outside while their drivers huddled around a brazier on the sidewalk, chatting amongst themselves.

Also milling about were the better-dressed patrons of the theater, and, as Jade made her way through the crowd, she spotted a tall figure standing under a lamp smoking a cigar. She recognized him instantly.

Danger.

No, surely not. Not twice in one day.

Jade stepped around an older couple, hoping to move past before he saw her. She hoped in vain.

"This is becoming quite the habit, Miss Bridges." His silky voice stopped her steps.

Jade turned back and was face-to-face with a very amused Count Armand Danger.

CHAPTER EIGHT

"IT MUST BE fate," she agreed. Then, nodding toward the opera house doors, she asked. "Any good?"

"The libretto? Superlative. The soprano? Divine."

"The chorus?" She raised her eyebrows. Jade was pleased when Armand laughed because that meant he knew she wasn't talking about the singers.

"Frankly, the chorus I could do without. My brother does his best, but my sister-in-law has *ideas*."

Jade grinned. "Ah, ladies with ideas. The most dangerous sort."

Armand issued a most put-upon sigh. "Answer me this, Miss Bridges," he said. "Do all sisters seek to meddle in their brothers' unwed states?"

Jade made an elaborate show of putting her fingers to her chin to ponder the question. Armand's expression lightened once again.

"After giving it consideration, my lord, I'm afraid the answer has to be 'yes'."

"Hmmm, I was afraid of that." Armand leaned in a little closer. Jade felt the return of the undercurrent of tension from this afternoon. "She's a nice enough lady, but..."

Jade held up a hand. "Say not a word more, my lord. A gentleman always has pleasant things to say about a lady and never notices anything less than her charms."

Armand shook his head, giving her a flash of a grin that warmed her from within. Then his expression became serious.

"I'm surprised to see you out after your *adventure* today," he observed. "What brings you out this evening? You didn't mention attending the opera."

"I've just come from a card party."

"What? Alone?"

Jade shook her head. "I was there for work. The host wanted me to, um, *value* some of his wife's jewelry."

She was conscious of Armand's eyes on her, taking in her evening dress and her own ornamentation. She ought to be offended by the man's frank appraisal, but she wasn't. Some part of her *wanted* him to look at her in that way. But when his eyes met her face, they'd hardened.

She knew a moment of disappointment colored by anger. She'd thought he was different. Just because a woman worked in the evening, it didn't mean she did it lying on her back.

"It's much easier to determine if a wife's jewels are still real if the wife doesn't know of her husband's suspicions," she said. "Now, if you'll excuse me. I need to get home."

She turned away. Armand grabbed her arm.

"I've offended you. I'm sorry," he said.

Jade shook her head but couldn't bring herself to look at him.

"You'll have not been the first to think that what I do is... *unsavory.*"

"It's not *you*, nor your profession. I just hate the thought of you being in a situation you couldn't get yourself out of."

At that, Jade raised her eyes to his. A flippant quip at her lips died. Armand's piercing dark eyes held her in thrall. They seemed to speak so much in a language she didn't quite understand, but she knew full well what it was doing to her insides.

"Armand? My dear count, why are you out here?"

The woman's voice calling his name broke the spell. Jade felt the absence of Armand's hand on her arm as he took a step back from her.

A beautiful blond woman approached them – a different to the one he'd squired to the Huntington's Ball.

"Ah, there you are," she said. "I've been looking for you. Intermission is nearly over."

Then the woman noticed Jade. She regarded her coldly with icy blue eyes.

"Go away. Ply your trade somewhere else."

How positively proprietorial.

She could almost smell the other woman's jealousy from where she stood. Before Armand could react, Jade burst into tears and put on a creditable French accent.

"Ah, mademoiselle, *pardonnez-moi!* Forgive me, please!" she said. "I did not mean to cause offense, but it is so long since I have spoken to anyone from my old home who knew my dear *Maman* that I just had to speak to *monsieur le comte.*"

Armand's eyebrows rose to his hairline.

"*Jouer le jeu!*" Jade hissed. *Play along!*

"*Etes-vous serieux?*" *Are you serious?*

"*Oui. J'essaie de sauver votre soiree.*" *Yes. I'm trying to save your evening.*

The woman looked bemused at the back-and-forth conversation in French. Jade was satisfied – not to mention relieved – that the woman didn't speak the language well enough to follow.

She addressed her next remarks to her. "Dear *Maman* died so many years ago, so to find a friend here in London whose family knew her? Ah, *je suis très heureuse.* I am so happy to have encountered *mon cher comte.*"

Jade leaned forward and placed her hand on that of the blonde's. "*I* do not wish to interrupt *your* evening. You have been most gracious in allowing me a few words with your – what is the word? Ah, *oui* – your *husband.*"

That seemed to do the trick. The woman gave Jade the most gracious smile.

"Of course, my dear," she said. "I *completely* understand. Armand, dear, would you like to introduce me?"

Jade offered him her most doe-like expression. His eyes narrowed. She fought a grin.

"Lady Cornelia Fairclough, allow me to introduce *Mademoiselle* Bridgette *Trublion.*"

Jade nearly choked with laughter.

Touche!

He'd called her Miss *Troublemaker!*

Armand took her hand, bowed over it briefly, and spoke to her in French once more.

"*Tu est incorrigible,*" he said. *You're incorrigible.*

"*Tu es sont trop gentil.*" *You're too kind.*

Armand shook his head, amusement playing at his lips. He hailed a hackney and helped her inside. Jade waved to Lady Cornelia through an open window. Standing behind the woman where she couldn't see him, Armand shook his head once more, but Jade was certain he was hiding another grin.

⟫⟫⟫⟪⟪⟪

ARMAND WASN'T SURE whether he wanted to throttle Jade Bridges or kiss her. He turned slowly to Lady Cornelia to assess her mood.

The woman was fanning herself vigorously.

"Oh, my lord, I am *so* sorry. I'm afraid I've offended *Mademoiselle* Trublion. I didn't mean to imply that… *well, oh dear!*"

He fought a temptation to laugh at Lady Cornelia's over-solicitousness and had it in him to feel just a little sorry for his companion. She had been most deftly put in her place by Jade.

To show no offense was taken, Armand offered Lady Cornelia his arm. She accepted, and they returned inside. At the top of the stairs, Charles and Arabella waited for them.

"You managed to find him in the end," said Arabella.

"Oh yes, I found him in conversation with an old family friend," said Lady Cornelia genially.

Charles' eyebrows raised in a silent question.

"From France," Armand clarified before escorting Lady Cornelia to her seat.

As the opera houselights dimmed, his thoughts turned again to Jade.

No, kissing Miss Bridges was a far more alluring prospect than wringing her lovely little neck…

The rest of the evening went by as though in a dream. Armand ensured he was a gracious host during the supper at his home, but, if he was honest with himself, his performance was by rote. He even had it in him to feel a small measure of pity for Lady Cornelia. She had tried her hardest to be witty and appealing. Even now, she was entertaining Charles and Arabella with a piece on the piano. Armand appraised her as he might a piece of artwork.

Objectively, she was everything a man was told he ought to want in a potential wife – beautiful, engaging, accomplished. Yet, as lovely she was, Lady Cornelia's appeal dimmed when he thought of Jade with whom he found himself by turns both intrigued and exasperated. Quite frankly, he didn't know what to make of her. In his experience, a young woman never went anywhere unaccompanied, but what did he know? All he knew were women of his own class, coddled at every turn by nurse, governess, *duenna*, and companion.

Yet Miss Bridges, like her namesake, he supposed, crossed the divide between the aristocracy and the mercantile class as though there was no division separating them.

It made him think about his own circumstances. He'd spent so most of his life embracing his new homeland that he hadn't allowed himself to think that he was as much French as he was English – by birth, even if not by upbringing.

A moment later, Armand became aware of three sets of eyes upon him.

Damn. He'd been caught deep in thought.

"Forgive me, I was transported by your performance, Lady

Cornelia," he said.

God forgive him for the lie.

Lady Cornelia blushed prettily. Arabella gave him a look of approval.

Charles wore an expression of disbelief which he quickly hid.

"Charles," Armand continued. "Would it be convenient to call on you tomorrow?"

"Of course!" said Arabella on her husband's behalf. "You do not need to ask."

Charles said nothing but continued to regard Armand with frank appraisal which made him wonder what expression *he* wore or what tone he carried. His stepbrother seemed to know instinctively that it wasn't intended to be a social call.

"Come by mid-morning," said Charles decisively. "We'll dine at White's afterwards."

Armand shot him a grateful look. Lunch at Whites meant they could talk with more privacy than they could at home.

At that, Charles suggested that they take their leave for the evening.

Armand kissed Arabella on the cheek, then took Lady Cornelia's hand. He bent over it, but did not kiss it, although she took the liberty of squeezing his hand.

"I hope to see you again soon, my lord," she said, flashing a flirtatious smile.

What the hell was the matter with him? An invitation like that should have him rising to half-mast at least. But all his body allowed was the faintest stirring.

He gave the lady a knowing look before releasing her hand.

Charles lingered behind a moment as the ladies retrieved their coats.

"You will have to tell me more about this old family friend when we meet tomorrow," he said.

Armand laughed uncomfortably. "It's not at all what you think. But I *am* interested to see if there is anything left of what our mother brought over from France."

"It's yours, whatever is there. It's your heritage – you ought to have it."

ARMAND COULD SEE the little boy, and his father, and realized he was seeing himself at three. And his papa. But the pair were unaware of his presence. *"Oh, papa! You've broken it. Maman will be cross."*

His father turned to him.

"I didn't know you were there, my boy! No, I haven't broken the clock. It still works."

"But the ball doesn't swing anymore."

"It's because I've taken off the pendulum," he said.

"Why?"

"I'm making a key."

Before his eyes, his father pulled apart the three bars that comprised the pendulum and reassembled them in a different order.

Armand's three-year-old self frowned. He knew what a key was. They were found in locks on doors and in drawers. He'd even seen the majordomo winding up the clock in the hall, but he had never seen a key like that.

"Why?"

"It's a key to fit a very special lock."

Armand didn't understand. He was about to ask when Maman hurried through the door.

"Robert, the Revolutionaries are marching northward. One of the serving girls said her beau on a nearby estate has gone to join them."

His mother, usually so gentle, seemed angry. At first, Armand had been worried until he realized that she wasn't upset at him.

"There is no need to worry, my love. Take Armand and ready yourself as we agreed. Armand, go with your mother and be good."

He nodded vigorously as his father rose from his desk, ruffling Armand's hair as he passed out the room.

He looked back at the statue of the Lady, looking lost without the brass pendulum that made the clock go 'tick-tick-tick'...

ARMAND FELT HIMSELF emerging from his dream. He squeezed his eyes shut, trying to keep himself there, but even now the vision of the study in *Chateau Ytres* faded to blackness. He sat bolt upright, wide awake.

The pendulum! That's what struck him as being odd about the reproduction. He *knew* it was supposed to come apart, but he didn't know *why* it should come apart.

He scrambled around for a striker and steel to light a candle, then, stark naked, rushed over to his desk and started writing down everything he could remember from the dream – the pendulum, the room, even what his mother was wearing.

He had no idea what was important. Hell, he didn't even know even if anything *was* important. His imagination could have made it all up out of whole cloth.

A *key*. A key required a lock. A lock presumed something to keep secure.

A door? Armand dismissed the idea immediately. The assembled key would be too large to work a door lock. A strongbox? Perhaps.

By the time he had finished writing, the fire within him had burned low, and the coals that lay banked in the fireplace could not ward off the early morning chill. Glancing to one side, he caught his reflection in a small standing mirror. How much resemblance did he share with his father? He regretted not pressing his mother for more details about him.

Who was he?

In that moment, Armand wasn't sure if he shouldn't be asking, *who am I?*

He stared at his image in the glass, trying to figure out which features came from his father. Most of them he could only surmise from those he did not share with his mother – black hair and dark brown eyes, a patrician nose. He lifted his chin, the lamplight illuminating the pale skin of his neck.

Unbidden, his mind's eye conjured the wickedly sharp blade of the guillotine plunging down. What was his father thinking in those final moments? Did he think of his wife and son? Was it quick? Was he aware of his head leaving his shoulders?

Gooseflesh covered Armand's skin, making him acutely aware of his nakedness.

The structure of his carefully ordered life he was now peeling off piece-by-piece until his soul was laid bare.

Who am I?

He rose from the desk and faced himself exposed.

He was Count Armand Danger of *Ytres*.

And for the first time in his life that meant something to him.

He extinguished the lamp and returned to bed.

Getting the clock was imperative. It was the key, the literal goddamned key to his future.

Armand squeezed his eyes tightly a moment before opening them and looking up at the ceiling. He was a grown man of twenty-seven years, and yet he was nearly undone by a vivid dream of his father, a man he couldn't remember. He took several deep breaths and forced himself to relax. It was the middle of the night. There was nothing he could do now.

Tomorrow... Tomorrow he would see what his mother had left. He might also visit the ever-surprising Miss Jade Bridges and entreat her once again to help him find the clock.

An image of her face swam before his eyes.

Ah, the very *pleasant* Miss Jade Bridges. He imagined yet again what it would be like to kiss her, and, in his mind's eye, he did. He closed his eyes, drifting off to sleep with a much more pleasant dream filling his thoughts.

CHAPTER NINE

"**T**HERE'S A GENTLEMAN here to see you."

Jade looked up from her inventory ledger and frowned. It was most unusual for there to be any clients before noon. During the Season, the *ton* rarely ventured from their homes until the early afternoon fashionable hour.

"Did he bring a card?"

Her maid handed it over.

Armand.

Perhaps he'd come to buy a trinket to appease the woman he was with last night. She was surprised by the little pang of jealousy she'd felt at seeing him with yet another beautiful woman.

Jade told herself off. The man was a handsome and wealthy eligible count. Why shouldn't he escort equally beautiful women by the score?

That truth provided no comfort. She had become used to considering him *her Armand*, as he always signed himself in the bidding register. *Armand Danger.* Never once had he used his title.

She rose, pausing by a mirror to run a hand over the stray strands of light brown hair that had escaped from her chignon.

You're primping for him.

Jade pulled a face at her accusing reflection, straightened her shoulders and went to meet him in the Oriental salon, where important clients were entertained.

When they had appointments, they were greeted with a drink of their choice and served little pastry delicacies on exquisitely decorated Imari plates.

The room featured expensive wallpaper patterned with branches that supported exotic blossoms. Equally elaborate pheasants flitted between the blooms. The furniture was finely proportioned. Black lacquer whatnots held priceless jade carvings in all shades from icy white to the darkest moss green.

Jade found *her* Armand admiring a large carving of a lion that measured nearly a foot long. He heard her enter and turned. Her breath caught.

Dear lord, he was *handsome.*

She had become so used to his rather plain attire at the sale room that to see him dressed as a man about town was particularly striking. His jacket was carnelian red, trimmed with brass buttons, over trousers the color of raw umber.

After a moment, Jade remembered her manners and offered a curtsy. "This is an unexpected pleasure, my lord."

He seemed to spend an inordinately long time looking at her face.

"I've just discovered where you got your most unusual name."

Jade blinked rapidly, allowing her eyes to slide to the display of jade pieces. She approached them.

"Those pieces were what made my grandfather's fortune," she said. "According to my father, grandfather foresaw there would be a great demand for treasures from the east. Much to grandmother's dismay, he sank the last of their funds into a syndicate going to China. He was down to his last farthing when the ship returned with enough porcelain and furniture to repay his investment a hundredfold. My mother was expecting me at the time, and my father promised if I was a daughter, they would call me Jade. So that is how I came by my name."

"A gem," said Armand softly.

Jade was conscious of his nearness.

Too conscious.

She was irresistibly drawn to him, like a pin to a lode stone. With a great deal of effort, she pulled away from his side and seated herself on a rose-pink velvet chair and nodded to indicate that he should take the matching settee. She prayed it was enough distance between them to break the spell.

"I'm here because you have something I want." There was something about the way he said those words that turned her insides to liquid. Her rational mind rang alarm bells.

Listen to his tone of voice. He's trying to seduce you!

She would be lying to herself if she didn't admit that part of her was thrilled by the prospect.

Perhaps she could turn the tables.

Jade lounged back in her chair.

"My lord, I have lots of things men want. You'll have to be more specific."

She watched with satisfaction as his nostrils flared and eyebrows raised at her very deliberate double *entendre*.

"The Thalatte clock," he said.

"You told me so yesterday. Have you abandoned your wager so quickly?"

Armand looked confused.

"You wagered you would find it before me."

"I hoped to elicit a truce and propose that we work as allies."

"To what end?"

Armand leaned forward, resting his elbows on his legs, looking at her intently.

"The clock is rightfully mine," he said softly. "It was stolen from my family by the Revolutionaries. I *will* get it back."

The determination that thrummed through his voice resonated with her too. But she couldn't forget that she was under obligation to another.

"I don't know how I can help you."

"Share with me what you know, and I'll promise to do the

same."

Jade opened her mouth to speak, but hesitated.

Obviously sensing a refusal, Armand spoke first.

"All right then. Explain to me why the clock means so much to your client."

There was only one honest response she could give: "I don't know."

Jade managed to pull her eyes away from his.

"Are you certain the clock was in your family?"

"Are you asking if I have the receipt?" he asked before adding mirthlessly, "I'm afraid a Revolution set fire to all of that."

"Then—"

"How do I know it's mine?"

Jade swallowed and nodded mutely.

There was silence. She raised her eyes to his, looking for truth in his expression. It was he who looked away first. It was clear he was carefully considering his answer.

"The pendulum is not one solid brass casting," he offered at last. "It's an assembly of separate rods which come apart. Is *that* something your client mentioned?"

Jade shook her head. "He gave me dimensions. He said the original is slightly larger than the copies, it's made of bronze, and it's signed."

"By Boyer."

She nodded.

"If I'm wrong, then you have a second pair of hands working for you. But if I'm right…"

"If you're right," she repeated, "then that is a bridge we'll cross when we come to it."

Armand seemed surprised by her answer. Perhaps he was expecting more of an argument.

"If the pendulum is constructed as you say, it will be something which is easy to determine, *if* we find the clock. But you do understand that I am obliged to my client?"

"Perfectly. All I ask is that you let me examine the piece first, before you send it to him."

Jade could think of no reason why she should refuse him that small request. She let out a breath. "I can do that."

Armand grinned, the smile giving him a younger, almost boyish look. He left his seat to kneel by hers. He picked up her hand. His lips caressed the bare flesh of her hand and sent a charge through her. "Thank you."

The two-word answer rumbled like distant thunder. She squeezed his hand in response. Yet he did not let go. His fingers stroked the downturned palm of her hand.

Her eyes searched his. She nervously licked her lips. His eyes flickered down to them, then back up to her eyes.

Never had she anticipated a kiss so much…

Never had she been so disappointed to not receive one. Instead, Armand released her hand and rose to his feet.

ARMAND ACKNOWLEDGED HIS low-key arousal. How tempting it was to kiss her. He could see himself doing it all too easily. And there would be no resistance on her part. It pleased him to see the invitation writ clear on her face, along with the flicker of disappointment that passed over it before the very proper Miss Bridges returned and schooled her features. But then, she also stood, looking every inch the composed businesswoman.

"Is there anything else I can help you with today, my lord?" she said coolly.

How odd that it was his turn now to be disappointed. He'd thought they had moved beyond formalities to being… *what* exactly?

Friends?

Colleagues?

Neither honorific seemed satisfying. His eyes fell to her lips once more, then the curve of her breasts beneath the cotton of her blue day dress.

Lovers?

Now that thought was appealing.

And yet, if he kissed her as he wanted, the truce they'd so carefully negotiated would come to an end. And as much as he wanted Jade at that moment, he needed the clock more.

He reached to stroke her cheek with his fingers, watching her lids flicker closed and her lips part with an almost soundless sigh. Temptation became too much. He leaned down and kissed her on the cheek. That got her attention.

"Wednesdays. We'll ride in Hyde Park," he said. "We can talk and not be overheard."

Jade let out a shuddering breath and nodded her agreement. Though she opened her eyes, she did not meet his gaze.

He had to stop now or lose the battle completely.

With business concluded, for now, Armand left the shop and stepped into the late morning sunshine.

The previous day, he could have rationalized his feeling towards Jade as one of chivalry – the desire to protect the lady from the blackguard who stole from her. Last night, as they bantered back and forth outside the opera house, his desire for her could be put down to comfortable teasing born of long familiarity.

Today was more difficult to explain away.

Tempting though it was to spend the rest of the ride to Charles' place indulging in a fantasy of doing more than simply kissing her cheek, Armand forced himself to think about the discussion he needed to have with his stepbrother.

He was admitted into the house and went directly to the drawing room to discover Lady Cornelia also in attendance.

She blushed prettily at him and said 'hello', presenting her hand. He bent over it but did not kiss it. Let her think him rigid with respect to proprieties.

Armand fought hard to hide his annoyance. He wanted to speak to his brother in private. He looked to Charles and knew him well enough to ken his thoughts. Lady Cornelia's arrival was unplanned – by him, at least.

His sister-in-law's expression, however, told him everything he needed to know. She had planned this 'accidental' meeting and looked rather pleased about it too.

Arabella rose to kiss Armand in greeting, then turned to her husband. "You didn't forget I was going to Countess Engelton's at home today, did you? Cornelia thought it best that we leave together."

They were leaving? That was a relief.

Arabella smiled at Armand. "Do let Cook know if you'd like to stay for supper," she said, then she turned to Cornelia. "Both of you. We have no special plans, do we Charles?"

Lady Cornelia wisely remained non-committal before departing in Arabella's wake.

Charles picked up a teapot from the tray on the low table and poured himself another cup.

"One for you?"

Armand nodded and sat in a nearby chair, picking up a plate and helping himself to a selection of small sandwiches from the platter beside the pot.

"Arabella has asked me to press you for information about what happened with Cornelia last night during intermission. I have no intention of satisfying her curiosity," he said. "But it did sound like you had something very particular in mind when you said you wanted to pay a call today."

Armand nodded, washing down the sandwich with a swig of tea.

"I want to go through the box of papers from France that *Maman* left. The one father gave me to look through when I was thirteen," he said.

"Are you sure she didn't take it back to France with her?"

"I don't think so. I recall returning it to the study for safekeeping. *Maman* hardly went in there after our father died."

"So, what's your interest now?"

Armand used the cover of scoffing down another sandwich to

contemplate his answer.

He found his place to begin.

"I've never told anyone this. Not even *Maman*. For years I've had dreams – nightmares, really – in which I am three years old, still in France. Until recently it's been pretty much the same dream. Except I don't think they're really dreams."

Charles set down his own plate and regarded him gravely. Armand didn't know whether to be pleased or dismayed. If his brother mocked, he might take it as a sign that he was being foolish. The fact that Charlie hadn't…

Armand reached for the teacup once more.

"I'm starting to think they are memories. Unreliable ones"

"You think that they're recollections of real events?" Charles asked.

Armand shrugged, trying to find a nonchalance he didn't feel. "I need to find out if they are."

"What do you expect to find in the papers?"

"Evidence of a clock."

Armand laughed at the comical expression that crossed Charles' face.

"Believe me, there's no one more surprised than me. But memories of this clock feature in my nightmares, and recently I've learned that the damned thing actually exists."

"What's so special about this timepiece?"

"I think it's a key to something left by my father, something that *Maman* has forgotten about."

"Or chooses not to remember."

And that's the nub of the matter.

Armand inclined his head in acknowledgement of his step-brother's observation.

Charles got to his feet. "Then let's not waste any more time. Let's see if we can find this mystery clock of yours."

Armand followed him into the study where Charles unlocked a desk drawer and handed him the set of keys to the cabinet.

"Anything you need, just ask," he said.

Behind the first locked cabinet door, Armand found the box his stepfather had given him. It was the first time he'd seen it in nearly fifteen years. He set it aside and continued his search.

Charles, too, rummaged through the many drawers of his late father's study.

"Do you remember the trunk that came with you after father and *Maman* married?" he said. "I was fascinated by it. I was convinced it contained pirate treasure."

Armand set down the paper he was reading. "I haven't thought of that old thing in years! I recall it being the only piece of furniture we had when we moved into the boarding house. It was our couch and our dining table. At night, *Maman* would pull everything out, line it with a blanket, and it was my bed."

"Did she get rid of it?" Charles asked.

He shrugged "I don't know. When they married, I was too much in awe of having a room of my own to care what happened to a trunk."

Charles got to his feet and tugged at the bell pull. A moment later, the butler answered.

"Danvers, do you recall ever seeing an old trunk, made of timber with iron strapping? Been knocking around here for years."

The servant frowned in concentration a moment.

"It doesn't spring immediately to mind, sir. However, if such a trunk exists, it might be in one-half of the old servants' quarters at the top of the house. That was given over to storage many years ago. I could have a couple of the footmen look for you, sir."

"Don't worry, Danvers. I'll go and take a look," said Armand.

"I'll come up with you," offered Charles.

Armand shook his head. "No, don't trouble yourself. I've taken you away from your work. I'll let you know if I find anything."

The upper floor room was illuminated by a set of three dormer windows. It reminded Armand of a dustier, less well-organized version of Jade's sale room. Canvas covers puddled around the feet of an old rocking horse. Several pieces of large furniture, unfashionable now, stood against the wall.

The butler who'd escorted him to the room returned with a lamp and left Armand to explore on his own. It didn't take long at all. There, half tucked under the leaves of an extendable dining table, was the trunk.

Heedless of the dust which coated the knees of his trousers and the sleeves of his jacket, Armand pulled the trunk out of its hiding place.

It wasn't locked. Thank God for that. It probably meant there was nothing in it.

Nothing of any value at any rate. He was probably wasting his time.

Armand recognized his prevarication, guarding against raising his hopes. If he expected to find nothing, he wouldn't be disappointed when he didn't.

He gripped the hasp of the lock and lifted. The heavy lid groaned stiffly on its hinges.

The trunk wasn't empty.

Inside it was a small box and a sheaf of papers. He lifted out the box. *It* was locked. Armand set it aside.

He hesitated over disturbing the papers, fearing the potential for a rats' nest or worse…

To his surprise, the paper, though yellowed, was clean and dry.

Seeing the box and the papers brought back memories of the boarding house. He recalled his mother bitterly crying as she ripped open the stitching on the lining of their clothes one by one and pulling out jewels and paper like a conjuring trick…

Armand removed what approximated a quire, then tapped the base and sides of the trunk to see if it might hold hidden compartments. Satisfied that it didn't, he brought the papers and the box closer to one of the dusty windows.

A densely written document in French was the first item he saw. He set it aside to read in better light.

The second document was a drawing. It took him a moment

to realize the shapes were not just random patterns, but rather landscape design diagrams.

He turned over another page and came face to face with Thalatte.

But not as a clock.

She was a statue – just like the one he'd seen in the book at the British Museum.

CHAPTER TEN

Dear Miss Bridges,

I cannot express the depth of my disappointment at your apparent lack of progress.

Jade raised her eyebrow at this. It had been four weeks since her mysterious client's commission, and there had only been one instruction on how to contact him to confirm her acceptance.

I believe I pressed upon you the urgency of my request. The passage of time has not dimmed my resolve.

I reiterate my sincerity in this matter by stating once again that money is no object. I will pay the owner whatever price he demands for the clock, so you should not fear about being out of pocket yourself.

In addition to the money advanced so far, I will pay double the usual commission for your service.

I expect an accounting of the effort you have made so far to find this object for me. You will write a letter addressed to…

Jade turned over a page hoping to finally find out the name of this client. If she had his name, she could track him as she tracked the clock.

…John Smith, care of 73 Edgeware Road, Hampstead Heath.

She set down the letter in disgust.

John Smith, indeed!

In a city the size of London there must be a thousand men with that name! Without doubt it was a pseudonym. Jade suspected the address to be a commercial premises – a bookstore, a stationer's – somewhere where one might expect a letter to be left for later retrieval.

With a deal of resentment, Jade started to fashion her reply – informing her client she had discovered that the clock itself was English and the statue was based on a late eighteenth century work by an acclaimed sculptor called Boyer. And as for its whereabouts, *that* was still a work in progress. She told him she had written to the manufacturer of the reproductions with enquiries about the original model and, closer to home, her brother had a pending appointment with a reclusive clock collector who might even own the clock in question.

Jade ended the letter and set it aside, waiting for the ink to dry. She did not mention what Armand had told her about the pendulum. That information she kept to herself.

Armand.

She smiled.

He'd kissed her.

Admittedly it was just on the cheek, but even that was enough to send tingles through her. Still, she thought she was smarter than to have her head turned by a handsome man. She'd vowed long ago that she would not be one of these missish young women who fell in love every other week with a pretty new face.

And Armand was wealthy in his own right, unlike some of the men who'd tried to call on her in the past. If she were of the right social standing, Jade would consider herself to be most fortunate indeed to have one of the *ton's* most eligible bachelors express an interest.

But really, where could it possibly lead?

Only to heartbreak.

Yet she couldn't help herself. She anticipated his kiss, *wanted* his kiss, and now she found herself anticipating Wednesday when she would see him again.

The clock struck eleven and her maid, Suzy entered the study holding a cloak and hat.

"Miss, the carriage is ready outside."

Jade frowned. Why? Was she going somewhere?

At her puzzled expression, Suzi continued. "When the master went out this morning he asked if you would go to the sale room and help him with inventory this afternoon."

Inwardly cursing, Jade glanced at the letter. She would just have to pen her reply later.

"I forgot," she said, allowing Suzy to help her on with the cloak and hat and gave her client's missive one last resentful glare before hurrying out the door.

She made it to the sale room before Edward. In fact, it was her brother who was late. When he did arrive, he looked harried and grim.

Work stopped. Jade and Dottie exchanged glances and joined the porters as they gathered around Edward.

"I have some bad news," he said. "Remember, Mickey Mattis, the Irish dealer?" Everyone nodded. He might only attend twice in a year, but they all knew Mickey.

"He's dead." There was a murmur of shock. Edward continued. "They found his body two days ago. He was stabbed to death in his warehouse."

"Robbery?" Peter asked.

"He was a bit of a shady character himself if you ask me," muttered Seton.

Edward shook his head slowly. "What's strange about it was the fact that not a lot was stolen, but there was plenty of damage."

"Someone was looking for something?" Jade suggested.

Edward nodded. "Most likely. The magistrate has asked me to value the remaining goods in his warehouse and contact his family in Ireland to find out what they want to do with them.

Unless they're promised to listed customers, we'll auction them off next month and send the money over to his family. That's it. I want you all to be careful when you leave here tonight. And if anyone remembers anything or learns of anything about Mattis, then come to me."

Everyone returned to their work, some muttering how London was no longer safe for the working man. Others agreed with Seton. Mattis was no angel, and perhaps if one lay down with dogs, one might get up with fleas.

Jade turned to go back to her work when Edward snagged her hand and nodded toward the back office. Clearly, he wanted to converse in privacy.

"There's something else the magistrate told me that I wasn't going to mention to the staff," he said. "Apparently in the days before Mattis's murder, someone was seen hanging about the warehouse, asking where one might buy and sell second-hand goods. He also told me there's been a spate of robberies recently, not just at the docks, but also more toward our end of town. In one of them, they threatened a female staff member to make her open the shop. I'm about to go out to instruct the porters here to make sure that Dottie and the other girls here are escorted home after they finish work," he said.

"And at the shop?" Jade asked.

"I'll send Seton to tell the boy the same thing."

She approved the idea with a nod. "A wise precaution."

Edward wasn't finished. "And that goes for you too. I don't want you attending client jobs on your own anymore."

No!

"I can't do my job with an escort, you know that," Jade protested. "I'm perfectly safe at card parties and balls."

"What about on the streets?"

There was something in his expression that silenced the counter argument on her lips.

Confident of having her full attention, Edward produced a silver vinaigrette from his pocket and held it in his palm.

Jade looked down at it and bit her lip. That was *her* vinaigrette. There was no mistaking it.

"Where did you find it?"

"Silas Hobthorn recognized it and sent me a message."

Jade nodded slowly. Silas had run a pawn shop in Cheapside for years. Every now and again, he would put the more valuable unclaimed pieces forward for auction. He was a useful source of information on who wanted to discreetly dispose of items of worth.

"When were you going to tell me?" Clearly, Edward was in no mood to be trifled with today.

Jade considered her position. If she told him that she'd been a victim of a cutpurse, it would only serve his point. If she lied and said she'd merely lost it, and he already knew the truth, this interview would go so much worse.

Her only choice was to dance around her answer and hope Edward wouldn't ask too many questions.

"It happened when I visited Eli at Hatton Garden."

"And you were alone…"

"Not exactly. Armand Danger happened upon me just after it happened. He saw me safely home."

Edward's lips pressed tightly as though sealing away the words he wanted to say. His face grew steadily red before the angry color receded. Jade felt hollow to the pit of her stomach. She had spent so many years as her brother's equal in the business. Now, to be treated like one of the staff, or worse, a *sister*, would undo her entire professional reputation.

She braced herself for his fury but stood ready to defend her position.

"You're a grown woman, Jade. You have your majority. I can't tell you what to do," he said softly. "But as head of Bridges & Sons, I have a duty to those who work for me. And – as your brother – I love you, and I worry about you."

What could she say to that?

If he had lost his temper and yelled at her, she could have

gathered together her pride and dismissed his concerns as being the fevered rantings of an overbearing busybody. But because he was reasonableness itself, she'd be churlish to dismiss his concerns for her safety out of hand.

Jade let out a calming breath. "I know you do. And I want to give you as little to worry about as possible," she said. "I promise I will take Seton as my driver from now on."

Edward nodded, not hiding his relief that he didn't have to engage in an argument with her.

In moments, the tension ebbed away.

"So, it's Armand, and not Count Danger of *Ytres*?" There was a teasing look of speculations in her brother's eyes. "I had no idea that you were acquainted outside the sale room."

"Don't you get any ideas in your head, oh brother of mine," she said in the most affronted manner she could muster. "For your information, the count is looking for the same clock as my mysterious client."

"Hmm, a professional conflict of interest if I've ever heard one," Edward mused. "How are you going to manage the expectation of both men?"

"I will solve that problem when I come to it," she said. "First I have to find the clock."

"Let's hope old Mr. Meddings has it tucked away in a corner somewhere along with all the rest of his timepieces and only wants a farthing."

Jade laughed.

"Fine chance that would be!"

She gave her brother a hug.

"Thank you for looking after me," she said softly.

Edward returned her embrace.

"Of course, I look after you. You're my sister," he said, then broke into a grin. "And my best valuer."

CHAPTER ELEVEN

B ARNET WAS HORRIFIED at the state of Armand's clothes on his return from Charles' place, and all but ordered him to change.

The newly pressed shirt laid out for him this morning was now black in places. The brocade on his waistcoat fared no better.

Armand allowed his valet to fuss over cleaning while he swiftly changed into at-home clothes – plain, simple, and functional – then went to his study to examine his finds in privacy.

He opened the red box he'd retrieved from Charles' study. To the contents of that, he'd added the papers and the small box retrieved from the trunk. He reached for the small box first and examined it closely for the first time.

It was simple, covered in canvas yet painted in the most vibrant colors. The background was a golden yellow onto which had been painted stylized tulips of white, blue, and red.

He was vaguely aware that it was a marriage piece, perhaps gifted to *Maman* by his father on their wedding day. The box was not large, only eight inches on its longest edge. Nonetheless, Armand had no idea how his mother had managed to bring it with her from France. They had fled with only the clothes on their backs. Or so he recalled.

It was closed with a simple hinged latch, secured in place by a locking escutcheon tarnished with rust.

A maid came in with a tray with freshly baked scones, a dish of butter, and a selection of condiments, and set it at his elbow.

Armand, fixed on his task, ignored her and concentrated on opening the lock. The latch held firm. And he had no key. He wondered how easy it would be to pick the lock before realizing he had no idea how to go about that.

Jade would.

He smiled at the thought.

How she had influenced him, and he hadn't even realized it.

Thanks to her, he'd found himself looking at objects with her eye. Now he asked, were they well-made? Were they pleasing to look at? He found himself appreciating craftsmanship and developing a curiosity about how a cabinetmaker created dovetail joints that were just *so*. He marveled at the skill of the glass blower in creating delicate pieces to drink from.

Armand set aside the little box to look through the larger one. The red-marbled cardboard triggered another memory – not just of his stepfather showing it to him for the first time, but of occasionally catching his mother, when he was much younger, looking in this box and seeming to be quietly reminiscing. At other times, there would be tears shining in her eyes.

He recalled trying to ask her questions then, but she simply dried her tears and fiercely reminded Armand that he was very lucky to be living here in England, and he ought not to forget that. Being the dutiful son, he'd done just that.

Maman…

His mother was a beautiful woman, but she was not strong. There was a delicacy in her manner and features that brought out the protective nature of men and that included her son. Whatever curiosity he had about his own father was tempered by the knowledge that the mention of his name would bring her to tears.

Anyway, it seemed disloyal to express too much interest for the past out of respect for his stepfather, who had always been so kind and generous with him. There had been many blessings to count, not least of which was managing to escape from France when so many had not.

Lady Nicole Danger, Countess of *Ytres*, had the beauty and the title which allowed her entrée into the British aristocracy. Their generosity was partly out of benevolence, but also an acknowledgment that republican tendencies easily spread. But for the grace of God, their English necks might have been on the block too.

How fortunate she was – *how they both were* – that the widowed Earl had fallen in love with her.

And how easy it was to forget there had been a life before England.

Not long after the Earl of Rosemont passed away, and Armand's stepbrother took the title, Lady Nicole's brightness dimmed. It would not be untrue to say that she had lost the second love of her life. Two men had loved her, and she loved them in return, but her heart always belonged to France.

Armand took out the papers. Among them were love letters between his parents during their courting days. He read them with an adult eye, appreciating the depth of this love between a man and a woman. It tugged at his heart, and not just because the words belonged to his parents. To experience that passion, that connection with another filled him with a moment's longing. For a moment, an image of Jade appeared in his mind's eye.

He set the letters aside disturbed by the unexpected direction his thoughts had turned. Armand picked up another piece of paper – a list of friends in England who would help them. It appeared to have been hastily written. Some of the names he knew. He'd grown up with their children.

Then there was the letter confirming the death of his father, and a newspaper clipping detailing the day in question.

The clipping was just a single paragraph.

We receive word that sentence was carried out on Wednesday, 16 October (old style) on enemies of the Revolution in Arras. Those who suffered the penalty of death for their crimes were Robert Danger of Ytres, Michel Cresse of Arras, Pierre Graves of

Arras.

Armand swallowed against a lump in his throat. What did his father think at that moment? Was he brave? Was his death mercifully quick?

He set letter and clipping aside and picked up another document – the landscape plans for the estate in *Ytres*.

Of all the things his mother brought with her, why those? Why had she sewn *them* into the lining of her cloak? He couldn't begin to fathom the significance of it.

From what he could see, the gardens of *Ytres* were formal, laid out in a geometric pattern away from the house and out toward the grounds. He could see where the architect had indicated plinths for statues.

He picked up the artist's illustration of Thalatte. The Great Lady of his nightmares. She was exactly the same as the clock, although the index finger of her right hand pointed outward, rather than holding a timepiece.

Clearly, the statue and the clock were significant. But how? *Why?*

He wished his mother was here now to talk to. In the year after his stepfather died, she begged him to return to France with her. Why had she not told him about this? Did she assume he already knew? Did *she* even know what it meant?

Armand had not wished to return to a place he barely re-membered. He had the courtesy title of Count, which he was happy to use to gain him *entrée* into society. But without the lands to go with it, he'd had very little interest in finding out more. It was like the Scottish title, *Laird*. It seemed that every man and his dog was a 'laird' in Scotland.

The statue was dated 1753, according to the paper before him. This was proof his family had owned an original Boyer sculpture. To be sure, it was not the clock, but if it was accepted that the clock was commissioned by his ancestors and inspired by the life-sized piece, then it could be argued that the clock was stolen from his family and was now his by rights.

However, it was a piece of the puzzle only.

Armand turned his attention back to the small box with its rusty lock. There were several keys in his desk drawer. Perhaps one of those could be used to open it. He sorted through them and found three that might suit.

The first wouldn't go into the small keyhole but, to his surprise, the second key was a perfect fit. However, it wouldn't turn. Was it useless, or was the lock just stiff and rusted?

He looked at the tray with the scones. The little pat of butter on the plate had softened. He wondered if he could use it to lubricate the lock and latch. He melted a dab of butter on his hand and smeared it across the keyhole and the key before reinserting it.

He twisted it gently back and forth a few times, then suddenly the key turned, and the latch opened.

Inside the box was a small cloth bag. He took it out and opened the drawstring. Afternoon sunlight from the windows lit the jewelry that sparkled on the inside.

The first items he withdrew were a pair of silver shoe buckles. On either side of the pin were two silver bow details, and in each corner, a stylized flower.

Next, he pulled out a pair of girandole earrings. There was a center stone, cased in silver, from which hung three smaller stones of the same reddish pink.

The final object was a delicate silver filigree heart pendant. Inside the heart, fine silver scrolls supported a round centerpiece of light blue enamel into which were embedded seed pearls and small cabochon rubies.

Obviously, these were the last of his mother's jewelry. He turned to the earrings. The stones were large. Surely they couldn't be real. Armand ran his thumb across the silver backing. Paste? Quite possibly.

Jade would know. Again.

Would he make a fool of himself by going over to Bond

Street to see her right now, as he had the urge to do?

"Sir?"

Armand looked up from his desk. He hadn't noticed Barnet enter.

"You have a visitor, sir."

"Who is it?"

"A Miss Bridges," he said with a slight note in his voice that suggested disapproval.

What? Here?

How strange that no sooner than he start thinking of her that she appeared, as though he'd conjured her up.

Armand rose immediately.

"Have the housekeeper serve tea in the parlor," he said, moving quickly past Barnet and into the hall where Jade waited. Unfortunately, the expression on her face suggested this was not a social call. He ushered her into the parlor.

Before he'd even invited her to sit, she spoke. "Do you remember the Irishman you were bidding against, for the clock?"

He was hardly likely to forget him. Armand nodded.

"He's been murdered. He was stabbed to death in his warehouse on the docks."

Armand rocked back on his heels. His jaw tightened a moment to prevent a string of curses from coming out. He let out a breath.

"I was there."

Jade looked alarmed. "When was he killed?"

"No, not then. On the day of the auction. I managed to catch up with him. He told me he had two more Thalatte clocks, and I wanted to see one up close."

She frowned, and at that moment he found himself longing to take her in his arms and smooth the worry from her brow. "He already had *two*?"

"Or so he claimed. I only saw one. It was already packed in a barrel, and he took it out to show me. It was seeing that one that caused me to recall the memory of my father pulling apart the pendulum."

"Edward hasn't mentioned coming across the clocks at Mattis's warehouse."

"He's there?"

"The magistrate asked him to make inventory."

A maid knocked at the door and came in with a tray with tea.

"Mary, leave that. Tell Barnet I'm going out."

If Jade wondered about his presumption, she didn't voice it. "I have a carriage waiting," she said.

JADE NOTED THERE was no surprise from Seton when she emerged from the Count's home with the man himself in tow, but he did look at her askance when she told him to take them to the docks. Nevertheless, he did as instructed.

While they made their way through London's crowded streets, she kept her focus outside the window so she could examine her thoughts.

As soon as she'd seen Armand's face as she delivered the news about Mattis, she knew she was right to have gone to him. She remembered how he had left abruptly after the auction and suspected that he'd tracked the Irishman down.

She felt Armand take her hand in his.

"This has really upset you," he observed.

"It isn't because Mattis was a good man," she said. "He *wasn't*. But no one deserves to be murdered."

He squeezed her hand in comfort.

"There's more to it than that, isn't there?"

She turned to him. "A man was spotted hanging around the warehouse for several days before Mattis was killed," she said. "I fear my encounter with the cutpurse is related to our search for the clock. If the copies are among the items missing, it might mean that someone *else* is also looking for the original."

Jade watched him consider her words. She thought herself fortunate that her brother had not yet put the two ideas together. It wouldn't take much for him to draw that conclusion. When he did, Edward would try to force her to give up the mystery client, which she had no intention of doing. She would be cautious, but she wouldn't be cowed into giving up her search. If it was important enough to kill for, she wanted to know why.

"It could be a complete coincidence," said Armand, although he was hardly convincing. "Or you were recognized for the nature of your business, or it might be something else entirely. But your conclusion cannot be ruled out."

Jade nodded, closing her eyes briefly.

It was as she feared. Armand knew it too.

Now she was afraid, and she wished for more than just the touch of his hand. As though he could read her mind, he pulled her into his arms in the reassuring embrace she needed. She breathed in the mint and ginger of his cologne, his undeniable maleness, the firmness of his thigh against hers as he embraced her. Then she became aware of her own femininity and the desire that warmed in her core. She looked into his eyes to find him watching her.

What would it be like to kiss him? *Actually* kiss him?

It would be foolish of course, with Seton so close above in the driver's seat, but she couldn't help it as her eyes flickered to his lips and back up again. A moment later, she had her answer. This time it wasn't a kiss on the cheek. It was his lips on hers. Soft at first, then firmer as he felt her response. He coaxed her mouth open, his tongue demanding entrance. She granted it, and he groaned.

Then he stopped.

"Let's not start something we can't finish," he said.

She blinked rapidly trying to make sense of what he was trying to say. After all, *he'd* kissed *her*.

Armand released her and she moved back to her seat, wondering exactly what he meant.

"I'm sorry," she said.

"Don't be. It was as much my fault."

The uniquely dank odor of the Thames intruded into the carriage as they neared the docks, a reminder of the reason why they were there in the first place.

The vehicle rolled to a stop outside the warehouse and Armand helped her step down as a middle-aged man emerged from inside the building.

"What are you doing here?" he asked. "This is no place for gentlefolk."

"I'm Miss Bridges, Edward's sister. I work in the business with him. I called on this gentleman because he wasn't aware of Mattis' death, but he did visit here with him a fortnight ago."

The stocky man regarded Armand with interest. "Did ye now, sir?"

Armand nodded once. "When Miss Bridges shared the news, I thought I might be of assistance. If there are items missing, I might be able to recall what they were."

The man allowed them to approach the warehouse, but Seton had climbed down from the carriage as they spoke and returned with her brother in tow.

Edward pointed a finger at her. "You. Go home. This is no place for a lady." Now he turned his attention to Armand. "And *you*. What the devil were you thinking in bringing her here?"

Jade had a retort for her brother ready on her lips when she felt Armand's hand briefly touch her back.

He addressed Edward. "I was here two weeks ago. I might be able to tell you what's missing."

Edward gave a curt nod of his head and beckoned Armand forward but didn't turn his attention from Jade. He narrowed his eyes at her. "Go home, Jade. I'll tell you everything there is to know when I get there."

Then he turned his back on her and walked to the warehouse entrance with Armand.

There was nothing else for her to do but go home and seethe.

CHAPTER TWELVE

A DARK STAIN on the hardpacked dirt floor was evidence of Mattis' fate. Although it didn't smell, Armand couldn't help but curl up his nose at it.

"Now you understand why I couldn't bring her in here," said Edward.

"I completely agree," said Armand. "Not that you need explain yourself to me."

"I know I don't, but I can tell you care for Jade. I suspected it before. But now, seeing you here, and seeing you two together, I am sure of it."

Armand made sure he looked at Jade's brother fully before replying. "I *do* care for her, more than you know. More than *she* knows, actually."

He hadn't intended to say the words out loud. In fact, Armand hadn't been fully aware of the depth of his own feelings until he articulated them. Now the truth was out there, laid bare before her brother.

What would Edward think of him if the man knew that not more than a few minutes before he was kissing his sister?

Edward nodded slowly, but Armand couldn't guess at his thoughts. The fact he hadn't warned him off ought to be taken as a sign that he didn't completely disapprove of their friendship.

Armand turned his attention to the space. Much of it was as

he remembered. There were pieces of furniture he recalled, but many of the surfaces which had been filled will small decorative items were now bare. A couple of small jewelry caskets that had sat incongruously on the shelves of a Welsh kitchen dresser were gone.

"There were a lot of small items about that aren't there now. Easily taken by a thief," Armand observed, "that is, if Mr. Mattis hadn't already packed them away."

Edward nodded. "Anything else which strikes you?"

Armand strode to the barrel from which Mattis had withdrawn the Thalatte clock. The lid lay discarded on the floor. He plunged his hand into the straw and pulled out an empty burlap sack.

"There's a clock missing," he said.

"What type of clock?"

As much as Armand didn't want Edward to draw the conclusion that Jade had done, there was no avoiding it. Bridges wasn't stupid, and *he* wasn't fool enough to assume he was.

"The Thalatte clock. The one with the Lady."

"The one you and Mattis made the mystery bidder pay far too much for?"

There was a hint of amusement in Edward's voice that irritated Armand.

He nodded once. "Mattis told me he had a second clock."

"Where?"

"I don't know. I didn't see it. Everything I wanted to know about the clock I found in the one he showed me."

Edward called to a couple of porters that Armand recognized from the auction room. He told them to let him know if they find another clock.

"I take it you're aware that a client of my sister wants the original?" There was more than just the obvious in Edward's question, and Armand didn't miss it.

"I want the original too."

"Do you? Well, it might be safe to assume that a third party wants it also."

"I think it would be fair to assume that."

"Is Jade aware of this?"

Armand nodded. Edward let out a long sigh in response.

"She's agreed to let me help her find the original."

The look of surprise on Edward's face was damned near comical. Armand might have laughed if the matter wasn't so serious.

"Now that *is* a turn up for the books. I'm sure it hasn't escaped your notice, but my sister values her independence rather jealously."

Armand couldn't help a grin. "I *had* noticed. But I can promise your sister will be safe with me."

Armand regretted his words even as he said them. They almost sounded as if he was assuring Edward Bridges of his honorable intentions towards his sister in a manner that suggested he was courting her.

Well, what are *you doing, old man?* For years, he'd been scrupulous in not allowing any young lady – or her parents – to assume an expectation of anything more than simply polite social intercourse. He'd cast that aside with Jade. He'd kissed her today and might have done much more than that under different circumstances. The question was how *much* further would he have gone? How much further would she have allowed him to go?

He waited for the almost inevitable man-to-man posturing in which the brother typically made dire threats of bodily harm should his sister's reputation be besmirched, or her heart broken. But Edward did none of these things.

Armand supposed that ought to wonder about her brother's intentional lack of curiosity, but frankly he was happy not to have to look that particular gift horse in the mouth – not until he had a chance to fully know his own mind.

"Since I've sent your transport away, you may as well pitch in to help," Edward said, matter-of-factly. "The sooner we're through, the sooner we can all be away from here."

Armand shrugged off his jacket, rolled up his sleeves, and briefly considered Barnet's dismay if he returned home with another set of clothing that needed laundering.

➤➤➤❮❮❮

"TAKE YOU STRAIGHT home to Bond Street, Miss Bridges?" asked Seton hopefully.

Jade look at the retreating figures of her brother and Armand and fought her annoyance at being dismissed.

Who did they think they were?

She was not some sheltered daughter of an aristocrat. She was a merchant's daughter. She was not naïve about the ways of the world. "No. To Hampstead Heath."

Seton did better at hiding his surprise this time. Hampstead Heath was nearly ten miles to the north of the city – and nowhere near Bond Street. Nevertheless, he'd gauged her mood a-right and wisely held his tongue.

Jade gave him the address and climbed back in the carriage. She took out the letter she'd written to her client. Her temper cooled on the ride. She reasoned with herself that there was little more she could offer than being an extra pair of hands, and ensuring Edward had all the help he needed.

She had a feeling that Edward would not find the clock that Mattis showed Armand. Her reasoning was nothing more than a hunch, but she trusted her intuition. And she trusted Armand. He volunteered that he had seen Mattis. Why do that if he had killed him? That made no sense. Was her mysterious client so fixed on the clock that he would resort to theft and murder?

It was possible. And yet, as dreadful as the idea was, it was better than the alternative – that there was someone else, someone unknown to them and murderous, who *also* wanted the original clock.

Short of their destination, Jade rapped on the roof of the

carriage. Seton brought it to a stop, some ways from the address.

She got out of the carriage and looked up the road. As she suspected, this was not an affluent area.

The street was lined on one side with three story buildings. There was a residence on the top two floors and a shop below.

The sun was casting long rays across the tops of the buildings, illuminating the windows of the upper floors.

"Stay with the carriage," she instructed. "I'm going to walk to the top of the rise and drop my letter into the shop. You'll be able to see me the whole way."

"Why do you have me wait here?"

"I want to know if my mysterious client is having the shop watched. He might be nearby. I also want to see if I'm being followed."

Seton was singularly unimpressed and conveyed it admirably on his wizened face.

"It is a journey of less than two hundred yards in which I will not be out of your sight but for the moment I step into the shop!"

The servant slowly shook his head.

"Ye brother won't be happy with me lettin' ye do this."

"If I'm accosted, you'll be upon him before he knows it. But if you accompany me, you are *guaranteed* to scare them off, and then we'll never know who this man might be."

Jade was well aware of Seton's sour look as he turned his head away. He muttered under his breath words that were likely to be less than complimentary. But that didn't deter her as she set off down the street.

The shadows caused by the falling dusk made for dark shadows in the corners and made the ugly buildings seem more gray and forlorn than they'd appeared from the top of the hill. The address brought her to, as she'd suspected, a print shop, and it was about to close for the day. But she entered it anyway.

"Good afternoon, young man," she said brightly to the young ink-stained apprentice who came to the counter. "I'm looking for a Mr. Smith."

The child, about ten, looked at her blankly.

"Mr. Smith?"

Repeating the name a second time didn't elicit any flash of recognition on the boy's face.

"I have a letter for him and was given this address to bring it. He might be a customer?"

The apprentice shrugged his shoulders and said nothing. He reached out for the letter in her hand. Jade didn't want to part with it until she received some kind of acknowledgment.

"Is your master in?"

No sooner had she spoke than a large, bearded man with a blackened apron emerged from behind a curtain.

"Jack!"

The boy started.

"What yer doin' standin' there like a tailor's dummy? Tell the lady you'll 'old the letter for Mister Smith."

The child repeated the words in an inaudible voice.

Jade ignored the boy for a moment and looked at the printer.

"Mr. Smith," she repeated. "Does he come in here regularly?"

"Lots of Smiths come in 'ere. If one comes asking for a letter, I'll give it to 'im."

With an eye on both the master and the apprentice, Jade handed over the letter she'd written in reply to her anonymous client and watched the boy place it into an empty pigeonhole fastened to the wall on his side of the counter.

She offered the boy a shilling along with her business card and asked him to send word when the message was collected. The child accepted the coin, as his master watched on with his arms folded. In truth, Jade held little hope of seeing any return on her investment.

The street was all but deserted when she emerged from the shop. She listened keenly for the sound of any footfalls behind her. Having her reticule stolen was not a mistake she would make a second time.

She kept her eyes on the carriage, now illuminated by its

lamps which she treated as a beacon. Jade trusted that Seton was watching her return with equal diligence. She covered the distance without incident.

Jade patted the horse's neck as she passed. Seton dropped down from his perch and aided her into the carriage.

"Anyone following me?"

"No. Not a one."

"No? How disappointing."

"Your taste for adventure is going to get you into trouble, Miss."

"It hasn't so far and probably won't, given that you're my watchdog."

The faithful retainer shook his head once more with more-or-less friendly exasperation. Jade touched his shoulder.

"Thank you," she said. "You've indulged my whims quite enough for one day."

Seton patted her hand.

"That mean we're going home?"

"Yes, we're going home. There's nothing more for it now but to go and wait."

ONCE AT HOME, Jade found she couldn't relax, not before Edward returned home. She occupied her time by addressing some correspondence, then rearranging the staffing roster for the auction. By the time she was considering whether she ought to rearrange the jade curios in the Oriental Room, she could hardly keep her eyes open. Still, she waited for Edward, quaffing probably more tea than was good for her, to stay awake. She was determined to find out what he'd learned.

It was well after midnight before Edward came home. He seemed surprised that she had waited up for him. He regarded her with bleary eyes and an ill-concealed yawn.

"It'll come as no surprise to you, I'm sure, but Mattis was supposed to have two clocks. Danger saw one of them, but not the other," he said.

"Did you find it?"

Edward trudged up the stairs while managing the feat of yawning and shaking his head at the same time.

"Missing out of the barrel it was packed in," he said around another yawn.

Missing?

Stolen.

She knew that as well as she knew her own name. Disappointment and exhaustion sapped the limits of her endurance. Jade squeezed her eyes tight until they watered to ease the grit then followed her brother up the stairs.

"We'll talk in the morning about what we'll do about your mystery client," Edward called down to her.

She knew what that meant – an order to cease her search for the clock. It was a bitter pill to swallow to announce to a client that she was conceding defeat.

Edward stopped part way up and glanced back at her. "Oh, by the way, your beau says he will pay you a call tomorrow."

Beau?

At her frown, Edward gave a tired laugh, shook his head, and continued up the stairs.

"He *likes* you, Jade."

Surely he wasn't referring to Armand. Belatedly, she realized he was.

Oh no. Her brother was reading far more into things than there was.

More than she herself wanted to hope for.

THE NEXT MORNING Jade told herself she was too busy to give any further consideration to her brother's words.

He likes you, Jade.

It would be so easy to ignore them if they'd been said in a teasing manner. But he hadn't. The words were in earnest.

What on earth had they spoken about at the warehouse yesterday?

Unfortunately, she'd had time to ponder those words as Madame Francine Dumont, the mantuamaker up the street, added the final touches to her new gown. A delightful seafoam green silk designed to set off the simple set of pearls that she hoped would attract the eye of one of this year's debutantes.

Her ensemble was for a ball held by the Duke of Auchen who had helped sponsor his distant cousin's debut. She had not met the Duke, although he was the most talked-about man in London this season. He'd lived in Scotland most of his life. And, perhaps most scandalously of all, if the rumors were to be believed, the man had actually *worked* with his hands for a living. He had *a trade.*

That alone was enough to commend him in her eyes.

Tomorrow night would be an opportunity to take a good look around Glenuig House. The Duke's late father had been somewhat reclusive in recent years, owing to bad health. It would be interesting to see how the fortunes of that particular Duchy fared.

And Armand would be there.

Of course, he would be, Jade reprimanded herself.

He was a count, his stepbrother was an Earl, and they were contemporaries of Lord Seth Musgrave, Duke of Auchen – all fast friends even, according to the latest news sheets.

And Armand would be there with a beautiful woman on his arm.

And it wouldn't be *her.*

She recalled how he kissed her in the carriage. It wasn't just a peck on the cheek either. Her cheeks grew warm at the memory. How much did that kiss mean? If it was any other man of his class, he might think she was someone to merely dally with. But Armand Danger was different to any other man of his class.

He really likes you, Jade.

She wanted to believe it to be true but wouldn't dare give herself that hope.

Today was Wednesday, the day Armand claimed as the day he would take her for a ride through Hyde Park. But, as she approached the shop, no curricle or carriage awaited her.

"A message came for you while you were out, Miss," said Suzy.

Jade accepted the note and unfolded it. It seemed the caution she gave her heart turned out to be warranted. It was from Armand, cancelling their engagement today. He was unavoidably detained and would call on her the day after tomorrow to discuss something of his mother's he had discovered. No mention of whether he would be at the ball. No inquiry about whether she would be attending.

She couldn't help but be disappointed.

CHAPTER THIRTEEN

"YOU LOOK QUITE beautiful tonight."

The words came out of Armand's mouth, and he meant them. She *was* beautiful. There was no denying it. But, in his mind's eye, he could not help to compare Lady Cornelia to another.

The lady in question acknowledged his words with the look of a woman who considered her beauty to be matter of fact, and the compliment only her due.

She had obviously dressed to impress him, Armand considered. Her gown was gold with an overskirt in net, embroidered with stylized leaves in black. The bodice was black velvet with gold satin ribbon embroidery on the bust and sleeves. Ostrich feathers dyed in black and gold trembled in her hair every time she moved her head.

Fortunately, she wasn't forced to bask in Armand's admiration for long. Arabella descended the stairs, and the two women expressed thrill and delight in each other's ensembles to a degree no man could possibly match.

Armand shared a wry glance of understanding with Charles.

Both men trailed the ladies out to the carriage.

Armand was looking forward to the ball at Glenuig House. He'd not known its owner Seth Musgrave, the new Duke of Auchen, for very long. Indeed, the man had only arrived in

London in October, much to the surprise of everyone who believed that the late Duke had no heir.

But there were a few people in this world with whom one felt a kinship instantly, and Musgrave was such a man. Armand had had nearly a lifetime to come to terms with the fact that the British aristocracy was not his natural home. For Musgrave, the discovery was more recent.

He liked that the fellow had common sense and a practical view of the world. He had passion for improving the lot of his workers and that was a credit to him. The fact he was leading by example was something rare among the bloviating classes.

And on that basis, Armand was happy to invest in his Glasgow textiles mill.

Glenuig House was just outside the city on prime acres of land bounded by the River Thames. No sooner had their party entered the gates than he could see the prized gardens in bloom, along with garlands of flowers and lamps leading up to the house which itself blazed with welcoming lights. Liveried footman aided them from the carriage.

"The Countess has outdone herself," said Charles.

"Do you think she has ambitions to be a Duchess?" said Cornelia.

"Surely not," said Arabella. "The Duke is twenty years younger than Lady Beatrice. He'll want a wife who can bear him children."

"If she's that fond of him, she might consent to be his mistress."

Armand hoped to put an end to the gossip. "That's not going to be the case."

It proved to be a mistake. The two women watched him as carefully as two cats with a cornered mouse.

"And why *not*?" Cornelia asked.

He silently appealed to Charles for help.

"For one, the Countess chooses a new lover every year," Charles interrupted. "I can't see her changing her habits now."

His stepbrother paused and grinned. "And secondly…"

Armand glowered as Charles batted the subject back to him. He sighed and the news he'd only become privy to this week. "His Grace's heart has already been taken."

"*What?* By whom?" Arabella demanded. She tapped Armand on the arm with her fan. "How dare you keep such delicious news from us. Who is she?"

Tempted though he was to say nothing, he also acknowledged that he'd receive no peace until he did.

"Her name is Lady Ruby McAllister. She's Scottish, like the Duke," he said.

"She's also an investor in his business, according to the Earl of Runcorn," added Charles.

"A woman of business?" Cornelia exclaimed. "How *novel!*"

"'Tis a pity Miss Bridges won't be here tonight," said Arabella. "They'd have a lot in common. Wouldn't they, Armand?" He knew his sister-in-law meant nothing beyond the observation, but it was enough for Cornelia to prick up her ears.

"You know another lady of business, my lord?" she asked. The question was lightly posed, but Armand detected a possessive note in it.

"Oh yes," answered Arabella, although the question was not addressed to her. "Surely you must have heard of the Bridges family. They own the most wonderful little shop on Bond Street. My dear, if you ever want a little trinket of the most unique sort, then you must go there. Did you know all the furniture you admired at Armand's home is all Miss Bridges' doing? She has very refined taste."

"The woman sounds like a paragon," Cornelia commented dryly.

The tone of the remark went over Arabella's head, but not Charles', who distracted his wife by pointing out some people they knew. Unfortunately, that left Armand to face Cornelia alone.

"I hope one day you'll afford me the opportunity to show my

domestic talents, my lord," she told him, sliding her arm through his.

Armand gritted his teeth and said nothing.

He'd never been alone in private with the woman, let alone kissed her. And he had no intention of doing either of those things. He'd accompanied her mostly as a favor to Charles in order to keep Arabella happy. But now the lady appeared to have *designs*.

Armand conceded the fact that one day he must marry, although until recently he'd not given it much of a thought. And yet the more he thought about it, the more he imagined the woman by his side having brown hair and green eyes. *Jade*.

He wished she was beside him now. He'd wanted to see her today and was sorry to have been so overrun by circumstances outside his control. He'd been really looking forward to seeing her, partly to show her what he had found in his brother's attic, but also to see if she was still mad at him, and her brother, for sending her away from the warehouse a couple of nights ago.

And above all, he hadn't forgotten their kiss.

IN THE BALLROOM, the orchestra had just started its first selection, and he found himself led by Cornelia. They made their way around the side of the room, looking for a seat and found several vacant beside a young woman whom he recognized as Lady Ruby McAllister. She appeared to be in conversation with someone he couldn't see, his view blocked by the fronds of a potted palm tree. The young Scottish woman looked up at their approach.

"My dear, Count," she said, rising to her feet. "How wonderful to see you again. And I believe you might already know my new friend. We appear to have a dressmaker in common."

The woman beside her rose also. Armand moved around so he could see her clearly. He felt a curious mixture of both elation and dread as he recognized her.

Miss Jade Bridges.

Although her gown of soft green was less elaborate than some, it suited her beautifully. The pearls around her throat and on her ears were adornment enough. Her hair was dressed in an array of curls secured by a silver filigree band.

He tried to read her expression but couldn't.

Cornelia's arm stiffened on his.

"You appear to know her, my lord," she said. "Will you not introduce us?"

⟫⟩⟩✦⟨⟨⟪

JADE HAD THE advantage of knowing Armand had been invited, so she had readied herself to encounter him. Rather, she'd thought she had. Now she realized how woefully prepared she was.

He stood before her, looking impossibly handsome. He did well to hide his surprise, but not enough to escape her notice – nor that of the woman on his arm.

And she didn't look especially pleased.

"Will you not introduce us?" the woman had asked.

Armand wore a fixed smile as he said, "Lady Ruby, may I introduce you to Lady Cornelia Fairclough."

The women, being of equal station, nodded their acknowledgement, one to the other.

"Lady Cornelia, may I introduce you to Miss Jade Bridges."

As Jade bobbed her curtsy, she witnessed a flash of recognition of her name, and some other, less pleasant expression on the woman's face.

"Lady Cornelia," she acknowledged. "I do hope you have a pleasant evening."

There was an uncomfortable moment's silence that even Lady Ruby had perceived as she regarded the party one-by-one. Jade curtsied to her. "I so enjoyed our conversation, I should go. I've monopolized too much of your time already."

"Not at all," the woman answered. "I shall call on you next

week."

Jade bobbed a curtsy again and walked away, glad to be away from the gimlet stare of Lady Cornelia Fairclough. The woman had recognized her from that night at the opera, of that could be no doubt. She had to walk away to prevent a scene she suspected Lady Cornelia was capable of making.

Her immediate impulse was to find Edward and ask to go home. He wasn't much for dancing and intended to spend most of the evening with the other gentlemen in the card room. Yet, the evening was still young, and it had been such an ordeal to get her brother to come along that to leave early was bound to require answers.

Perhaps if she pleaded a *megrim*…

Jade cursed herself for a coward.

Be honest with yourself. The fact that Lady Cornelia recognized you was not the only reason why you left.

The jealousy was not all one-sided. It was one thing to harbor a secret fancy for a man who was above her in station and see another woman on his arm. It was another thing entirely to have kissed the man in question – and quite passionately too – *and* see another woman on his arm.

Jade felt a tap on her shoulder; a young man whose name eluded her requested a dance. She accepted, grateful for the distraction.

Better still, the dance was a cotillion. She concentrated on the steps and keeping up a pleasant façade when she felt the touch of another gentleman's hand on hers as she passed.

"I wish I'd known you were attending tonight," he said.

Armand.

Jade took a deep breath.

"Would it have made a difference?" she asked before stepping into a *pas de deux*.

His hand left hers as they stepped back into their respective lines, but his eyes never left hers. They skipped back into the center. His hand held hers as their arms touched, wrist to elbow as they slowly turned in a circle.

The only face she could see was Armand's. She was aware of every point where his body touched hers.

"It makes a difference to me," he said.

Then they parted once more.

Jade corrected a misstep and concentrated on the rest of the dance. When it was over, she thanked her partner and hurried outside for fresh air.

Damn her traitorous heart. Why did it have to pound like that whenever Armand was nearby? Why did she seem so utterly aware of him?

She raised her head and blinked back tears until she felt her composure return. Jade breathed in a deep lungful of night air, then five times over as the heat of her cheeks cooled.

Tonight is a night like any other night, she told herself. *These people are not your friends. They're your customers, they're acquaintances.*

Jade repeated the words to herself over and over again until she was ready to face the throng once more.

SHE MANAGED A pleasant smile and walked back into the ballroom. Immediately, another young man asked her to dance. She demurred on the one just beginning but granted him another a little later in the evening, telling him she needed to seek some refreshment.

At the refreshment table, Jade found the newly engaged Lord Tarquin Asquith and Miss Jeanette Millarstone. She offered her best wishes to the couple. They had a pleasant discussion of nothing of any consequence when Miss Millarstone's attention was drawn to someone over Jade's shoulder.

She stepped to one side to admit the newcomer to their conversation.

And it was the very person she didn't want to face.

Armand greeted the newly engaged couple warmly with the familiarity of close acquaintances.

Then he turned to her.

"May I claim the next dance, Miss Bridges?"

Jade's reticence was noticed by Miss Millarstone.

"Oh do, Miss Bridges, the Count never dances enough! He and the Duke of Auchen usually sit out the dances, but Lord Musgrave dances tonight, and so should Lord Danger."

Jade glanced at Armand who'd raised his eyebrows in silent appeal. There was no way she could refuse graciously, so she offered an exaggerated sigh of forbearance instead.

"Well, if I *must*, to prevent the gentleman from becoming a wallflower, then I must."

Millar Millarstone and Lord Asquith laughed. Armand grinned and proffered his arm. Jade accepted it.

"You're under no obligation to do this just because we are acquainted," she said as he led her to the dancefloor.

"You were under no obligation to accept."

"It would be churlish to not oblige the guests of honor."

"Then I thank you for sparing my blushes."

Curse her bad luck. The music that began was a waltz.

How could she possibly not be aware of Armand's hand at her waist and the other holding her wrist? And despite his alleged reluctance to dance, Armand did it exquisitely.

She closed her eyes a moment and relaxed into his arms, feeling the music around her and through her and cherished this one chance to be in his arms. She remembered his kiss.

Jade opened her eyes and looked straight into his.

As wonderful as this was, it couldn't happen again.

Lady Cornelia stood on edge of the dancefloor, watching them carefully.

"Your companion does not seem to approve of your choice of dance partner, *Monsieur le Comte*," she said.

"I suspect she might be jealous."

"Of whom?"

The dance increased in tempo. They were now near the musicians where it was too loud for them to converse. His full attention was on her, the subtle pressure of his hands showed her each next move until they moved as one.

It took her by surprise, but not him. He smiled and subtly drew her closer. Almost close enough to embrace.

Did he remember their kiss as she did? His eyes fell to her lips. Unconsciously, she licked her lips, and his nostrils flared, setting a spark of arousal coursing through her, unchecked.

The dance came to an end. Armand's hand firmed on her arm and, with a determined expression on his face, steered her toward the door to the gardens. Jade glanced back but couldn't see if Lady Cornelia still watched them.

"She has every reason to be jealous of you," he said once they were alone.

No, this was too much.

She turned her face away lest he see the war waging within her. Jade shored up her composure to answer.

"That Gallic charm will get you into trouble one day, monsieur." Her voice was shaky.

"I never say what I don't mean."

"And what *do* you mean?" she said.

The pull into his embrace was swift. The depth of his kiss left her unable to stand on her own feet. Jade could do nothing more than be swept by the tide of his passion. She clung to him, returned kiss for kiss, before wrapping her arms around his neck to draw him even more tightly. His hands stroked her back. Sensation coursed through her like the thousand fireworks that were promised for tonight's entertainment.

This could not go on.

Jade broke away.

"That's twice you've done that," she said, "And you've never directly answered my question. What do you mean by it, sir?"

She supposed she ought to be flattered that Armand was breathing hard as if the kiss affected him too. He took a deep breath before he answered.

"It's obvious to Lady Cornelia that my interest lies elsewhere," he said. "Hell, it's probably obvious to everyone who cared to watch us dance."

Jade's fingers tingled, then her toes. She looked away to steady herself. How ridiculous that she could be acting like an ingenue when she was nothing of the sort. She turned to him and raised her chin.

"Are you going to declare your intentions? Seek my brother's approval?"

He really likes you, Jade.

Edward's voice in her head was not helpful, right now.

Neither was the expression on Armand's face. Hesitation made a brief appearance on his fine features before that masterful control returned. "All I'm certain of is how much I want you."

The answering call of her own desire responded to his words, but somehow Jade managed to find the power to resist him. How could she not when she could be nothing more to him than a mistress?

And she refused to settle for that.

Jade offered him her haughtiest expression instead.

"You're an attractive man," she said. "No doubt you would be an excellent lover. But I have a reputation to keep."

Armand grinned. She knew it was a reflexive action, but at that moment it annoyed her.

That was good. It enabled her to take a few paces away from him.

"It's clear you don't fully understand. I wouldn't expect you to," she continued. "Yes, the young women in your social circle have reputations to guard also. If they show themselves too free with their favors, they will not marry well. But you forget, *Monsieur le Comte*, that *I* have to work for a living."

Armand folded his arms. A defensive posture. But to his credit, he seemed prepared to listen without mounting an argument for himself.

"Can you imagine the damage it would do to my livelihood, to my family's business, if it got out that all it took to tup Miss

Jade Bridges was a bit of flattery?"

He winced, looking down at the grass a good long moment before returning to her.

"I've greatly offended you, and for that I humbly apologize, Miss Bridges," he said softly. "You may rest assured that this will not happen again."

Jade did not doubt his sincerity. She nodded her acceptance. "Given the difference between our stations, my lord, professional courtesy is the only thing there can be between us," she said. "I was wrong to let you believe there could be more than that."

Jade moved past him to return to the house before her resolve to resist him founded.

You may rest assured that this will not happen again.

How come she already regretted eliciting that assurance?

ARMAND WATCHED JADE walk towards the house, her head raised, back ramrod straight. In short, there was pride in every step she took away from him.

He cursed himself for being the worst kind of fool.

What had he been thinking? In truth, he had not been thinking at all. And, yet she couldn't deny that she'd responded to return passion equal to his own.

Armand turned away and walked in the lamp-lit gardens, avoiding the shadowed nooks where lovers met. He headed toward the riverbank and watched men being rowed out to the fireworks barges anchored in the middle of the river.

So, what *did* he want from her?

The truth of the matter was, he didn't know.

Was he in love with her?

The thought was shocking. Not because he was necessarily averse to the notion, but rather that he'd never before considered it. Not with Jade. Certainly not with Cornelia. In fact, not with anybody.

Being in love carried certain expectations – marriage the primary one.

He wasn't sure how he felt about *that*.

Armand gritted his teeth as he headed back towards the house, making his way through the outward flow of guests spilling out onto the lawn in search of the best vantage point for the fireworks display. When he returned to the ballroom it was nearly empty. But waiting for him were Arabella and Cornelia.

"There you are!" Arabella greeted him brightly. "Charles went to look for you in the card room. We thought it would be nice to watch the fireworks together."

He smiled in return and agreed that would be a pleasant thing to do. Cornelia did not smile, he noted.

Armand used his superior height to scan the edges of the room, ostensibly looking for Charles, but in truth he searched for someone else entirely. Someone with chestnut hair and cat-like green eyes.

He wasn't hopeful of finding her. Lady Cornelia continued to regard him with a great deal of interest. No doubt she'd seen him leaving with Jade and returning alone.

"Perhaps I should go look for Charles," he said.

If Jade's brother remained in the card room, it was likely she was still here and…

Charles appeared. He spotted them and hurried their way with a huge grin on his face. "There you are! Come on, hurry now, we don't want to miss the start of the display."

Armand was glad for Charles' infectious enthusiasm because it prevented anyone from noticing his distraction or Cornelia's ill-disguised irritation.

Given the lateness of the evening, it was doubtful he would see Jade again tonight and he was forced to console himself with the notion that he would see her on Wednesday. He planned to hold her to that, regardless of what she thought of him now.

Charles took his wife's hand while Cornelia claimed Armand's arm.

Outside in the darkness, Lady Cornelia stepped close to his side, pressing herself against him. "I'm not sure I like loud noises," she murmured close to his ear. "Even the sound of thunder frightens me."

Armand knew he was expected to offer words of comfort, a willing ability to show gallantry. Against his better judgement, he put his arm around her shoulders and drew her to his side. He tried to keep his touch as light as possible, but Cornelia wasn't having that. He felt her arms slip around his waist while she rested her head against his shoulder.

He watched the fireworks display with very little interest. Even though he knew it was a futile effort, he glanced about with every colorful burst of light to see if he could spot Jade among the silhouetted guests.

The display continued, with Lady Cornelia hanging onto his waist. He felt nothing for her, and everything for the woman who had so adroitly put him into his place. He needed a distraction, and an escape from the marriage-minded machinations of his sister-in-law. Armand decided then that he would lick his wounds by preparing for a trip to France, where he would see his mother for the first time in two years.

It was time he moved on. He'd ignored his past for too long.

CHAPTER FOURTEEN

Two days later
The Meddings' Residence
London

EDWARD'S EYES WIDENED the moment the door was open. Lining the entrance hall behind the elderly servant were no fewer than four long-case clocks. All kept time with metronomic proficiency.

Jade lowered her head a moment to hide a smile as the old retainer addressed them.

"Good afternoon, Mr. Bridges, Miss Bridges. The master will see you in the orangery."

The man led the way, his slow walk kept pace with the ticking of the clocks, as though he himself was a clockwork automaton.

Still, it gave her plenty of time to examine the artwork on the walls and peer inside some of the rooms as they passed. They too boasted several timepieces within.

Eventually, in exactly sixty-eight ticks of the clock – Jade counted them – they arrived at the orangery. To her surprise, there were no clocks in here. In fact, with the door to the house closed, she could not even hear them.

Their host sat in a bath chair, a blanket over his lap even

though it was pleasantly warm amongst the potted trees and shrubs.

"Mr. and Miss Bridges, sir," the servant intoned gravely.

Edward stepped forward. "Mr. Meddings, sir, thank you for taking the time to see us today."

The man nodded, letting out a cough as he did so.

"Sometimes the clocks are wearisome," he said, as if he knew what Jade was thinking. "Don't mistake me. I love my timepieces. They are beautiful, intricate little miracles. Works of art. But occasionally the noise becomes a bit too much. Especially when they all strike twelve."

Meddings swept a bony hand across his body, indicating they should sit. Edward and Jade took up positions on a cushioned wicker settee opposite him.

"I am an old man, but I have not lost my wits, despite what my nephew might believe. I've called on you to value my collection and give me an honest appraisal. I have given the young man items to sell in the past, and if I receive half what I believe they're worth he tells me to count myself lucky. I won't be made a fool of."

Edward nodded in sympathy only to be peremptorily dismissed with a wave of the old man's hand.

"I will converse with the young lady here, while you go about your business. Value my clocks in the library, morning room and my study. And the paintings too."

She and Edward exchanged glances as he slowly rose to his feet.

"Well, what are you waiting for?" Meddings snapped. "Manfred will show you where to start."

Jade gave Edward a barely perceptible nod. This was not the first eccentric they'd encountered in their line of work, and Lord knew it wouldn't be the last.

"Manfred, return with tea for my guest and myself."

The elderly servant bowed and left with Edward trailing behind in the same slow, methodical gait. This time the door was left open, and Jade clearly heard the ticking of the clocks from inside the house.

"Tell me about your clocks," she said. "From what I saw, you have a very fine collection."

Meddings preened at her words. It was quite remarkable how forthcoming most men were when a pretty young woman took an interest in them and their hobbies. He proceeded to tell her everything about his beloved timepieces.

Jade listened without interruption, making sure she showed her host genuine interest. People who knew things she did not had something to teach her. One never knew when an arcane or little-known piece of knowledge might prove useful to her in the future.

Eventually, the time was right to address her business.

"Do you know anything of the Thalatte clock?" she asked. "I believe it is French."

Meddings held up his hand. Jade frowned, then listened. She heard a ratcheting sound from one of the clocks, before a split-second pause then a veritable orchestra of gongs, bells and chimes deafeningly announced all at once that it was four o'clock.

"I have a particularly fine reproduction," he answered after the sound of the final gong decayed, "but alas, not the original. I did hear that it arrived on our shores. There was a rumor that it had been purchased by some gentleman's group here in London, a private drinking fraternity I believe, sometime before the end of the last century. But sadly, I've never seen it."

Meddings continued describing the clock in minute detail as if he were a lecturer and she a pupil. He seemed very proud of the fact that he knew the original statue was a miniature of a life-sized version sculpted by Boyer for an aristocratic French family. She schooled her face to hide her disappointment. Apart from mention of the men's club, she had not learned a thing she did not already know.

Eventually, sounds of much quicker footsteps approached the orangery. She dearly hoped Edward's afternoon had been more productively spent than hers.

"Boyer? Those French statues?" The voice did not belong to Edward. "Prendegast loves the things."

Jade turned to see a rather pudding-faced man approach them. His attempt to hide baldness with a few remaining strands of long brown hair was a distinct failure.

He noticed her for the first time.

"Well, Uncle," he said, smacking his lips. "Who do we have here?"

"This is Miss Bridges," said Meddings. "She's accompanied her brother on a task for me."

"Oh yes, I saw him. I thought he was a tradesman by the way Manfred was hovering, but you... you're quite the lady, aren't you?"

Jade swallowed down her distaste and offered him a simple, "How do you do?"

"Miss Bridges, Rufus Mayditch, my nephew." It was clear in Meddings' tone that he had no love for his relative.

The man joined her on the wicker settee and sat himself a good deal closer than was proper. Jade adjusted her posture to put the maximum amount of space between her and this odious individual.

"Prendegast? The man is a libertine," Meddings spat.

Mayditch shrugged dismissively. "Nevertheless, you have to admit he has money and taste," the younger man replied. "Those statues he has in his own personal pleasure garden are worth quite the pretty penny."

Mayditch turned his attention to Jade. "What do you think of statuary, Miss Bridges? Particularly nudes?"

His amused grin became a leer. She ignored the double *entendre* and pretended his uncouth manner was beneath her notice. He wasn't the first of his type she'd encountered.

"Boyer's works are considered the finest ever created in France," she said. "Did you know he studied in Italy? He was inspired by the works of the great masters of anatomy including

Michelangelo and spent fifteen years learning to reproduce their techniques."

Rufus blinked rapidly a moment, apparently speechless. She used his confusion to rise to her feet and put distance between them. She smiled sweetly to Meddings.

"I've monopolized too much of your time already. Perhaps I should look for my brother. I'm sure he must be nearly finished by now."

Mayditch rose to his feet and held out his hand. "I'll escort you."

Jade lightly side-stepped him. "No, no. I won't put you to the trouble."

At that moment, Edward returned to the orangery. His expression told her that he'd correctly assessed the situation. He addressed her. "I'm sorry to keep you waiting so long, sister dear," he said. "Mr. Meddings has an outstanding collection."

Then to Meddings he said, "Sir, you will have my written valuation by week's end."

Jade noticed Rufus Mayditch shifting uncomfortably with a sheepish expression on his face.

"Excellent," the old man replied, looking smugly at his nephew.

Jade went to her brother's side, and they left, not waiting for Manfred. This time it took them only forty ticks of the clocks to reach the front door.

As soon as Seton set the horses in motion, Jade released a nervous giggle. "Well, that was an afternoon I won't forget."

"Please tell me you learned something of value, at least," said Edward.

Jade recapped her conversation, concluding, "I presume Prendegast is Lord Kingston Prendegast, and the inheritor of something called the Dionysus Club, so that is something worth inquiring about."

She watched amused at Edward's lips thinned in distaste.

"Do you know what the Dionysus Club is?"

"Well, I know who Dionysus was, so I can guess this club has more to commend it than just being an all-male drinking club," she said innocently, then chortled at her brother's reddening face.

"Do not make any enquiries about it," he said. "*Promise* me."

"No direct enquiries. I promise."

Edward nodded, and nothing more was said. He either did not notice, or chose to ignore, that her promise did not include *indirect* enquiries.

She leaned forward to open the aperture to the carriage driver. "Seton, please take me to the library at the British Museum."

ARMAND SPOTTED HER the minute she walked into the library. He drank in her appearance, pleased almost to the point of irrationality at seeing her again.

So far, Jade hadn't spotted *him*. He remained where he was at one of the reading tables, happy to simply watch her graceful movements as she made her way to one of the librarians. He saw the young clerk gesture in his direction. She frowned, no doubt, at being told that the books she wanted were already being read by someone else.

Her head lifted imperceptibly at seeing him. Armand kept his own expression neutral. The librarian approached him.

"Excuse me, sir, have you finished with the books you requested? The young lady here wishes to peruse them."

Armand kept his attention on the librarian. "Alas, I have not, but if the young lady would consider sharing the table, there are two books I have not yet started on."

The librarian turned at Jade in silent appeal.

Jade offered a put-upon sigh and nodded her head. Yet Armand like to think he knew her well enough to know her performance was mostly theater.

Armand got to his feet. "Do take a seat, Miss Bridges."

"I prefer to remain on this side of the table, *Monsieur le Comte.*"

The librarian looked back and forth at them, slightly confused at their familiarity before he decided it was safe enough to retreat to a discreet distance.

Jade picked up one of the reference books from the stack on his left and began reading. Armand returned to his own book, making the occasional note, but before long her presence became a distraction – the faint scent of lemon from her soap, the tap of the pencil on her bottom lip as she became engrossed in the book.

Armand slammed the large tome shut. *Whump!*

"Miss Bridges, I believe it is safe to assume that we are in the same place for the same purpose, so will you at least *talk* to me?"

Jade slowly lifted her head from the book, meeting his eyes. The pencil remained at her slightly open lips. Deliberately. Armand felt the stirrings of arousal.

"What is it you'd like me to say, my lord, which wasn't already said at the Duke of Auchen's spring ball?"

Armand could feel his lip curl. He turned his face away from her to give him time to master his flash of annoyance. "So does that mean we are not even to be friends?"

His words seemed to surprise her, although she said nothing.

There was plenty more he wanted to say, but a library was not the place for it. He glanced down at his notes and decided he'd done enough. He rose from his chair.

"I bid you farewell, Miss Bridges," he said, then made directly for the entrance.

Bloody annoying females. Every last damned one of them! They either come on too strong, or they treat you like a pariah.

"Wait!"

Tension thrummed through him. He needed to move. He was in no mood to spar with Jade today. She had firmly put him in his place last night. While he never intended any dishonor or disrespect towards her, she clearly saw it otherwise. And what was particularly galling was he could see how it might appear from her point of view. Now she was here with apparent intent of rubbing salt into the wound.

Armand heard Jade call out, but he ignored her. He quickened his pace and lengthened his strike to put distance between himself and the library.

"Armand!"

She had obviously followed him out.

The street noise was loud. He used this as an excuse not to hear her and kept walking. Armand crossed the street to take a shortcut through the park as so many Londoners were doing to get about their day. By the time he got halfway across, the stiffness had left his body, and he was beginning to feel more like himself to the point that he entered White's whistling – something which did not endear him to the footman at the door.

Inside, he was hailed by a group of men he knew, led by the Earl of Runcorn.

"Ah, a friendly face!"

Armand cocked his head. "Why, what's been bothering you?"

"The number of free men seems to be diminishing by the month – first Lady Amber Honeyfield hooks the Earl of Castleford, and now there's news that Musgrave has got himself engaged to a Scottish lass." Runcorn lifted an eyebrow. "You're not going get yourself shackled soon, are you?"

"Not bloody, likely!" Armand averred.

The man laughed. "That's the spirit!"

Armand slumped into an empty chair. Runcorn ordered more drinks.

"So, what's been occupying your days?" he asked.

"I've been brushing up on eighteenth century French sculptors, as it so happens."

"Ah, you've become a man of refinement since moving to Mayfair."

"There's one artist in particular, Boyer. I believe my family once had some of his works – classical pieces inspired by the ancient Greeks."

Runcorn dropped his usual clownish demeanor. He was thoughtful. "Have you spoken to Kingston Prendegast?"

Armand shook his head. "I know of the man, but I wouldn't say we were friends."

"His family have been collecting things like that for ages," Runcorn continued. "In recent years, young Prendegast created his own private garden full of sculptures. You might find your Boyer there."

"Would he be open to offers, do you think?"

The earl sucked air through his teeth. "I don't know, old man – he guards it jealously. But…" Runcorn glanced about before leaning forward conspiratorially. "He carries on the family tradition of the Dionysus Club, you know – *drinking parties*. I've been to a couple over the years, and they're not for the faint hearted, let me tell you. Wine, wenching… they're veritable orgies, but joining in one of those is probably the best way of ingratiating yourself if you want something from the man."

"I'll keep that in mind," Armand replied dryly.

"No, really. My offer is genuine if you're truly interested. He's planning one for two weeks hence. I can get you an invitation."

Armand nodded slowly. It sounded like a useful lead to pursue. A little indirect reconnoiter.

Something Jade would do.

And right now, the idea of besting that woman at her own game had very strong appeal indeed. Drinking and whoring were not Armand's usual vices, but the idea of doing something so alien appealed greatly. He wanted to forget—forget himself and forget Jade.

Armand drained his drink and set it heavily on the table. "Yes. Do that. It might be worth going along."

Runcorn grinned. "Make sure you bring your stamina. The last party went for two days straight."

CHAPTER FIFTEEN

J ADE WATCHED ARMAND leave the library.
Her stomach plummeted.

Had she so grievously offended him? She had no idea that he'd take her rejection so personally.

But what else was she to do? She had to put a stop to this, no matter how much the taste of his lips on hers awakened a desire in her that she struggled to master.

Jade swallowed against a lump in her throat and returned to the table they'd shared. She closed her eyes a moment to stop welling tears and took a deep, unsteady breath. She needed to make him understand. It was not a rejection of him as a man, as a friend. And they could still be friends and get back to the way things were before. A mutual acknowledgement of attraction to be sure, but with the realization it could never go any further than that.

Jade was honest enough with herself to admit that the idea of being so much more than friends was tempting, so very tempting, but she couldn't allow herself to fall for him. She had meant what she said about her reputation. If she lost that, Edward would also lose the respect of their clients.

She opened her eyes and reached for one of the books Armand had been reading. Classical French sculptors.

He was following the same path as she was. They'd made a

deal to work together. Did he no longer trust her?

It wasn't until she realized she'd read the same passage for the fifth time over that she decided to close the book.

Her mind kept going back to what that odious Rufus Mayditch had said.

Lord Kingston Prendegast...

She would ask the porters at the auction house to make enquiries after the man, and she knew that Edward would do the same with some of his street contacts. And that was all well and good, but the only way to be certain that he didn't possess the Thalatte clock was if she could take a look at his collection for herself ...

Not that she *would*, of course. Her brother was right. Prendegast's reputation was quite irredeemable – not that the man cared a whit. He was tolerated by the *ton* because of his pedigree, but young ladies of quality were also directed away from his attention.

Jade reached across to take the last book Armand had been studying. Beneath it was a sheet of paper. She frowned as she tugged it out from beneath the hard bound book.

It was a series of crudely drawn sketches. Of a pendulum? Strange. It seemed that Armand was trying to sketch each part of it. He was adamant that the pendulum and its decoration came apart in the original and was not a single casting.

What was so fascinating about a gridiron pendulum?

Jade sighed.

There you go... so much for your vow not to think of him.

Setting the volumes aside, Jade reopened her notebook, took Armand's sketch and slipped it inside. She would write Armand a note apologizing for the offense she had clearly given him and ask for a chance to meet.

When she emerged from the library, the sun was lower in the sky. Jade considered sending a page with a message to Seton who waited with the carriage at a nearby coaching inn. But the idea of waiting for him didn't have much appeal. She would walk to the inn. It would give her time to think.

She had done the right thing by Armand, so why did she feel so awful?

Why did her heart ache when she thought about it?

Jade set off at a clip and crossed through the park, catching sight of families, of nannies with children, couples walking hand-in-hand. A touch of longing speared through her.

A family of her own…

Edward teased her every now and again about her unwed state. And to be fair, she gave as good as she received regarding her brother's own bachelorhood. Never once had his words wounded. But never before had she experienced this yearning.

Jade paused at a park bench to adjust the laces on her walking shoes. When she glanced up, she noticed a man who was watching her. He wore a dark gray peacoat that seemed a little out of place on such a fine afternoon.

She paid him no heed and continued on her way, given she was not far from the end of the park and in sight of the inn. And yet, something prompted her to glance behind.

The man was still there.

Their eyes met. The man looked away hastily.

He is following me.

She could hurry to the coaching inn, or…Jade turned and marched toward him with all the determination of a soldier. She got no further than a dozen feet before the man hurriedly stalked off in the other direction. Nevertheless, she followed, keeping his gray coat in sight until they reached the street where he disappeared into the throng.

Who was he?

How long had he been following her?

And why?

It *had* to be about the clock.

It was the only thing which made sense.

First her purse was stolen along with it the detailed sketch of the clock. Then was Mattis' murder. The dealer only had copies and not the original of the clock.

And there were only two people to her knowledge who were so desperately interested in it. One she knew. Armand made no secret of it. But the other did.

Was it her mystery client? Was he so disappointed with her lack of progress that he was sending someone to spy on her?

The more she thought about it, the more furious she got.

Enough.

Either the man revealed his identity and motive, or she would return his fifty pounds and wash her hands of the whole affair. Her mind was made up by the time she reached the inn. While Seton readied the carriage, she drafted the letter in her mind.

Dear Sir,

I do not appreciate being harassed by my clients. Being followed and spied upon is utterly beyond the pale. I demand a full explanation of your actions and to do so at a face-to-face meeting.

If you wish me to continue working for you, I will consider it, but only if you agree to certain conditions of my own. Otherwise, I will resign herewith, return your fifty pounds, and consider the matter settled.

Yours sincerely,
Miss Jade Bridges

"Ye not had a good afternoon, Miss?" Seton observed as he aided her into the carriage.

She forced a smile.

"Am I that obvious?"

"Only to the ones that know ye."

Jade shook her head slowly. "I've decided I've had enough of being deceived."

WEDNESDAY CAME. ARMAND was supposed to visit her today, however she doubted he would call. So, Jade did what she'd always done when there was too much to think about – go down to the auction house to inventory and catalogue. Anything to keep her mind busy.

Besides, if she was not at home, and he did not call, she couldn't be disappointed.

Jade lifted her eyes from her papers and watched the hands on the mantel clock tick away the time. He had not acknowledged the note of apology she had sent around to his house. She even attempted a little bit of coercion by letting him know she had his sketch if he would be interested in collecting it.

Edward had left on a trip to Wales that morning and would be away for several weeks. She considered herself lucky that she had so much to occupy her. It certainly made the hours pass a little more quickly.

She wiped her hands down the front of her apron and picked up the next piece – a set of enamel bowl coffee spoons. Jade picked up the first and found the hallmark, then reached for her loupe to identify the assay office, date, and silversmith's mark.

Too quickly the clocks struck one o'clock. She moved to her little private office with a plate of cold meats, some cheese, and a cup of tea. The Times, which had remained unopened from breakfast, beckoned. She scanned the advertisements and found the one she had placed the day before.

Jade had used the same introduction she had been told to use in the commissioning letter, but with an altered message:

TKA to VMA

Grandmother has taken a turn.

Need to see you urgently

She would prefer a face-to-face meeting to register her protest. The letter that sat on the desk was a second-best option.

Billy, one of the porters, poked his head through the door.

"Excuse me, Miss. Master Edward said you were interested in information on Lord Prendegast."

Jade set down her cup and motioned the young man into the room. She noticed him glance at the thin cuts of meat beside her. She offered him the plate. He grinned, liberated a slice, and wolfed it down in a couple of bites before sitting on the chair on the other side of her desk.

"So, what can you tell me?" she asked.

"Well, I heard he has some pretty expensive parties in that place of his."

"I heard that too. I also heard they're not the sort of parties that ladies are invited to."

Billy acknowledged the truth of her statement with a nod and an "umm…".

"He hires big, though. Employs at least fifty extra staff for each party. Mostly servants to cook and to serve guests. He also has musicians and jugglers and contortionists for the entertainment."

"I can just imagine what other kinds of entertainment he has on offer," she said dryly. "I'm led to believe it's quite the bacchanal."

"I don't really know what that means, Miss, but if it means what I think it does, then yeah, there's plenty of drinking and lightskirts."

"*How* do you know this, Billy?"

"My sister did a couple of 'em – oh!" He caught himself in what his words inferred and leaned forward, lowering his voice. "Just as a kitchenhand, mind! Nothing else. She was in the kitchen all night, didn't even see any of the guests. She's a respectable girl."

Jade nodded. "Yes, of course. I know Joanie. She's a good girl."

Billy nodded, satisfied that he hadn't accidentally maligned his sister's character.

"And what you say matches what Edward was able to find

out. Prendegast doesn't keep a large household, so it would make sense to hire extra servants for an event that extravagant." She paused a moment, "Do you remember that statue clock we sold that the bidding went high on?"

"The one with the lady? Yes."

"Joanie didn't happen to mention seeing a clock like that the last time she was there, did she?" she asked hopefully.

Billy shook his head. "No. Why should she?"

"It was just a thought."

He shrugged. "All she really said was once the dishes were served, there wasn't a lot for her to do for hours and hours before it was time for cleaning up the dining hall. Nice pay, though. She earned a good bit of coin that night, she did." Billy looked her directly in the eye. "I reckon she could get you in if you wanted. And that's what you want, right? To go in and find that clock?"

Jade held her breath. Indeed, that *was* what she wanted, but one couldn't exactly come right out and ask. After all, it was a little different from the kind of events she usually attended. Never was she at a home to snoop for another client. Mostly she attended to showcase jewelry for sale or to discreetly conduct a valuation.

And she was *invited*. Going in the guise of a servant was another matter entirely, somewhat akin to spying.

Dangerous.

She suppressed a shiver.

"You know what my brother would have to say about that, don't you?" she said at length.

Billy rose to his feet. "Best ye don't tell him then, Miss," he said with a sly grin. "It's neither here nor there to me, but you wanted to know about Prendegast, and our Joanie has been to his house a time or two, so I thought it was worth your while knowing."

"Thank you, Billy. I think I will have a talk to your sister. There can't be any harm in doing that. Here," said Jade, pushing her plate forward toward him. Billy accepted the offer and took a couple of more slices before returning to work.

Jade ate the remains of her meal, thoughtful. A voice in her head that sounded suspiciously like Edward's warned her it was foolish to attend.

But what an opportunity…

Edward's voice lost the argument. Besides, what he didn't know wouldn't hurt him.

Jade considered her plan. She'd met Joanie a couple of times, and she *was* a nice girl. If Billy's sister could manage one of these parties with her dignity and virtue intact, there should be no reason why *she* could not. With the decision made, Jade turned to inventorying a silver cutlery box when there was another sharp rap on the door frame.

In her quest to find the hallmark, she didn't look up. "If that's the next box, Dottie, just leave it by the door."

There was no reply. From Dottie, at least. Another, familiar, deeper and more welcomed voice rang out.

"Am I welcome, even if I'm not Dottie?"

Jade recognized the voice and nearly dropped her loupe.

Armand filled the doorway.

She immediately got to her feet and tried to hide an expression of delighted surprise.

Unsuccessfully it would seem, because Armand grinned back.

She gave up trying to hide her pleasure at seeing him. The fact that he was smiling meant that he'd forgiven her, and everything was back to normal between them. Relief and joy bubbled inside her, and she was honest enough to herself to admit that she missed him.

"You're always welcome," she told him warmly.

She waited for Armand to cross the threshold, but he didn't. For a moment he looked as though he was going to say something but then he appeared to change his mind with a shake of his head, and the silence between them stretched on.

"You weren't at home," he said then, softly, cautiously, as though he thought she might lose her temper with him as she very nearly did at the library.

"I didn't think you would come," she replied, matching his tone, wondering whether he could hear the apology in it.

Armand broke eye contact, looking down at his boots a moment. It appeared that he was gathering his thoughts. Jade's stomach effervesced. Perhaps this was not going to be a good meeting, after all.

Finally, he lifted his gaze to hers again. "Are you free to ride with me today, Miss Bridges?"

Yes.

No.

She was not a young lady of leisure whose days consisted of waiting for someone to call on her. She had to work to do. Edward was in Wales. She needed to stay at the shop.

"Yes." The answer was as much a surprise to herself as it was to Armand. She watched a smile dance across his face. He quickly mastered his expression, though. Here was the face he showed to the world – the proud, slightly austere aristocrat. What a far cry he seemed from the easy-going man she had come to know in the auction house over the past months.

He did not move from his position in the door frame. Jade rose from her seat and approached him. He did not reach for her hand and indeed, maintained a proper distance as they made their way through the sale room.

"I'm just going out with the Count," Jade announced to Dottie who was working at the counter. The woman raised her head and gave Jade a knowing look. Jade pulled a face in return.

Yes, she knew what her friend thought. Best she keep *that* view to herself, Jade reflected sourly. There would be no fairytale ending. Merchant's daughters do not marry counts.

As they emerged into the sunshine outside the auction house, she caught a brief glimpse of a figure in a gray peacoat stepping back into the shadow of a building across the street. Jade stopped and stared after the figure, trying to identify where he had disappeared to.

She felt Armand put a hand on the small of her back to guide her to the curricle that waited. "Change your mind?" he asked mildly.

"I thought I saw someone across the way. A man. I think he was watching us."

Jade glanced up at Armand, expecting him to dismiss her concern, but he didn't. He frowned and, moving away from her, prepared to cross the street. She reached out and caught his arm.

"There's no need. I expect it will all stop soon."

"I trust there is an explanation of just what '*it*' is?"

Jade squeezed his arm.

"I will tell you everything on our ride."

ARMAND ACCEPTED THAT for now. He aided her up into the curricle, thoroughly enjoying the feel of her waist beneath his hands as he lifted her to the first step.

Stopping by the auction house had not been part of his plans for today.

After he'd gone to the shop in Bond Street and learned Jade was not there, he'd intended to be done with her and damn his own feelings. But before he knew it, he'd been halfway across London Bridge.

Now that Jade sat beside him, he regretted those uncharitable thoughts.

They crossed the noisy streets of London's South End, making their way across the Thames until they reached the oasis of calm that was Hyde Park.

"Lately I have discovered that I am being followed," she said at last. "I had my suspicions ever since my reticule was stolen, but two days ago I spotted a man."

"Where?" he asked, trying not to let his concern appear too obvious.

"In Russell Square. I left the library a little while after you did and decided to walk to the coaching inn to find Seton."

Armand listened in silence as she described spotting the man while retying her bootlaces and how she had intended to confront him. He felt a simmering of anger. Something might have happened to her. If he had not lost his temper at the library, he would have been there to offer a degree of protection. He searched her face. "Tell me that you've told your brother about this, at least?"

Jade wrinkled her nose. "Don't be ridiculous. What would have there been to say? Nothing happened. Besides, I've addressed the issue now. I expect it to be righted in the next few days."

Armand slowed the curricle and turned to her. "Oh, yes? How so, *Miss Bridges*?"

"I've sent a message to my client to demand the spying stops. I intend to return the fee he paid in advance."

"And you're sure it's your mystery client?"

"It has to be!" Her exasperation was plain, not directed at him but at the circumstance in general. "I've been working in this trade for as long as I can remember. I've never encountered anything like this before. And I don't wish to again."

As tempted as Armand was to offer a litany of warnings, he did not, judging that to be the wisest course. Instead, he snapped the reins, and the curricle emerged from under the shade of the spreading tree. The light brown strands of hair that escaped her bonnet glinted gold.

She flashed him a grin. And damn if it didn't contain a hint of a tease!

"Are you not going to scold me?" she asked.

Armand raised an eyebrow. "Do you wish to be scolded? If you are, let me assure you that I'm very much up to the task."

He was not wrong. A lovely blush pinkened her cheeks, before she hastily changed the subject.

"I meant what I said in my note. I'm sorry I offended you.

You've been nothing but gentlemanly, and if I gave you the impression that you took more liberty than I was willing to give, it would not be the truth."

Armand shifted in his seat as several things occurred to him at once. First, Jade Bridges had apologized to him – a red letter day indeed. Secondly, she'd all but told him that she desired him. And thirdly – he'd received no note from her.

"You sent me a note?"

He chanced a glance at Jade whose attention was fixed on securing her hair pins and bonnet. "Did you not receive it? I sent a messenger to your home on the same day I saw you at the library."

Armand shook his head.

"Ah well," she shrugged. "It contained nothing more than what I've said to you now."

"Thank you."

Jade offered him a half-smile.

"I mean it, Jade," he said. "I needed to be reminded of what was important – my past, my heritage. I wanted to let you know that personally before I left."

Now he had her full attention.

"Left? Where are you going?"

He drew breath to answer, but she did it for him.

"You're going to France?"

"It seemed to make sense that if I was going to find out something about my past then I should go back to where it began."

"When do you plan to go?"

"In a month. There are preparations I have to make first."

Armand slowed his horse to a stop under the shade of a large oak tree. Jade nodded, and, if wasn't mistaken, she swallowed hard.

"Is there any hope you might miss me?" he asked. The question was only partly a tease.

"Would you prefer it if I did?"

Parry, thrust.

"*Touché*, Miss Bridges."

She smiled. A full, genuine smile. The tension between his shoulders which had been plaguing him for a week now eased.

"Does this mean you have no further interest in the clock?"

Armand shook his head slowly, drinking in her beautiful features. The verdant green of the park paled in comparison to the color of her eyes.

"I'm still convinced the clock is the key to understanding the events that happened the night my mother and I fled. But there is so much more I don't know. *Maman* has returned to France, so that's where I will go to seek answers."

He watched Jade take in the news of his decision and its implications.

He knew it as well as she – if there was the chance his land could be restored to him, and with the title recognized by the French Court, there was every chance his stay in France would be a permanent one.

He wasn't sure how he felt about that. As a result, he refused to give it anymore thought than it being just a vague possibility, something that only *might* be over the horizon.

Her eyes fell from his. She looked down at her hands in her lap. "I'll miss you," she said softly.

With those simple words, something changed. He couldn't describe why or how, but suddenly he loved her. He knew it to the core of his being.

He reached for her hands, bringing them up to his lips. The act surprised her, but she didn't pull away. "I'll miss you too," he said. "More than I can say. You've changed me, Jade. You've done so much for me."

She frowned. "What have I done?"

"Without you, I would never have considered searching out my past. And your offer of sharing what you learned of the Thalatte clock, even though you were committed to your client…"

"It seems so little."

"It means everything to me." He invested every word with significance.

He saw her eyebrows rise with surprise, then her expression softened. She squeezed his hands.

"I don't know what to say."

"Then say nothing."

He released her hands and touched her cheek, gently drawing her to him. Her lips parted, ready to receive his. He took his time kissing her, savoring every moment of his lips on hers before gently coaxing her mouth to open to allow him to taste her again.

Jade sighed.

Then her tongue met his, and his desire increased ten-fold.

He pulled back, delighted to see the dreamy expression on her face. He'd done that. He made her feel that way.

Now all he had to do was convince this proud, independent businesswoman that her place was at his side forever.

CHAPTER SIXTEEN

THE MOMENT HIS lips touched hers, Jade's resistance was lost. She returned his ardor without hesitation, drinking it in as though parched. For one reckless moment, she fully surrendered. He could ravish her here, in public view, and she might go along with it willingly.

Thank God he had the willpower to stop, for she had none.

The tenderness of Armand's expression left her totally undone. She took in a shuddering breath and let out a shaky laugh. "You tell me you're leaving, then you kiss me like that? That makes you a cad."

Armand smiled, but there was a knowingness in his expression. When he replied there was gentleness in his tone as well as levity.

"Indeed. You're right, Miss Bridges. You've caught me out again."

"Well, see that it doesn't happen again, Monsieur le Comte," Jade continued as breezily as she could manage. "You know what young girls are like – a moment's lingering attention with your magnetic brown eyes will have them in a swoon."

"I am so pleased to have you warn me of such things! You will forgive me if I'm forced to prevail upon your wisdom in this matter."

She laughed, pleased to find Armand's face animated.

"Now," she said, "we have important things to do before you go, such as finding your clock."

"Ah, then have I won a victory, Miss Bridges. You concede that the Thalatte clock *is* mine."

She reached across to take his hand. "I know it is."

Armand's hand squeezed her.

"Then I should not want to take up any more of your time," he said. "I'll return you to the auction house."

He gathered the reins, and they were in motion once again.

What just happened? Jade wondered.

His breezy joviality was as forced as her own. Just before he'd kissed her, there was a look in his eyes she'd not seen there before that delighted and scared her all at once.

It was a look of love.

How easy it would be to give in and love him back – she was already halfway there.

But to do so would be unwise, ill-advised, foolish – even so, he was as irresistible as her favorite sweets. She could not stop at one mouth-watering tidbit of Turkish Delight any more than she could stop herself from kissing him back. It was clear he felt the same.

But the humorous exchange was, perhaps, good. It meant at least they were back on safe ground, even if only for the moment.

And she *would* help him find the clock, she told herself, because he was her friend, and it interested her to do so.

But where should she look next?

It would have to be at Prendegast's Dionysus Club dinner.

And all too soon, they had returned to the auction house.

She spotted Billy carefully cleaning a black lacquer screen decorated with colorful hardstones carved to create chrysanthemum flowers, foliage, and vases.

"Billy," she called out. "Do have your sister pay me a call tomorrow to further discuss that matter we spoke about today."

"Will do, Miss Bridges," he answered. "Oh, by the way. This message just arrived for you."

He dipped in the pocket of his apron and handed over a sealed envelope before returning to his work. Jade opened it and immediately recognized the particularly spidery handwriting.

"My mystery client has agreed to speak with me face-to-face," she said to no one in particular.

"When?"

For a moment, Jade had forgotten Armand had walked her inside. Looking up, she found his expression determined.

"At my earliest convenience."

"Then let's not keep the gentleman waiting."

Jade folded the letter slowly and made a great show of opening her reticule and popping it inside, all the while keeping her eyes locked to his.

Armand had obviously guessed her intent. "You're not going alone."

"Quite right. Seton will drive me," she said airily.

Billy raised his head from his cleaning task. "Seton's gone to deliver furniture this afternoon," he called.

"It looks like you're stuck with me, Miss Bridges." Armand's voice left no room for contradiction.

Aware that the staff in the saleroom were now surreptitiously watching them, Jade raised her head confidently. "Then I thank you, *Monsieur le Comte*. We'd best be on our way."

Jade waited until she was safely up on the curricle's high seat before she spoke again. "This man is a client of mine, and you are both after the same object. It's most inappropriate for you to be there."

"Then don't consider me a client. Consider me a friend who will have more than his conscience to answer for if anything untoward happens to you."

She heard the voice of her brother in her head, warning her to be cautious.

Jade sighed. "I'm not trying to be difficult, you know."

Armand flashed a grin before turning his attention back to driving.

"My dear Miss Bridges, you don't have to *try*."

THE ADDRESS WAS in a fashionable part of the city, stately and quiet. The courtyard at the front of the house was bordered by raised garden beds filled in the heady scent of daphne bushes displaying flowers in various shades of pink.

Armand urged the horse to a stop at the bottom of half a dozen steps up to a door painted dark green. In the center was a bronze door knocker that took the form of a woman's head in a classical style. The hinged knocker extended from her shoulders in an oval shape reminiscent of a gilt mirror frame.

"It seems a respectable enough place," said Jade.

Armand picked up the knocker and dropped it on the striker several times.

"Looks can be deceiving."

Jade gave him a sidelong glance just as the door opened. A stern-looking woman, solidly built and not quite into her middle age, opened the door.

At first Jade thought she was the housekeeper, but the uniform she wore resembled that of a butler, right down to the fitted knee breeches and the short jacket tailored to her generous frame.

"I am Miss Bridges," said Jade. "I've been invited to call upon your master for business." At that, the woman's mouth quirked into not-quite-a-grin.

"You are expected, Miss, but your man will have to wait outside," she said.

"Oh, he's not my man – this is Count Armand Danger who is accompanying me today."

The woman eyed Armand up and down.

"Nevertheless miss, he is still a *man*."

Jade and Armand exchanged glances.

"The Baroness allows very few men through her door," she

explained, then addressed Armand for the first time. "You will wait in the retiring room, my lord."

The woman stepped aside to allow them admittance, then moved to open a door immediately on her left. Jade caught a glimpse inside. It seemed a pleasantly appointed, if cozy room.

Armand lifted his eyebrows to Jade.

She had no idea if he was questioning whether or not she felt enough at ease to venture off on her own or was dismayed at the position of being made to wait in another room, like a servant.

Regarding the former, Jade would have naturally been seeing her client alone if Seton had been available to drive her; regarding the latter, though surprised, she found the situation amusing.

At the nod of her head, Armand, defeated, walked into the room.

"I will send one of the maids with refreshments," said the woman. "Your man will be quite comfortable there."

She struggled to contain a smile. The woman gave Armand no more heed than if he were a lap dog who required a bowl of water for his comfort. "Very good," Jade replied, adding a measure of imperiousness to her voice. Over the woman's shoulder, through the open door, Armand stared at her to suggest future retaliation was a possibility.

The majordomo drew the door closed, leaving Jade to follow her farther into the house.

From what she saw as she passed, the home was immaculately kept. They paused a moment while her escort asked a passing maid to send tea and refreshments to the gentleman in the front retiring room.

The maid's eyes widened a moment before she ran off to do as she was bid.

They eventually reached a pair of closed double doors. "Please wait here, Miss Bridges," she said and entered the room, closing the doors behind her.

Jade waited alone in the hall for a minute, then the majordomo reappeared and ushered her into a large and airy drawing room.

"My lady, Miss Jade Bridges."

An elegant woman rose to her feet. Jade judged her age to be about sixty. Her hair was silver-gray and styled short.

Jade bobbed a curtsy. The woman noted the action with approval.

"I am Baroness Gretchen von Hoecker. I understand you wish to speak with me about the clock I commissioned you to find."

⤜⤜⤜✦⤛⤛⤛

IF HE WERE to be locked in a cell for a while, one could do a lot worse than this room, Armand decided. Nonetheless, it might have been once a large cloakroom. It was narrower than it was wide, and decorated in a chintz wallpaper of mid-blues, golds, and greens.

A green leather Chesterfield chair and footstool were the dominant pieces of furniture in the room which was lit by a narrow casement window. But the thing which caught his interest stood on the mantelpiece over a small fireplace.

A reproduction Thalatte clock.

Armand approached. This one seemed of better quality than he saw in Mickey Mattis' warehouse – the casting was crisper and better defined. It would be easy to imagine this was the original, except that the pendulum was, again, a single casting.

He was about to reach for it when there was a small scratch at the door.

"Enter."

A young woman carrying a tray entered with downcast eyes. She placed the tray on the side table just inside the door without once acknowledging his presence.

"Thank you," he said. The maid looked up at him, then looked swiftly away, as though ashamed to have raised her eyes to him. Once she had set the coffee pot and plate of sandwiches on the table, the girl turned hurriedly to the door. She was about to exit when Armand asked, "What is the name of your master?"

The girl giggled but did not turn to face him.

"Oh, there be no master here, sir," she said, her hand on the door handle. "Only a mistress."

Armand opened his mouth to ask another question, but the girl scuttled from the room and closed the door behind her.

The aroma of the freshly brewed coffee was tempting. So too was the clock. He stilled the pendulum and picked up the piece carefully. It was too light to have been cast in bronze. Spelter then. The sweep of Thalatte's robes and the well-defined features suggested it was an early casting copy.

He placed the piece back on the mantle, setting its pendulum swinging once more.

The coffee called to him again, and he poured himself a cup, leaving the sandwiches alone for the moment. They'd not filled the plate, so there was the expectation that Jade's interview would be short.

He hoped.

He took a sip and pulled a face.

Bitter.

Armand set the cup back on the saucer.

Perhaps it was going to be a long wait after all.

"COME, MISS BRIDGES, sit beside me. You'll be much more comfortable," the Baroness suggested. The woman swept her skirts aside and patted the gold velvet seat cushion beside her.

It was not a large settee. Jade angled her back towards the arm to put a little space between herself and her host. Nevertheless, she could not help their knees touching.

"Now, I want a full explanation for your extraordinary advertisement in *The Times*."

Jade outlined what she knew of the clock and its origins, her discovery that it was based on a life-sized sculpture, and her intent to concentrate her search on that in an effort to trace the clock.

She was dissembling, and she knew it. There was something particular about the Baroness, but she couldn't put her finger on it. The interview felt as though she were giving an accounting of some misdemeanor to a school mistress. What made matters worse was the majordomo standing haughtily at attention near the door.

Jade watched the Baroness raise an eyebrow when she told her how she had been followed. Then she informed her of Count Armand Danger's interest in the piece. How his mother bravely escaped from France with her only child.

"This is the male you brought with you today?"

Jade nodded.

"Wilkie," the Baroness said, "Go fetch our other guest. I wish to speak to him."

The woman bowed before disappearing into the hall.

The Baroness leaned into Jade with an almost tender expression on her face.

"You believe *I* had someone follow you?" She reached out and gently took Jade's hand, patting it. "That must have been quite frightening. Tell me about it."

She did so, all the while conscious of the fact the Baroness watched her face with unnerving interest and had not let go of her hand.

"And you said it was a *male* who followed you?"

"I could not have been mistaken on the matter, my Lady."

"Then I am most pleased to assure you it was not me or anyone in my employ." The Baroness paused a moment, allowing herself to look faintly amused. "If I had sent anyone to follow you, it would have been a *woman*."

"Why so?"

"For the very same reason I hired you, Miss Bridges. Men are such *cumbersome* creatures, are they not? They lack grace, subtlety, and most oftentimes wit."

"But your letter to me – that was very much a masculine hand."

The Baroness regarded her observation with approval. "I didn't say they don't have some uses. I have Fitzsimon, he was my father's young valet, whom I inherited thirty years ago. He is useful if I need a male presence in the house – or in a letter. Now there," she added, patting the back of Jade's hand again, "have I done enough to assure you that I have no nefarious intent?"

She drew breath and nodded, not completely reassured, but enough to appreciate the Baroness' ways were likely to be much more indirect. The woman released her hand only as the female butler returned with Armand. Jade noticed the firm line of his jaw soften when he saw her. In turn, she gave a small nod of reassurance. Then he turned his attention to the Baroness.

"Mistress," said Wilkie. "Count Armand Danger of *Ytres*."

On the introduction, Armand bowed, looking every inch the masterful young aristocrat.

"At your service, my lady."

Armand knew the full power of his charm, but so did the Baroness it appeared, and *she* was having none of it.

"I very much doubt that, young man. According to my Miss Jade," she began, patting Jade's knee as she did so, "you claim to be the rightful owner of the original Thalatte clock."

"I am."

"Then we are in a quandary, because I have commissioned the best curio finder in London to locate her for *me*, and I will not have you using your *attractions* on her to try to trump me."

Jade witnessed a flash of annoyance cross Armand's face, but he mastered it and forced deference into his voice.

"Madam, it is not my intention to interfere in the business arrangement you have with Miss Bridges. My interest in the matter is entirely *personal*."

The word was used deliberately, Jade kenned, and the Baroness knew it too. The shades of meaning were laid bare. Before the

Baroness could make remark on it, Armand continued.

"You have an exceedingly fine reproduction of the clock in your retiring room."

"Thank you. But a copy is not as appealing as the original, wouldn't you say?"

"Indeed, which has me wondering if we might come to some arrangement."

The Baroness's laugh filled the room. "I have never come to *any* arrangement with a man. And, at my time of life, I don't intend to start. But you do intrigue me, nonetheless. What is it you propose?"

"If I'm not very much mistaken, your interest is in Thalatte, rather than the timepiece specifically, am I correct?"

"You're observant for a male of the species."

Armand obviously treated it as a compliment or sought to give the impression he'd taken it as one. He offered another small bow.

The Baroness was unimpressed. "Get on with it!"

Armand shrugged and continued. "I believe my family had the original life-sized statue from which the figure for the clocks was produced."

"Had?"

"I return to France in a few weeks to confirm whether or not it is still on my family's estate. Should the redoubtable Miss Bridges be successful in finding the original clock, and I am successful in reclaiming the statue, would you consider exchanging one original for the other?"

The Baroness cocked her head, clearly giving the proposal some thought.

"Explain to me why you'd make such an extraordinary offer. A statue by Boyer – *that* statue – has far more monetary value than the timepiece. What is it about the clock which interests you so?"

"I wish I could tell you. I don't fully understand it myself. But my only lasting memory of my father is with the clock. He was killed by the Regime."

Armand's voice dropped. The Baroness had to lean forward a little to hear him continue.

"My mother risked her own life to flee France with me when I was only a child. She remains the most remarkable woman I know. Her courage and resilience made an indelible mark on me. The return of the clock would be of comfort to her."

The older woman was not so entirely immune to Armand's charm as Jade first supposed. Her expression lost its hard, suspicious edge and softened, if only marginally.

There was a long silence before she gave her answer.

"I will consider it."

CHAPTER SEVENTEEN

JADE WAITED UNTIL they were outside the Baroness' gates.

"Do you mean it? You'd give her the statue of Thalatte?" she said.

"If I can find it," Armand answered. "I have the plans for the garden that my mother brought with her. They have to be of some significance."

Once again, it was a reminder that he was leaving her.

"Will you write to me?"

He looked confused for a moment.

"While I'm gone?" he asked.

Jade nodded.

"Would you like me to?"

The corner of his eyes crinkled a little. Damn the man, he was trying to hold back a grin.

She raised her chin. "If you think it is because I will miss you, then you have another thing coming. If you do not write to me, how will you know when I have acquired the clock? I certainly won't be able to tell you."

"Ah, so this is to be pragmatic correspondence," he said.

"Of course! What else could it be?"

"No long lines of poetry revealing how much you miss me?"

"If you want purple prose, I suggest you look elsewhere, *Monsieur le Comte.*"

"Ah, you cut me to the quick once more, Miss Bridges."

Jade returned his grin.

It was good to laugh after that, quite frankly, unsettling interview with the Baroness. Even now, Jade wasn't sure where she stood with the woman. She had come to confront her about being followed and to quit her assignment, only to leave convinced by the woman's honesty, if not her strangeness.

"She says she wasn't having me followed," Jade offered in a more serious tone.

"Do you believe her?"

Jade nodded.

"Then if not the Baroness, who do you think it is?"

"I don't know. Perhaps I imagined it."

Armand shook his head. "Come along, you know better than to spin that nonsense with me. A little while ago you were adamant that you were being followed."

"And you believe me?"

"You above all women? Yes."

She chanced a glance at him then. Armand met it without hesitation. She looked away first, unable to stand the weight of his gaze. Jade swallowed and looked down at her hands, fingers threaded together. She let out a slow breath.

Yes.

How remarkable that one simple word could put her so off-balance. At that moment it meant more to her than a declaration of love. Armand *believed* her. Believed *in* her.

"So, if it is not the Baroness, who might it be?" Armand asked again. "Anyone else you've dealt with in business? Someone with whom your brother may be at odds?"

"I've asked myself those questions, and I do not have an answer."

They pulled up outside the auction house. Armand jumped down and came to the other side of the curricle to help her down. His hands gripped her firmly at the waist as he lowered her, taking his time to do so. He paused when they were face to face, her tip toes barely touching the pavement.

His hands around her waist seemed more intimate than the kisses they'd previously shared. She felt an arousal build. Her hands gripped his shoulders. How tempting it was to wrap her arms around his neck and press herself to him, to feel the hardness of his body against hers. Then her heels met the ground, and he released her. It was most disappointing…

"Will you call on me again?"

Jade hated herself for asking the question. It was the question those silly little debutantes asked as they made calf-eyes at eligible young men. Still, the expression on Armand's face told her the inquiry was not unwelcome.

"Yes, I'll call again before I leave. I don't know when that will be."

Jade swallowed back emotion and nodded, her eyes falling from his.

Then she gathered up her pride and found an expression to show him.

"Until then, *monsieur le comte.*"

She turned away, but he snagged her hand. She turned back. And he drew her closer before bending over her hand to kiss it. His hooded expression made her heartbeat faster.

"Until then, Miss Bridges."

⟫⟫⟫❁⟪⟪⟪

JADE SURVEYED HER appearance. She wore the oldest dress she owned – simple, serviceable, and faded. She'd removed every piece of jewelry she customarily wore and pinned her hair back under an old straw bonnet.

There. She *could* pass as a servant.

She thanked Providence that her brother was so frequently absent. If he caught her looking like this, his suspicions would doubtlessly be aroused. As it stood, all she had to do was to evade the household servants and meet Joanie on the street corner a block from Prendegast's home. There they would go to the servants' entrance to sign on to serve at the Dionysus Club dinner.

Joanie was already waiting for her. "Ah, Miss Bridges, I hardly recognized ye."

"No, you mustn't call me that. No one must know my real name."

"Then what shall I call ye then?"

Jade blinked rapidly. She hadn't thought that far.

"Addie," she decided. In truth, it was the first name that popped into her head.

With that matter sorted, they walked to Lord Kingston Prendegast's house and found the side gate. Within, people milled about a small courtyard that was part of the servants' area.

"There are so many servants here... does Prendegast really need this many?"

"Not everyone will be chosen," said Joanie. "He's right peculiar, is this gent. You'll have to satisfy the housekeeper first."

Joanie caught Jade's look of concern and grinned. "Don't you worry about that. I'll look after ye."

The young woman took her hand and walked right up to one of the footmen. She looked up at him and gave him a seductive smile.

"Hullo there, Stanley."

The man stood tall and grinned back.

"Joanie, back for another one, I see."

"I brought a friend with me," she said, thrusting Jade forward. "Her name's Addie. She works with me, and when I told her how much money I made last time, she was right keen."

Jade bore Stanley's scrutiny with a pleasant and hopeful smile on her face and acted as though she ignored the way he eyed her up and down like she was a piece of horseflesh.

"I tell you what, Joanie," he said, "since you've been 'ere before, I'll send you directly to the housekeeper with your friend, so you don't have to wait in line with this lot.

Joanie patted Stanley's cheek. "Ah, you are a love."

The young footman gave her a plainly comic leer in return. "Just give me a chance to show you how much of a love I can be."

Joanie giggled and dismissed the remark. They went round to a side door that Stanley had pointed out.

Jade grinned. "A beau of yours?"

She received a half-shrug in answer "A little flirtation never did anyone any harm," she said.

They waited at the door with a group of other young women, much fewer in number than those who were in the courtyard.

An older woman guarded the entrance. She cast her eye over the young women and pointed to Joanie and four other girls. Jade held her breath and kept her fingers crossed that she was to be added to that number.

"And you." The woman pointed directly at her. "Come inside with me. The rest of you can go."

The other girls shook their heads and muttered their disappointment, departing back toward the courtyard.

"That's Mrs. Greenwood, the housekeeper," Joanie whispered.

The woman gave each one of them a cursory, individual inspection then addressed them all.

"I recognize some of you," she began. "For the rest, I am Mrs. Greenwood. I am Lord Prendegast's housekeeper, and I am here to tell you now that this is no ordinary event at which you'll be expected to serve. It is a costume party his lordship hosts for his friends. You will be given a costume and expected to wear it all evening. You will be expected to behave with discretion. Speaking outside these walls about what goes on within them will result in you being barred from this and any other household where his lordship has influence. Do you understand me?"

Jade joined in the chorus of, "Yes, Mrs. Greenwood."

"Now go down to the next room. Girls who've been before,

lead on for the newcomers."

Jade glanced to Joanie who waited until the other girls had gone on ahead.

"Hiring extra servants for the party takes two full days," Joanie whispered.

"I'm not surprised at this rate. Why are they so particular?"

"You haven't seen the costumes yet," Joanie giggled. Jade raised an eyebrow but didn't get a chance to ask any further questions as they entered the next room.

Another woman, stood before a table piled high with garments, told them to line up. She was a seamstress, judging by the row of pins threaded through the bodice of her dress. They glinted in the light like some strange kind of military decoration, and the woman walked along the ranks, inspecting the new troops.

She eyed them up and down, seemingly noting their measurements in her head before reaching into the pile of clothing. In turn, she gave each girl a thin shift, a skirt, and soft, under-bust, front-laced stays.

Jade wondered if she was, in fact, a seamstress for one of the theaters. The woman noticed her attention and snapped.

"What are you waiting for? Try them on. Make sure they fit. I don't have all day to waste."

Jade followed Joanie and found a corner that gave the illusion of privacy. She untied the laces on the back of her dress, removed her stays and slipped on the chemise. Then she pulled on the skirt which had ties on the back. Jade bent over to pick up the stays and noticed the neckline of the chemise gaped open alarmingly.

She didn't need a mirror to see how she looked. Any sudden movements would see the deep scoop of the neckline drop over her shoulders and risk exposing her breasts. Perhaps that was the intent.

Nearby, one of the other girls tugged at the neckline and burst into tears.

"I can't do this! It's *indecent!*" She hurriedly removed the costume, scrambled to change back into her own clothing, and ran out of the room.

Joanie ignored the girl's perturbation and adjusted her own costume to give the right proportion of practicality and slutty enticement.

Mrs. Greenwood bustled in from the hall and called out. "Have you finished with the girls, Suzette?"

"These are the ones who have stayed from this audition," the seamstress answered.

The housekeeper addressed them.

"Your job is to serve food and drink, and to clear tables." The older woman smirked. "For those of you in fear for your virtue, rest assured there will be other ladies at the party who will fulfill that particular duty. They will be very distinctly dressed.

"Should you wish to be *generous* with your charms, that is your affair. But if you neglect your serving duties, you will have the extra coin confiscated, and you will forfeit the balance of your night's wages. Are we understood?"

Jade glanced at Joanie and matched her hardened expression. A character a little more forward, a little less deferential was what was required here.

Mrs. Greenwood inspected her from top to toe, then slowly nodded her satisfaction.

"You'll do," she said. "Get back into your ordinary clothes and bring your costume to the first room."

Jade did as she was ordered, feeling somewhat sordid already. Every scintilla of common sense warned her to leave and find some other way to discover the clock. She might have slipped away except Joanie came bounding over, her eyes bright and cheeks flushed.

"This will be so much fun!" the girl exclaimed.

They walked together back to the first room where Mrs. Greenwood bundled their costumes and pinned a numbered piece of paper to each one. "You are number nine," she told Jade. "Remember it. What is it?"

"Number nine, mum," Jade replied in as close a mimic of Joanie as she could manage.

"Good. Don't forget it." Jade found a couple of small silver coins in her hand. "There will be more than that when you come back at the end of the week. And if you can keep your mouth shut."

Second thoughts hit Jade the minute they passed the side gate. It was one thing to have an idea of what went on at these types of parties and another entirely to participate in them. When they were clear of the grounds, she stopped and placed her hands on Joanie's shoulders.

"Your brother told me you worked as a kitchenhand at these parties, not as a serving girl."

"I did work in the kitchen the first time, but then I found out how much the serving girls were getting, so the next time I put my hand up for that."

"Does Billy know?"

Joanie's eyes widened.

"No, of course not! Do you think he'd let me, if he knew? It was a hard night's work in the kitchen for not a lot. But as a serving girl, I flirt with some gentlemen, and I earn a nice bit of money. And what Billy doesn't know won't hurt him."

"Joanie, it's an orgy!"

The girl looked at her with disdain.

"I *know* that. But the more they drink and the more wiggle you put in your step the more coins get slipped your way."

Then her expression changed, when it dawned on her what Jade was thinking.

"Don't go thinking I've let those gentlemen have their way with me because I haven't. I'm no slut," she protested. "But there's no harm in giving them a quick peek at my bosom. I earned nearly a pound on top of my wages at the last event," she added proudly.

"You know the risk of something truly dreadful happening, don't you?" Jade countered and dropped her voice lower, "If you were to be assaulted – *raped* – then what would you do then? Your brother wouldn't be able to do anything against these powerful men."

Joanie dismissed her concerns with a shrug. "This will be my third time serving, and nothing bad has ever happened to me."

"There are other ways to get money," said Jade.

"There might be for *you*."

The words stung.

"I'm sorry," said Jade.

Joanie shrugged her shoulders, and they continued on toward town.

After a while, Joanie sighed. "It's not just that, not just the money. It's the excitement of doing something a bit naughty," she continued. "And I get to tell the other girls who aren't as brave as me all about it. It's not so different than what you do, dressing up for those fancy balls and things."

"It's not the same thing at all," Jade countered.

Joanie shot her a disbelieving look.

"I've heard of rich ladies who like to pretend to be one of us common folk so they can have fun with the gentlemen while in disguise. When Billy told me you wanted to speak to me about Prendegast's party, I promised myself I wouldn't ask questions of my betters. Told myself it wasn't my place to ask why. But you didn't give me the same courtesy. You asked me, so I ask you – why are *you* doing this?"

It was a fair question.

"I'm doing this for work – just like you," Jade answered. "I believe Prendegast may have an object my client would like to buy from him. But I won't know if it's there unless see it myself."

Joanie looked decidedly unconvinced. "There are other ways you could do that, you know. Your brother could ask. Your fancy man, the count – *he* could ask. Billy's told me about how he's been hanging about. He'd do anything for you."

"It's hardly the same thing," she said. "The client is mine, and she only trusts me to work for her."

The excuse sounded weak to her own ears, and it was. Joanie was right. There were other ways to discover the clock. She had a company of staff that she could send out on errands. But the truth was that she liked what she did and was good at it.

She was conscious of the privileged in-between world in which she lived. She enjoyed many liberties that young women of the upper classes did not on one hand. On the other, her family's relative wealth also insulated her from hardships experienced by women of the working classes.

So why *did* she do what she did?

An honest answer was the only one she could give.

"I'll tell you truly. I enjoy the excitement of it too," Jade confessed.

Joanie nodded smugly.

"There, then. That wasn't so hard was it?" she said. "And I don't need a lecture from you about the risks, since we're taking the same ones together."

"You're wrong about one thing though," said Jade.

"What's that?"

"Lord Armand is *not* 'my fancy man'."

CHAPTER EIGHTEEN

OVER HIS MORNING coffee, Armand opened a much-welcome letter from his second cousin, Gerald Perrin.

The two men had corresponded in an off-and-on fashion for the past year or so.

The connection had come out of the blue from Gerald's mother, Giselle, about three years ago, not long after the death of William, the Earl of Rosemount. Armand's mother recalled her to be the wife of his father's first cousin, now widowed.

It had been a pleasant surprise for Armand and his mother to hear from any members of their family in the years following their escape to England. It was an unexpressed understanding that the rest of the family had either been executed or scattered to the four winds by the revolution.

The letters, full of family reminisces and cheerful news, were regular and always welcome. A year later, another correspondent joined. Gerald, who was ten years older than Armand, had travelled extensively but now had returned home to Arras to look after his mother, Giselle.

It had been Gerald who asked if *Maman* would like to pay his mother a visit following Charles' wedding. The invitation had been eagerly accepted.

And if Armand was honest, it had come as little surprise when his mother announced her visit would become a permanent stay.

A few weeks ago, Armand had written to Gerald of his intention to come to France to pay his mother a visit.

Armand read through Gerald's reply:

Cousin, how good it would be to meet face-to-face at last. Of course, you must come and stay with us. You are welcome here as your maman is welcome. We live simply, nothing as grand as you have in London, or indeed, the old chateau at Ytres, but you will find us hospitable.

News of your plans have given Tante Nicole much joy. In fact, Maman says she cannot recall the last time her friend was so full of joie de vivre.

We too have much to discuss. I'm intrigued by your search for the clock. I did mention it briefly to Tante Nicole, but she seems to recall nothing of it.

Do write when you are sure of your travel plans.

Your cousin,
Gerald.

Armand quickly penned a response, knowing Barnet waited for him upstairs to try on his costume for Prendegast's party. It wouldn't be untrue to say he was having second thoughts about attending the Dionysus Club.

His misgivings started the moment the Earl of Runcorn introduced him to Prendegast. Frankly, there was something about his soon-to-be host that made Armand's skin crawl. Oh, to be sure, the man was charming. He dressed impeccably and had fine manners to match. Some might even consider Prendegast to be handsome.

Yet there was something about him which caused Armand to be immediately wary.

Kingston Prendegast had a way of looking at you – *through you* – as though he could see the darkness in one's soul and knew how to exploit it.

Nevertheless, Armand said the right things to ingratiate himself. He hinted at an invitation and received it, along with a list of rules. Costumes were to be worn. No one was to be addressed by their real names – a pseudonym was to be used. If a fellow was recognized, the knowledge was to be kept to oneself and communicated to no one. No one was to speak of what went on in the den of Dionysus.

However, despite his *arrière-pensée*, it would all be worth it if he found the clock there.

How so?

Armand ignored the little voice that whispered caution in his ear and set aside the addressed letter to Gerald to be sent out with the morning's post.

His course was set. He had to own his past to find his future.

And every time he thought of a future, it always included Miss Jade Bridges.

Was this how *she* spent her days? Doing things she didn't wish to, in order to curry favor with people she wouldn't choose to associate with, all in the name of business?

He shook off the thought and went upstairs to try on his costume.

Once dressed, Armand evaluated his reflection in the mirror and barely recognized the man who stared back at him.

"Sir, I think you look splendid," Barnet said approvingly.

Splendid was not the word that came to mind when Armand first saw what had been suggested for him. In fact, he nearly returned the costume on the spot. Pantaloons that were a rich cherry pink with a matching waistcoat. A coat with tails down to the backs of his knees in a mint green. Both were lavishly embellished with gold braiding. His own hair was covered by a curly black wig.

It was the embodiment of the rococo fashion his great-grandfather might have worn in eighteenth century France.

It was on his lips to make some self-deprecating remark, but he couldn't do it. Clothes indeed maketh the man. There was something about wearing it, seeing not his own face in the looking glass, but that of a wealthy French Count, which struck something in him hitherto unexpected.

The man before him didn't just *carry* a title. He *was* the *Comte de Ytres*.

He caught Barnet's reflection behind him in the mirror.

"Vous avez bien fait."

You have done well.

"Merci, monsieur," Barnet replied, looking most satisfied with himself.

Nevertheless, Armand found himself wound tighter than a clock spring as his carriage rolled through a second set of gates into Prendegast's estate. He thought the evening was to be held in the main house. It never occurred to him there was a second residence until a footman holding a lantern aloft directed them to the road to the left.

Out of the gardens, ghostly forms gleamed in the moonlight. It took Armand a moment to realize they were statues made in the Greek style. Mostly figures of naked women – of course – but 'tastefully' done to give a fig leaf of respectability to the display.

One of the tall, graceful figures struck him as familiar. For a brief flash, Armand was the three-year-old boy of his nightmare, afraid of the giant lady who loomed over him.

He squeezed his eyes shut briefly as the carriage rolled to a stop. After taking a deep breath, he was ready. He settled the mask on his face then disembarked and approached the life-sized feminine feature. On her plinth, she stood about a foot taller than his own six feet.

A plaque revealed her name – not Thalatte, but Athena.

He crouched down, pretending to adjust the silver buckle on his shoe, so he could look up at the statue from a lower view-point. Yes, he could see how imposing a statue of Thalatte would be to a young boy.

Armand rose and looked about.

Roughly a hundred yards away, separated by a great expanse of lawn and a thick hedgerow, was the main house. It was in darkness, apart from a couple of lights in what he deduced to be the servants' wing.

What if the clock was in the house and not this *building?*

The idea of wasting his time here, doing something he didn't really want to do with people he didn't even know, let alone like, was maddening.

A footman approached. "Sir, can I help you? You will find the party waiting for you this way."

Apparently, he'd tarried alone outside for too long. Armand gave a single nod of acknowledgement and followed the servant along the stone path. It wended its way between large yew trees into a private courtyard that surrounded a large outbuilding two stories high, almost square in shape.

He followed the sound of music and gales of laughter. Reports had not been exaggerated. Prendegast really had turned the place into a private Vauxhall Garden. Jugglers tossed clubs back and forth, fire eaters breathed flames high into the air, exotic dancers wearing what seemed too little in the cool night air performed sensuously around the guests, accompanied by wandering minstrels.

All were masked.

Naturally.

A large tankard was offered to him by a rather voluptuous serving girl who grinned and winked at him knowingly, as though she somehow kenned he was out of his depth here. He took a sip. It was a dark and malty ale, not something he favored. However, given the size of the vessel, he could stay on the one mug for much of the night, and no one would be the wiser.

He felt conspicuous despite there being others dressed in costumes more or less outlandish as his. He looked for the entrance to the building, skirting the edges of a group of men who had women draped over them. The females were barely dressed in brightly colored silks and matching masks. They were, without question, prostitutes.

The girls laughed gaily at every bawdy jest, whether truly amusing or not. One of the women gave him a frank appraisal as he passed. Armand avoided her direct gaze, but not before he noticed her faintly amused smile at his diffidence.

This is hopeless. A wild goose chase.

Armand wondered how long he would be obliged to stay before he could slip away unnoticed. He scanned about for his host. Despite the fact that all were lavishly costumed, Lord Prendegast was easy to spot.

His costume hinted at a Tudor style – a close-fitting doublet in red satin edged in black which featured mameluke sleeves of red satin slashed with black. His hose was the same shade of scarlet. His shoes were red leather held by gold buckles and black bows, while gold rings and a striking collar made of large square links sat around his shoulders and neck.

Armand imagined this would be how a libertine Sir Francis Drake might dress. But who *was* he representing?

Mephistopheles?

It seemed appropriate.

Prendegast headed his way. Armand acknowledged him with a nod, but not his name.

His host clasped him by the shoulders. "Come now, do you see nothing to your liking?"

Armand forced a laugh. "I see plenty – too much to take in all at once."

"Then greed is not your deadly sin. Very wise of you. The virtuous say to delay gratification is to make the conquest more satisfying. Perhaps there is something to it, perhaps not. Every taste is catered for here. You must be one of my first-time guests."

He nodded over to a clutch of colorfully dressed prostitutes.

"Nothing is off-limits to my guests. If *they* do not whet your appetite, you may wish to sample the serving wenches as well as the food."

He watched as Armand took it all in – the spectacle, the displays of flesh. More welcome than any of that was the smell of freshly roasted meat on a spit.

Prendegast noticed his interest.

"Lust and gluttony can be a potent combination. Enjoy."

Armand bowed, took another sip from his ale, and put a lightness in his step to stop himself from looking entirely sober and used the opportunity to wander around the gardens.

There was more here than just the statue of Athena. There were at least a dozen magnificent life-sized figures from the pantheon of Greek deity. Armand had no idea who the sculptor was, but he could appreciate the workmanship. It was tempting to run his hands along the shapely calf of Aphrodite, so he did and ignored any strange glances that might have been directed his way.

Why not? Nothing was off-limits.

The anonymous sculptor was a master of his craft. Armand understood how Prometheus thought, his desire to create a beautiful woman – *his* perfect woman captured in marble and yet brought to life.

Armand allowed himself to feel a measure of hope for his mission.

Given the sculptures in the grounds, perhaps it wasn't outside the realm of possibility that the Thalatte clock was in this building after all.

He stood back and examined what he could see of the structure. The ground floor, which he imagined to be public rooms, were lit with lamps. The floor above, he guessed were bedrooms and private suites.

Before he could give it any more study, Armand's hands were grabbed by two women, both blondes. He could smell gin on their breath as they giggled and dragged him away from the shadows and towards the building. The smell of roasted meats and vegetables reminded him of how hungry he was. He clasped the girls' hands tighter and stepped up the pace, so he was the one leading them. The women stumbled along behind, falling into gales of drunken laughter.

Out of the corner of his eye, he saw Mephistopheles watch on with approval.

Armand and his two escorts tumbled into a ballroom which had been decorated in the style of a medieval banqueting hall with long tables and benches. Colorful pennants were suspended from the ceiling. In a minstrel gallery above, another set of musicians were tuning up.

Across the room, he spied double doors that led further into the house. They were closed.

On another wall, a smaller entrance. Servants filed out carrying jugs of ale and wine, followed by others hefting large trenchers of food.

Other guests were flooding in as the musicians struck up, and soon the noise in the banquet hall was deafening, a constant hubbub of noise punctuated by howls of laughter and the occasional feminine squeal competing with the music from the gallery.

Armand's two female companions continued to cling to him like leeches and sat him down at a table.

One of the trenchers, filled with roasted meat, dropped before him. Armand looked up and caught an eyeful of a soft white bosom barely contained in a blouse. He quickly raised his eyes and saw a familiar face.

No.

He was *wrong.*

He *had* to be mistaken.

It was just someone who looked like her.

Armand cut the meat absently and offered it to his companions on his knife. Instead, they preferred to take the beef directly from his hands, sucking his fingers as they did so. Reflexive arousal stirred in him.

Despite the distraction, he kept his eye on the serving girl and watched her make her way around the room. On first glance she'd appeared to have the disinterested, even bored expression that many of the servants wore. But though a yard or two separated them now, he could see the tension in her jaw as she moved away at an angle to him.

She made her way to the end of the row of benches and walked without a backward glance toward the servants' entrance. He knew the walk. He knew the color of the light brown hair escaping from the white cap.

Armand bit down on all the curses he knew in both English and French.

Mademoiselle Bridgette Trublion!

CHAPTER NINETEEN

I T WAS INDEED, as promised, a bacchanal.

The guests had been relatively well-behaved to this point, but it couldn't last. So far, Jade's bottom had been pinched twice, and the night was still young. Joanie gave her a commiserating smile in passing. A man had snatched a half-full pitcher from Jade's hands and sent her away with a slap on her bottom.

Little did the man realize that he'd done her a favor. With her hands unencumbered, she could now take her time to get back to the kitchen.

Jade waited until she was back in the service corridor before wiping her forehead of sweat. She had only been working for two hours but it felt like she'd been doing it for a lifetime. It was grueling, trudging back and forth from the kitchen, first carrying trenchers of meat and now pitchers of ale. Her arms ached.

Never would she take her below stairs staff for granted ever again.

Still, the effort had not all been fruitless. She'd kept her eyes open during the running back and forth from the kitchen had given her a familiarity with the layout of the building.

If there was a clock here, she guessed it would be in a library or a study.

Raucous laughter followed her down the hall. Jade glanced back to see that no one actually followed. She was alone for the moment. She shook her head. Never had she seen men and women imbibe alcohol so freely. It was as though the conventions that governed behavior were defenestrated in this place.

She glanced behind her once more and, seeing she was still alone, slipped through a side door into the entrance hall.

Here it was surprisingly quiet. Jade went to the right of the grand staircase to finish her exploration of that passage. It was deserted. Rooms led off to the right. She tried the doorknobs.

Of the four, three turned under her hand – they were unlocked. The fourth did not turn.

She didn't enter the unlocked rooms – not yet. Jade hung on to the housekeeper's promise that there would be a lull in the proceedings after the main meal had been served. She planned to use that time to slip away to complete her exploration when the servants sat down to *their* dinner.

Jade hurried back to the kitchen. It would not do to be missed. On seeing her, the butler pointed to two filled pitchers. Jade nodded, grabbed them by the handles, and headed back to the banqueting hall once more.

She passed off one of the pitchers to another girl who was empty-handed, and stopped a moment to survey the room, looking for the 'thirstiest' guest first.

Some of the men had abandoned the food, preferring to make a meal of the women beside them. One satin-clad woman sat astride a man's lap, her breasts exposed, her back arched in some kind of ecstasy.

She glanced away from them, but not before prickles rose on the back of her neck.

She was being watched.

And not simply by some lascivious guest. It was as though whoever it was touched her, although she was quite apart from anyone.

Jade looked around for the man who had followed her in the park and had waited outside the sale room but did not see anyone that fit his description.

There was only one who was directing his gaze at her. It was a man in the long black curly wig of the King Charles era. Jade approached him with what she hoped was an appropriately pleasant expression.

The closer she came, the more intense his countenance appeared. She went around the table to approach from behind, ready to fill his tankard when his hand gripped her wrist. His other hand steadied the pitcher. He took the weight of it, forcing her hand down until the jug rested on the table.

He was close enough now for her to smell his cologne, a familiar mix of ginger and mint that cut through the smell of alcohol and smoke.

Jade chanced turning her head and looked at the man up close.

Her heart leapt into triple time as knowing dark eyes bored into hers.

Armand!

His mouth was set in a grim line.

She licked her lips and drew breath.

What on earth was he *doing here?*

Before she could consider that further, Armand roughly pulled her onto his lap, causing her to accidentally kick one of the prostitutes at his side, sending the woman face first into the crotch of the man on her other side. Those around them howled with laughter.

Jade struggled fruitlessly against Armand's embrace. His arms were like steel bands. His breath against her ear sent shivers through her and sparked an ember of desire in spite of everything.

Damn him!

She struggled once more. His grip tightened.

"I want to talk to you," he whispered in her ear. "The statue of Persephone in the garden. Know it?"

She'd seen it. It was the one furthest from the building and deepest into the shadows.

Jade ceased her struggling and nodded wordlessly, waiting for him to release her. But he didn't. His eyes bored into hers, watching her carefully as his hand slid up her leg, over her knee to her thigh, setting every nerve ending alight. She drew breath to tell him off when his lips descended, capturing hers.

This was no attempt at seduction. Armand's tongue plundered her mouth, taking what it wanted from her.

She knew she ought to object, to struggle harder to free herself. Yet her body responded to his, making demands of its own until she was returning his kiss in equal measure. After a moment, he loosened his grip. She rose on shaky legs, her attention still on him, and not on the lewd comments directed their way.

His eyes left hers and traveled lower. She'd almost completely fallen out of her blouse. Her breasts heaved with her heavy breathing.

She hated how her hand shook as she reached for the pitcher. Of course, that wasn't helped by the dark and stormy look Armand continued to give her. She hastened away, thankful the buzzing in her ears drowned out the lecherous comments cast after her.

Jade continued through the room to retrieve empty jugs from the tables, mindful that Armand watched her.

Perversely, part of her was pleased he was here. She expected Joanie to be a fair-weather friend if trouble arose, and, despite Armand's obvious displeasure in seeing her here, she knew he would protect her if it came to that.

Was that why he'd mauled her so openly? To mark her as his?

That was just positively barbarian.

And yet she had to own to her reaction to it. If it had been anyone else, she'd have screamed blue murder and fought back. Not with Armand. If she was honest with herself, if he did that again – in less public circumstances, of course – she would not object.

Far from it. She would encourage him further…

She shook her head.

What on earth was she thinking?

Before heading back down the servants' passage, she looked back across the hall. The volume had increased with the amount of drink consumed. A small crowd of people surrounded two men arm wrestling, betting coin on the outcome. Another group were showing similar enthusiasm over some kind of dice game.

However, most were preoccupied with attractions of the feminine sort. Some of the men were holding court, opining on who-knew-what to a clutch of lightskirts who, despite being three sheets to the wind, still showed the requisite amount of interest.

Yet more had found one or more women to their liking and were openly groping them, and some were–

Oh my God, there was a couple actually copulating in front of everyone!

Jade turned away, cheeks flaming, and dashed back to the kitchen.

There, at least, was normality. The scullery maids were cleaning pots and pans, some of the serving staff were eating a late supper at the servants' dining table. She spotted Joanie in playful conversation with Stuart and another of the young footman.

As a consequence, no one paid her heed when she entered. She buttered a slice of bread and wolfed it down along with a mug of cider. She watched the housekeeper remove a small set of keys from her belt and place them on the sideboard while she adjusted her uniform. The older woman put her hands to her lower back and stretched just as the butler emerged from the dining room and beckoned her.

The two disappeared into another room.

What luck!

Using the keys would be much quicker than picking a lock – which she was quite capable of doing. Many a locked item had come into the auction house without its key and required nothing more than wire and a degree of patience to open.

Jade stood, swiftly glanced about and pretended to wipe her hands with a dish cloth and slipped the keys into her pocket unnoticed.

She could check *all* the rooms now, including the locked one. It wouldn't take her long to examine the four of them, return the keys, and meet Armand outside as he'd demanded.

Jade started with the furthest of the two rooms. Thanks to the light of two low-wicked lamps in the first, she had no need of the candle stub and steel striker she'd hidden in her pocket.

Covered under dust sheets in the middle of the room were the familiar shapes of a virginal and harp.

The music room.

Jade quickly walked the perimeter. There was no clock on the mantle nor in the bookcase.

Search completed, Jade opened the door and peered down the hall. There was no one about. Given the sound of revelry coming from the banqueting hall, she felt safe enough to continue her search.

Jade quickened her step. It wouldn't do to tarry. Armand was clearly furious with her for being here tonight. She feared what he might do if she left him waiting. If he called her out in front of everyone, or let it be known among members of the *ton* that she'd been here, her family's reputation would be destroyed.

Why was she so weak when it came to him? All it took was one smoldering look, and she lost all good sense. Why was that?

A search of the second room, the morning room, was similarly fruitless.

Now, the final, unlocked room. She put an ear to the door to listen for anyone inside. There was no doubt in her mind that they would soon be occupied for more than their intended functions. A shudder of revulsion went through her.

She slipped around the door and closed it behind her. Like the others, this one was empty.

The room had no lit lamps, but the fire in the hearth was banked. Even without the small amount of illumination, the smell of aged leather, glues, and paper alone told her that she was in a library. Jade went to the mantle and lit a spill from the embers in the grate to ignite her candle.

She stood with her back to the fire and glanced about the room.

"It's not in here. I've already looked."

Jade held back a scream and almost dropped the candle, but a firm hand steadied hers. She breathed in deep. Her nose filled with his familiar scent.

Armand.

"I told you to meet me outside," he said softly, but with an undercurrent of steel.

Jade covered her fright by returning his angry glare threefold.

"I haven't spent all evening in this scrap of a costume being leered and pawed at to meekly wait for *you* outside."

She could see his face, dark and menacing, but for the first time appreciated his elaborate Jacobean costume, expertly cut to accent his physique.

She wanted to kiss him.

She wanted *more* than a kiss.

"So, if you're looking for the clock, what exactly *were* you going to do once you found it? Sneak it out under your dress?" He eyed her up and down.

She felt warm again.

"No, I would arrange to make a call to see if the Earl would be interested in selling and—"

There were voices outside.

Armand blew out the candle, plunging them into semi-darkness.

Jade held her breath and listened. The voices moved on.

"Get the candle relit," said Armand. "We only have a moment to search."

"I thought you said it wasn't here."

"I lied. Get on with it."

Jade did as he said and didn't question the fact that Armand helped himself to a lamp from his host's desk and lit it. He explored the opposite end of the library.

"Are you sure you want to call attention to ourselves?" she

asked.

"I have an excuse to be here."

"Oh? Like what?"

Armand turned and looked at her. "You."

Jade swallowed. She could guess what he meant by that.

She turned to examine a large bookcase glad he could not see her face redden. Meanwhile, her traitorous body reminded her of what his kisses could do to her.

A moment later the disappointing search ended with them together at a sizeable oak reading table positioned by the curtained windows.

"Well, where next?" Armand whispered.

"There's the room next door. If not there, then we'll have to try upstairs. That is if it's here at all."

It was a gloomy thought, but one that had to be faced.

At Armand's dismayed expression, Jade took a step forward and brushed his cheek with her fingers. "It's a risk we'll have to take," she said. "It's an occupational hazard."

"I'm not cut out for the world of cloaks and daggers."

She smiled. "Neither am I. I'm usually looking round a house with the owner's permission." She eyed him appreciatively. "I will own that you wear that costume well."

He flashed her a grin in response.

"Not half as well as you wear yours."

His words were a caress. And he knew it too. He followed up with a feather-light touch to her shoulders, playing with the neckline of her blouse. Without meaning to, she leaned toward him. He responded by snaking a free arm around her waist, drawing her to him. He moved forward until Jade could feel the edge of the table at her backside.

"You do know your reputation would be ruined if anyone here knew your identity," he said.

Jade tried to remain focused on her thoughts instead of being distracted by the press of his body against hers.

"Apart from one of the other girls, no one knows I'm here but you, and she won't tell. Will you?"

"I might be persuaded to silence."

Armand's kiss was soft and full, less brutal than the kiss in the banquet hall, and more sensuous. Jade returned it fully, giving license to her own desires. Every part of her body was aware of him. Wanted more of him.

She wrapped her arms around his neck to deepen the kiss. *Click!*

Before she could identify the sound, Armand had hoisted her up onto the table and pushed her back. He covered her mouth with one hand and, with the other, pulled down the bodice of the peasant top then bunched her skirts up to her thighs.

Once the blood stopped rushing through her ears from the shock of being thrust onto the table, she heard other voices in the room. Inebriated voices.

Armand drew a hand along her leg. He kissed her passionately for several moments then moved to her ear.

"Turn your face away from the room," he whispered. "They will notice your body, but not your face."

The hoarse instruction sent eddies of gooseflesh along her body. She responded, how could she not? She threaded her fingers through his hair, drawing him closer to use his body to shield hers from view.

They ignored a lewd comment directed their way, then the drunken group departed the library, leaving the door wide open.

Jade kept her eyes on Armand, acutely aware of his body over hers. She nervously licked her lips. His eyes flickered down to them and back to her eyes. They were so dark as to nearly be black. Before she could disentangle herself, more people stumbled in. A couple by the sound of it.

There was no conversation from them, no words spoken, just the sound of rustling fabric, then panting, and moans accompanied by the creaking of the leather couch that Jade had seen just inside the doorway.

Her eyes widened. Armand's lips compressed. Good Lord,

there was a couple having sex in this very room, heedless of the fact it was occupied!

Jade was acutely aware of her semi-clad state, her breasts against the satin of Armand's waistcoat, her bare legs wrapped around his hips. The way he stroked her hair to comfort her now took on a more erotic meaning.

He watched her carefully, his eyes flicking down to her exposed breasts. She could feel his growing erection between her legs and her own body's answering call.

It was maddening.

It was arousing.

If he touched her, she would be completely undone.

And she desperately, desperately wanted to kiss him.

As if he'd heard her, Armand lowered his mouth to hers and kissed her with deliberate slowness.

She willed his hands to touch her, explore her. And as though she had commanded it, he did.

It was madness. All of her senses were filled. The taste of his lips, the scent of his cologne, the sight of his handsome face, the feel of his hands as they made free with her body, even the sounds of the other couple in the room with them.

Armand's touch sent fire through every part of her being. That secret place between her legs ached to be touched, wanting what the gasping, moaning woman with them in the room was receiving from her lover.

Silently she pleaded with Armand.

His expression darkened.

Lightly, almost tentatively, his fingers reached between her legs to find and brush against her clitoris. Jade squeezed her eyes tight, unable to hide her own cry of desire. She wrapped her legs around Armand even tighter, holding him to her, desperate to make the erotic sparks last longer.

She thought it was impossible to desire him more at this moment, but she was wrong. His touch became bolder. His fingers deftly rubbed and stroked until the crescendo of her orgasm was reached. Jade no longer heard the other couple, the rush of blood through her ears deafened her to everything else.

Sweat glistened on Armand's forehead, his expression focused. She could see that he was holding himself back for her sake.

Using his shoulders for support, she raised herself to a sitting position and touched his erection through his breeches, feeling its firmness. His eyes shuttered closed a moment, as though he were in pain. Then his hand clamped over hers, holding it there a moment. She buried her face in his shoulder and stroked him as he had stroked her.

Armand released her hand and held her to him before snaking a free hand between her legs once more. Her body welcomed his attention eagerly, and the sensation of bliss rose again swiftly.

The other woman screamed her fulfillment, apparently unknowing or uncaring of their accidental audience. Soon the man let out a series of grunts, loudly encouraged by the woman he'd been pleasuring.

Jade cried out too, pressing herself tightly to Armand's chest where she could feel his heart pounding.

The man groaned his fulfillment as the woman giggled drunkenly. A moment later, the strangers stumbled out the door, slamming it loudly behind them.

CHAPTER TWENTY

A s soon as they were alone, Jade released him as though scalded.

Armand cursed himself the worst names under the sun. He turned his back to give her a moment of privacy to right her clothing. The sight of her laid out bare before him was indelibly scorched into his memory.

The disgust was with himself.

Never with her.

The fault was his entirely, and he hated himself for it. He'd intended to cover their presence in the library by giving the interlopers what they might expect to see – not a couple searching the shelves but doing what was no doubt being done all over the house by now.

But he had come perilously close to losing control and actually taking her there on the table. Even now he sported a full erection.

And if he hated himself, he could only imagine what she thought of him.

He stalked over to the library window and opened the large sash. He deeply breathed in the night air, welcoming its coldness. He looked down. It was only a couple of feet to the ground. They could avoid the orgy taking place all about the house if they left this way now. And he could send her away safely, back to her home, and far, far away from him.

"Quickly," he said gruffly. "We're not going to be alone for long."

He straddled the sill then twisted until his feet dangled over the edge. Then he aided Jade up onto the sill beside him. Her face matched his own grim expression.

Armand launched himself to the ground, then he turned and reached up. Jade eased herself forward off the sill until his arms could take her at the waist.

He knew just about every inch of her body now. And his own responded unbidden once more.

As soon as she was on solid ground, he grasped her hand and together they ran into the deep shadows of the garden to put as much distance between *that place* and themselves as possible.

"Wait! I can't run as fast as you," she gasped.

He ignored her complaint until they reached the statue of Persephone.

How appropriate – he was Pluto, Jade was Persephone, and he had just dragged her into Hades.

Beside him, she panted heavily, which recalled *other* activities that he was trying very, very hard not to think about.

There, through a break in the hedgerow, he could see the main house. He guessed that the coaches and coachmen would be accommodated at the main stables. If he didn't tarry, he could get Jade to his coachman and instruct him to take her home before Prendegast discovered his absence.

Armand bared his teeth in the struggle to keep himself under control which made him sound gruffer than he intended.

"You must have known what this event would be like," he said. "What if I hadn't been here? What if some other man had grabbed you?"

Jade's beautiful green eyes widened; so did her mouth. Armand ignored his body's continuing reactions and went on.

"Believe you me, dressed as *you* are, he wouldn't have stopped at a grope. And at another time and place, *I* might not have stopped either."

Jade turned flame red, not only because of embarrassment but also anger too, he guessed.

He was right. She shoved him in the chest with both hands.

Hard.

Armand staggered back a pace.

"I can take care of myself," she hissed. "I'm not some woolly-headed debutant, naïve in the ways of the world."

The violence of her response, ironically, quenched his own. Armand could now regard her calmly. And when he spoke it was measured.

"I know. And I love you for it."

Her mouth closed with a snap. That was not the response she was expecting.

Now was the time to extend an olive branch.

"I am not dismissive of your abilities or your knowledge. And more recently I have become even more aware of your beauty and passion. If I came across as a brute it was not my intent."

Emotions swirled across her face. She slowly lowered herself onto the garden wall. Her hands shook as she steadied herself.

Shock.

Armand removed his coat and laid it across her shoulders. And he was irrationally pleased to see that she wrapped it around her. It was a form of embrace he was afraid she would never grant him again.

"I know what I did in coming here was foolish," she admitted. "As soon as I saw what they wanted us to wear, I knew. But…"

"…you had a job to do," he finished for her.

Jade looked up at him and nodded.

"And here we are… no closer to finding the clock," he added.

"There is still the other room."

"Which is locked."

Jade smiled slyly. "I have the key."

She fished it out of the pocket of her skirt and dangled it in front of him. Armand sucked air over his teeth, unable to hide an exaggerated pained expression.

Jade giggled. It was a sound that made him suspect not all was lost between them.

"They just happened to be sitting there by the butler's pantry."

Armand processed the news. "Give them to me. I'll go back in and look."

Jade got to her feet and shrugged off the coat.

"No, that won't work. You need me to return the key to the kitchen, and I need to finish the evening and retrieve my own clothes. It will look suspicious if I disappear. I promise I'll stay in the kitchen once we're done. I won't go anywhere near the revelers."

Armand accepted his coat back and shoved his arms into the sleeves, watching her evaluate his mood. Dear God, she was temptation itself. All luscious curves. Now he'd sampled her passion, he knew that once would never be enough.

Oddly, rather than leaving him feeling frustrated, he found a sense of calm.

He leaned forward to give her a chaste kiss on the cheek. Even in the moonlight, he could see her blush.

She didn't hate him. In fact, Jade had emerged from the whole encounter with a better equilibrium than he had. For that he was profoundly grateful.

With less hurry and more stealth, they returned to the house. Armand boosted Jade back through the library window after determining that it was all clear. He hoisted himself in after her.

"I found a connecting door between this room and the next on our first search around," he said. "But it was locked too."

Jade fished the keys from her pocket once again. The first one she tried fit the lock perfectly, and it opened almost without a click.

Outside the library, the drunken revelry was getting louder. People were approaching.

"Quickly," he whispered. He herded Jade through and shut

the door, before taking the key from her and locking it.

The room was in complete darkness. Clearly this was a space not intended to be used tonight.

Their eyes quickly became used to the relative lack of light so that what light was spilling under the door out to the hallway provided illumination enough to search for the fireplace.

Jade found it first. He heard the rasp of steel on flint and saw a small shower of sparks. After several attempts, a flame from a paper spill ignited and, soon after, a lamp.

This was a drawing room and a surprising space, distinctly feminine in its décor. It seemed, dare he say it, somewhat *normal*.

Armand turned back to the fireplace and was stunned. There, up on the mantle, he saw it.

The Thalatte clock.

"Jade, the lamp. Hold it up! Do you see it? On the mantle."

Her gasp told him that she did see it. She set the lamp on a table and raised the wick, giving the room an intimate warm yellow glow, and Armand knew at a glance now that it was not a fine copy like the one in the Baroness's retiring room.

It was the original.

It was even more magnificent than the sketch made out. More incredible than he remembered from his dreams.

He couldn't stop staring at it. Somehow it had mesmerized him.

He forced himself to move forward. At first it was enough just to reach up and touch it.

The metal was cold beneath his fingertips. At twenty inches in height, and made of bronze, he knew it would be damned heavy.

He quickly looked around and found a small step stool. It was enough to give him a few extra inches of height to safely lift the clock from its position.

He stepped up and gazed at Thalatte, a goddess in miniature, a work of art in her own right. The fine features which made her beautiful were exquisitely rendered. The way her robes draped and flowed over her body gave her life. The tick-tick-tick of the movement might well have been her heartbeat.

But, as beautiful as she was, the thing which interested in the most was the clock. He stilled her heartbeat and carefully removed the pendulum from the crutch behind the escapement, bringing it down to the lamp for a better view. He glanced up to find Jade keenly watching.

Then he returned to the clock and lifted that down. He placed it on the table with the pendulum and stood back a moment – and his entire world changed. No longer was he in the London pleasure palace of the notorious rake Prendegast. The scene before him was his father's study in the chateau at *Ytres*.

"What are you doing?"

It wasn't Jade's voice, but his own at three years old.

He observed hands not his own dismantle the three vertical steel and brass bars from the pendulum and reassemble them differently.

They fit together perfectly.

They fit together perfectly to form a *key*.

He felt a hand on his shoulder, but all he could see was a key. He held it up to the lamplight where it glinted gold.

The key.

The hand squeezed his shoulder then shook it over and over until he'd returned to a semi-darkened, London drawing room.

"ARMAND!" JADE WHISPERED his name harshly several times before he returned to her. Seeing him go into a trance, watching him dismantle and reassemble the pendulum so deftly frightened her more than anything else she'd experienced tonight.

He raised his head and looked her way without seeing her at all.

He held the key in his hand. If she hadn't seen for herself, she would not have dreamed that the three distinct parts could form such a perfect *other* whole. Jade reached for it. Armand released it into her hand, exhaling as if a sigh.

The key was unusual. The shaft was long and slender. There was a T-shape at one end, and it terminated to a small hook at the other end.

She'd never seen the like before – not in person, at any rate. There were elements of it that were reminiscent of keys from the medieval period.

"The key?" she said.

Armand nodded.

"But to open what?"

"I don't know." She could hear the frustration in his voice. "I keep having these dreams of when I was a *garconnet*. But I don't understand…"

Outside the drawing room door, there were drunken shouts and at least one object crashed to the floor and shattered.

"We can't say here," Jade whispered.

"We can't leave it here," Armand responded.

She rested her head on his shoulder and softly rubbed his back.

"We can't take it out under my skirts," she quipped.

That elicited a bitter laugh. Obviously, he remembered the words he'd spoken to her.

"We have no choice," she said. "Leave the clock here. We'll relock the room. It will be safe."

Armand set down the key and folded her into his embrace. Not one of raw animal passion this time, but of comfort. Jade accepted it whole-heartedly.

After a few moments, he gave her a light squeeze then released her, turning his attention to the object he'd created.

She watched him turn it back into three separate pieces of metal then back into what looked like a gridiron pendulum, and was, but also was *not*. With exceeding care, Armand lifted the clock back onto the mantle, rehung the pendulum, and set the clock going once more.

Another timepiece somewhere in the house chimed one o'clock. Armand adjusted the time on the Thalatte clock to disguise their interference and stepped down again.

He took her hand and kissed it gallantly. She giggled at the chasteness of the gesture, given how much more they had shared tonight. His returned smile was tender.

He placed the door key in her hand and fished out a gold sovereign from a small purse tucked in his belt. He held it out to her.

"What's this?"

"It's your alibi. Trust me. You'll have been noticed missing, and so will have I. If anyone asks… well, we'll just leave it at that."

Jade blushed and nodded her understanding. "What are you going to do?"

"I'll accompany you as far as the servants' hall, then I'll make sure I'm seen out and about for a little before making my excuses. When are you released from your duties?"

"Two o'clock."

"I'll be waiting for you."

The words sent a shiver of delight through her which she tried to suppress.

"You can't. Joanie will be expecting me."

"Billy's sister?"

Armand laughed at her shocked expression. "I do know everyone who works at your auction house, I've been there often enough. I'm presuming she was the one who got you in. Tell her she has a ride home – unless she's otherwise occupied."

She and Armand left the drawing room. Everyone they met were drunk on sex, alcohol and high spirits. They paid no heed to anyone or anything not already in their hands.

Still, his arm wrapped around her shoulder, he steered them through a throng of revelers, pretending to be as drunk as they were. He even managed a stagger. Jade wrapped her arms around his chest and giggled uncontrollably.

It wasn't all for show.

She loved him.

What a damned inappropriate time to come to that realization.

But once acknowledged, there was no avoiding it. Her heart knew, and her head could mount no argument why the notion was ill-advised and untenable anymore.

She loved him. There was nothing she did not love about him. His looks, good humor, thoughtfulness, and intelligence. And to have experienced the raw, carnal passion in his hands, her desire grew for him in equal measure.

CHAPTER TWENTY-ONE

JADE SLEPT RIGHT through the next morning. Soft gray light in the center parting of the curtains suggested the day was overcast. A moment later, she heard the splatter of rain against the windows.

If not for the gold sovereign hidden away in her reticule, she might have been able to imagine the previous night was a strange sort of fever dream.

Surely, Armand never touched her like *that*.

Surely, she never allowed him to…

The blankets caressed her body, and for a moment Jade closed her eyes and imagined she was in Armand's arms once more.

But as much as might try to deny it, her body knew and reacted instantly to a need that would remain, sadly, unfulfilled.

Just one more moment imaging his embrace…

Several moments later, Jade sighed and rang for her maid.

There was nothing to be gained by staying in bed all today, especially when there was work to do.

First on her list was to convince Edward to visit Prendegast with an offer for the clock without letting him know *how* she knew it was there. Then would come the difficult part – negotiating a price.

Prendegast wasn't short of money, and he spent it lavishly.

He was also a collector. His passion appeared to be the classical Greeks. It was a pity Armand didn't have an endless collection of Boyer sculptures to offer as a trade.

She went down to breakfast and found Edward there finishing a noon meal.

"Ah, awake at last!" he said. "I got back two hours ago. I wasn't sure I was going to see you at all today. Are you not well?"

"Well?" Jade asked, pouring herself a strong cup of tea.

"You don't usually sleep so late."

"I was up late," she said.

Edward regarded her expectantly. Jade considered her answer, a steppingstone of truths to cross a stream of lies.

"I know where the Thalatte clock is."

Edward threw his hands in the air. "Hallelujah, at last! That thing has become a millstone. Arrange a price and deal with your two clients."

"I need you to approach the owner for me."

"Why? Who is it?"

"Prendegast."

At that, Edward gave her his full attention.

"The man keeps himself to himself when he's at home," he said. "The only people he sees there are by special invitation, and I know you know what I mean."

Jade speared a pork sausage from the warming dish and put it on her plate.

"You don't need to beat about the bush. I do know what you mean. Prendegast had one of his 'events' last night. Billy's sister Joanie was there."

Jade sat down at the table to face her brother's scandalized gaze.

"Don't worry, she works as a kitchen maid."

Edward's expression changed to relief, then skepticism.

"Joanie has no idea what you're looking for."

"I told her."

The truth… sort of.

Jade crossed her fingers under the table.

"And Armand Danger was there."

A truth.

Although it didn't paint Armand in the best of lights…

"It seemed he suspected the clock might be there, so he got himself invited," Jade continued.

"And you know that *how?*"

Jade opened her mouth to speak, then closed it instead of speaking a lie.

After staring at her in silence for a full five seconds, Edward raised his hands. "Don't tell me, Jade. I really don't want to know."

"Eddie… I—"

He pointed a finger at her. "I can't be angry with you without cause. So don't give me cause. And before you ask, yes – I'll go to see Prendegast. That is, if you are completely certain, in your professional opinion, that the clock is the original."

"It is. In my professional opinion."

Jade endured several more long, uncomfortable moments of scrutiny before Edward nodded his agreement.

"What is the most you are prepared to pay for the clock?"

"Two hundred pounds."

Edward's jaw dropped. "You do realize how much we'd need to clear to turn a profit on that?"

Jade knew – double the price paid, plus a percentage. The Baroness would need to pay five hundred pounds. Saying the amount in her head didn't inspire her with confidence.

"Perhaps it won't cost two hundred," she said. "What if you offered Prendegast one of the engravings you have from the *La Pucelle D'Orleans* series? That would *definitely* appeal to him."

This time it was her brother who looked uncomfortable.

As well he should.

They were not your classical nudes. They were pornographic, and some would even say blasphemous, depictions of Joan of Arc, inspired by Voltaire's satirical poem about the French heroine and her many alleged lovers.

"You've seen them?" Edward asked cautiously.

"Of course, I have. They're in the back corner of the auction house – five of them. You forget who catalogues and takes inventory."

Their grandfather had held them there in safe keeping for a French *émigré* during the early part of the French Revolution. The owner never returned.

"Given the subject matter, they can never go to an open auction. If you're looking for a prospective buyer, there's no one better than Prendegast," she added. "You never know – if he wants one, he might take the lot, and we'll be in profit just like that. Unless you have other plans for them, that is."

Edward hid his flushed face behind a swig of coffee. He got to his feet.

"I'll call on Prendegast tomorrow. In the meantime, you need to untangle the competing interests of your clients. I hope you won't let your feelings toward Danger color the responsibility you have towards your commissioning client."

Jade was affronted. "I won't."

Edward rose, dropped a kiss on the top of her head.

"I know you won't."

He left. Jade listened to the sounds of his booted feet disappear down the hall then sighed. That went a lot better than she thought it would. She thanked her lucky stars and the heavens above for her brother's studied lack of curiosity.

That would have taken a lot of restraint on his part.

She would do her best not to let him down.

THE PAPER GLOWED, became flame.

The beating of his heart became the sound of the tattoo of drums outside where the fire chased him, faster and faster away from the safety of his bed to the place where he dreaded to go.

The giant lady pointed the way. He went where she directed.

The building was the home of the Dead.

The *rap, rap, rap* of the drums became a *tick, tick, tick* of a clock keeping time. The giant lady was now tiny, but the *tick, tick, tick* she made was insistent.

Maddening.

So much so, that papa ripped the cage from her hand and broke it apart. The lady was now silent.

Armand's breathing grew rapid and shallow, and he forced himself to look closer at what his father was doing.

Never before had Armand had control of his dreams, but now, knowing the secret of the clock, he forced his dream-self to pay attention to his father now despite the dread that coursed through him.

Armand watched his father put the key against a plaque on the mausoleum wall. It seemed to swallow the shaft whole.

The drumbeat outside grew louder. The *sans culottes* must have broken down the gates and were now in the grounds. The pounding in his ears became the pounding of his heart.

Rap, rap, rap.

Armand forced his eyes open.

"Come in."

Barnet opened the door. There was a towel over one arm and a bowl of steaming water in the other.

"Sorry to disturb you sir, but the day is getting on, and you mentioned several matters you wanted to attend to today."

Matters?

He'd be damned if he could remember what they were.

Barnet seemed to read his mind.

"You mentioned discussing – *ahem* –a delicate matter with Lady Arabella," he said.

Now it came back to him. He'd almost forgotten about Lady Cornelia. In fact, he *had* forgotten about her. He needed to break it off with her, even though there was nothing to break, not as far as he was concerned. But women regarded these matters differently, which was why he sought another woman's advice.

Arabella wouldn't be best pleased. But if he was honest with her about why he could no longer squire Cornelia about, she might show just a little understanding about it.

"Yes, of course," he said, almost forgetting that Barnet was there ready to shave him. "I won't be back until at least early evening. There are several things I need to do."

"Very good, sir."

One of these things was to see Jade. This madness had to stop now. He had hopelessly compromised her – whether she accepted it or not. He was not at all convinced that someone would not have recognized her serving at Prendegast's party, and that was quite beyond the culpability of his own behavior last night.

It had been a deuced uncomfortable ride home afterwards. He'd sported a partial erection all the way home, thanks to his lack of *relief* and Jade's proximity in the carriage opposite him. He considered himself lucky that Joanie was there to act as an unwitting chaperone. If he had been alone with Jade, the temptation to pick up where they'd left off might have been too much.

Her response to his touch in the library was beyond arousing. How much more could he coax if he were to make love to her properly? The possibilities of bringing them both pleasure was intriguing. He wanted to see those green eyes, wide with arousal, beneath him again.

Soon.

Very soon.

Armand washed himself and dressed, still deep in thought.

He loved her, so what was the point in dissembling? He would ask her to marry him. He wanted her, needed her, loved her. And he would spend a lifetime showing her how much.

And, after all, he had confessed his love to her already.

He frowned.

Hadn't he?

He recalled the words he spoke last night but couldn't remember whether she had shown any reaction to them at all.

Did *she* love *him*?

He didn't know but felt arrogant enough this morning to be sure he could persuade her.

A grin reflected back at him in the mirror.

Persuasion could be most pleasurable.

He checked his watch. As he recalled, he was to call on Arabella at three o'clock.

It was one o'clock now. He had time for something else he needed to do. Armand elected to drive himself in a curricle and headed over the bridge to Southwark. About thirty-minutes later he walked into the auction house.

Billy greeted him brightly. "Good morning, my lord. If you're looking for Miss Bridges, I'm afraid she's not here. She's at the shop on Bond Street."

"Good morning, Billy, I'm here to see Edward Bridges, if he's free."

At the sound of his name, Edward emerged from his office. It struck Armand how many features the man shared with his sister – the same light brown hair and green eyes as well as an open expression.

"Danger," he said. The greeting wasn't exactly warm, and curiosity was writ large on his face. "To what do I owe the pleasure, my lord?"

"I've come on a private matter," Armand answered.

Edward stepped out from the doorway and gestured Armand in.

"If it's about the clock, you'll have to talk to Jade about it," he said without waiting for Armand. "I don't interfere with the way my sister conducts business."

"It's not about the clock," Armand said, "but it *is* about your sister."

Edward lowered himself to a chair and indicated that Armand

do likewise.

"Do I really need to know?" he said. "Is it something about Prendegast?"

Armand frowned. "I beg your pardon?"

Edward looked as though he was about to say something then thought better of it. He shook his head. "Never mind. Speak your piece."

"I wish to marry your sister."

Edward's eyebrows shot up a moment then plummeted into a furrow.

"I don't wish to disparage anybody, but why would someone of your standing wish to even pay court to my sister, let alone marry her?"

"Because I love her."

Armand made certain to keep his eyes firmly on Edward's. They remained locked together like that for several silent seconds before Edward nodded slowly.

"I believe you."

Armand relaxed somewhat, and Edward's expression lightened considerably.

"Does Jade know your intentions?"

"Not yet. I wanted to speak to you first."

"She has her majority. She doesn't need *my* approval."

"But I know she does value it."

Edward rose from his desk and walked over to a small wine table in the corner of the room. He picked up a bottle of claret and poured two glasses, setting one before Armand.

"Ah, well – she might lead you to believe that, but my sister has a mind of her own and very firmly so."

"I've encountered that already."

Edward openly chuckled.

"I have no doubt. Does Jade love you?"

Armand took a sip of the claret. "The honest answer is, 'I'm not sure'."

Edward offered a smile and raised his glass in a toast.

"Man-to-man, I wish you every success."

Armand returned the salute.

"I knew this day would happen eventually," said Edward, retaking his seat. "I always wondered how I would feel when some man seriously announced his intentions."

Without sisters of his own, Armand could only guess at what the man before him was feeling. But he imagined under the circumstances it would be more than just fraternal concern for a beloved sister. The man would also be losing a business partner.

"I must say I'm glad it's you," Edward added.

"Thank you. It means a lot to me to have you say so."

Edward sipped his wine thoughtfully. "Are you going to see her today?"

Armand shook his head and gave him a disappointed expression.

"I would like to. Unfortunately, I have another engagement I can't postpone. I intend to call on her tomorrow."

"Hmm. I'll just have to keep my face straight until then, eh?" said Edward with a smile.

He drained the rest of the claret. Armand did likewise.

Both men got to their feet, and Edward thrust out his hand.

"You're all right, Armand," he said. "I hope to welcome you to the family soon."

CHAPTER TWENTY-TWO

ARMAND ARRIVED A few minutes early. He greeted his sister-in-law with a kiss on the cheek and followed her into the parlor where she poured tea for them.

"I've been positively burning with curiosity when you said you wanted to talk to me especially," she said. "May I guess the reason?"

"If you so wish," he answered, accepting a cup from her hands.

Arabella's smile broadened. "You wicked man, keeping your intentions such a secret. Cornelia hasn't a clue. I asked her. Oh, this is so exciting! When do you plan to propose?"

Armand took a sip of the tea and set the cup down deliberately.

"I'm not planning to propose to Cornelia."

The woman opposite him blinked rapidly, her mouth falling ever so slightly open. He took advantage of her momentary silence.

"There is a woman I love deeply to whom I plan to propose on the morrow."

Arabella's teacup rattled on its saucer a moment before she set it on the table beside her.

Armand watched the play of emotion on her face – surprise, disappointment, even a touch of anger.

"Well, you've kept that one dark," she managed at last. "I can't imagine who it might be. Is she someone we know?" His sister-in-law was trying her hardest to maintain her poise with studied politeness.

His answer would only frustrate her more.

"She is, but I won't give her name until she accepts me."

It was not the answer Arabella was wanting. She blinked rapidly, pressed her lips together, and clasped her hands on her lap. Armand set his own cup aside, then leaned forward to squeeze her hands gently for a moment.

"I've come here, dear Arabella, to ask for your advice."

"Mine?" Her laugh was shaky. "I hardly know what advice you need from *me*. You've found your own bride without recourse to my help. All I ever wanted was to see you happy and settled as Charles and I are."

"I want that too, and with this particular woman as my wife, I would be very content indeed."

Arabella pulled one of her hands from his and swiftly swiped away a tear.

"Oh, poor Cornelia. She had hopes that you would, well…"

"That's *why* I need your help. I don't want to hurt her. But I do want to let her know that any expectation on her part has always been her own, not mine. I am hoping you will counsel me on how I can best broach the topic with her."

Arabella's expression became even more distressed. Armand wondered if she'd heard him properly.

"I invited Cornelia to drop by this afternoon!" she said. "I knew you were coming, of course, and I thought if she just happened to… and you were here… *Oh dear!*"

Arabella removed her other hand from his and covered her eyes. A tear fell down her cheek. Her distress tore at him.

"Perhaps it is better this way," he said. "I'll ask Cornelia to stroll in the garden, and I'll speak to her privately. She will need a good friend and a confidante. And Cornelia has no better friend than you."

Arabella's tears sprang anew.

"I've let her down, Armand," she wept. "I gave her reason to believe you might feel tenderly towards her."

Arabella's sorrow swiftly switched to annoyance. "Oooh – and you have made me feel like such a fool too! Why didn't you tell me about your mysterious lady? I have no idea who she might be. As far as I know you've shown no partiality towards anyone. I would have welcomed her, Armand, truly I would!"

Armand offered her a sympathetic smile. "Yes, I know you would. It's just that *I* was uncertain about my feelings for her until very recently. In truth, I am not certain that the young woman feels the same way towards me as I do about her."

Arabella brought a napkin to her eyes to wick away the moisture.

"And it would serve you right if she refused you," she said tremulously. "Armand Danger, *Comte de Ytres*, having his heart broken as he has broken other's hearts."

"Yes. It *would* serve me right," he said softly.

She regarded him then, eyes wide and bright with new, but unshed, tears.

"You're serious, aren't you? You *love* this woman."

It was less a question than a statement, a coming to terms with her own feelings on the matter.

He nodded gravely.

Arabella sniffed delicately and rose to her feet. She took his hands in hers.

"Then I promise to do what I can."

Armand squeezed her hands in return.

"Charles is in the billiard room," she said, her voice now composed. "Do join him. I'll let you know when Cornelia is here."

He kissed her on the cheek.

Merci, ma petite soeur.

Armand found his brother.

"Well, did all go well?" Charles asked. He deftly potted the red ball. "I'm presuming the matter had to do with Lady Cornelia."

Armand picked up a cue, He joined his stepbrother at the table and lined up a shot.

"In the kindest way possible I told Arabella that I will not be offering for Cornelia, and, as luck would have it, I get to clear the air with the lady in question shortly."

Armand's shot missed.

"Don't envy you, old chap." Charles's next shot, a carom, was perfect. "Still, I suppose it's for the best. I could tell your heart wasn't in it."

"That's not the end of my news."

Charles straightened up and set down his cue. Armand did the same.

"That sounds serious."

"I still plan to get married. Before I leave for France, if possible."

"But not to Cornelia?"

Armand shook his head. "And don't ask me who she is, because I haven't even asked her yet."

"But she does know your intentions?"

Another shake of his head was his answer. Charles laughed out loud.

"You! Of all people! I never imagined you to be such a gambler. We will get to meet her, won't we? If she says 'yes', that is."

Before Armand got a chance to reply, Arabella came to the door.

Charles shot him a sympathetic look.

Arabella tucked her arm in Armand's as they made their way down the hall. "I didn't speak of the matter," she said softly, "but she knows something is amiss. Be gentle with her, won't you?"

He patted the arm in return. "Of course, I will."

Indeed, Cornelia, waiting in the drawing room, regarded him with a bravely cautious expression. His heart went out to her. He thought he had been sufficiently circumspect when it came to expectations, but obviously not nearly cautious enough. He drew breath to speak, deciding that directness and a firm but not unkind tone was required.

"Good afternoon, Lady Cornelia. Could I impose on you to walk with me in the garden?"

Cornelia cast an uncertain look in Arabella's direction. The young matron nodded in reassurance.

Armand said nothing until they were clear of the house. He found a path that would still allow them to be in view of the windows. He knew Arabella would be watching and thought it best that she witness the scene.

"Lady Cornelia, I would like you to know that I hold you in the highest esteem. But I need to address a matter of some delicacy."

"Of course, my lord," she said. "I hope I have earned your respect sufficient to the task."

Armand acknowledged her with a slow nod. This was one of the most difficult things he'd ever had to do. It was one thing to have a falling out with a fellow – a few harsh words, hell, even a few punches, then there was always a better than fifty-fifty chance they'd shrug it off and patch up their friendship over drinks.

The fairer sex operated with a different set of rules and reactions. Once a slight, intended or not, had been given, there was very little chance of repairing the relationship. Armand chose his next words with care.

"I hope I am not too presumptuous in believing that you have developed a tenderness towards me?"

Cornelia blinked rapidly a few times.

"Are you asking, my lord, if your manner towards me has given me hope of an affection beyond the commonplace?"

Armand nodded the once.

"I confess I did harbor such hopes," Cornelia said. "However, I've been aware for several weeks that affection has been misplaced."

It was not the answer Armand expected. He frowned.

"When did you know?"

"I had an inkling at the opera. But it was at the Duke of Auchen's ball when it all became clear. I was introduced to a Miss Jade Bridges, and I knew her face was familiar, but I couldn't recall where I'd seen her before. It was only when I saw you dancing together that I recalled our night at the opera. You introduced her as *Mademoiselle Trublion*. I don't know why you'd forgotten you'd told me that."

He *had* forgotten the opera, but the name had certainly stuck…

Cornelia continued. "I knew for certain when Arabella and I came to pay you a call one day. You were out, but your man was kind enough to serve tea while we waited. We were there an hour or so before we realized your absence was going to be longer than we anticipated. Just as we were leaving – we were outside on the steps – a boy arrived with a message for you. I took it, and, as it was not sealed, I saw what was written on it. It was a woman's hand, hastily written I think, apologizing to you for something or another. It was signed by Miss Bridges."

Lady Cornelia paused until she was satisfied of having his full attention.

"I was angry and jealous," she went on. "So, I took the note, and I'm ashamed to admit I destroyed it. I hoped it would cause you trouble. So, it seems your esteem of me is misplaced."

Armand shook his head. "No, the fault is entirely mine. I have caused you distress, and I can only ask for your forgiveness and give you my sincere wishes for your future happiness."

Gamely, Lady Cornelia offered him a small smile. "I own it's been difficult to disabuse Arabella of the notion that we were a match," she said.

"It's very difficult to dissuade Arabella of anything once her mind is made up," he agreed.

They shared a small smile. The weight of his burden lifted somewhat.

"Will you be kind enough to answer a question for me, so

there will be no further misunderstandings?" Cornelia asked.

Armand nodded his assent.

"Tell me truly," she asked, keeping her voice light, "is a shop-keeper's daughter the one who has captured the heart of the most intriguing eligible bachelor in London?"

"She is."

Cornelia visibly swallowed and looked away.

Armand felt like a cad.

"I intend to speak to Miss Bridges tomorrow morning," he said. "I have told no one else her identity, not even Arabella. Only *you* know it. I owed you a full explanation, and I hope I can be granted your pardon."

"It is easy to forgive when there has been no offense."

Armand was about to respond when Cornelia turned to face him and laid a hand on his arm, just briefly.

"No, truly. I meant what I said earlier. The misapprehension was mine alone. I thank you for telling me in person. I know of some whose only inkling that their affection was unrequited was seeing an engagement notice in *The Times*."

Armand winced. Cornelia noted it and gave a genuine laugh.

"Put your mind at ease, my lord. My heart will soon mend."

THE DAY PASSED without word from Armand. Jade was surprised at how much she missed him.

Absence makes the heart grow fonder? Yes, she supposed that was very true, indeed. Her heart had grown more than fond. And anxious.

Did Armand still feel the same way about her today? Last night before last he'd said he loved her, but surely that was to mollify her anger in Prendegast's garden. Was it an off-hand compliment, meaning as much as saying one loved a good cup of tea or a freshly baked slice of bread with butter and strawberry jam?

He *did* find her attractive. Of *that* there could be no doubt. But there was no guarantee that desire was the same as love. People had loved without desire; others desired without loving.

And then there was the class difference between them. Hadn't she told him in no uncertain terms that she was not part of his world?

But was it wrong to want something for its own sake? Would she regret not accepting him if the opportunity presented itself?

She shook her head. No, she was getting far too ahead of herself.

Jade returned to her letter to the Baroness von Hoecker announcing her success in discovering the original Thalatte clock. She read it through one more time, then added a paragraph promising to let her know when she could make an appointment to inspect it. She sealed it with satisfaction. It felt good to finalize that particular commission.

She smiled in recollection of Edward's face when she mentioned the lurid Joan of Arc etchings. Did he truly think she did not know they were there? What was he going to do with them if not offer them directly to the likes of Prendegast?

With one job done, Jade turned her mind to a new task, compiling the list of auction items and their descriptions to be sent to the printers for the auction the week after next.

Edward tapped on the door frame of the study and came in.

"You don't have any plans to be out tomorrow, do you?" he asked.

"No. Should I?"

Edward shrugged. He walked over to the credenza and picked up a folio of documents but gave them scant attention. "I suppose not. I just wanted to make sure that you'd be home when I returned with the clock."

"And for no other reason?"

Edward tilted his head to the side and raised his eyebrow in silent answer. Jade returned a look of his own. Edward shrugged.

"You just tell that client of yours that the clock will be available to view at the auction house on Wednesday. And you can tell the Count himself when he comes in tomorrow."

Jade's eyes narrowed. "What makes you sure Count Danger will be paying a call tomorrow?"

Edward shrugged his shoulders in an exaggerated insouciant manner.

"He knows where the clock is. He knows where you are. And he knows that you will get the clock. Doesn't it make sense that he would call?"

The logic made sense, even if it plainly wasn't the truth.

"I suppose so…"

Her brother flashed her a grin and left the room.

Jade shook her head with affectionate exasperation at his disappearing figure and returned to her work.

She'd given a great deal of thought about how to deal honestly with both Armand and the Countess. The only fair thing to do was to hold the clock here or at the auction room until both parties worked out an agreeable settlement.

The image of Armand, trance-like, rearranging the parts of the pendulum into that strange medieval style key, flashed before her mind's eye. It made her wonder if it was really the clock Armand wanted, or just the pendulum mechanism.

The *key*, he called it.

The 'key' to what?

She couldn't imagine what kind of lock it would fit. The shaft was extraordinarily long for a key and brass was a relatively soft metal. The torsion required to actuate a lock of consequence would surely twist or break the metal.

Then again, there was every chance Armand could be wrong about it. Maybe it wasn't a key after all.

But if not a key, then what was it?

A new thought crossed her mind.

Would the countess allow Armand to take the pendulum if the original casting of Thalatte was what she truly wanted? Eli

Rosenbaum, the jeweler at Hatton Garden, could make her a replica pendulum, right down to the separating pieces.

Then again, by the same token, would a reproduction pendulum suit Armand's needs?

She rang the bell for one of the servants.

"Is Seton here?" she asked.

"No, Miss Bridges, he's making deliveries all afternoon."

"Oh yes, I'd forgotten about that."

She glanced at the clock. It was a quarter past five. While it would have been convenient to have Seton drive her to the nearby print works, she could easily walk there before closing time at six.

"Is there anything else I can do, Miss?"

"No, no, that's fine. It will do me good to go outside. I'll take the next sales catalogue to the printers. They'll be glad to receive it early, I'm sure."

She wrapped the handwritten catalogue items in brown paper and tied them with string. There had been too much work done in those twenty pages for them to go missing in a gust of wind.

The late afternoon air was brisk, the sun casting long shafts of light between the buildings.

Despite the fact that she was familiar with these streets, Jade was mindful of what may lurk in the shadows. She had not seen the man who was spying on her since she confronted the Baroness. Perhaps the woman *had* been foxing, in the same way she'd ordered her ancient manservant to write to her in the first instance.

Nevertheless, Jade paid extra special attention to her surroundings – just in case.

She arrived later than expected at the print shop. It had just gone ten-to-six when the exhausted-looking apprentice took down the particulars and promised the catalogue would be typeset by next Friday afternoon for approval.

Jade stepped out of the shop just as clocks across the city sounded six, the end of another workday. By the last peal, the streets were a crush with people trying to make their way across London in order to enjoy the last couple of hours of sun before twilight descended.

She turned down Bond Street, only a block and a half away from home, when a strange feeling assailed her. One of being watched.

Despite the sizable number of people about, Jade was disquieted. She picked up her pace and headed towards a shop she knew where the lights were still ablaze.

She ignored the part of her mind that told her she was merely jumping at shadows. Better to be thought of as a foolish young woman than make a dangerous misstep.

She bustled through the door and closed it behind her, watching the passing parade of pedestrians for any that resembled the man who followed her in the park, or watched outside the auction room. But it was nearly impossible to pick one face from another.

She breathed in the scent of freshly varnished furniture. The Lennox family must still be working.

"Toby!" she called.

A gangly lad of about seventeen emerged eventually from behind a curtain that led to the workshop.

"Evenin', Miss Jade! What can I do for you?"

"I know this may sound strange, but I was wondering if you would walk me the rest of the way home."

He frowned.

She knew what he was thinking. Her shop was little more than a block away. In fact, if you stood at the door of Lennox's Fine Furnishings, you could just make out the shingle of Bridges' Antiques and Curios. She'd walked this road hundreds of times and never once asked for an escort.

"I'd be glad to, Miss Bridges. I'll just tell mum I'm going out," he said.

Jade kept a watch through the windows in case anyone lurked obviously outside.

Toby returned a moment later, along with his mother.

"Some unsavory gent bothering you, Miss Bridges?" she asked.

"I'm not sure, Mrs. Lennox," she said with just a touch more confidence than she felt. "But I'd prefer not to be wise after the event."

"Oh, I quite agree with you!" Mrs. Lennox turned to her son. "I'll lock up the shop, Pet. When you get in, just run upstairs and wash up for tea."

Jade shot the woman a grateful look and preceded Toby out through the door.

The boy walked by her side, looking left and right occasionally. *Bless him*, he took his role as escort seriously.

After a few yards of silence, Toby spoke. "I *have* seen someone hangin' about near your place recently, Miss Bridges," he said.

Jade made sure not to inject her voice with too much concern.

"Oh? What does he look like?"

"He's always been too far away to get a good look at him. About my height, a bit older – nothing to make him stand out though. Only caught me eye 'cause it was odd he was just hanging about outside and never goin' in."

Outside Bridges' Antiques and Curios, Jade paused.

"Do you see him now?"

Toby looked around.

"No. I haven't actually seen him in like a week or so."

Well, that was something, Jade supposed.

She reached into her reticule, half embarrassed that she'd taken Toby away from his work for no reason. "Let me give you something for your trouble."

Toby refused the offered coin. "It's no trouble at all, Miss Bridges. We're all friends and neighbors here. I was glad to help."

CHAPTER TWENTY-THREE

I T HAD BEEN a spur of the moment decision to purchase a bouquet of flowers, but Armand felt the burning obligation to bring *something* when he proposed marriage.

Most men, he imagined, would buy an expensive piece of jewelry with which to plight their troth. But given Jade had access to a collection that might make a Duchess green with envy, it seemed rather pointless to give her what she already had in abundance.

He elected to arrive earlier in the day than one would be expected to go calling, but this was the Bridges family. They worked for a living. Eleven o'clock meant their day was already well underway.

Besides, he didn't want to wait. His mind had been made up the night before last. He would have proposed to Jade then, if he hadn't been sure he'd be swiftly rebuffed.

And now?

In truth, he wasn't sure whether he'd be accepted, but he already had an answer for that.

He announced himself at the door and, once again, was directed to the Oriental Room.

While the jade carvings were indeed spectacular, this time Armand was drawn to a little cabinet of curios. On the shelves were rows and rows of figurines about the size of an acorn. He picked one up and marveled at its intricate carving. All of them depicted people. One figure reclined with his head propped up on one arm. The next sat playing a flute. Another stood, burdened by a heavy pack.

Nearly all of them were ivory, but others were lacquer or were carved from boxwood.

"*Monsieur le comte*, it is an unexpected pleasure to see you again."

He turned.

Jade's light brown hair was piled high in some sort of chignon, her eyes shone with mischief that carried in the tilt of her chin and that expressive mouth of hers.

His gaze lingered there a moment until he noticed color rising to her cheeks.

"Unexpected?" he asked, imbuing his voice with a seductive tone.

"Of course," she answered, approaching him until she was close enough to take into his arms.

It was tempting to do so.

She noticed the hyacinths in his hand.

"They're pretty," she said, but she did not reach out to take them.

"They're for you."

"Oh?"

He held them out to her. She accepted them and brought her nose to the bouquet.

The innocent tone didn't fool him for a second. She knew what she was doing to him. Unfortunately, before he could do anything about it, they were interrupted by the appearance of a maid bringing in tea.

"Hetty, do take these flowers, and put them in a vase for me. Then return them here, please," she said.

Armand released a breath as soon as the door closed. They were alone. Before he could take Jade's hand, she turned away from him and took a seat on a chair.

"I'm afraid you're too early," she said. "Edward has not yet returned from Prendegast's, so I don't know whether he's been successful in getting the clock."

"That's not the reason I'm here."

"Oh?"

Armand shook his head and sighed. "Are you really going to make this difficult?"

Jade fussed with the tea pot and didn't even look at him.

"I'm sure I have no idea what you're talking about."

The prim little display was becoming tiresome. Armand took a step closer.

"Perhaps you need a reminder," he said silkily.

Jade shot to her feet.

"I prefer to forget that night, and I wish you would too."

He took another step forward.

"On the contrary, I have no wish to forget it. Ever."

Armand took another step forward until she was a mere hand span away.

"I want to repeat it – and more…"

It seemed Jade realized her mistake in not moving away from the chair. She looked past him as if to find another means of exiting. He swiftly hauled her into his embrace and took advantage of her open-mouthed shock to possess her lips, to stoke up the passion he'd so intimately experienced that night.

Her resistance lasted only a moment before her kisses matched his in intensity.

When his mouth eventually left hers, she had the same heavy-lidded expression she wore when he brought her to fulfillment on the library table.

"I'll never be your mistress," she whispered.

"I don't want you for a mistress. I want you for my wife."

JADE PULLED AWAY and swore she must have misheard him.

"Your *wife?*"

Armand nodded. "To make it as plain as I possibly can, I'm asking you to marry me."

No, this couldn't be happening. A count needed a countess, someone from the *beau monde.* She had no idea she was shaking her head until he continued.

"Are you refusing me?"

Her eyes shot to him.

"What? No! Yes! I mean this is impossible. I can give you a hundred reasons why a marriage between us could never work."

Armand grinned. "Believe me, I could probably give you a hundred more, but nevertheless, that doesn't change the way I feel and what I want."

He gently took her hands and maneuvered her until they could sit on the settee together.

"I love you," he said.

Tears sprang to her eyes. "And I love you. If it was just that alone, I'd—"

Armand stopped her with a press of a finger to her lips.

"The first four words were enough. Will you marry me?"

Jade had composed herself enough to give him a stern look.

"I'd be doing you a service if I refused – especially when there must be a dozen titled ladies whom you wouldn't have to ask twice for the honor."

Armand turned away from her with a sigh, but he didn't get up off the seat. Rather, he stretched his long legs out.

"Then you leave me with no other choice."

There was something in his tone of voice that put her on alert immediately. She straightened her posture and turned towards him, narrowing her gaze.

"I will be forced to tell Edward about Prendegast's party, and how I hopelessly compromised you."

He spoke the words lightly as thought the conversation was no more serious than whose turn it was to deal cards at whist.

Jade was aghast.

"You wouldn't!"

Armand turned to face her again, his expression focused.

"Dare me."

He looked very much like the cat that got the cream. And dammit if her heart didn't beat a little faster at the look.

"You'll regret this, you know."

Armand flung an arm across the back of the settee. His fingers tickled the nape of her neck. She sighed at the shivers of delight that coursed through her.

"Uh-hmmm…" he purred.

"There will be gossip."

He slid closer until his thigh touched hers.

"Uh-hmmm…"

"They will say dreadful things about us both."

He leaned in and kissed her earlobe.

"Uh-hmmm…"

Jade fought the arousal beginning to stir in her.

"Will you stop that?"

Why did her protest sound like a sigh?

He shook his head. "Uh-uh."

His arm was drawn around her shoulders now, and he was pulling her gently toward him. His lips found the column of her neck.

Now she was firmly in his embrace and all the very good, most excellent, supremely logical reasons why she ought to refuse him flew out of the window.

"There's no point in fighting this, Jade," he murmured. "Just say 'yes'. You know you want to."

"My brother…"

"I've already spoken to him."

Jade shook herself awake and struggled to a more upright seating position. Armand released her. She slid to the end of the settee, putting an appropriate amount of distance between them once more.

"When?"

"Yesterday."

At her open-mouthed expression, Armand gave a put-upon sigh.

"You are your own woman, but a man doesn't just marry a wife, he marries her family. I wanted to be sure that if you accepted my proposal, I would be welcomed by all."

Of course, Armand would be welcome, she thought. Edward was a very affable man and had come to know the count over the past six months. If he had not been welcome, Edward would have made his views very clear on the matter. So, the fact Armand was here now meant…

Still, she felt the need to continue arguing her case.

"And if you were not?"

"I would still be here asking the question only you can give the answer to."

All the clouds of indecision and doubt broke. The love in her heart for this man shone through to vanquish any lingering doubts.

"Yes. I will marry you."

Armand drew her into his embrace. His sigh was one of relief. Then he rained kisses on her forehead, her cheeks, and her hair, leaving her giggling.

"You were always going to say 'yes', weren't you?" he asked between kisses.

Jade pulled away so she could see Armand's face.

"Yours is not the first marriage proposal I've received, you know, so I have practice in refusing." She touched his cheek tenderly. "But I needed to feel certain you'd have no regrets."

Armand took her hand, kissed it, and kept it firmly in his.

"I'd only regret letting you go."

A light tap on the door caused them to move apart just as Hetty came in with a blue enamel vase, the bouquet of blue, pink, and violet-colored flowers artfully displayed. The maid was discreet, but even she couldn't have avoided noticing the tension in the air.

Jade resisted the urge to tell her the news and simply smiled at the young woman, thanking her as she placed the vase on a sideboard. The girl glanced back at them inquisitively from the doorway.

"Was there anything more, Miss Jade?"

"Not right away, Hetty, but let me know when my brother has returned."

The girl curtseyed and left the room.

Armand got to his feet, bringing Jade with him. "How shall we celebrate our engagement? A ride in Hyde Park? Lunch at Rules at Covent Garden?"

"Let's wait for Edward," said Jade.

"Do you think he'll be back soon?"

"Probably. His appointment with Prendegast was for nine, so I expect he's not far away."

"I think you're eager to share the news with your staff as well. They're 'family' too, aren't they?"

Jade kissed him on the cheek.

"What was that for?"

"For recognizing that the people who work for us aren't just servants, they're also friends and, yes, 'family' in a way. Many people wouldn't give them the time of day, let alone get to know them as you've done. Thank you."

"Ah, you mustn't forget that I hold my title lightly. Unlike Charles who has the weight of his family history and holdings, I have nothing to speak of. Unless I can lay claim to my family's lands in France, then my title is nothing more than a courtesy. My wealth is not substantial, but it's sufficient and entirely made on the fortune of good investments."

Armand stopped and looked thoughtful.

"Perhaps I shouldn't have told you that. Now you know my true state, you might think you've agreed to marriage under false pretenses."

"If I were a grasping woman, I'd have run a mile already," she said breezily. "But now I've said yes, you're stuck with me."

Armand kissed her sweetly.

"And gladly," he said.

***

"WHAT IS THIS? A half-day holiday?" said Edward, striding into the Oriental Room fifteen minutes later.

"Sort of," said Jade with a brimming smile. "I'm getting married."

"So, you got her to agree," said Edward to Armand. "What did you have to do?"

"Blackmail!" he answered.

Jade blushed deep red, but said nothing, hoping Edward would let the comment pass without probing.

Her brother clapped Armand on the back, then turned to give her a kiss on the cheek.

"I'm pleased for the both of you. Truly. But celebrations will have to wait until later. I have returned with a certain curio for the count – and your mystery client. I'm sure there's no harm in letting you get the first look at it, Danger."

Seton entered the room with the clock under a black cloth. Edward directed him to set the heavy bronze piece down.

"Dare I ask how much you paid?" asked Armand.

"A whole lot less than I thought we might have to," said Edward, casting a meaningful glance Jade's way. "I was able to exchange it for some engravings that Prendegast found 'intriguing'."

Armand looked to her and then back to Edward, his brow furrowed in inquiry as to what meaning lay behind Edward's words and the glance between brother and sister.

Jade held her tongue, as did Edward, and Armand raised his hands in surrender. "No, I won't ask. Every business must have its trade secrets."

Edward removed the black covering with a flourish.

"When I saw it for myself, I could see why you were so taken with it. The crispness of the casting and the fine detailing on the figure is just superb. The clock mechanism is high quality."

"Believe me, you don't need to sell it to me," Armand answered, his attention fixed on the clock. "I know how special it is. This is more than a superbly crafted timepiece. It's worth more than money to me."

"So, when is the wedding?" her brother asked, changing the subject.

Jade and Armand looked at each other uncertainly.

Edward burst out laughing. "You haven't even discussed it?"

Armand kept his eyes on her "As soon as possible. In three weeks, as soon as the banns are read?"

Jade nodded.

Yes, a short engagement, she'd prefer that.

EDWARD OFFERED CONGRATULATIONS once again then returned to work, leaving them alone in the parlor.

"Ah, my lovely fiancée," Armand announced. "Do I have you to myself at last?"

Jade picked up on his teasing mood instantly. She made an exaggerated show of looking around the room.

"Why, yes indeed. What did you have in mind, *monsieur le comte?*"

"A light luncheon, perhaps, followed by that ride in Hyde Park. Then afternoon tea with my brother and sister-in-law."

Her smile faltered a little.

"Are you sure you wouldn't rather tell them about our engagement in private? To give them warning?"

Armand took her hand and kissed it. He drew her close and brought up her hand to kiss the inside of her wrist.

Her full mouth, those pouty lips opened at his liberties, but she didn't stop him. He drew her closer to kiss the crook of her elbow, delighting in the fact her peridot green eyes widened.

"They knew I was going to propose today."

Jade raised an eyebrow. "Was *I* the last to know?"

"Not exactly. I told them I was planning to ask. I just didn't tell them who."

"Won't they be in for rather a shock when I come through the door? I imagine they'll be thinking your fiancée is one of the crop of this year's debutantes."

"It doesn't matter. You already know Charles and my sister, anyway. Charles bought pair of earrings from you."

"That's different. It is one thing to be acquainted by trade, but quite another to be presented as an equal."

"You are an equal. More than equal."

Armand coaxed her into his arms. "I love you, and my family will love you. I promise it."

"Only if I can change my dress first. I can't go calling in this."

Armand took his time looking her up and down, making no secret of his desire for her.

"What's wrong with what you're wearing?"

"I have finer day dresses than this."

"You look lovely, and I'm sure Charles and Arabella won't mind."

Jade gave him a peck on the cheek and turned out of his arms.

"But *I* mind," she said. "I want to make a good impression. There will be invitations to meet the rest of your friends. I want to make sure I fit in. I'll be a curiosity. I'll be tested to ensure I pass muster. Believe me, do not underestimate the power of fashion to establish one's credentials."

Waiting for Jade to get changed, Armand sent his driver on to tell Arabella to expect them to call for afternoon tea, then return for them.

In four weeks, he would be heading to France. His preparations were already partly made. Now they would have to be altered to accommodate a wife.

His wife.

Armand smiled.

He thought of his mother. How pleased she would be to see her son settled at last. He would write to her and to his cousin Gerald to ensure they were ready to receive them both.

To his surprise, Jade returned to the parlor quicker than he expected. He was used to Arabella whose promptitude generally fell between fashionably late and grossly so.

It had been one of the reasons why Charles bought the billiard table. Practicing for three-quarters of an hour past the appointed time for every social engagement had turned him into a superbly good player.

Jade appeared in a day gown of bright green and yellow flowers, a bright touch of early summer on this on this fine day.

She caught him staring, and a small furrow marred her brow. "Is it too much?"

"It's perfection. *You're* perfection. The color of the dress matches the green of your eyes."

His vote of confidence was enough for her to give him a smile. His own eyes softened, and he leaned forward for a tender kiss.

So, this is what being in love feels like? he mused. So far, he approved of it.

Knowing that the woman he loved loved him in return was like the sun parting through clouds. It made everything brighter.

CHAPTER TWENTY-FOUR

L ADY ARABELLA WITHERICK, Countess of Rosemont, personally greeted them at her door.

"Arabella, I would like to introduce my fiancée, Miss Jade Bridges. Jade, this is my sister-in-law, Arabella."

Jade bobbed a curtsy.

"It is an honor to be invited to your home, my lady."

She witnessed a moment of surprise, but the expression was gone in an instant and replaced with a pleasant smile of welcome.

"I… ah, the honor is mine. You will forgive me for being shocked, Miss Bridges, but Armand has kept your courtship a closely guarded secret. When he told me yesterday he was going to propose marriage, I thought… well – I didn't know *what* to think. It was just a surprise, that's all."

Jade's heart went out to the Countess.

"Please don't trouble yourself," she said with all sincerity. "It was a complete surprise to me as well."

Lady Arabella led them to a tastefully furnished drawing room where the Earl of Rosemont waited.

The introductions were barely over before Lady Arabella started speaking. She described the *objet d'art* on the walls, told her about the latest news from court.

Jade nodded politely, which Arabella took as encouragement. Armand's half-pained, half-apologetic expression told her that his sister-in-law's reaction was not unexpected. She accepted that Lady Arabella was doing her utmost to make her feel welcome, but she did wish the woman wouldn't *try* so hard.

"Now, dear," said her husband, the Earl. "If you monopolize the conversation now, then what shall have to talk about over tea?"

Jade saw her opportunity and took it.

"Lady Arabella, I noticed your beautiful garden as we arrived. May I see the grounds?"

"Oh! Yes, of course," the woman said hurriedly. "I'd be delighted. I mean I wish I knew more about the plants."

Jade caught Armand's eye and gave him a smile of reassurance that all would be well.

Arabella continued to chatter like a magpie from the near edge of the gardens until they reached a fork in the path. From what Jade had seen so far, one way would circle around to the drive, the other would lead to what appeared to be ornamental gardens.

At the fork, Arabella hesitated on which direction they should go. Jade had started the turn to the right. Arabella fell into step with her, apparently having now exhausted her store of light conversation.

"Might I speak frankly, my lady?"

"Why, yes, of course you may," she said. "And we don't be so formal, do we? After all, when you and Armand wed, your rank will equal mine. Do call me Arabella, and I shall call you Jade."

Jade acknowledged the offer with a nod of her head. "I know my engagement to Armand has come out of the blue, and I'm sure you have many questions for me. I think it would help set your mind at ease to ask them freely and banish any fears you have about Armand making an imprudent match."

Arabella blinked. Her mouth opened and closed twice as though considering and dismissing responses.

"Do you always speak so plainly?" she asked at last.

"I've found it's served me well to do so."

They walked in the shade of spreading oak trees until they reached a stone bench lit by a patch of sunlight. They sat down, taking in the elevated view of the sunken gardens and the pond which was its centerpiece.

"Well, I suppose the natural question to ask is 'do you love Armand?'," Arabella began. "But words are so cheaply spoken, do you not agree? I suppose the better question to ask is 'why do you love him'?"

Jade nodded. They were *both* good questions to ask. She had asked them of herself, but this was the first time she spoke her heart out loud.

"I love him for his thoughtfulness and kindness."

The answer seemed to take Arabella by surprise because she said nothing. Jade continued.

"He is kind to everyone. I remember the first time I came to think of him as more than someone who attended our business. We have two dear old ladies who are present at all our auctions. Oh, they never buy anything. For them it is a game in which they guess what the bids will be. Most of the regular dealers don't pay them any heed, and the other bidders are there on their own business. But Armand would go out of his way at each auction to spend time chatting with them. He didn't have to do that. Now the ladies affectionately call him their nephew."

The more Jade spoke, the more the words came.

"Armand is also quick-witted. I find I have to be on my mettle around him. He is smart, humorous – and handsome as well. I won't deny it."

"Your engagement won't be easy for some people to accept, you know. There are quite a few families who are interested in a match with Armand. Even though his title, being French, doesn't confer as much weight as an English one, the fact he is well-to-do and, as you say, *handsome* counts a lot in his favor."

"I'm prepared for that. No doubt, some people will see me as an upstart, grasping, ambitious. But, alas, I'm not in control of other people's thoughts. If they wish to see me that way, I can do nothing to dissuade them. I would simply hope that those who truly love and respect Armand will judge me by my actions and see that I love him and wish only for his well-being and happiness."

Arabella surprised her by taking her hand. "And I love Armand as much as my own brother. All I've ever wanted since I married Charles was to see him settled. On many occasions I thought I'd found him the perfect bride, but I can see now that he needed no help from me."

"I would so like us to be friends, Arabella. He speaks of you and Charles with such affection. Family is important. I too am close to my brother, and I would welcome a sister."

An unsettled expression flitted across Arabella's features for a moment, and Jade wondered if she had presumed too much. She watched the young woman beside her stare out across the landscape then turn to her again.

"May I ask a personal question?"

Jade nodded.

"Is it hard to work for a living?" she asked. "To run a business as you and your brother do?"

It was not the kind of question Jade was expecting, and it took her a moment to gather her thoughts.

"It can be," Jade began. "There is a lot to know. It's somewhat of a puzzle. So many pieces need to fit together precisely to make a business work. It can be worrying if trade is not going well because it's not just *your* livelihood at stake, but also of those you employ. On the other hand, it does give you the opportunity to try new things. To innovate."

"I'm not sure I could do that," Arabella admitted.

Jade turned to regard Armand's sister-in-law. She was pretty and they were about the same age. Her face was unlined, her hair coiffed *just so*, and she wore the latest fashions effortlessly. She had mastered the world of the *ton* but seemed somewhat perplexed by the world outside it.

Not that Jade could blame her for that. The working men and

women of England had no idea of what went on in the fine drawing rooms either, and little appreciated that the *beau monde* was sometimes not so 'beau'.

The fact that Arabella had given it some thought, however, was a credit to her. Jade considered her answer.

"It is not a role that suits everyone – man or woman alike. It's been ingrained in Edward and me since childhood. It was our father's business, and *his* grandfather's, before him. I have been very fortunate that trade has been successful and afforded me opportunities to live comfortably."

"And you work because you wish to, not because you have to?"

"Exactly."

Arabella turned to face her. "Will you be sad to leave it when you marry Armand?"

Now it was Jade's turn to pause. She hadn't considered it. As a Countess, she could hardly show up on auction day in shirt sleeves and apron.

"I… I hadn't thought about it," she confessed. "There will be a period of adjustment, I expect."

Then a thought occurred to her. Jade leaned toward Arabella and said conspiratorially, "Still, I might just encourage my brother to find a wife for himself, instead of relying on me. I will need your advice on how to find wives for brothers."

Arabella laughed. "Given my success with Armand, I'd be the last person I'd take advice from!"

Jade laughed also, pleased the tension between them was broken.

Then Arabella added, "And, to give you fair warning, I plan to monopolize a lot of your time between now and the wedding."

There was a twinkle in the young matron's eye that hinted at a good sense of humor. Any reservations Jade had about her welcome into the family were allayed. She reached out and took Arabella's hand.

"And I'll be glad for it. I want to make Armand proud."

Arabella returned the gesture with a squeeze. "You already have."

⇶⤙⤙

ARMAND HADN'T REALIZED how on edge he'd been at the prospect of Jade meeting Charles and Arabella until he saw the two women return from the garden arm-in-arm.

And he was not the only one to express relief. Charles did also. The four of them lingered in the drawing room until late into the afternoon where his brother held court, delighting in telling Jade stories of mischief the two of them would get into as lads.

He sat back and watched his bride-to-be with pride as she participated in conversation as though she had known Charles and Arabella all her life.

In that moment, he learned something. He had once thought to be in love was a one-time thing. One day one was *not* in love, and the next day one was *in* love. What he didn't expect was that feeling to grow and expand, to be conscious of being *more* in love in a moment of time than the moment previous.

Eventually Arabella banished both men to the billiard room because wedding arrangements needed to be made and male input was not required.

Charles set the balls as Armand selected his cue.

"I can see you're not going to ask the question, but I'll answer it anyway," said Charles. "I like Jade. She's a charming young woman. More than that, I can see already how happy she makes you."

Charles' endorsement, although not required, was welcome, nevertheless.

"I've never known a woman like her," he said. "I thought it mere coincidence that she knew my tastes instinctively when she helped me furnish my home, but the more I got to know her, the more my regard for her increased. Until one day…"

"It was love."

Armand nodded, grateful his brother understood.

"Has Jade seen your townhouse?" Charles asked. "She really ought to, given she selected all the furniture in it."

⫸⫷

INSPIRED BY CHARLES was how he and Jade ended up pulling up outside his townhouse at twilight. The excitement of the day had banked into a warm, comfortable contentment. Jade's head rested on his shoulder, his arm around her.

Soon, in mere weeks, he would be falling asleep with her in his arms and waking up with her every morning for the rest of their lives.

It was because of that distraction that he didn't see the man hurrying along the pavement towards toward them as they disembarked from the carriage. Jade started and tugged at his arm.

"Armand!"

He turned just in time before the man nearly crashed into them.

"It *is* you!" the man exclaimed in a strong French accent.

Putting himself between the excited man and Jade, Armand looked at him. He seemed youthful but had a liberal amount of silver showing in his black thatch of hair.

"I'm sorry, my friend, do I know you?" Armand asked politely.

"But of course! It is your cousin! I have written to say I was coming, but sometimes people move faster than the post, do they not?"

Armand rapidly took in the man's features more closely, struck by a chord of familiarity. "Gerald?"

"*Bien sur!*" the man grinned. "Business brought me to England unexpectedly, so of course, I must call on my cousin."

The door of Armand's townhouse opened. Barnet looked at the party on the step expectantly.

"My dear Gerald. After all these years! Won't you come in, so we can make introductions properly?" said Armand. That was the cue for Barnet to direct the party into a drawing room and to anticipate that refreshments would be required.

"Jade, I'd like to introduce you to my second cousin, Gerald Perrin. His father and mine were cousins. We've been corresponding for years, but this is the first we've met. Gerald, this is Miss Jade Bridges, who today consented to be my wife."

"*Affianced!* How wonderful!"

Gerald raised his right arm stiffly, took Jade's hand, and kissed it.

"It is a day for meeting families, it would seem," she said politely. "First Charles and Arabella, and now you, *Monsieur* Perrin."

"Ah, you must call me Gerald as we are to be family," he said.

Gerald was certainly a garrulous fellow, Armand noted.

It was one thing to perceive his exuberance in letters, another thing entirely to experience it in the flesh. It took a little getting used to. The man gushed over Jade and insisted on knowing everything about her. Who was she? How had they met?

From anyone else the questions might have come across as intrusive, but Gerald's effusive Gallic nature had charm enough to get away with it.

He clearly won over Jade.

"What happened to your arm, cousin?"

The animated chatter came to an abrupt halt. Jade and Gerald looked at him curiously.

"Your arm," repeated Armand, indicating Gerald's right arm. "You seemed discomforted by it just before."

Gerald blinked rapidly. "My arm? Ah, *c'est rien.* The passage was rough, I fell and bruised it."

"When did you arrive?" Jade asked.

"I have been in London for only a few days," he said.

An unasked question hung in the air.

"Then you must stay with me," Armand announced. "If your business doesn't take you long, we could travel to France together."

"I do not wish to be an intrusion," said Gerald looking meaningfully at Jade. "And now you are to be married..."

Jade smiled in acknowledgement and turned to Armand. A silent conversation flowed between them.

Gerald was family – if only newly met.

But the chance to be alone...

Gerald seemed to sense his imposition.

"I refuse to be an imposition to you. Like I say, I have business to conduct in London also. I expect to be out most of the time, so I have taken simple lodgings. I need little more than a place to rest my head. Please don't bother yourself."

Armand made the decision. "Nonsense. It's no bother. Quit your lodgings. You must stay with me."

Jade nodded her agreement. "I'm sure I would like to know more about Armand's family, Gerald, and I'm sure you have news of Armand's mother."

"*D'accord!* Then knowing we will have more time together, I will take my leave and return tomorrow," said Gerald.

Armand rang for Barnet.

"This is my cousin, *Monsieur Perrin*," said Armand. "He is leaving now, but he will be staying here from tomorrow."

"Very good, sir. I'll prepare the guest room in the morning."

Gerald took Jade's hand and kissed it and extended his hand to his cousin. Armand shook it with his normal grip but saw the man trying to cover a wince. He gave a tight smile, then quickly gave him an embrace before departing.

Jade touched Armand's arm. "It's getting late, my love. I should be getting home."

He couldn't hide his disappointment. They'd spent the whole day together, but it seemed since he had proposed, they'd had not two minutes alone. Jade seemed to sense his mood. She smiled at him which took the sting out of their premature parting.

"Wait. Not yet," said Armand. "I have something for you. Stay here."

He took the stairs two at a time until he reached his bedroom. Opening a dresser drawer, he extracted a small box and returned downstairs.

"It's customary for a groom to give his bride-to-be a token," he said. "I hope you will accept mine."

He opened the box to reveal a silver filigree heart pendant.

"When we fled France, my mother sewed some of her jewels inside her coat and sold them when we first moved to England. In the end, there were only two pieces left. I want this to be yours."

Jade touched the piece reverently her thumb, caressing the centerpiece of blue enamel into which was embedded seed pearls and small cabochon rubies.

"It's not the most expensive piece of jewelry," he said, half-apologetically "If you don't like it, we can go to a jeweler's tomorrow, and you can pick anything you want."

"Oh, no. This is beautiful. It's a true love token," said Jade.

"Yes, a love heart," said Armand. *"My heart, my love."*

"Oh, but it's so much more than that, don't you see? It's more than its parts," she said breathily. "Silver is symbolic of strength. And the light blue enamel made to look like turquoise? It means good luck and protection. The little rubies are red for passion, and the little pearls? They're associated with Venus, the goddess of love. This was your mother's?"

Armand nodded.

"This pendant must have been something your mother treasured above all things. Perhaps it was given to her by your father while they were courting."

When she looked up at him, there were tears in her eyes. "This means more to me than all the diamonds and rubies in India."

Armand swallowed against a lump in his throat.

Jade removed it from the box to examine more closely before allowing him to take it and fasten the clasp of the silver chain around her neck. It sat beautifully, just below her collar bone. Armand squeezed his eyes shut a moment, knowing if he did not, tears would well in his own eyes.

Damn.

He thought his heart full before, but this moment only increased its capacity.

This was why he loved her. She had brought something more of his past back to him. Until a moment ago, he valued the pendant simply as a piece which belonged to his mother. Thanks to her, he now saw it as an enduring symbol of love between his mother and his father.

"Thank you." He wrapped his arms around her, hoping to impart a small portion of the emotion which filled him.

"It is I who should be thanking you," she said.

Armand shook his head.

"I had lost so much of my past that I thought *none* of it mattered. But you've showed me in so many ways how important it was. I have you to thank for helping to restore it. And I have joy beyond measure now you are to be part of my future."

JADE HELD HIM tight, reveling in the strength of the man who held her. She never expected to fall in love – work was as much her mistress as it was her brother's. Now she realized that, as much as she enjoyed it, it didn't disguise an aching desire for love.

Armand loved her.

It was a miracle she would treasure now until the end of time.

"And you have saved me from being an old spinster," she said lightly. "I might have made work my life and found myself old and never having loved. You love me for who I am. You *see* who I am. How can I not love you in return?"

His lips on hers were tender. They began a gentle exploration, leisurely, but oh, so wonderful.

"I am counting down the weeks until I can take my time to taste you fully," he whispered in her ear. Eddies of sensation spread down her body.

"But time is against us for now," she said.

"Sadly, yes."

Armand offered her an exaggerated sigh and kissed the top of her head.

"Come on, let me take you home knowing we are one day closer."

"We're going to France for our honeymoon?"

"Yes, I mean, I assumed... given that you knew my plans, I..."

"You never actually told me the specifics of your plans. It will give me the chance to practice my French."

"I'd almost forgotten, *Mademoiselle Bridgette Trublion*."

Jade laughed and tucked her arm in his.

"You know, my mother made sure I had a lady's education, but my French lessons came from the wives of the *émigré* goldsmiths who settled in Spitalfields. Now that England and France are at peace, I will get my chance at last to see how well I did at my lessons."

Armand settled his cloak over her shoulders as they walked to the door to the waiting carriage.

"My cousin's arrival was unexpected," said Armand in reflection. "I hope you don't mind that he'll be accompanying us on part of our honeymoon."

Jade settled on to the bench beside him. "Not at all. He is family. I see plainly the resemblance between you. Gerald's hair might be more silver, but there are many features you have in common."

Armand grinned. "Like the nose?"

"Ah, you noticed it too."

"It's quite distinctive."

"I call it distinguished."

"Then you are a shameless flatterer, and I love you for it."

The ride was a short one, but the parting at Jade's home was longer. Edward insisted Armand stay for supper. Jade watched her brother and Armand converse as thought they had been lifelong friends.

By the time Armand left, the clock had struck eleven.

She went into the study to wish her brother a good night and found him there checking through the household accounts.

"News travels fast around here," observed Edward. "Madame Francine Dumont has already left a card inviting you to a wedding gown fitting."

Jade settled into the chair on the other side of the desk. Edward set down his pen.

"So, you've finally gone and done it. Gotten yourself engaged, and here you are leaving me on my own," he teased.

"It's sudden, I know."

Edward smiled tiredly and closed the lid on the inkwell. "Not so sudden. I wondered for months whether or not there was something between you two."

"The attraction was always there," Jade admitted. "But I refused to allow myself to believe that it could be anything more."

"Why?"

Jade frowned. "Why? Our worlds are so different. I would not be accepted as a wife of a Count. And there was you. *We* are Bridges and Sons. If I left, I would be leaving you to run the business on your own. Even now I feel guilty about leaving you in the lurch."

Edward rose from the desk and hugged her.

"This day was always going to come. You're too beautiful and smart to remain a spinster. Believe it or not, I've already given some thought about what to do. We have some good people working for us. I have my eye on one or two who are ready to take on additional responsibilities. More than that, I'm glad for you and happy to welcome Armand to the family."

Jade left her seat and approached Edward. He rose. She wrapped her arms around her brother in a full embrace and took heart that Edward did not demure from returning it in full measure.

CHAPTER TWENTY-FIVE

A RMAND HANDED GERALD a balloon of brandy and took his own to his chair.

The man smiled at him. "You stare at me, cousin," he said with a hint of amusement. "The family resemblance is striking, is it not?"

"After so many years believing there were no relatives left, I'm just surprised at seeing familiar features that aren't simply reflections in a mirror."

"I am taken the same way. There is no doubting the Danger family connection even if I do bear another name."

Gerald took a long sip of brandy and set it down.

"You've never returned to France, have you?" he said.

"Only long enough to see *Maman* settled. I didn't even bother going to *Ytres*."

"That means you'll be coming back to your homeland as a stranger."

Armand inclined his head, conceding the point. Up until now he'd never really considered himself anything other than English, albeit with unusual Christian and family names that were usually both mispronounced.

He'd grown so used to it that his own name from the lips of a Frenchman again sounded damned odd.

"I suppose I will be a stranger. In truth I'd never given consideration to how I would feel about it."

"It will be good for you to see France through fresh eyes," said Gerald. "I look forward to showing you and your bride."

His cousin took another sip from the glass and set it aside. "I didn't know you were planning to wed. I thought you were to be the very last of the Dangers. You said nothing about your intentions in your correspondence. Was it intended to be a surprise for *Tante* Nicole?"

"It was a surprise for me too. I only asked Miss Bridges yesterday."

"The Danger name will live on then," said Gerald mildly. He picked up the brandy balloon and raised it to Armand before taking another sip, letting the conversation lapse. Several long moments passed before he spoke again.

"Your mother will be pleased to see you – and to see you settled."

"How is she? She doesn't correspond as often as she used to. I really appreciate the notes from her that you slip in with your letters, even if they don't make much sense."

Gerald drained his glass. The conviviality of his features faded to a serious mien.

"That was another reason why I decided to come to England to meet with you. There is something I could not explain in a letter. Even now I don't think I have the words."

Armand frowned. "Is *Maman* unwell?"

"Yes. But not in the way you might think. Her mind wanders. And her memory, it is becoming forgetful."

Armand did the sums in his head. His mother was only in her early fifties.

"But she is in otherwise good health?"

"You will see that she is. She suffers no physical infirmities apart from tiredness. The doctor cannot find anything wrong with her."

"How long has she been like this?"

"For a few months now. At first the signs were not clear. We thought she was simply distracted or in low spirits when she would not do the things she enjoyed doing. Then *Tante Nicole* would rally, as she always did when she received your letters, but she never went back to the way she was before."

Guilt speared Armand's gut. He could have been a better son. He saw how unhappy she was after the death of his stepfather. She had become listless and reclusive. The only time that state changed was when there was a new correspondence from France. Then she became more like her old self.

When she announced that she wanted to return to France, he encouraged her. And she told him she understood her son's life was in England and that he ought to remain with his stepbrother.

Charles had witnessed his stepmother's decline with equal alarm and was in complete agreement that a return to France was the best course.

Had it been a mistake?

He saw how Gerald watched him beneath hooded lids, gauging his reaction to the news.

Armand picked up his brandy and took a draught, allowing the burning heat of it to bring him back to the present.

"Charles and I thought we were doing the right thing…"

"And you *were*! You have! *Tante* Nicole has been very happy. She *is* very happy. Her forgetfulness has not altered her disposition, but I wanted you to be aware that you would find her changed."

"Then I'm glad we're going to see her," he said.

Gerald pulled a cigar from his pocket. He rose, approached the fireplace, and pulled a spill from the mantle. He touched it to the fire to light his cigar.

"The lady you are going to wed, she is not titled? I recall you saying your sister-in-law was – how did you say it? – *throwing young ladies your way*."

Armand started at the change of topic, but he welcomed it. There was little he could do about his mother until they arrived in France.

The clock struck eleven. Barnet entered the room to ask if there was anything the gentlemen required before he retired. Armand dismissed him for the evening.

Warmed by the company and the fine brandy, he told Gerald the story of how he and Jade met, delighted to find his cousin showing genuine interest. The conversation flowed on long into the night and Armand told him about their search for the clock. That was something he hadn't even shared with Charles.

A twinge of conscience pricked at him. It wasn't as though he was deliberately hiding his search from his stepbrother; it just never came up in conversation. Charles had a title of his own with the responsibilities that came with it. He couldn't expect him to be invested in such a quest other than out of fraternal interest.

But it was different with Gerald, for some reason. He listened without interruption, and, it would appear, with genuine interest. And why not? He had visited the Danger estate at *Ytres* as a young man. He was familiar with the setting and the house in "the good old days".

The clocks in Armand's Mayfair townhouse had been silenced for hours. In the after-midnight quiet, the glow from the fire on which Armand focused seemed to invite revelation. Soon, he found himself telling his cousin about his recurring dreams of his father, and the night he and his mother fled for England.

Gerald hung on his every word.

"This is *formidable*! You are convinced this key unlocks something your father wanted to keep hidden from the Revolutionaries?"

"You must think I'm mad."

Gerald hastened to reassure him. *"Mais non*, not at all! Did you find the clock?"

"Jade did. Her brother negotiated the purchase with the current owner."

"Excellent! Do you have it?"

Armand shook his head and yawned deeply.

"Ah, there's the rub. I'm not the only one who wants it."

"Oh? Who else?"

Armand rose to his feet. "That's a long story. It'll have to wait until morning. It's been a long day, and I have a lot to do to be ready for a wedding and a trip abroad."

Gerald rose also and clasped Armand's shoulders.

"It will be good to have you home, cousin. But one more question before it slips from my mind?"

Armand paused in the doorway.

"The key. Do you know what it opens?"

Armand shook his head. "No, I don't."

Gerald's face registered disappointment a moment. Or did it? In his exhausted state, Armand might have imagined something else in the man's expression.

His cousin shrugged.

"Do not let me keep you from your bed. I will explore your library and sample a little more of your brandy, if you don't mind."

"Not at all. Make yourself at home."

BEFORE BARNET HAD gone to bed, the exemplary valet had laid out Armand's night shirt and his clothes for the morning. On his dressing table was a note reminding him of various appointments on the morrow, and a personal note from the man congratulating him once again on his engagement.

Armand undressed, reflecting on the incredible day it had been. He had begun it as a bachelor with little family to speak of. He ended it as a man engaged to marry and with a cousin staying under his roof.

Gerald was indeed a good sort of fellow. Armand couldn't say he knew him intimately, despite their correspondence. The missives between them were friendly and familial, but nothing out of the ordinary.

But when *Maman* became a less diligent correspondent, Gerald had taken up the slack with his own letters from Arras, and

Armand meant it when he thanked his cousin for adding his mother's notes to his own correspondence. But for Gerald encouraging her to write the rambling little scraps, he might not have heard from her at all for months.

Still, he didn't tell Gerald about his suspicion that the key had some connection with the family crypt at Ytres. The two things were inextricably linked in his mind although he couldn't say why – the only thing that connected them was the recurring dream of his childhood.

There was no reason why he *shouldn't* have told him – given how he had revealed everything else, but there was a little inner voice that cautioned him to not reveal everything to his newly-met family member.

⊱⊱⊱❈⊰⊰⊰

THE NEXT AFTERNOON emerged overcast, giving a premature end to the twilight. The entrance of Bridges & Sons Auction House was well lit in preparation for Baroness von Hoecker.

The woman had insisted she would not attend the Bond Street shop. Instead, she would come to the auction house at Southwark incognito, and, to that end, she would do so after dark.

There was another stipulation – only Miss Bridges was to be present.

To the latter demand, Jade refused point-blank. The Baroness returned her own tersely worded message that she would only concede to the presence of Armand and Edward if they made themselves inconspicuous.

Jade stood in the doorway as the Baroness's coach approached. The vehicle was of superb quality. It was black, as were the matched pair of horses. The driver was female, as was a liveried attendant who sat beside the driver and another who stood on the step at the back. When the conveyance rolled to a stop, the young woman leaped from the back with the grace of an Amazon. She set down the step and opened the door.

The Baroness emerged wearing black from head to toe. A lace veil obscured her features.

She completely ignored Edward and Armand standing off to one side and went straight to Jade. "You have found my beauty."

"I have, my lady," Jade answered gravely.

"Then I wish to see her."

Jade led the way through the auction room and into a back storeroom where the Thalatte clock stood on a cloth-covered table. Armand and Edward remained just outside the doorway, the Baroness's Amazonian standing guard behind them.

Lamps had been lit in preparation for the inspection. They cast the bronze sculpture in a warm glow.

Jade stepped aside to allow the Baroness to fully examine the timepiece for herself. She caressed the figure as a lover might – running a finger down Thalatte's cheeks, mapping her waist, and tracing the line of her limbs.

"She is more beautiful than I dreamed," the woman announced at last. "You have done well, Miss Bridges. I will gladly pay your price."

Jade glanced through the doorway at Armand, then at Edward, both of whom remained out of the Baroness' eyeline. Edward responded with a raise of his eyebrow, silently signaling Jade this was her sale to handle as she saw fit.

"Do you recall the bargain you offered to consider at our first meeting, my Lady?"

"With that male you brought with you? Of course, I do. I have given it much thought. But I hired *you*. You have found my Thalatte, and I am willing to pay your price for her. I will only be convinced to give up my claim if the life-sized statue of her exists as he claimed, and it must be in as fine condition as this one. That was the proposal, I believe."

Jade nodded once in confirmation. "My other client is prepared to honor this agreement," she said. "The clock is yours."

"A word, Miss Bridges." Armand's voice was tight.

She curtsied to the Baroness and left her in the room with the clock.

Armand was angry. He followed a pace behind Jade towards the office. Edward trailed behind them both.

The door closed, and Jade turned to face Armand.

"The pendulum," he ground out.

Jade unlocked the desk drawer and opened it, motioning for Armand to look inside.

The pendulum, minus the bob, lay within on a blue cloth.

Armand took it out and examined it.

"This is–"

"A copy, perfect in every way," she interrupted softly. "Same materials, same dimensions. I had Monsieur Rosenbaum make it."

Armand pulled it apart and reassembled it as the key. His expression was still dark, but not as thunderous as it was a few moments before.

"When did you do this?"

"Today. The jeweler's apprentice delivered it along with the return of the original an hour ago."

"That was quite a risk, Jade," said Edward. "What would have happened if Rosenbaum hadn't completed this in time?"

"I was wondering that myself," Armand added.

Jade straightened her back. She loved these two men dearly, along with their good opinion. But as Edward was always reminding her, this transaction was *hers* to control. She'd made a decision – a risky one given the time available, she would concede – but it worked. Mr. Rosenbaum was able to do it straight away, and the original was back on the clock before the Baroness arrived, so there was nothing to get upset about.

After a moment, Armand let out a long exhale.

"I hope this works if we can find the lock it fits," he said, holding up the key.

"It will," Jade replied confidently. "It really is a perfect copy. It even weighs exactly the same. I could have put it on the clock and kept the original except Mr. Rosenbaum needed another day to make the bob. And I couldn't do that anyway – I promised the Baroness *the* clock and that meant *all* of it. Even if you are to get it back when – *if* we find the statue, I couldn't cheat a client and deliver something even a partial fake."

"I understand – but I just lost years off my life," Armand said with a self-deprecating chuckle. "You might have warned me."

Now it was Edward's turn to laugh. He slapped Armand on the back.

"Now you can see what I've had to put up with. And once you're married, she's *your* problem."

Jade pulled a face at her brother before turning back to Armand.

"The plan only came to me yesterday morning. I wasn't even sure it could be done."

Armand placed the replica pendulum pieces back in the drawer, leaning forward to kiss her softly.

"We'd better get back to your client and finish the deal, because I want to get home for supper and—"

Pop! Pop! Pop!

A series of percussive sounds came from outside.

Edward, closest to the door, started at a run. He threw open the front door and ran into the darkness. Armand followed swiftly behind.

Jade could hear the baroness's horses whinnying in fear along with the shouts of the driver trying to keep the beasts under control.

She hurried to the storeroom to check on the Baroness.

"What's going on?" the older woman demanded.

"Nothing to worry about, my lady. Some miscreant letting off fireworks, I expect," Jade said with more confidence than she felt.

"Then order them to stop immediately."

Jade bristled at being ordered about by the woman. She raised her chin imperiously. "I've sent the men outside to so."

The baroness nodded her satisfaction.

Now was the time for Jade to press her advantage.

"Five hundred guineas."

"I beg your pardon?"

Jade now had the baroness's full attention.

"For the clock," she continued. "The price covers my time and expenses, and, as you'll agree, it's reasonable for a Boyer sculpture in such a beautiful form."

The woman slowly removed her veil to reveal lips quirked in a half-smile, then eyes that showed a measure of respect.

"You don't need to sell it to *me*, my dear. I know its value. Very well. I agree to your terms. Your money will be delivered here tomorrow morning."

Armand came into the room without so much as a by-your-leave. The baroness cast a sour look his way before righting her veil to cover her face once more.

He spared a glance to Jade but addressed the baroness directly.

"My lady, I think it is best for you to leave now."

"I beg your pardon? I've never taken orders from a man, and I don't intend to begin now."

"Someone deliberately scared your horses. Your driver and maidservant had difficulty keeping them under control. They insist you will not require our escort home, but I would appeal to your good sense, madam, and beg you to leave now."

The older woman stiffened and said nothing for a moment.

"Mistress?" One of the liveried women appeared at the door. "We are ready to depart."

The baroness nodded in the servant's direction, then looked at Armand.

"Make yourself useful and bring the clock."

CHAPTER TWENTY-SIX

ARMAND FOUND HIMSELF relieved of the clock by the solidly built coachwoman who dealt with the weight of the bronze almost as easily as he had done.

He warred with disappointment and regret at seeing the Thalatte clock in someone else's hands even though he himself had suggested the solution. One way or another, this minor Greek goddess was part of his earliest memories, and even now he felt the urge to snatch it back.

The pendulum. That was the most important thing for the moment and the replica of that was safe in Jade's desk drawer.

The coachwoman passed the clock inside the carriage to the other assistant who lowered it gently into a wooden crate brought along especially for the transportation. The servant who guarded the Baroness aided her up into the coach before returning to her station on the back step.

Armand saw the baroness lean forward in her seat momentarily and caress the statue's cheek again before allowing it to be covered with a black cloth.

The assistant emerged and closed the door, then climbed up onto the seat beside the driver. The coachwoman directed the still-nervous horses away from the auction house.

Armand turned as the sound of scuffling reached him. Edward held a scrawny man by the scruff of the neck. Both men wore evidence of a struggle in their disarrayed clothing.

"'Ere!" Armand's coachman, Lawson, approached. "That's the one who set the crackers off in front of that lady's coach. I had the devil's own time keeping our two under control."

"C'mon, let's get him inside and have a quiet word," Edward growled with menace. He propelled the miscreant headfirst into the auction house.

Jade stiffened as they entered the well-lit room.

"You!" she said. "You're the one who's been following me. Why?"

Edward roughly shoved the man into a wooden chair and placed a heavy hand on his shoulder. Surrounded by three angry people, the man apparently thought it wise not to attempt escape.

Armand watched the man's expression change rapidly – surprise, fear, denial – before it fell. A moment later, he slumped in apparent resignation.

"You'd better speak now," said Armand quietly, forcing the man's attention to him. "Or I cannot vouch for what will happen."

Armand glanced up to Edward, who remained behind the man, holding him in the chair. Jade's brother gave him a tight nod to indicate that he should conduct the interrogation.

"Why did you set off those firecrackers?"

The man shifted in the chair and remained silent.

"Your idea? Or someone else's?"

The man's eyes dropped, lids fluttering a moment. Armand had his answer.

"However much they paid you, it will not be enough to compensate for going to jail for attempted murder."

The man's eyes rose and fixed on his.

"That's right. You might have killed someone tonight with that stunt."

The only answer was silence.

Then something occurred to Armand.

"Why did you kill Mick Mattis?"

He had no idea whether he was right, but he went with his gut feeling.

The man's lids fluttered, a rapid semaphore that revealed much without words.

"Who wants the clock so much they'd pay enough for you to risk the gibbet?" Armand pressed.

The prisoner's mouth pressed into a thin line. There was also a bob of his Adam's apple that suggested the man swallowed hard.

"You'd better answer him, matey," added Edward.

The man sighed. "Yeah, all right. I was paid. But all I was asked is to get the clock."

"Why?"

The man would have attempted a shrug, except he was prevented by the press of Edward's hands.

"I dunno. The man just told me where to go looking for it. Mattis was alive when I left his warehouse, so you can't pin that on me."

Armand folded his arms. "You're going to have to do better than that to convince a magistrate. We are all in agreement to swear out a charge of murder against you unless you tell us the whole truth."

The man considered the argument.

"What's the name of the man who hired you?"

"I don't know."

"What's *your* name."

"Smith."

Edward hissed his displeasure.

Armand slapped "Smith's" face hard.

"Jade, leave us a moment," said Edward. "Go find some rope in the back room."

Armand didn't dare look at her. He braced himself for an argument against being rough with the man that he could well do without. But there wasn't one. He heard the swish of her skirts as she walked out of the room, presumably to do as her brother

asked.

"Smith" raised his chin defiantly.

"Shall we try this again while the lady is out of the room?"

Instead of a slap, Armand stepped forward and jabbed the man hard in the solar plexus.

"Farthing. Tom Farthing," he wheezed out when he could talk again.

"Better," said Edward. "Who employed you?"

After a few gasps of breath, Farthing spoke. "He told me 'is name was Smith."

At Armand's glare, Farthing raised his hands to cover his face.

"I swear to God, that's the name he gave me! I know it's fake, but his money was real enough."

"I suppose you don't know what he looks like either."

"I dunno. Tall like you. Dressed plain. Spoke like a gent."

"Hair color? Beard?"

"Always wore a hat. No beard."

Sensing the other men's frustration, Farthing continued.

"I can lead you to him."

"That's better."

Armand felt a touch on his arm. He started and turned to see Jade looking at him, mouth set in a grim line. In her hand were the lengths of ropes her brother had asked for.

Edward hauled Farthing to his feet and pulled his arms back while Armand bound the man's wrists behind him.

"You'll have overnight to think about how much more you want to tell us because, my friend, your neck is well and truly on the line."

Edward pushed the man toward a small windowless storeroom just off the room where they'd shown the clock just twenty minutes earlier. He shoved him in, then swept the man's legs out from under him with his right foot. Farthing dropped unceremoniously to the floor with an "oof", and Edward immediately knelt on him.

"Tie his ankles," said he ordered.

Armand used the second length of rope to do it.

They stood and regarded Farthing in the dim light coming from the other room. "Don't try to get away, either," Edward warned him. "Do any damage and you'll pay for that too."

He slammed the door to the man's tiny cell and locked it.

"I'll stay here for the moment," said Edward. "Send Seton back with a couple of the footmen to keep guard on him overnight. Our guest needs time to think on things. We'll see where this inquiry leads us in the morning."

He wrapped an arm around Jade and kissed her on the top of her head.

"I'll see you at home," he said. "I think you'll be in safe enough hands with your fiancé."

Armand shot him a grateful look.

"But don't bring her back too late," Edward said with a tired grin. "You're not married yet."

The moment of levity was exactly what was needed to break the spell of this strange evening.

But the good mood lasted only until they left the auction house.

"What made you ask that man about Mattis?" Jade asked.

Armand shrugged. "I don't know. The fact that you recognized him, maybe."

Jade sighed. "More disturbing is tonight's incident proves that the baroness was telling the truth. She *wasn't* having me followed. It confirms that someone else wants the clock. I can understand *her* reason for wanting it, and I can understand *yours*, but not this third party. It's only a statue, only a clock – a very nice one to be sure – but not something to kill over. What interest could it have for someone else?"

It was an excellent question, and one Armand didn't have an answer for.

"Could someone else know the significance it has for you?" she asked.

That was the question that lingered in the back of his mind.

Now Jade had asked it.

They crossed London Bridge in silence.

"It's possible," he conceded.

A more worrying thought occurred to him.

"You're not going to accuse Gerald, are you?"

He chanced a glance at her, wrapped up warm in a voluminous forest green coat, sable fur framing her face.

"Why would you think that?" she asked.

Armand shrugged. "I don't know. The key unlocks something important, possibly only important to someone in the family, and he's the only other male left in the family line."

"Well, someone knows," she said. Jade paused, then shook her head. "No, it can't possibly be him. We've been searching for the Thalatte clock for months, and it's been about that long since I had my reticule snatched by Farthing. Gerald only arrived in England in the past week."

"Well, this is the end of it for tonight," he said. "One way or another, Farthing will tell us what he knows, and the Magistrate will deal with him and his paymaster."

He pulled Jade across into his arms. "We have other things to think about."

She snuggled in close. "We'll be married in less than three weeks," she said softly.

"Believe me, I've not forgotten," he said.

"You should see the trousseau Madame Dumont is making for me."

The thought of seeing Jade in diaphanous shifts and, frankly, in nothing at all, stirred him down below.

"You're really determined to make these three weeks the longest of my life, aren't you?"

She raised her head from his shoulder and gave him a knowing look. She started stroking his back.

"I still think about that night," she said.

So did he. He turned so he could hold her properly. Her face raised to his begged for a kiss, so he obliged. Here in the semi-darkness of the carriage, they were truly alone for the first time in days. But not quite…

The small door up to the driver opened. Jade slipped out of his arms. Armand tamped down his disappointment.

"Sir, we've arrived at Bond Street."

"Thank you, Lawson." Armand turned to Jade. Her lips were full from the kiss they'd shared. In the dull glow of the lamplight, her brown hair seemed burnished copper. He wanted to touch her, to kiss her, to have her call out his name in ecstasy.

"Did you want to go home?"

He held his breath waiting for her answer.

"No. I want to stay."

COLD NIGHT AIR swirled in as Armand opened the carriage door to get out. Jade wrapped her cloak about her to wait. If she was of a mind to be sensible, she would have bid Armand a good night and informed Seton of Edward's instructions herself.

But she no longer felt like being sensible.

What she wanted more than anything was to be in Armand's arms and to feel safe.

Frankly, she didn't know how she felt about Farthing's capture. On the one hand there was relief that her instinct was sound. There *had* been someone following her. On the other hand, the fact that it *wasn't* the product of an overwrought mind was *also* unsettling.

The man admitted to having robbed Mickey Mattis, and he most likely murdered him too – despite his protestations to the contrary. Would Farthing have killed her? Perhaps Armand? Edward? Or any other of their staff, for that matter?

With the business with the baroness settled for the time being, and the excitement of the evening gone, Jade still remained on edge.

The door opened once more, bringing in the chilled air. Armand seated himself beside her.

"Seton and some of his men are on their way to the auction house." He cocked his head, looking at her quizzically. "Are you all right? Wouldn't you rather go inside?"

No, she wouldn't. She would rather stay with him.

Jade opened her mouth to say as much, except an unexplained lump rose in her throat and barred her words, so all she could do was swallow, fight the tears that were welling in her eyes, and shake her head 'no'.

Armand told Lawson to take a slow drive. The carriage lurched back into motion.

"Come here."

His voice was like the grumble of distant thunder which sent lightning through her veins. Jade slid across the bench, letting him hold her. She let out a sigh and settled against his chest.

This was what she needed now, Armand's presence to eclipse the fear and doubt that was in danger of taking root.

The gentle sway of the carriage and the tender touch of Armand's hands caressing her arms soothed her into a warm lethargy. She tilted her head to find that he was watching her intently.

Her lids lowered as his lips descended. Jade gave herself into the slow languorous kiss. For several minutes they simply kissed. Slowly, deliberately. Desire rose steadily, not an instant conflagration of passion, but rather a rising tide. She willingly allowed herself to be pulled into his lap where his kisses became deeper and more insistent. Jade followed willingly, returning kiss for kiss, touch for touch as they explored one another.

His hand snaked through the opening of her coat and unerringly found her breast. His fingers teased her fresh, brushing over her nipples until they stood proud and ached. She felt his erection pressed hard at her hip.

Her own body responded. Jade lamented the layers of clothes that separated them. She wanted him. She wanted him now. She needed to feel his strength around her. Over her. In her.

Arousal made her brazen.

"Make love to me, Armand," she whispered. "I cannot wait three weeks."

He shook his head. She frowned.

"Two weeks and two days," he said.

"That far away?" she pouted, tracing a hand down his chest.

"The time will fly before we know it."

Jade's fingers spread across his abdomen and moved lower until she reached the bulge in his breeches.

"What will we do until then?" she asked coquettishly.

"I would suggest exactly what we are doing."

"More kissing. Less talking."

"My, you are a bossy woman, aren't you?"

Feeling bold, Jade cupped his erection. Armand groaned, which quickly became a growl as he took charge of the seduction. He slid her off his lap, positioning her until she straddled him. Her stockinged thighs were exposed to the late-night air, but that was more than offset by the heat building between her legs.

The cloak slipped off her shoulders as he leaned forward to kiss her sensitive neck.

"Before I go to sleep, I think about you… about us in the library that night," he said. "I close my eyes and imagine that we don't stop, that I take you. Your cries of pleasure are loud. My lips on your breasts, tasting you. Your legs are wrapped around me."

The more he spoke, the more his words became real in her mind's eye, stoking her arousal further.

Jade's eyes fluttered shut as his hands slid from her back to her waist, his thumbs teasing her breasts. She pressed her core to his erection, desperate for the contact, her arousal growing with each breath.

"I don't want to wait," she said. "I can't wait. Take me home and make love to me Armand."

CHAPTER TWENTY-SEVEN

JADE ALLOWED HERSELF to be man-handled once again until she sat on the padded leather seat once more. Armand slid off the seat until he knelt before her. He slid the hem of her dress slowly up her calves and over her knees to her thighs until it was bunched at her hips. His fingertips trailed the bare flesh of her thighs and parted them.

"I also dream of doing this."

Slowly he lowered himself between her legs. The anticipation became an agony of want, desire, lust. His breath on her bare skin heated her so intensely that when she felt the feather-light touch of his tongue on her center, she jumped, but his hands firmly gripped her hips.

Jade was transported on a tide of ecstasy as he used his tongue to bring her such pleasure. Her fingers wended through his hair as Armand continued his exploration of her, then tension inside rose higher and higher until it exploded into a universe of stars.

When the last glimmer of light faded behind her lids, Jade opened her eyes to Armand's smoldering gaze.

Nothing in her life had prepared her for the overwhelming sensations he brought out in her. Having experienced it once, she wanted it, *craved it* again.

"Take me home, Armand, she said.

Quickly adding so there was no misunderstanding, *"Our home."*

Armand took Jade's hand in his and brought it to his lips, then instructed Lawson to take them home to Mayfair.

The short trip was made in silence. As the carriage rolled to a stop, Jade had righted her clothing and made some headway in fixing her hair, somewhat hampered by Armand's insistence in taking out a hair pin every time she set one in place.

In the end, she let her hair tumble loose over her shoulders and back. The heated look she received from Armand told her he preferred her hair that way.

They were met at the door by Barnet who discreetly departed after being told his services would not be required for the night.

How could a place she'd only set foot in once feel so much like home? In every room she passed, there were pieces of furniture and decorations she recognized. But, after all, they were objects that she, herself, had chosen.

It was only after they climbed the stairs and entered the master suite that she entered a room she knew nothing about.

Two lamps had already been lit which bathed the room in a golden glow.

"I think I'm nervous," said Armand.

"You?"

He smiled. "This is the only room I've decorated on my own."

Jade cast her eye across the room with the practiced eye of an antiques dealer. The bedroom furniture was solid English oak and distinctly masculine in style. A good-sized bed, not outsized in the space offered by the room, was already turned down.

The rectangular dresser mirror reflected light from the lamp on it. The second lamp was on a desk by a window.

She pronounced her verdict.

"It's a bachelor's room, but nothing that can't be fixed."

Armand laughed and hauled her into his arms once more.

The tension was broken, and any unease Jade might have had

in committing herself to Armand this night was all but over. This would merely be the first of many nights together, a union of souls, of hearts and bodies. What was there at all to be nervous about?

Jade stroked his cheek which now had a hint of late-day stubble. She recalled the feel of him between her legs and wondered how dark his beard may grow overnight. Armand remained perfectly still, allowing her to set the pace.

Provocatively, she brushed her breasts against his arm as she slid past him to sit at the dressing table seat. During the ride here the laces on her dress had loosened. When she bent forward to work free the laces of her walking boots, she knew full well she was giving Armand a good view of her breasts.

And he was looking his fill.

Tonight, she was a wanton. Perhaps she would be every night, particularly when her husband-to-be made her feel such glorious things.

Armand had made short work of his own boots, along with his waistcoat and shirt. He extended his hand to her. Jade took it and allowed him to bring her to her feet and draw her to him. She stroked the black, wiry hair on his chest. The smell of his cologne, the feel of his warm skin was intoxicating.

She touched and caressed him, only peripherally aware of the fact that his hands were behind her, unlacing her gowns and the stays beneath with the deftness of a man, she knew was well-practiced at seduction.

The dress slid from her shoulders, taking the shift with it. Jade lowered her arms. Armand grasped the neckline and tugged until the fabric pooled at her hips.

He kissed her then, urgent and demanding. Her arms twined around his neck, pulling him closer. The feel of her bare breasts on his chest made them sensitive. She brushed them across the hair on his chest until her nipples stood proud.

Armand's hands slid down her back, cupping her bottom. His lips left her and trailed a line of kisses down her neck to her collar bone where he nipped and sucked her flesh. Jade threw her head back to give him greater access. She let him support her weight as he bent forward to kiss her breasts and took one of her nipples into his mouth.

Jade cried out in pleasure, grinding herself against him. He continued with one bud, then the other.

"Please, Armand," she breathed.

He looked at her, his eyes dark with passion, then kissed her lips with an urgency that swept her into a surging wave of desire. He swept her up into his arms, and they headed for his bed.

In several swift seconds, she was lying on the bed and spread naked before him. Something in his hungry gaze answered a call within her. Jade touched her breasts as he had done, causing him to groan. He continued to stare as he made hasty work on the buttons of his breeches.

At that moment, she felt as powerful as a goddess. One who could bring this powerful man to his knees. She drew her fingers lightly across her stomach, anticipating his touch there, and started to trail lower.

Her mouth grew dry when she saw his unsheathed erection for the first time. He was magnificent.

Jade reveled in Armand's gaze running over her. Love, desire, honor – everything she ever wanted in a husband was in the man before her now.

Armand kneeled on the bed. Her legs parted as he drew near. She reached for him, but he remained just out of reach between her knees. She watched him lower himself to her core and dart out his tongue to touch the swelling nub between her legs. He teased her with his tongue over and over until she cried out as pleasure overtook her once more.

"Even better than in my dreams." He rose over her. For the first time she could feel his cock touch her most private parts.

He didn't take her then and there, as she thought he might. Instead, he worked his way up her abdomen and her ribs with kisses, before lavishing her breasts with more kisses, laving her nipples with her tongue until they stood out red and full.

Jade no longer fought to master the sensations. She gave into them completely, floating along with each new tug of desire. She met his lips eagerly, investing each kiss with all the love within her soul. Her fingers spread through his hair, held him to her while he rocked his fully engorged cock against her sensitive clit.

His fingers stroked her, as they had done at the library. The memory was still fresh in her mind. Another orgasm swiftly followed.

Armand began to enter her deliberately, slowly. She opened her eyes and watched him join with her.

It was too much; it was not enough.

"I don't want to hurt you," he said. The look of studied concentration on his face was erotic, and she fell in love with him all the more.

"Now Armand, please," she begged.

He reached the limits of control. He entered her fully and began to move. Jade wrapped her legs around him, holding him close. Armand increased his pace, the friction against her sensitive skin bringing her to the peak once more. She cried his name over and over again until he shouted his own release.

In one fluid motion, he rolled until she was laying on top of him, her legs splayed over his muscular calves. Jade couldn't resist the sated, pleased expression he wore. She leaned forward. He prepared himself for her kiss, except she ignored his lips and kissed the tip of his nose.

He mock-growled. Jade giggled and dropped a kiss on his forehead, his cheek, his ear – anywhere other than his lips.

Armand tried to stop her tease with his hands on her hips, which then slid up her waist until they cupped her breasts.

Jade pressed herself into his hands, reveling in the sensation of his touch.

Now she had been thoroughly distracted, Armand's lips found hers. She gave herself into the kiss, expressing the depth of her love for him without words.

"I love you Jade," Armand whispered into her ear. "You have made my life complete. The missing pieces of my soul that I didn't know were lost, I've found in you. Together, like this, I feel whole."

Tears welled. The fullness in her heart made words impossible to find, so she kissed him instead, Over and over again, until she was breathless with it. Tears that threatened to spill over turned into giggles as he started tickling her in an attempt to make her stop.

In the end, Armand rolled them both over until she was beneath him again.

"I love you, Armand," she whispered, looking up at him. "Always."

⇻⟫⟪↢

BY MUTUAL AGREEMENT, Armand took Jade home early in the morning.

That the mistress did not sleep in her own bed last night would no doubt be a source of gossip, but he also assumed that Jade's servants were hired for their trustworthiness and discretion.

What he hadn't counted on was her brother already being up. Armand readied himself for an uncomfortable dressing down.

Edward glared at the both of them as they walked in the door. Armand squared his shoulders, refusing to be intimidated. It was Jade who broke the tension.

"Oh, stop that, Edward. You look like you've sucked on a lemon. I don't make a fuss when *you* stay away overnight," she said. "Make yourself useful and order some tea and have breakfast served. I'm going to get changed. I'll meet you in the morning room."

She flashed a smile and bounced up the stairs as though this were a usual conversation between brother and sister. Armand

and Edward were left staring after her in the hallway.

Now they were alone, he waited for Edward to say his piece.

Perhaps *he* ought to say something.

An apology?

For what?

He and Jade certainly had no regrets. As far as he was concerned, they were married in all but name, and even that would be rectified in the space of a couple of weeks.

As Armand girded himself for an argument, Edward's upright posture deflated like a balloon.

"I can't stay mad at her. Even when there's good cause," he said.

Armand returned a look of sympathy.

Edward shook his head, quickly finding his good humor. "Don't you give me that look. I've told you already – she's going to be your problem soon."

"I think Jade would strenuously object to being described as a 'problem'," Armand said wryly.

His observation was dismissed with a wave of a hand.

"I'm not going to stand here debating it before I've had bacon and eggs and at least one cup of coffee."

And with that, he strode off, and Armand followed his host into the morning room where servants were setting out the table.

"Another setting, please, Nigel. The count will be joining us for breakfast."

As soon as the servant had departed, Armand directed Edward's attention to more serious matters.

"How do you want to approach there being a man currently tied up in your sale room?"

"I called for someone to meet me here this morning. Will you join me? It wouldn't hurt to have a well-connected member of the aristocracy there, given that you're also a witness."

Armand gave a swift nod of his head.

"Do you truly believe he killed Mattis?" Edward asked.

"It was a guess on my part. It made sense because the connection is the clock. All we need is to ascertain the veracity of Farthing's story and track down this Mr. Smith."

"The name is clearly a fake, so the chances of finding him, if he exists, are slim-to-none."

Armand poured himself some coffee. "It's the only lead we have."

"Do you think someone else knows the trick with the pendulum?"

"Jade asked me the same question last night. The truth is, I don't know. I can't imagine who or why. If we find them, maybe we can ask *them* what it unlocks, because I still don't know. I'm almost certain that the return to the *Ytres* estate will yield nothing. It has been thirty years since the Revolution, and, according to my cousin, the house is all but destroyed, and the grounds gone to wrack and ruin. I don't even know if what I'm looking for is still standing."

"It may not be about the pendulum at all," Edward proposed. "A miniature sculpture from Boyer is worth something to a collector. It was worth five hundred guineas to Baroness von Hoecker, to be precise. Did you see how she admired it?"

"I did. So perhaps it's worth more to someone else."

Edward shook his head.

"Not a chance. As lovely as the clock is, we see sculptures of equal quality come into the sales room often enough, and they make only a fraction of that price. The baroness bought the piece out of, um, *sentiment*, shall we say. If she put the item up for sale now, she'd lose money on it."

"Whoever Farthing's accomplice is, hopefully he'll give up when he learns he's arrested, and we can go about our lives in peace."

Jade entered the morning room wearing a white muslin gown decorated with green and dove gray ribbons that had been fashioned in a diamond pattern across the skirt.

She was lovely, but what pleased Armand more was seeing his mother's silver filigree heart pendant around her neck.

He rose to his feet, along with Edward.

Jade looked at him with a warm smile, and then to her brother with a less certain one, evaluating his present mood.

He merely gave an exasperated shake of his head. Jade approached the table and dropped a kiss on top of Edward's head before filling her plate and taking a seat opposite Armand.

"I've had another thought," she said while buttering some toast. "Why don't you take this man to the pawnbrokers? If he was the one who tried to pawn my vinaigrette, Silas may recognize him. That should help prove that he stole my reticule at least."

Armand nodded in agreement and addressed Edward.

"It will be something to charge him with if we can't find 'Smith'."

At that moment a servant entered and announced a Mr. Allard was here.

"He's the man I mentioned," said Edward to Armand. He hastily finished his breakfast and left the room.

Now alone with Jade, Armand got up from the table and went to her side. She stepped into his arms and kissed him.

"I'm going with Edward today to see about Farthing," he said. "Do you need me to stay?"

"Certainly not! There is still a wedding to prepare," she said, before adding with a grin. "I'm about to embark on a mission more dangerous than yours – shopping with your sister-in-law."

❧

CHAPTER TWENTY-EIGHT

T HE MAN WAITING in the Bridges' oriental room was in his early fifties. He had a lean, muscular build, and he nodded at Edward, who greeted him by name.

Armand recognized Allard, although they'd never actually been introduced.

The man acknowledged Armand's expression.

"That's right, sir, I was in Mattis' warehouse when you came with Miss Bridges."

"Allard is from the Thames River Police," Edward explained.

"Not Bow Street?"

The man in question shook his head.

"No, sir. Me and my men look after the docks and the goings on along the river. The Bow Street boys have enough on their hands, and they don't get paid nearly well enough for it. At least we get a stipend. Anyhow, Mattis got himself killed on the docks, and that's our patch."

"We might be able to help you with it," said Edward. "We have a man in custody."

"Aye, so your note said. Let's not keep the gentleman waiting."

Three of them travelled to the auction house. On the way, Edward went over the events of last night. They found Pete guarding the door of the makeshift cell.

"He's been quiet enough since we got here this morning," he said as he unlocked the door.

The man inside had lost much of his bravado lying overnight on a cold floor with his hands and feet bound.

"If it isn't my old mate Farthing," said Allard, peering in at him. "Murder's a bit of a step up from petty theivin', innit?"

"I didn't kill no one Mr. Allard, that's God's own truth."

"I want to believe ye," replied the policeman as he untied the man's wrists and ankles. "But these two upstandin' gentlemen with me beg to differ, and ye did set off them fireworks to spook the 'orses. Now why would you do that?"

Farthing admitted that a Mr. Smith had paid him to do it. The man had been very specific about the time and place, and a sovereign was a sovereign after all.

Allard hauled Farthing to his feet and the man limped into the main storeroom where he didn't resist when pressed down onto a wooden chair. And when he was ordered to recount everything, starting with his first meeting with Smith, he didn't stint.

They learned that his first meeting with Mr. Smith was not by the docks, but rather at the coaching inn, The Swan with Two Necks. Farthing had been there "on business". Prodded, he admitted he was picking the pockets of newly arrived travelers when he was approached by a well-dressed gent who asked him if he knew Mattis.

"He was after something particular," said Farthing. "He asked me if I knew Mattis' warehouse, and if I'd go and see if he had this clock."

Armand straightened. "Describe it to me," he ordered.

Farthing cast him a baleful look. Apparently, he hadn't forgotten the punch he'd received.

"It's a clock held by a statue of a woman," he said.

Allard nodded thoughtfully, drawing Farthing's attention back to him. "Then you went to the warehouse as instructed. What happened next? Did Mattis disturb you, and you killed him in self-defense, like? Or did you stab the man to death for the hell of it?"

Farthing looked horrified.

"No! I didn't do neither! I went there the next night. I got in, looked about a bit, and got out. I saw no one, and no one saw me. Then I told Smith what I'd seen, and he paid me. Then he asked where I usually drank because he might have a few more odd jobs for me."

"Was one of those to follow a lady?" Armand asked.

Farthing turned his head away. "Yeah. But I ain't proud of it. One day she saw me following her, and she started after me. I told Smith I wanted nothin' more to do with it after that. I don't hurt no women."

But you scared horses which might have killed a couple of women.

Armand kept the thought to himself.

"You were happy enough to steal the lady's reticule."

Armand waited for the denial, but it didn't come. He exchanged a quick glance with Edward, and then with Allard who addressed Farthing.

"Did this 'Smith' always meet you at the pub?"

"No, I met him at a rooming house once."

"You'll take us there, won't you, Farthing?"

Farthing would.

Edward and Armand emerged from the storeroom, while Allard continued interrogating Farthing.

Edward led the way into his office and poured himself a brandy.

"Yes, I know it's early in the day, but I want to clear my mouth of the bile," he said.

Armand couldn't reprove him.

"Pour me one as well," he said.

Edward gave him a knowing look and reached for a second glass.

"THERE, THAT IS fitting beautifully."

Madame Dumont sat back on her heels after pinning the piece of embellished ribbon in place.

Despite her French name, Francine Dumont was actually Scottish, but she could put on a creditable Continental accent to appeal to those customers for whom appearances mattered above all.

She exchanged a knowing look with Lady Arabella. Both women said nothing.

"Well?" Jade asked, hoping she didn't sound too impatient.

"Would you like to see how you look in the dress?"

Jade touched the blush pink net overskirt that seemed to float over the cream silk skirt.

She took a deep breath. "Oh, yes please."

Francine got to her feet and nodded at a young seamstress who held the edge of a piece of muslin that covered a full-length mirror.

"Et Voila!"

The fabric was tugged away.

While the skirt was unadorned, save for the overskirt, the bodice showcased the mantuamaker's skill. Satin ribbon roses in the same blush pink decorated under the bust. The bodice itself, front and back, was decorated with finely detailed roses picked in gold thread. It was simple and, without doubt, refined.

"You look superb, my dear!" said Arabella. "And now I see the gown, I insist you wear the Rosemont family pearls. I believe Armand's mother wore them when she married Charles' father, so it is only fitting that you should do the same as Armand's bride."

Jade had trouble finding her voice. Francine had no such difficulty.

"As soon as you told me what you wanted, I had this vision in mind for you."

"It's magnificent," Jade breathed, raising a shaking hand to her mouth.

Francine grinned. "Ah, if only all my brides were so easy to please," she said. "Mind you, you've not left my girls a lot of time to make a trousseau for you."

"I'm more than happy with everything you've done for me so far. I've never owned so many fine negligees."

"Ah, they're not for you alone; they are for your husband to enjoy as well."

Francine stepped behind her and loosened the ribbon on the back of the gown. Soon, Jade was in her undergarments again, and her beautiful wedding gown had disappeared along with the seamstress to the back room for its finishing touches.

Arabella approached and kissed Jade on the cheek. "Armand won't be able to keep his eyes off you," she said. "I'm sorry I cannot stay longer, but I will see you and Armand for supper tonight?"

Jade nodded and shared one last smile with Arabella before the woman left.

Francine rang for some tea while Jade dressed.

"I'd had always wondered which lady would finally land the Count of *Ytres*," she said, her affected accent gone and a soft Scottish brogue in its place.

"I'm not really a 'lady'."

Francine laughed. "You're more of a lady than half the clientele who come in here. Believe you me. The things they say…"

"So, they're talking about me already?"

Francine dismissed her with a wave of her hand.

"They talk about everyone."

Jade picked up her cup and took a sip of tea.

"What are they saying?" she asked mildly. Jade knew there would be gossip. In the past it never bothered her because she was not of that world. But, as a countess, that was another matter entirely. It was Armand's reputation too.

Francine shook her head. "Nothing worth reporting."

Jade skewered her with a look.

"Does it really matter?" Francine protested. "Does their opinion truly count for anything? Most of them are jealous on behalf of themselves and their daughters. The rest like to cement their reputations by repeating any old rubbish. Once you and the Count return to England after your honeymoon, there will be a fresh crop of victims for the gossipmongers to savage. Besides, as Countess, related by marriage to the Earl of Rosemont and his Countess, you will both be the most fashionable young matrons in the city."

Jade shook her head, letting her amusement show.

"There's no need to tout for business, Francine. I will have no one else make my gowns – if I can ever make an appointment. The new Duchess of Auchen is said to monopolize all your time."

Francine leaned forward and patted her knee. "I will always make time for you. You're my favorite client."

"I bet you say that to *all* your clients."

Francine burst out laughing.

"We've always understood what we're about here in Bond Street. We give the aristocracy something they cannot do for themselves. We provide grand illusions and get the privilege of witnessing what is behind the curtain."

"That is true enough," said Jade. "Some of the stories I could tell…"

"I don't want to hear them!" Francine raised her hands. "All I need to know is who's tardy in paying their bills."

The dressmaker stepped behind her to adjust the ribbons on Jade's day gown, then gave her a hug. "I cannot be more pleased for you, *cherie*. You deserve this happiness."

Jade returned the embrace fully.

"Now. The girls will deliver your trousseau two days before the wedding," the dressmaker continued, "so you will have plenty of time to pack. And I'll be at your home at seven o'clock on your wedding day to help you dress."

IT WAS ONLY a two hundred yard walk along Bond Street from Madame Dumont's salon to Bridges & Sons' shop. It took Jade three times longer than usual to get there.

Her engagement to the *Comte de Ytres* had become quite the thing to talk about among the Bond Street retailers. By the time she had got to her door, her cheeks ached from smiling, and her voice was hoarse from talking.

The merchants on this street were more than colleagues. They were friends. She would be lying to herself if she refused to admit experiencing a pang of regret that she would be leaving this community.

Going upstairs to the family's private apartments, Jade was greeted by her maid, Suzy.

"Miss Bridges!" said the young woman, "I'm glad you're home. There is a pile of calling cards and invitations waiting on your desk. The doorbell has been ringing all day."

Jade flipped through the calling cards, noting the names. Those she did not know personally, she wrote back to, thanking them for their call and their kind wishes.

She rang for Suzy.

"Has Mr. Bridges or Count Danger returned?" she asked.

"No, miss they haven't, but the Master sent word to say he won't be home for supper."

Jade would have to wait for news of their investigation.

She looked down at the invitations and cards in her hand and supposed she ought to be grateful that she had more than enough to occupy her time.

When Jade had expressed a desire for a wedding breakfast after the ceremony, Dottie had offered to organize the catering. It was a touching offer, and Jade was delighted to accept. She now added the callers with whom she was close to the invitation list for that event, then began deciding what to do with the invitations for her to attend at-homes and lunches.

THE BOARDING HOUSE was located in a street that was the very definition of genteel poverty. The paint on the buildings was either faded or peeling off to reveal the brickwork underneath. The number Farthing directed them to was in the middle of the street. It was four stories tall with a basement dwelling below. A sign in the street-level front window announced rooms to let and to inquire of Mrs. Crofts within.

Armand received a sideways glance from Edward. He shrugged and led the way up the steps and into the plainly furnished entrance hall. There were no servants to greet them. On each side of the tiled hall were two rooms with doors wide open.

On one side was a communal sitting room, on the other, a dining room with a long refectory table and a dozen mismatched chairs. From up the bare wooden stairs they heard the sound of slamming doors and booted feet tromping along uncarpeted floors.

A moment later, two men, speaking rapidly in Italian, descended, and walked past them without any acknowledgement.

"What room number did Farthing give us?" Edward asked.

"Thirty-two," Armand replied.

"There aren't thirty-two rooms in this place."

"Let's try the third floor and the second door."

The two men found it without difficulty. The door was locked.

They knocked. There was no reply.

Armand stood to one side blocking a view of the door from anyone coming down the passageway. Edward stepped forward toward the door with a skeleton key borrowed from Allard.

This place brought back memories to Armand of his arrival in London. He and his mother stayed in a place very much like this one. They all seemed alike – run by widows who, threatened with penury, opened up to lodgers the houses they could no longer afford to keep on their own.

Season after season, year after year, the property would resemble a family home less and less. Internal doors would acquire locks and painted numbers. Inside, the furniture that would have given the room its individual purpose and character was sold off and replaced with a basic bed, a chair, a table, and, if one was lucky, a wardrobe.

Allard's key turned in the lock effortlessly. They slipped inside.

The room was exactly as Armand imagined it would be.

The bed was made. The wardrobe door was ajar. Nothing hung within it. The room was bare, the only thing left behind was the faint odor of cigar smoke.

"Well, that's that," said Edward.

"Let's look around first," said Armand. "Smith may have left something."

He turned to the bed and cast his eye over it. Behind him, Edward sighed.

Armand pounded the pillows, then stripped back the sheets and found nothing. He lifted the mattress. Nothing. He knelt down to peer under the bed. Nothing.

"Oi! Who are you two? What are you doin' here?"

Armand stood up and faced a short and stout middle-aged woman who filled the doorway. Her look of alarm vanished, and her eyes narrowed as they fell on him.

"It's *you!*"

The woman marched up and prodded him in the chest with her index finger.

"What are you playing at? Thinking you can sneak back here and take the rest of yer belongings without paying what you owe?"

"I…"

He was cut off.

"No excuses out of you. I've dealt with your sort before. Your things are locked away. You're lucky I didn't call the Runners after you. I had me doubts when ye gave yer name as Smith. *Humph!* Like I haven't heard *that* before."

"Now... Mrs. Crofts—"

"Don't you Mrs. Crofts, me! Did you think you could fool me with that bootblack in your hair? Now you pay me five quid right now for yer rent in arrears and the trouble you've caused me, and for the storing of your junk."

Armand frowned thoughtfully and pulled out his purse to put the requisite sum into the woman's outstretched hand and didn't say a word.

"You nobs always cause me the most trouble," she muttered. "Sneaks and frauds to a man. Come and collect your rubbish, and then you can get out."

The landlady turned on her heel and headed down the stairs. Edward gave Armand a quizzical look. Armand shrugged and followed the woman downstairs.

Yes, five pounds was extortionate, but if Smith had left something behind...

Mrs. Crofts opened a door off the kitchen. She pulled a small wooden crate out of the dank cupboard and dropped it into Armand's hands.

"If you're goin' into trade as a clockmaker, you're doing a pretty poor job of it. Now, out!"

She bustled them into the hall.

"You know your way, so go. And don't come back."

Armand didn't dare look at the contents until the front door slammed resolutely behind them, and he and Edward were safely out on the street.

Inside the crate, in a hundred or more pieces, was a reproduction of the Thalatte clock.

CHAPTER TWENTY-NINE

A LL IN ALL, it was a disappointing end to the day, made even more bitter by learning that Baroness von Hoecker refused to press charges against the mystery man or even Farthing. She wanted no part in the proceedings.

Furthermore, they learned from Allard that Farthing could be charged with nothing more serious than purse-snatching. Even then, they were lucky that Silas the pawnbroker remembered him, given his trade saw many, many people each day.

Allard threw them a small bone of hope when he suggested a little time in the gaol might shake Farthing loose of some more details about Smith, but admitted the man was hardened enough to simply do his time and keep his mouth shut.

The only clue left was the box of clock parts. If there was anything missing, that could be significant in and of itself, but that seemed a forlorn hope.

Armand considered that if there was any comfort to be had from the day, it was dining with Jade. Arabella had insisted on a family dinner which meant Edward and Gerald were invited as well.

After a long soak in a bath, Armand decided he would dress himself instead of calling for Barnet. He stood in front of the mirror, tying his cravat when the voice of Mrs. Crofts came into his head.

Did you think you could fool me with that bootblack in your hair?

He paused and studied his reflection a moment. He resembled the man they were looking for?

How closely? Obviously, his hair wasn't black.

ARMAND FOUND GERALD reading the afternoon edition of the newspaper in the drawing room.

He much did he really know about the man? He hated himself for having asked the question. But once Jade had pointed out that the person who wanted the clock may know its secret, he'd wondered.

He shook his head.

How? Would his cousin know? The only reason *he* knew was because of the nightmares that had plagued him since childhood. Even now Armand had no idea what the key unlocked – or even if it was there to find.

And if Gerald knew, then why didn't he say something? Apart from the one conversation many nights ago when they both got on the brandy together, he'd expressed no especial curiosity about the clock or the key that was formed from the pieces of the pendulum.

No. It had to be someone else.

His cousin looked up. He set the paper down and got to his feet, adjusting the sleeves of his jacket.

"You look every inch a count, cousin," Gerald said. "I hope my more modest attire doesn't offend our host."

The charcoal gray of his suit and the silver streaks of his hair might have made the outfit seem austere, but a large ruby tie pin added a striking punctuation of color.

"You look fine, Gerald. Charles and Arabella will welcome you as you are."

"So, tell me of your day. The man caught by your fiancée's brother, what happened to him?"

Armand briefed him on the events of the day.

Gerald shook his head sympathetically. *"Courir après la lune."*

Chasing after the moon.

How appropriate.

"Ah well, you've done all that you could," Gerald continued. "You have the clock. The villain does not. So, all is well. And, next week, you and your lovely bride will leave behind England and your troubles."

Barnet entered to let them know the carriage was ready and waiting for them. That was another thing Armand knew he would have to address. It was well enough for a bachelor to simply have a valet and a few housekeeping servants, but as a married man, he would need a butler, footmen, a lady's maid…

Lady Jade Danger, Countess of Ytres…

Armand smiled to himself.

He wondered how his Countess-to-be was faring.

JADE STRETCHED OUT a cramp in her hand. Following her dress fitting, she had spent the rest of the day responding to the many invitations that had come her way.

A secretary. That's what she would have when she was married.

If endless invitations were to flow in day after day, she would insist on it.

She heard the front door close. Edward's voice echoed in the hall. Jade shut the lid of the ink well and got up to greet him.

"Do you know what, sis? Your fiancé is not a bad chap."

"I'm glad you think so. Over the past week, you've seen more of him than I have," said Jade, adding a mock peevishness to her voice.

"Ha! You'll have enough time alone with him soon enough."

Jade ordered coffee to be brought to them and made Edward tell her everything that had happened with Tom Farthing that day.

"The man who bought the other clock at auction also signed himself Smith. It's likely to have been the same man." She shook her head ruefully. "I wish I'd paid more attention to him at the time," she said thoughtfully.

"You couldn't have known then. No one could have," said Edward. "By the way, I've asked Eli to reassemble the clock. We'll see if that reveals anything of import. But that's the end of the matter as far as I'm concerned – Farthing is in prison, and Smith has gone to ground."

A clock of their own chimed five somewhere in the house.

"We should start getting ready for dinner with Lord Charles and Lady Arabella," Jade observed.

"No, not yet," Edward shook his head. "There is something I need to give you first. Wait here."

He crossed to a locked cabinet, unlatched it, and removed a thick envelope. He set it on the desk before her.

"What's this?"

"Open it."

Jade did. Inside was five hundred guineas.

"That was the amount you negotiated with Baroness von Hoecker, correct?"

"That's right."

"It's yours."

"No, Edward, it can't all be mine. At least a third goes back into the business."

He ignored her protest. "Look further."

Jade withdrew a piece of paper. It was a banker's certificate for three thousand pounds. She stared at it, reading it four times over to make sure she had not misread it. She held it up to the lamplight and found the tell-tale watermark.

"That's a tremendous sum," she breathed. "It's too much."

Her brother regarded her with wholehearted affection.

"You earned every penny of the five hundred guineas. It's yours," said Edward. "The rest is your dowry. Our grandmother and our mother made provision for it in their wills."

"I seem to recall, but I had no idea it would be so much."

Her brother leaned forward and squeezed her hand. "Well,

don't tell anyone, but I added funds to it too. Partly for your share of the business as my partner, partly as a gift from me."

Jade returned the squeeze. "I can't imagine no longer being a part of Bridges & Sons."

"Me either." Silence fell between them a moment before Edward added, his eyes twinkling, "But if you happen to see something worth picking up in France for an auction, you're more than welcome to be paid on commission."

Jade was glad Edward made the joke, otherwise she might have burst into tears. She blinked them back, nevertheless.

"I'll be looking for a lot more than ten percent," she said.

"Fifteen. That's my best offer."

"Twenty. Then you have a deal."

Edward rose, leaning forward to kiss her on top of her head.

"You'd better go upstairs and do whatever it is you females do to look beautiful," he said. "I'm reliably informed that men don't like to see their brides-to-be all bleary eyed."

Jade gave him a mock scowl and playfully slapped Edward's arm.

"I love you," she said.

"I love you too, sister, and I wish you a world of happiness."

Two weeks later.

JADE STRETCHED HER nude form languorously beneath the crisp linen sheets as the longcase clock in the hall chimed seven o'clock in the morning.

For members of the *ton*, it was early – too early to wake, too early to arise from bed.

She was awake from habit but felt no desire to leave her bed – especially when the man she loved lay as naked as she was beside her.

They'd made love again last night, for the first time as husband and wife.

Armand still slept, so she watched him, taking in the dark, new-day's stubble on his chin. The lean muscularity of his body half-hidden under the sheet stirred possessive desire in her once again.

Armand Danger was *her* husband. Of all the women in the world he could have chosen as his wife, he'd chosen *her*.

Jade raised her left hand and studied the band of gold on her finger. Tangible proof, if such a thing was needed, that they were bound to each other.

What a wonderful day yesterday was. It was a modest wedding by society's standards but filled with so much laughter and love.

Edward, she had learned, had given the ladies from both the shop and the auction house full rein to prepare the wedding breakfast.

The feast, no doubt, would be spoken about for weeks to come.

The menu was French inspired.

Carp a la Chambour

Partridge a la Peregueux

Petit Nougat aux Raisins de Corinthe

Choux au gros Sucre

The meringues were a particular favorite. Jade had learned that the wedding cake had been decorated only a few hours before the wedding, and the fruit was set to soaking in brandy on the day of their announcement. The three-tier cake was covered in a layer of marzipan and then a thick portion of sugar icing onto which roses and fleurs-de-lis was piped.

Aristocrats rubbed shoulders and danced with those who wouldn't have ordinarily been given their time of day, and, by the time the bride and groom made their farewells, it was agreed that the celebrations would continue in their absence.

Jade smiled at the memory.

"Good morning."

Armand's sleep-roughened voice drew her back to the present. She turned to face him.

"Good morning," she replied.

He took her hand and brought it to his lips. He leaned up on his elbow and kissed her softly setting a hum through her.

Outside their door, the household was coming to life, and their private retreat coming to an end for the time being. They would sail on this afternoon's tide.

"How do you feel about returning to France?" she asked.

Armand huffed. "It doesn't feel like I'm returning. It was the same as last time, when I accompanied *Maman* to Arras. I felt like a stranger who spoke the language but knew little else."

"What about seeing your mother? Gerald mentioned she is not in the best of health."

"It's one of my greatest regrets," he whispered. "I wish I had paid greater attention, maybe visited or written more often—"

Jade kissed him slowly, and with deep tenderness.

"Your mother wanted to return home, and you helped her. She also wanted you to have a prosperous life in England. I'm sure she would never resent you staying here. What of the chance to reclaim your legacy?"

"That's long gone, I expect. What I want more than anything from my mother now is what memories of my father she can share before what she remembers is gone. Going back to *Ytres* is more about saying goodbye to the past than anything else."

Jade lay her head on his chest and counted the steady beats of his heart.

"If you felt that your mother would be better off back in England, then we should bring her back to live with us."

"You wouldn't mind?"

"Of course not."

Armand pulled her into his arms and trailed his fingers softly across her back.

"Thank you," he whispered.

How much she loved this man.

CHAPTER THIRTY

France

THEY SPENT A leisurely week travelling the one hundred miles south-east from Calais to Arras.

Gerald was an entertaining tour guide, ebullient and knowledgeable, who seemed to recognize how much of his company was appropriate. He was there to help and guide when needed and absented himself often enough to give the newlyweds privacy.

When they first landed in France, Jade was surprised to find herself as much at home in Calais as she had been in England. In fact, it seemed there were just as many English people there as there were French.

Many of the Englishmen were in uniform, waiting for their turn to cross the Strait of Dover and go home at last after the long campaign against Napoleon. Relations between the English and the French were cordial here. Gerald explained that the Revolution had hardly touched the port town at all.

In fact, there had been a healthy two-way smuggling trade that went on even through the war. The English enjoyed barrels of brandy while one particular entrepreneur "acquired" lace-making looms from Nottingham and established a now thriving industry in the St Pierre quarter.

Jade took full advantage of purchasing a decent amount of the fine lacework, much to the delight of Armand, who encouraged her to spend as she wished.

A couple of days later they continued on their way, breaking the journey at Lumbres and taking a walk in the picturesque countryside, dotted here and there with historic river mills. The town of Bethune featured architectural delights, and Gerald pointed out the belfry on the Grand Place, built in 1388, and the round brick tower of Saint Ignace of the same period.

On the seventh day, they arrived at Arras.

ARMAND SAW HOW Jade watched him closely, perhaps wondering what memories would be sparked by returning to this place.

His own memory of it was relatively recent, from when he had accompanied his mother to come and live with *Tante* Giselle. But there was also this town's bloody history during the Revolution.

He was well aware that Arras had been the home of Maximillian Robespierre. Hundreds of people had been executed here, and many more starved to death. Religious buildings – the Arras Cathedral and the Abbey of St Vaast among them – were either destroyed or desecrated.

The madness was purged through the fever of war at the cost of countless lives, both French and the opposing allies. The rebuilding continued to this day, with Gerald explaining that in the past year work had begun to repair the medieval cathedral.

However, despite his wife's worries and to Armand's own surprise, the nightmares of his past did not bother him here. He was a tourist, just as his wife was.

Nicole and her cousin Giselle lived in a modest little home in a street just off the *Parc du Rietz*.

Gerald had sent word ahead to his mother. She greeted them warmly with an animation that hinted at the beauty she must have been in her youth.

"I cannot believe that we meet at last, Armand!" she said in rapid French. "We are together at last."

The older woman turned to Jade. *"Tres jolie!* You make Armand a wonderful bride," she said.

Jade bobbed a curtsy, *"Merci beaucoup, Tante Giselle."*

"Ah, I did not know you spoke French! Why did you not tell me, *mon fils?"*

The expression on Gerald's face gave the answer away – all the time they'd been in London, they'd conversed in English. He simply didn't know. And, for the briefest moment, Armand had the impression that Gerald was shocked, even alarmed, by the revelation.

But the look disappeared as quickly as it had crossed his features.

"I didn't know, *Maman,"* he replied.

Jade seemed to have noticed his surprise too. She gave him a smile. "Your English is so excellent, Gerald. I didn't know you were speaking it solely for my benefit."

Gerald found a smile, gave her a formal bow, and said nothing.

They were led to a comfortable parlor where a young maid served coffee.

"Where's *Maman?"* Armand asked. "Has she become bedridden?"

"Oh no, she is only out in the garden," said Giselle. "She likes it there, tending her flowers."

Giselle set down her cup. "I thought it would be wise to speak here first as so not to distress her. I take it Gerald has told you about her health?"

Jade reached for Armand's hand and took it. He welcomed the reassurance of her touch.

Armand nodded once in answer.

"Answer me truly," he said. "How does she fare?"

Giselle shrugged. "She has good days and bad days. She clings to routine. Change is difficult for her now. It took nearly a month for her to get used to the fact that a new boy from the bakery delivers to us in the morning."

Armand took a deep breath. What would he do if his own mother did not remember him?

"May I suggest that you approach your mother first, Armand?" said Gerald. "*Maman* will go with you. Your bride can stay by me. It would not do for *Tante* Nicole to be overwhelmed by so many people at once."

Jade's nod gave Armand the reassurance all would be well.

Giselle led the way out to the large walled garden. A spreading tree in one corner provided shade for a little table and chairs, but the rest of the garden was bright and sunny. Garden beds were bordered with lavender and filled with honeysuckle, and bloomed with roses of every hue, along with geraniums in white and red.

It was the very definition of a *jardin curé*. A curate's garden. It was charming.

A woman wearing a plain dress and a large sun hat had her back to him as she tended a garden bed filled with irises. Purple, pink, yellow, white – all of them seemed to flourish under her hand.

"Your mother is a gifted gardener. This is all her work," said Giselle. "When she first came here, she joined a group of local gardeners and entered competitions for the best blooms."

Giselle called out, "Nicole! We have some visitors."

The woman rose to her feet, removed her gloves, and dusted her hands on her apron.

"Were we expecting guests today?" she asked.

Her eyes widened as she spotted him. Her hand rose to her mouth. Armand's heart clenched. His mother looked ready to cry.

He crossed the yard to be at her side.

His mother threw herself into his arms and smothered his face with kisses.

"Robert! Robert! I cannot believe it is you!"

Armand's heart fell.

Robert was his father. His long dead father.

Armand held his mother close to stop her seeing his shocked face, and to give himself a chance to recover. A moment later, he released her from his embrace and took a step back.

"No, no, Nicole," said Giselle, stepping forward. "This isn't Robert. This is your son, Armand. Remember? He wrote to us that he was coming to visit."

He glanced between the two women. The difference between *Tante* Giselle and his mother couldn't be more stark. Despite the fact they were similar in age, his mother seemed much older. The lines around her eyes and mouth were more pronounced, and she carried with her an air of frailty that her cousin did not.

Armand found a smile and presented it to his mother.

"That's right, *Maman*. It's Armand. I have made the trip from England to see you."

She looked over to where Gerald stood with Jade and frowned.

"Aren't *you* my son?"

"No, *Tante* Nicole, I am your nephew."

Nicole blinked rapidly as though she was trying to put the puzzle pieces of her life together in the correct order.

"Of course. You are Gerald, and this is Armand," she said as though she had known it all along. She gave Armand an uncertain smile. "You look so much like your father that for a moment I thought he had returned to me."

She turned to her cousin.

"Did Gerald get married?"

It was Giselle's turn to look startled. She shook her head.

"Then who's the girl with him?"

Armand reached forward, took his mother's hands, and kissed her on each cheek.

"I want to introduce you to my bride," he said softly. "Her name is Jade."

He held a hand towards her, and she came forward to stand at his side.

"Jade? That's an unusual name," said Nicole.

Jade curtsied and greeted her in French.

His mother looked up at him. "She's not French, is she?"

"No, *Maman*. Jade is English."

"And England. That's where you live?"

"That's right."

Her brow furrowed a moment.

"With Charles?"

"That's right. He is your stepson."

"He married too, didn't he?"

"Yes. To Lady Arabella."

Nicole breathed out in apparent relief at getting everything correct. She gave him a tentative smile.

Armand's heart broke.

Yes, his mother was before him, more-or-less the same in appearance as when he last saw her, but she *was* different.

"Come," she said to Jade, holding out a hand. "Let me look at you."

Jade dropped a curtsy once more.

"My lady."

Nicole took Jade's hand and squeezed it. "You are my *belle-fille*. You must call me *Maman*, as Armand does."

"I would be honored."

"*Très bien.* You will tell me all about your family, yes? And whether my son is a good husband to you?"

Jade gave him a smile that eased at least some of the tension in his chest.

It would be all right.

"I see by the look you give him that he has been a very good husband, indeed." Nicole retained hold of Jade's hand and reached out for Armand's and squeezed it too.

"Since it has been such a very long time since I saw my son, I want you to tell me all your news. My memory isn't as sharp as it used to be, so do be kind to me."

JADE HID HER dismay. Gerald had told the truth about Nicole's memory.

Her heart ached at seeing Armand's reaction when his mother did not recognize him at first.

She knew the pain of losing her own parents, but there was something more tragic about seeing the past being erased in a living person.

But after the uncertain beginning, things brightened considerably through the afternoon. Jade could see how the constant, kindly attention of Giselle and Gerald had been such a comfort to Armand's mother.

Nicole became very much as Jade had imagined her to be – a charming, gracious hostess. She ventured to ask what Armand was like as a boy.

Nicole's eyes lit up, clearly delighted by the question.

"He was a *good* boy," she said. "I know all mothers are supposed to say that, but in the case of my son, it is true. I have him to thank for introducing me to my second husband."

Armand's eyebrows rose in surprise, which did not go unnoticed.

"Yes, it *is* true, Armand. You became friends with Charles after we would meet after church. It was the Earl's idea that you boys should be tutored together. He thought Charles would benefit from having a friendly rival."

"I didn't know that," said Armand.

His answer brought a pleased smile to Nicole's face.

"They were happy days indeed."

By mid-evening, Nicole's reserves of energy were expended. She excused herself to bed early. The four remained in the living room to play cards.

Gerald offered to teach her and Armand how to play *jeu de tarot* with a traditional deck of seventy-eight cards.

The cards on their face were familiar. Jade recognized the suits of spades, hearts, diamonds and clubs and their values on the diagonal corners. This deck was elaborately decorated with scenes of aristocrats at their leisure.

Fortunately, Gerald was kind to them as they played. It was just as well. Jade won only once in a dozen games before she finally learned the way of successfully taking tricks.

"Of course, you are welcome to stay with us for as long as you wish," said Giselle, "But you are on your honeymoon. You must have places you want to see. Paris perhaps? Venice? Or even Rome?"

"Ah, a Grand Tour," said Gerald.

"Yes, Venice and then Vienna, but before that, I want to go back to *Ytres*," said Armand.

The hands of cards slipped in Giselle's grasp, threatening to tumble onto the table.

"I don't think you'll find anything of interest for you there."

Armand raised an eyebrow. "My family's estate was there. I should like to see what remains of it."

The words were calmly spoken, but Jade heard the edge in them.

"Oh, Armand, I don't mean to distress you," Giselle hastened. "But your beautiful home – it's nothing but rubble. It was destroyed the night you and your *Maman* fled. It's hardly a place of happy memories."

Gerald broke the uncomfortable silence that descended.

"Is it my turn to deal? Why, yes. Yes, I believe it is."

It was about eleven o'clock when Giselle announced she intended to retire for the evening. Jade too proclaimed she was ready for bed also. She suspected that now Armand had seen his mother, he would have more questions for Gerald, and it was better to let the two men speak in private.

Still, once in their sleeping quarters, she didn't hasten in her routine, hoping to remain awake by the time Armand joined her. She was still brushing her hair when he entered their bedroom.

He approached her to drop a kiss on the top of her head and another one on the neck. Jade sighed with pleasure and put down the brush.

"Did you find out more about *Ytres* from Gerald?" she asked.

"How did you know that was what I was going to ask him about?"

"I saw the reaction Giselle had when you mentioned it."

Jade left the dressing table and climbed into bed. With sleepy eyes, she watched her husband undress.

She'd gotten to know his body well over the past couple of weeks. She knew it by sight, touch, and taste. Until the end of eternity, she would never tire of the way he brought her a world of pleasure every time they caressed. She loved him to the very depth of her soul. She believed she would climb mountains and fight lions for him and stand at his side no matter what the future brought.

Soon, he climbed into bed, and she snuggled into his arms.

"There's been something which has bothered me since before we left England," he said.

She lifted her head from his chest and rolled on her side to look at him.

"It was the landlady at the rooming house. She thought I was her tenant and that he'd dyed his hair as a disguise. I dismissed it as nothing more than coincidence at the time, but when my mother thought Gerald was me this afternoon..."

"I know what you're thinking," Jade offered, "but I would hate to believe that Gerald and Giselle, who have been so kind to us – *and* to your mother – would deliberately thwart your efforts to find out more about your past."

Armand sighed. "It doesn't make me feel better to raise the prospect, but now the idea is in my head, I can't seem to let it go."

Jade frowned. "It would mean Gerald was in London for many weeks, not just a few days as he claimed. And he would have had to have known of the clock before you told him of it.

How would he know about it? Let alone its significance?"

"I don't know. Perhaps my mother's memories are clearer on the matter, or at least they may have been. It might well have come up in conversation at some time."

Armand stopped looking up at the ceiling and turned on his side to face her. He reached out to tuck a length of hair behind her ear and stroke her cheek.

"Then what are we to do?" she whispered.

The look of tenderness in his eyes was her undoing. Jade tilted her face to him to receive his kiss. She surrendered to the taste of him, of warm brandy and cigars.

"We go on as we mean to," he whispered. "I've never made any secret of my intent to dig up the past. In a few days, we will thank Gerald and Giselle for their hospitality and make our own way to *Ytres*."

Jade reached for Armand and brought him down to her for a kiss. He allowed her to lead, and she relished in possessing his mouth as he so often commanded hers. She trailed fingers across his back, across his neck until he had enough of her teasing.

He rolled her beneath him and raised her arms above her head to stop her teasing. Armand settled himself between her thighs. His eyes darkened with desire. She received a feral grin from him. She put up a playful struggle that served to rub herself up against his growing erection.

He nuzzled the opening of her night gown, dropping kisses across her breasts until he found her nipples. He licked the buds, then blew across them until they hardened.

"Have I told you you're the perfect wife?" he asked.

"Show me instead," she whispered.

CHAPTER THIRTY-ONE

WHEN JADE SUGGESTED she might accompany Giselle and
Gerald to the markets, Armand could have kissed her
then and there.

Her suggestion would leave him and his mother alone in the
house. They could reminisce privately without the well-meaning
but constant presence of their hosts.

As the day was cool and overcast, Nicole wanted to sit in the
morning room and knit. Armand picked up a skein of wool and
wrapped it around his hands to aid her with the task.

"I remember sitting in the boarding room in London in the
evenings just as we are now," he said. "You would sing me songs
while you knitted."

"I did, didn't I?" Nicole looked up from her work and smiled.
Then she sang:

"By the light of the moon,

My friend Pierrot,

Lend me your quill

To write a word.

My candle is dead,

I have no light left.

Open your door for me

For the love of God."

"I remember that," she said, "but sometimes these days I can't remember what I did last week. Isn't that strange?"

"Some memories have a way of living on forever," he said, releasing another yard of wool from his hands. "You used to tell me stories of Papa."

"He was my first love," she said. After a pause, she added, "I remember the night I fled with you."

Armand's pulse quickened. Given her reticence to speak to him of his father ever since they got news of his execution, he had wondered how he might broach the topic with her now.

"I was very young," he ventured.

"You were three years old."

"I remember a clock."

"Ah yes, not just a clock – *the* clock. Your father used to keep it in the study."

"I knew even then there was something special about it."

"It was your grandmother's. Your grandfather had it made as a wedding gift for her because she was so taken with the statue in the garden. Do you remember the statue? You were so fascinated by it as a boy."

He chuckled. "It gave me nightmares."

"Did it? Really?"

He nodded. "It still does."

"I thought you liked it. You used to look at it so much."

Armand was heartened to see his mother smile at the revelation. He sought to press the advantage.

"I seem to associate her with the family crypt. I've never been able to work out why."

Nicole did not respond. The *clack-clack* of her knitting needles adding row upon row of knitting was hypnotic in the silence of the morning room.

"I remember the night the Revolutionaries came," he added.

There was no reaction from his mother save her agile fingers, the moving wool along the needle as more rows of knitting were added.

Did he dare ask more of her? He might learn nothing if she became distressed thinking of it. But when she spoke at last, it was in calm reflection.

"My heart broke that night," she said softly. "It was the last time I saw your father."

"Tell me, *Maman*," Armand almost pleaded. "I want to remember him. Tell me what he was like. What happened that night? I dream of it, but I don't know if what I see is true or just the make-believe of a child."

His mother took a deep breath. "Your father was a wonderful man. A good man in the truest sense. After the declaration of the republic, life went on as normal for a while. We were not worried. Whatever politics happened in Paris, they were too far away to affect us in the north. We treated our tenants well and enjoyed a good relationship with the villagers. It came as a shock when the revolutionaries started making threats against us."

Her eyes on her knitting as she spoke.

"The troublemakers were from *here*. From Arras. They came down to *Ytres* and stirred things up with their talk of overthrowing the old order. Then the cathedral was looted. Soon after that we learned they were rounding up prominent families. Your father warned that we might have to flee. He spent weeks preparing."

She stopped speaking for perhaps a minute, but her fingers worked the knitting needles dexterously, furiously. He waited to see if she would continue speaking.

The knitting needles stopped.

"I remember it as clearly as it were yesterday, but how I wish I could not."

The words were nearly inaudible, Armand had already leaned forward to catch them. He dropped from the chair to his knees before her and leaned in so close to his mother that their foreheads touched.

"I love you, *Maman*. I know this is difficult for you to remember..."

He received a wan smile as she looked up, then a kiss on the forehead as though he were but a little child once again.

"Did you know your father was an excellent swordsman?" she said brightly. "He was also an excellent dancer. I remember the first time he led me out to dance. That night, I knew he was the man I wanted to marry. My father pretended to be dismayed. He refused to consider the match when I pleaded with him. But Robert quickly convinced my papa of his true feelings for me. You are so much like your father."

She paused to cup his cheek, then took up her knitting again.

She spoke without looking up.

"Your grandfather had a secret hiding place made in the crypt."

The statement was delivered so matter-of-factly, so abruptly that Armand nearly felt dizzy from the sudden change of direction her conversation took.

The place the dead lived! Armand fought to keep his voice gentle and not disturb her with his urgent curiosity.

"Why did he do that?"

"Who can say?" Nicole shrugged, adjusting her knitting. "But who would think to rob a place that was only home to mere bones?"

"I remember being in there the night we fled *Ytres*."

"That's right. We were. Your papa told us to meet him there. There were papers or something he hid there. He told us to remember where they were, then we went back to the house."

"There was the clock. The parts of the pendulum made the key," he said.

Nicole looked up. "Have I told you this before?"

Armand shook his head.

"Oh. I thought I had," she said. "I'm sure I've told someone."

"No," he replied and unwound another length of wool from his hands. "I saw Papa take apart the pendulum in his study that night."

Nicole smiled at him fondly.

"That was probably when I was upstairs. I was opening the lining of my biggest coat and putting inside all the jewelry that would fit, and I was packing a little bag for you."

"You said there were papers in the vault, *Maman*. Do you know what they were?"

"No," she shrugged. "I left all of that in your father's hands. He knew better about such things."

She stopped knitting and suppressed a small yawn. "You always ask me questions about the clock. I don't understand your fascination for it. I don't wish to talk anymore about it. The memories make me sad."

"I understand, *Maman*," said Armand, but he most certainly did not. Disappointment reared its head. He tamped it down. He had the key, and, if the mausoleum still stood, he could find whatever his father had hidden.

"I suddenly find myself tired," Nicole announced, setting aside her knitting. "I should like to lie down before dinner."

"Of course, *Maman*." Armand put down the skein of wool and helped her to her feet.

She jumped at something over his shoulder.

"Gerald, I didn't hear you come in."

Armand turned, and his cousin stood in the doorway, looking as though he'd just been caught doing something he ought not.

Armand frowned, and Gerald glanced at him nervously before addressing Nicole.

"I've only just come back, *Tante* Nicole, I didn't mean to interrupt the audience with your son."

"Have Jade and Giselle returned with you?" Armand asked.

He suspected he already knew the answer. The three of them would not have been able to enter the house without making some kind of noise. But one person could…

"No." Gerald hesitated, then continued with more certainty. "They stopped at a *patisserie* to select a *gateau* for tonight's supper. I left them there."

The excuse sounded plausible enough, but still…

Ignoring his mother's protests that she could manage the stairs well enough on her own, Armand insisted on escorting her up to her room.

"Are you happy here, *Maman?*" he asked when he was sure they were out of Gerald's earshot.

"But of course! I am home among my people. The English were very kind to me, and your stepfather was a good man. But I am French, as are you."

"It's strange. I never felt French. Not until recently." Armand smiled. "You have my bride to thank for that."

"And so, I do thank her." Nicole patted his arm before tiredly lowering herself onto the bed. "It is good to have you home, *mon fils.*"

She lay down.

"Yes, Giselle and Gerald have been so good to me," she continued around a yawn. "Gerald is like you. He asks lots of questions about the family."

He kissed his mother on the cheek as her eyelids fluttered closed.

When Armand returned downstairs, he glanced into the salon. Gerald was sitting there with a copy of the afternoon paper.

His cousin seemed engrossed in his reading, so Armand continued quietly toward the front door and over the hall floorboard that squeaked ever so slightly when one crossed the threshold.

He would have entered here, wouldn't he?

Armand went to the back of the house where the housekeeper and the maid-of-all-work were preparing the evening meal.

"Have you seen *Monsieur* Gerald?" he inquired.

"*Non, monsieur,* not since he left with the Mistress and your wife," answered the housekeeper, up to her elbows in flour. "They should return soon."

He returned to the salon feeling perfectly ridiculous in entertaining the thought that his cousin was somehow being duplicitous. And yet he couldn't shake the feeling that not everything was as it seemed.

The answers he sought lay in *Ytres*.

Armand made sure he trod heavily to announce his presence.

"Ah, *Tante* Nicole is tucked up in bed?"

At Armand's nod, Gerald continued.

"*Maman* will wake her before dinner, and she'll be most refreshed. Shall we have a brandy before the ladies return?" he suggested.

Armand accepted the offer and took a seat opposite Gerald's.

"You've been to *Ytres*, haven't you?" he asked.

Gerald shrugged and poured two glasses of the amber liquid and handed one to Armand.

"Years ago," he said. "There was not much to see. There is a little village, smaller now than before the Revolution apparently. Many people left because of the war with Napoleon and did not return. I looked for your family's estate, but only half-heartedly, I'm afraid, out of curiosity mostly. The woods are thick, so I didn't get far. Only enough to see the chateau was a ruin."

Mindful of his cousin's curiosity, Armand took a sip of the particularly fine brandy, swirling it about his mouth before letting it burn a trail down his throat.

"Are you still determined to go there?" Gerald asked. "I'm afraid you might be disappointed."

Armand gave a shrug. "I can't be disappointed if I have no expectations."

"Will you be travelling alone? I can't say it would be an enjoyable trek for your wife."

"Did I hear my name?"

Jade entered the room. Armand was warmed by the smile she cast his way. He rose, as did Gerald. She settled herself on a chair to Armand's right.

"We're talking about venturing on to *Ytres* in the next few days," Armand said, keeping his manner easy.

"Yes," Gerald agreed. "I was saying there is very little to recommend it as a destination for a lady."

Jade reached over, took Armand's hand, and addressed him.

"I don't require grand locations as long as we're together, darling," she said.

"I promised you there would be hiking, my dear."

"Yes. I *adore* walking."

Armand turned to Gerald.

"It seems we are set for *Ytres*."

Gerald saluted them with his glass.

"When do you plan to go?" he asked.

"The day after tomorrow, I shouldn't like to overstay our welcome with yourself or *Tante* Giselle."

⊁⟫⟫⟩⟨⟨⟨⊱

JADE CAUGHT A frisson of tension between Armand and his cousin from the moment she stepped into the salon.

She wasn't sure what to make of it, so she followed Armand's lead and backed him up in the conversation, half wondering which of her boots would be best for a country hike.

When the conversation sputtered to a stop, she squeezed her husband's hand and suggested they take a walk in the nearby park before dinner.

It was only a couple of streets away, but perfect for having a truly private conversation. They crossed through the gate into the park.

To anyone observing them, they were lovers out for a stroll. Only Jade could detect the tension that thrummed through her husband.

He remained deep in thought, so she said nothing until he was ready to speak. They walked along the boulevard in silence for a while. The morning's overcast had lifted, and the line of trees provided welcome shade in the warmth of the early August afternoon.

"Did things not go well with your mother today?"

"Yes… no… She's trying hard to be here in the present, but it is a struggle. My heart breaks for her. She is as bright and as sharp as ever when she recounts happy events of long ago, but talk about more recent things, and she struggles to keep up."

Jade took his hand.

"You being here gives her a chance to share those happy memories with you."

Armand briefly gave her hand a squeeze.

"She tires so easily."

"She can rest knowing you are settled and that your father's memory will live on," she said, returning his comforting gesture. "Will you tell me what caused the tension between you and Gerald when I returned?"

She looked at him, waiting for an explanation, uncertain whether one was to be forthcoming. Armand worked a tic at his jaw while he thought.

"When did Gerald leave you and Giselle at the markets?"

Armand's voice was calm, but she knew he considered the answer to the question significant.

"When we were about halfway around. He said had some other errands to run. We told him we'd be home after we visited the *patisserie*."

"How long was it after that before you came home?"

"About an hour, I suppose."

Armand led her to a garden bench. They sat.

"I cannot be certain, but I believe Gerald was eavesdropping on my discussion with *Maman*."

"Could it not have been a coincidence?" she asked.

"Yes. Certainly. And I want to believe it is. But I can't forget the nervous expression on his face when my mother spotted him. He also lied to me. He said he had only just left you at the *patisserie*." He sighed deeply. "The landlady who berated me. My mother getting us confused. I don't think I can deny it any longer. Gerald is Smith."

HER HEART SANK. She had hoped so much it wasn't true.

"*Maman* told me there's a secret hiding place in the family mausoleum. She said father hid some papers there."

"So, what's his purpose?" Jade mused. "The papers? Could Gerald want your title? He may believe the papers could be used to prove a claim in the French Court."

"Who knows? But whatever he thinks it is, he thinks enough of it to commit murder for it."

"What do we do? We can't leave your mother with him. And what of Giselle? She is close to her son."

With a long sigh, Armand leaned forward, resting his forearms on his thighs. He stared into middle distance.

"If what we are supposing is true, Gerald has been planning this for a long time," he said. "There is no reason to harm *Maman*. She is his source of information. Remember when she believed Gerald to be her son. Through her he learned the secret of the clock, but not the whole of it, which is why he came to England. He only made himself known to me when he could not get the clock for himself."

"You must have had your suspicions before we traveled, when you insisted the pendulum pieces were secured in my trunks, instead of yours," she said.

"It was only an inkling. Placing the parts in your trunk instead of mine was a last-minute decision.

"Then what is our plan?" she asked.

"We do our best not to arouse suspicions. We have been straightforward all along about our intent to visit *Ytres*, so that's what we'll do. But we do it with our eyes open, and the expectation that, one way or another, we won't be visiting the estate alone."

⁂

CHAPTER THIRTY-TWO

Ytres, France

JADE HAD TO concede that Gerald was truthful about one thing – there was very little in *Ytres* to attract a casual visitor. It was a farming community centered around a little church and an inn. A blacksmith's workshop occupied a prominent location on a cross street.

It was obvious to the locals they were strangers. The carriage they'd hired had attracted no shortage of curious glances.

The innkeeper, at least, was happy for the custom. He slid across the guest registry. To Jade's surprise, Armand signed it as 'Smith'.

"English, eh?"

"Yes! How did you know?" said Armand in less than perfect French. Jade said nothing, not trusting herself to keep a straight face if called upon to say anything. There was no harm in letting the innkeeper believe she spoke no French at all.

Their room was small, but perfectly clean and well kept. Their host opened the shuttered window, pointed out, and said in a tone often used with young children.

"Une vue sur les arbres, uh?"

A view of the trees.

"Ahhh," Armand nodded, as though mentally translating the

simple phrase from French into English. "Oui, une forêt," he agreed.

The man muttered something uncomplimentary under his breath before closing the door after him.

Jade folded her arms and counted to ten to ensure the innkeeper had fully departed.

"Smith?" she said.

Armand pushed on the mattress which didn't sag too much.

"It was good enough for Gerald, so it's good enough for us."

He plopped onto the bed and bounced. The bed had an unfortunate squeak. He grinned at her.

Jade shook her head and granted him an indulgent smile.

"I know it's been nearly twenty-five years, but I have no idea if the Danger name is remembered fondly, if at all. I thought it best not to borrow trouble if we didn't need to."

"The forest. Is that the beginning of the family estate?" she asked.

Armand reached inside his jacket pocket for a map and unfolded it on to his lap.

"I believe so. It should only be half a mile from the beginning of the tree line. We'll make an early start tomorrow."

"Do you think Gerald will follow us?"

"Oh, I'm certain he will. But we have the key."

Jade received a come-hither look from Armand who patted a place beside him on the mattress. She joined him, placing her arms around him, and resting her head on his shoulder.

"Surely this scheme of his can't work. You and your mother were recognized by the English when you first arrived. That must count for something, even if French records were destroyed. Your stepfather recognized your title, didn't he? As your stepbrother does now."

Armand nodded in response to both questions.

"Perhaps it's *not* my title he wants. It might be my mother was wrong about the papers, and my father left clues to buried treasure."

Jade glared at him in mock exasperation. Armand put his arms around her and pulled her back onto the bed and started raining soft kisses on her face. She refused to be distracted – not just yet, at any rate.

"What about you? What do *you* hope to find?"

He ceased his kisses with a sigh and lay beside her, looking up at the ceiling. He was giving his answer some consideration.

"I have everything I need right beside me. I'd give up everything I have, everything I'm supposed to be, for a lifetime with you. The only title worth a damn to me now is husband. Perhaps one day, father."

Jade placed her head on his breast, listening to the strong beat of his heart. His words touched her deeply. Still, he hadn't answered the question.

Before she could ask again, Armand continued.

"What do I *want* to find? A simple memento from my father. Gerald is welcome to the buried treasure. If it exists."

ARMAND WOKE SHORTLY before dawn. He spent a few moments watching Jade sleep. His gaze lingered on those lips he'd kissed to fullness well into the night. He meant every word he said to her yesterday.

She was his treasure, the fulfillment of the restless yearning he hadn't known he possessed. Jade helped find who he really was. And now his past, present, and future were reconciled – or soon would be.

Careful not to wake his wife, he slipped out of bed and opened the curtain at the window. He stared out at the view. The forest was black, silhouetted against a rosy sky.

The rhyme about sailors and skies came to mind.

In the soft, early morning light, he looked at the preparations they had made. A knapsack sat beside two pairs of sturdy boots.

Still, Armand couldn't help himself. He opened the bag and pulled out the replica pendulum one more time and prayed it would work if they found the lock it opened.

"Good morning."

The voice behind it was thick with sleep but could not have sounded sweeter. He turned to admire Jade as she stretched.

He loved the way she blushed as his eyes roved over her body. He loved her shy smile, although there was nothing timid about the way she responded to him in bed.

Dressed for their hike, they went downstairs. The innkeeper's wife, Madame Leroy, showed more curiosity than her husband and asked them where they planned to hike.

Armand indicated the woods.

"There's not much in there to see but a ruin," she said.

"Do you know much about it?" he asked, trying not to display too much curiosity as he settled a small wicker basket of food into the knapsack.

"It has been a ruin for as long as I've known it, Monsieur. And my husband and I have lived here for twenty years. They say a family of aristos lived there, but they all disappeared during the Revolution. I imagine they're all dead now, but who cares? It was a long time ago."

He knew Jade wanted to say something, but he silently warned her against it with his eyes. The innkeeper's wife meant no malice, and no offence was taken by him. Except it wasn't *that* long ago.

Armand checked his pocket watch. It was just before nine o'clock. He was keen to be on their way.

"*Merci beaucoup, madame,*" he said in his deliberately labored French.

THE PATH TO the forest narrowed as they reached the tree line. A grass expanse curved to the right and extended on for some yards. A driveway or a road? It looked as good a direction as any, so they followed it.

For the first hour or so, they were as they'd proclaimed to the innkeeper – English newlyweds on a honeymoon walking trek.

Crested larks and blue-throated warblers fitted through the branches at their approach. Distant knocking drew attention to the black woodpeckers at work, high in the more mature trees. Closer to the ground, a hare or two bounded in the undergrowth. They heard larger animals moving too – deer, most likely.

The sun was high in the sky when the forest thinned a little and the first piece of a manmade structure came into view, a low stone wall. They followed it until it intersected with another wall, this one larger, the foundations to the gatehouse if Armand were to guess.

They walked along farther, and grass gave way to gravel underfoot.

They left the trees completely to emerge out onto a grassy meadow. Goats had the run of the grounds. They looked up at the human intruders without much interest and returned to their grazing.

Beyond was the chateau itself. Only one of the round towers with its conical roof remained intact.

The front of the building had been razed to the ground; the central courtyard, now exposed to the elements, had a tree almost as tall as the tower growing through it.

To the right, the remnants of a hexagonal wing thrust forward. It would have been three stories high once upon a time, but now only the fire-ravaged façade of the lower two floors remained intact.

Suddenly, it all came back to him in his mind's eye – the manor as it had been. The moat that would have surrounded it in medieval times had long been filled in before Armand's day, but one portion still remained. He remembered it as a large rectangular pond full of carp.

Jade's hand touched his shoulder, and he was returned to the present once more.

He smiled, offering her more reassurance than he felt himself.

"Now we've found the chateau, the mausoleum can't be too far away, perhaps down the hill to the right. We'll rest and eat then go on," she suggested.

Armand was in full agreement. They found a shaded spot within the ruins and set out their repast.

"Do you remember much of how it was?" Jade asked.

"Only bits and pieces," he admitted. "I remember the carp pond. It would overflow in wet weather. I think my father's study was on the ground floor somewhere to the left. I had a wooden rocking horse in the nursery on the second floor. It was gray with a real horsehair mane. Papa promised me a pony of my own when I turned five."

Armand was surprised at how many memories came back in this place. Of his beautiful mother coming in to kiss him good night while dressed in her finery. There had been a ball in the grand hall. She was dressed in a gown of pale blue, he remembered, and the color seemed to perfectly match the diadem in her chestnut hair. She was as beautiful as a queen as far as he was concerned. He remembered being caught halfway down the stairs by his *nounou*. He'd heard the music, he'd explained, and the kindly woman let him sit on the stairs for a few minutes to listen before returning him to his room.

What might have been his life had his father lived? If the Revolution hadn't happened?

He closed his eyes and imagined the chateau whole again. And yet the feeling of longing for that past didn't bite as deeply as he thought it might. In all, he'd had a very fortunate life and he couldn't regret it, despite the loss of his father.

Most of all, he couldn't imagine a life without Jade in it now.

She watched him cautiously, no doubt to see how he fared. He picked up her hand and kissed it.

"I'm fine," he told her. "Truly."

Jade acknowledged his statement with a nod and a squeeze of his hand, but she did not mask her disbelief.

Armand shrugged.

"I confess to feeling anxious about coming here today. I didn't know what memories might come back, but I've dealt with them. This property ought to be mine, but it certainly isn't home. That much I am sure of."

"What are you going to do with this place?" she asked.

"I don't know. Gift it to the people of Ytres?" he shrugged.

"Do you think you could do that after what they did?"

"Why not? It wasn't their fault the madness infected them. You heard what Gerald said – they caught it from Arras, Arras caught it from Paris."

He got to his feet and aided Jade to hers.

"But let's not forget the reason we came. I want to get this done before Gerald catches up with us with whatever madness *he's* been infected by."

Jade pointed out the remnants of a path away from the house towards the now overgrown gardens. Here and there through the weeds and the bracken, stone-edged garden beds were visible.

They had just arrived at a line of pine trees now become a grove when a voice called harshly out to them.

"Go no further!"

Gerald stood about twenty yards away with a pistol in his hand. Sweat beaded the man's brow.

Armand stepped forward to put himself in front of Jade.

"I was wondering what had taken you so long," he called to his cousin. "I expected you to join us at the inn this morning."

Gerald laughed mirthlessly. He approached slowly without lowering his arm, panting from exertion.

"I was an hour late, or so I was told. I've run all the way here."

Armand glanced at the gun and back up at his cousin.

"Would you mind putting that thing away?"

The menace on Gerald's face turned to an expression of uncertainty.

"Don't underestimate me, Armand, I'm a desperate man."

"You're also family."

Gerald's breathless panting became a half sob. He lowered the pistol. Armand saw the gun hadn't even been cocked.

He let out a breath of relief and relaxed a little, although he remained watchful.

"It's a mess, everything is a mess. I can't go back," said Gerald. "I mean it. I've done much I'm not proud of. I thought I could justify it to myself, but it's too late."

Armand and Jade exchanged glances.

"Why are you here, Gerald?" Jade's voice was soft and soothing. "What do you hope to find?"

"I am in debt. Tremendous debt…" The man's face wrinkled as he tried to hold back tears. He took a gulping breath and composed himself.

"I'm sorry, Armand, really sorry. The two hundred pounds a year you send for your mother has been the only thing which has kept my mother and I from *pénurie*. When I was in Belgium, I gambled on a business venture. It went well at first, but then Napoleon's War began. I lost everything and ran up debts. Mother does not know this. I dare not tell her this is reason we moved to Arras."

Gerald took a few more steps forward. Armand shifted his position again to ensure his wife's protection. His cousin noticed his movement and came to a halt. He looked down at the pistol in his hand and tossed the weapon away. He held out his hands like a supplicant.

"I also have not told *Maman* that I pretended to be the Comte de Ytres in my business dealings," he continued. "You see, I knew about our connection with your late father and that he had been executed. At the time I did not know what had happened to you or your *Maman*. So, I came to Arras not only to escape my debts, but to see what remained of the estate. I thought I could claim it, you see, as the sole-surviving heir. I would use a mortgage to discharge my debts and have the title to rebuild my fortune."

Armand listened without interruption despite simmering anger against his cousin's deception. Gerald seemed to be looking for absolution, but Armand had none to give.

He'd put his mother in this man's care – the same man who arranged for Jade to be robbed, and who was quite likely a murderer as well.

"When did you find that Armand and his mother survived?" Jade asked.

Gerald let out a hoarse laugh. "It was by accident. We were in Lille on our way to Arras. I bought a newspaper to pass the time. There was an article on the death of the Earl of Rosemont. It said the widowed Lady Rosemont was the dowager Countess of Ytres. It was *Tante* Nicole, and the newspaper said the title was currently held by her son – *you*, Armand."

Rage threatened to boil over. Armand clenched and unclenched his fists, using all of his self-control to not advance and knock the man to the ground.

CHAPTER THIRTY-THREE

JADE BRACED HERSELF against the rising tension. She silently prayed that Armand could keep his temper. Satisfied that neither man was paying her heed, she backed away from both of them and quietly retrieved the pistol. She looked down, the iron was pitted with age and disuse. The wooden stock was grayed and dried. Obviously, it had been years since it had seen oil.

She'd seen enough firearms come through the sale room to know the weapon was in poor condition. It was doubtful it could be successfully fired.

"So, you got to Arras and encouraged your mother to write," said Armand through gritted teeth.

"I didn't know she had written until we received the first reply from your mother!" Gerald insisted. "My mother was lonely, and they corresponded so warmly, so following news of your stepbrother's marriage, I suggested *Tanta* Nicole come live with us."

Jade stepped closer and put a hand on Armand's arm to draw attention to the fact she now held the pistol. She slipped it into the knapsack he wore.

"Armand, the day is getting away from us," she said softly. "We should go to see what we can find."

He searched her face as though looking for answers for what to do about Gerald.

After a moment of silence, Gerald pleaded again. "Please cousin, forgive my deception. I swear I love your mother as though she were my own. I would not harm her. I would not shame you."

Jade believed the man was in earnest, but the decision as to what to do was not hers to make. Armand stared his cousin down until the man hung his head and shoulders slumped.

"I have no expectations about what we will find," Armand said. "Clearly, cousin, you *do*. What is it?"

"Your mother talked of something your father left behind," Gerald replied. "At first, she did not say what it was. Only that it was important. I thought at first that if I could find it, it would please her. I swear! That was my true purpose."

"What changed?"

Gerald's face crumpled. "One of my creditors from Belgium tracked me down. He wants money. He says he'll see me jailed. Then your *Maman* said what had been hidden was of tremendous value, and the clock and the statue had the answers to it."

"Did you find the statue? Is it still here?" Armand demanded.

Gerald nodded and led the way into the grove.

Jade spared her husband another glance before falling into step and following Gerald. Now the pistol was secured, she felt more at ease. She didn't believe Gerald to be an uncontrolled lunatic. Most of all, the poor man seemed out of his depth, but still, he was desperate and therefore potentially dangerous.

He led the way in silence for about fifty yards before he spoke.

"How did you know I'd be here?" he asked.

"You *are* 'Smith', aren't you?" said Armand. "You've gone to such great lengths to try to find the clock, you had to know its secret."

Gerald laughed. "If only it was that simple. When I found the chateau in ruins, I thought my hopes were dashed. Then *Tante* Nicole mentioned the statue and the clock, how they were alike, but not alike. It took me another visit to realize what she meant."

He moved purposefully ahead until turning right, moving down a gravel path barely visible through the weeds.

"I had begun to despair that her story was make-believe until I found this," he said, stepping aside and holding out his arm.

There, where he gestured, surrounded by wild-growing gentian flowers, was the life-sized bronze statue of Thalatte.

Jade covered a gasp with her hand.

The likeness to the clock was remarkable. But instead of a clock in her hand, she simply pointed.

Armand approached the statue slowly, almost cautiously and stared up at it as though mesmerized.

"My visit to see you in England was a genuine one," Gerald continued. "I had fully intended to call on you as soon as I arrived, but then I found a flyer for the auction with an illustration of the clock. I thought it lost in the burning of the chateau, but here it was, so I attended the auction. When I saw you there, I was convinced you already knew the clock's secret and were planning to take what was mine."

He let out a bitter laugh.

"Little did I know that these clocks are everywhere."

"Do you admit to hiring Tom Farthing?" Armand asked.

A rapid series of nods was the reply as Gerald put the heels of his hands to his eyes and bit back a sob.

"Why did you kill Mattis?" Armand demanded.

"It was an accident!" Gerald cried, his hands falling from his face, his eyes pleading. "*He* attacked *me*. I went to his warehouse to look for the other clocks that Farthing said were there. The Irishman came at me with a knife. We scuffled. I was frightened for my life. He wounded my arm, then somehow the knife was in my hand with his blood on it. I found the clocks and took them, only to discover they were as worthless as the first."

The man was close to tears. "Once I started, I had to go on."

Armand kept his expression tightly controlled as a cloud passed overhead, plunging the glen into a dim coolness which seemed to match the mood.

Assured Gerald was no longer a threat, Jade walked away from the two men to give them both a moment of privacy.

The cloud passed and, just for a moment as the shadow lifted, she perceived a vertical straight line, the edge of some man-made structure through the tangle of overgrown bushes and boughs to which Thalatte pointed.

She followed the path around the shrubs and the Danger family's mausoleum came into view.

It was here, as Armand described it from his dreams.

And, unlike the chateau, the wide, squat octagonal structure was whole.

She approached it. The entrance was barred by iron gates. She tugged on the bars. They didn't move. She peered through the metalwork lattice into the vestibule. A single flat-topped sarcophagus stood in the center of the space. In the walls around it, tarnished brass plaques marked niches representing generations of the Danger family. Everything appeared intact despite the destruction wrought on the chateau itself.

"Armand!"

He and Gerald approached at a jog, then stopped and stared at the building.

"There's a lock on the gates," Jade said. "How do we get in?"

"The hinges are rusted," Gerald observed. "Perhaps they are weak."

Armand positioned himself on one side. Gerald took the other. The two men pulled and shook the gates. The hinges didn't give way – the mortar that once anchored them to the stone did, and they suddenly sagged outward and fell.

Armand set down his pack and pulled out the folded cloth containing the pendulum.

Recalling the key's finished size, Jade examined the crypt to see if anything resembled a lock.

"Anything?" Gerald asked after her hopefully.

She shook her head. "Nothing."

A GIANT LADY pointed the way. He went where she directed.

The building was the home of the dead.

The rap, rap, rap of the drums became a tick, tick, tick of a clock keeping time. The giant lady was now tiny, but the tick, tick, tick she made was insistent, maddening, so much so that papa ripped the cage from her hand and broke it apart.

The tiny lady was silent.

The dream of his childhood hit Armand with full force.

He forced his eyes open, and, for a fleeting moment, the key was not in his hand but his father's.

Queasiness assailed him, and he swallowed down rising gorge.

He had the key, but where in hell was the lock?

A deep breath. Then another. A third for good measure.

He opened his eyes and started looking.

"They are already in the grounds Robert! Why have we stopped here?"

"Be quiet! Only a moment, Nicole."

Young Armand had never seen his parents argue. It frightened him more than being woken from his bed and hurriedly dressed in his warmest day clothes.

"When this is over, we will return here."

"Yes, yes, but hurry!"

Robert seized his wife by the shoulders, forcing her to look at him.

"Pay attention, beloved, I implore you. This is important. See this plaque? Remove the dowels and use this key. Come back when it is safe. Everything you need is here."

Armand squeezed his eyes tight, trying to force himself to remember what else his father told *Maman*. The sound of the drums and the encroaching mob filled his ears.

"Make your way to Calais. Remember the little inn, Le Chat Noir? Wait there with Armand. If I haven't joined you there by the end of the week, take the next passage to England."

His father's words had been urgent.

"Remember, Nicole."

So many years spent trying to forget.

A hiding place. *Where?*

See this plaque?

Armand rose and looked at the array of tarnished brass plaques on the wall, at least two dozen of them bearing names and dates speaking of the arrivals and departures of his forebears whose mortal remains lay in each niche. A dozen or more yet blank, awaiting Dangers who would never lie here.

Which one? He was only three, for God's sake!

He moved along reading the names, hoping for something that jogged his memory – his grandfather Achille, his grandmother Cyrille, his uncle Patrice who died before he was born... Who was this?

Sylvie Boyer Danger.

He knew of no such ancestor. The only Boyer he knew was – Sylvester Boyer. *The sculptor.*

"Jade! Fetch the pocketknife from my pack..."

Each of the plaques was held in place by a dowel of brass, its round dome-shaped head about two inches in diameter.

He forced the knife blade between the edge of the dowel in the top left corner and the plaque. A gap opened, and he prized the soft metal out. It fell to the floor leaving only a round hole half an inch in diameter and perhaps two inches deep into the wall behind. It was not wide enough to fit the key which was at least an inch and a half across.

Undeterred, he attacked the top right dowel. This time, it exposed a hole almost as wide as the head of the dowel and only half as deep. And at the bottom of the hole was a horizontal slot plainly the correct size to accept the key.

Jade and Gerald watched over his shoulder as he inserted it into the slot. It reached the end of its travel with three inches of the shaft exposed.

Armand turned it. At forty-five degrees, the key went in a

little further, then – nothing. He hesitated a moment, loath to try to force it in case the slender key broke in the lock. Taking a deep breath, he applied just a little more force, and the key suddenly turned again. As the key reached ninety degrees from its starting position, the plaque moved a mere fraction of an inch.

Gerald reached in and tugged on it, but it held fast.

"The other dowels. There has to be another lock," Armand muttered to himself. He prized out the remaining two. One was like the first – a genuine dowel – the other revealed another key slot.

Turn one. Slip in. Turn two… the plaque shifted again. Gerald pulled at it. It came away in his hands, and he stepped back to put it on the floor.

"They're coming! Go now, take Armand."
"Come with us, Robert!"
"No, I've got to hide the clock back in the house. The secret panel behind the fireplace in my study – don't forget, Nicole!"

Inside the funereal niche lay a large leather purse. Beneath it, what appeared to be a sheaf of papers covered in waxed cotton.

Armand opened the purse. Inside was a small fortune in gold and some jewelry – necklaces and rings. Among them, he spied his father's signet ring with the fleur-de-lis crest.

He took the ring, then tossed the bag in Gerald's direction. The man fumbled. The purse fell to the floor atop the plaque. Shiny gold louis spilled out.

"That should be enough there to satisfy your debtors. Take it. You can have the jewelry too."

Gerald stared at him wide-eyed for a moment before bending down. He scooped up the coins and peered into the bag.

"You got what you came for, cousin. Go back to Arras, make your excuses to your mother, and leave," said Armand, making no effort to hide his distaste. "Never go back there again. And if you value your neck, I suggest you never set foot in England again. Accident or no accident, Mattis is dead at your hands. If I see you again, I'll have you in irons before you can draw your next breath."

The tension in the dim enclosed space was thick. Gerald looked to Jade as though she might perhaps side his way and beg to ease the banishment Armand had placed upon him. She did not.

Regret and sorrow filled the man's features, and Armand had to own to a moment of fleeting sympathy for his cousin.

Gerald had a fortune in his hands but was nevertheless the poorer of them.

He faced Armand again. With a nod of acknowledgement and tears in his eyes, he turned and walked away, not looking back.

"Let's go," Jade urged after a moment. "I don't think I want to stay here anymore. What if Gerald comes back, or does something rash?"

Armand realized his hand was clutched tight around the signet ring. He unfurled his hand and stared at it.

His father's ring. He did not go to the guillotine wearing it. He left it here that night.

Did he know he was going to die when he hid it?

It was now Armand's by right. He slipped it onto the index finger of his right hand. It fit perfectly.

"I don't think he will," said Armand.

His cousin was weak-minded, but he didn't believe there was true malice in him. It was just a moment of weakness that sent him deeper and deeper into the quicksand.

With a full steadying breath, Armand went to the sarcophagus across which the lowering afternoon sunlight now fell through the doorway. He put down the waxed cotton wrapped bundle and untied the leather thongs that held the papers together. Among them was the deed to the estate and a letter of introduction to a bank in England with details of a safe deposit box.

Lastly, there was a sealed letter.

It was addressed to him.

Jade, looking over his shoulder, gasped. Armand swallowed hard against the emotion rising in his chest. He dare not look at his wife, lest his sentiments overtake him.

He broke the seal and carefully unfolded the decades-old paper.

Beloved son, Armand,

I don't know when or if ever you will receive this letter, but it gives me comfort to write it. We live in highly uncertain times. The things we took for granted a few short years ago are now gone and there is no guarantee they'll ever return. What is certain is that you will grow up in a world so very different to mine.

In France, the thirst for revolution will inevitably lead to baying for blood. We have seen it with the executions of our own king and queen, but that will not be enough because the revolutionaries seek to remake the world in their own image.

There is no room for nuance, no wish to sort the guilty from the innocent. For them, to be an aristocrat is not simply an accident of birth, but an original sin. That is why I am sending you and your mother to England. You will be safe there until I can join you and you will be safe if I cannot.

I write this not to frighten you, my son, but to instruct you.

There are so many lessons I was looking forward to sharing with you as your father. Now time has run out and I am forced to leave you in the safest hands I know. Be kind to your maman, Armand. If you feel her arms around you embrace too tightly, just remember that it is because she had already lost much. She loves you for the both of us.

Hold to what is true – honor, valor, integrity. That will not be easy when it seems the tide is against you, but in the end it is the only thing a man truly owns.

And love unreservedly. It is easier to risk your life than risk your heart, but when you find someone to love, hold nothing back, and she will do the same for you. You will know passion, strength, comfort, and joy without measure.

This is what I have experienced with your maman, and she with me.

If what I have left here reaches you, then I know that I am at peace in the hereafter.

With love,
Your father

Armand's eyes filled with tears, blurring the flourishing signature of Robert Maximillian Danger.

His father was a man he could barely recall… In those few lines, Armand now knew him.

Tears fell, and the son wept unabashed.

He mourned the loss of a good man.

He mourned the loss of his mother's first love.

He mourned the years he had been denied his father.

He mourned never having the chance to hear him say how proud he was that he had become the man he wished him to be.

The tears were as cathartic as they were finite.

Armand held his wife's embrace, comforting her now as she comforted him.

The late afternoon sun now streamed through the door of the mausoleum, lighting the names of Armand's ancestors for whom this was their final resting place.

He packed the contents of the bundle into his backpack and walked around the room, tracing the embossed names of his forebears with his fingers, committing them to memory. He would not return here again.

Ytres might have been home once, but no longer.

He reached out his hand to his wife who took it. He drew her to his side and kissed her.

Wherever they were together – that's where home was.

And it was where the future lay.

EPILOGUE

London
December 1819

JADE WATCHED HER reflection in the mirror as Suzy, her maid, dressed her hair for the Earl of Castleford's ball. It was a special event with the Prince of Wales announcing his attendance.

She and Armand had returned to London just a month ago from their honeymoon on the Continent, and this was the first event of the season to be attended by the Count and Countess of Ytres.

It was only now she was experiencing nerves. Armand went out on business earlier this afternoon and, to her knowledge, had not yet returned.

There was a knock at the door and another maid entered.

"A letter has arrived for you, ma'am."

Jade took it and smiled. It was addressed to Miss Jade Bridges. There was only one person in London who would write that.

And indeed, it was a short note of thanks from Baroness von Hoecker for making her aware of the arrangements for transportation from Ytres of the life-sized Boyer sculpture of Thalatte. She wrote that she would reserve judgement on whether or not to return the clock to Jade's possession until she had inspected the condition of the statue on its arrival in England.

Jade smiled. She expected nothing less from the woman.

Suzy placed the last of the hair pins in place. "Are you sure you won't let me put ribbon there, Miss – er, my lady?"

Suzy still stumbled over her title every now and again. She couldn't blame the girl –Jade herself was still getting used to the sound of a title attached to her name.

The woman before her in the dressing table mirror still resembled the one she had been a year before, and yet she was different. She was a wife. In time she would be a mother. In fact, she was nearly certain that she'd felt the quickening of new life in her womb.

"No, thank you, Suzy. I feel like I'm wearing a king's ransom in jewels as it is."

She rose from her seat and examined her reflection in a full-length mirror. Her gown was pale blue, almost silver, and trimmed with ribbon from Habetrot Textiles in Scotland, exclusive to Madame Francine Dumont of Bond Street.

The connecting door to her dressing room opened. Armand appeared resplendent in his dinner dress. He eyed her with unabashed appreciation.

Jade felt heat rise to her cheeks at his appraisal.

"I didn't know you had returned," she said.

"My errands took longer than I intended. When I returned Barnet was pacing the floor, so I thought I'd dress first before he wore a hole in that Turkish rug you suggested I purchase."

Jade laughed. "So, you're more afraid of displeasing him than me?"

Armand returned the grin. "I hope this little token makes up for my tardiness, beloved."

In his hand was a leather box, taller than a normal fitted jewelry case. He unsnapped the leather straps holding the two halves of the box together and opened the lid.

Jade gasped.

Inside was a diadem of small diamonds and emerald cut aquamarines. It was magnificent.

"This has always been worn by the Countess of Ytres," said Armand. "I feared it had been lost. But my father had it sent to England."

Jade removed the piece from the box and admired the way it scintillated in the lamplight. She did not need to examine the stones with her loupe to know they were genuine.

Suzy set the jewel in her hair, then curtsied and left the room with a smile on her face, satisfied that she had pleased the master of the house as well as its mistress.

Now alone, Jade received a lingering kiss from her husband.

"I cannot tell you how fortunate I am," he whispered. "I love you."

Jade returned his kiss. "And I love you."

His dark eyes promised passion which perforce would have to be postponed for now. He raised her hands to his lips and kissed them.

She sighed and savored the anticipation.

"That wasn't all that I found in the deposit box at the bank," he said. "It seems that in the early days of the Revolution, my father saw fit to open an account here. There is the equivalent of five thousand pounds."

"Oh, Armand! And your mother never knew?"

He shook his head.

"It's hers by right. She will not return to England, but I want to see her and Tante Giselle properly cared for. The reason I was late home was I went to see my solicitor. He will make arrangements with a lawyer he knows in France to manage their affairs. They will want for nothing."

Jade drew Armand closer and into an embrace. She knew his decision had not been easy – they'd both wanted Nicole and Giselle to join them in England – but it was for the best. They kissed, savoring the moment until Barnet discreetly knocked on the door to let them know it was time to leave for the ball.

A moment later, the clock struck seven.

Armand admired her once more before they left.

"You're beautiful."

"I'll be considered a curio by some."

"Let them look. I'll be the envy of every man there."

THE END

No hand can make the clock strike for me the hours that are passed.
—Lord Byron

About the Author

Elizabeth Ellen Carter is an award-winning historical romance writer who pens richly detailed historical romantic adventures. A former newspaper journalist, Carter ran an award-winning PR agency for 12 years. The author lives in Australia with her husband and two cats.

www.ingramcontent.com/pod-product-compliance
Lightning Source LLC
Chambersburg PA
CBHW072011190726
48293CB00001B/239